I0712890

HOME
OF THE
HARPIES

VANESSA JOYCE

Home of the Harpies by Vanessa Joyce

Book Cover Illustration by Angie Liu
Editor: Jasmine Barry
Allison Johnston-Crosier

ISBN: 9798265707406
ISBN: 978-1-17635600-5-5

First Edition.

Genre: Fantasy, Adult Romance.

Summary: When Aliera and Beau face the Harpy Queen, every realm trembles.
But in the aftermath of war, their greatest battle is choosing who they are without it.

For those who rise, even when it hurts.

Foaming
Elgak's Rest
Heluva Village
Faun Hall
Faunmoor
Cliff's of Gideon
Underfoot Forest
Aravena Lake
Sula Mounds
Stink Horn
Point Pore
Honey Hills
Three Sh
Howling Clifes
Harpian City
Pyre
Salted Sands
The Bog
Buo
The Cradle
Dunya Portal
Lioli
Cloplands

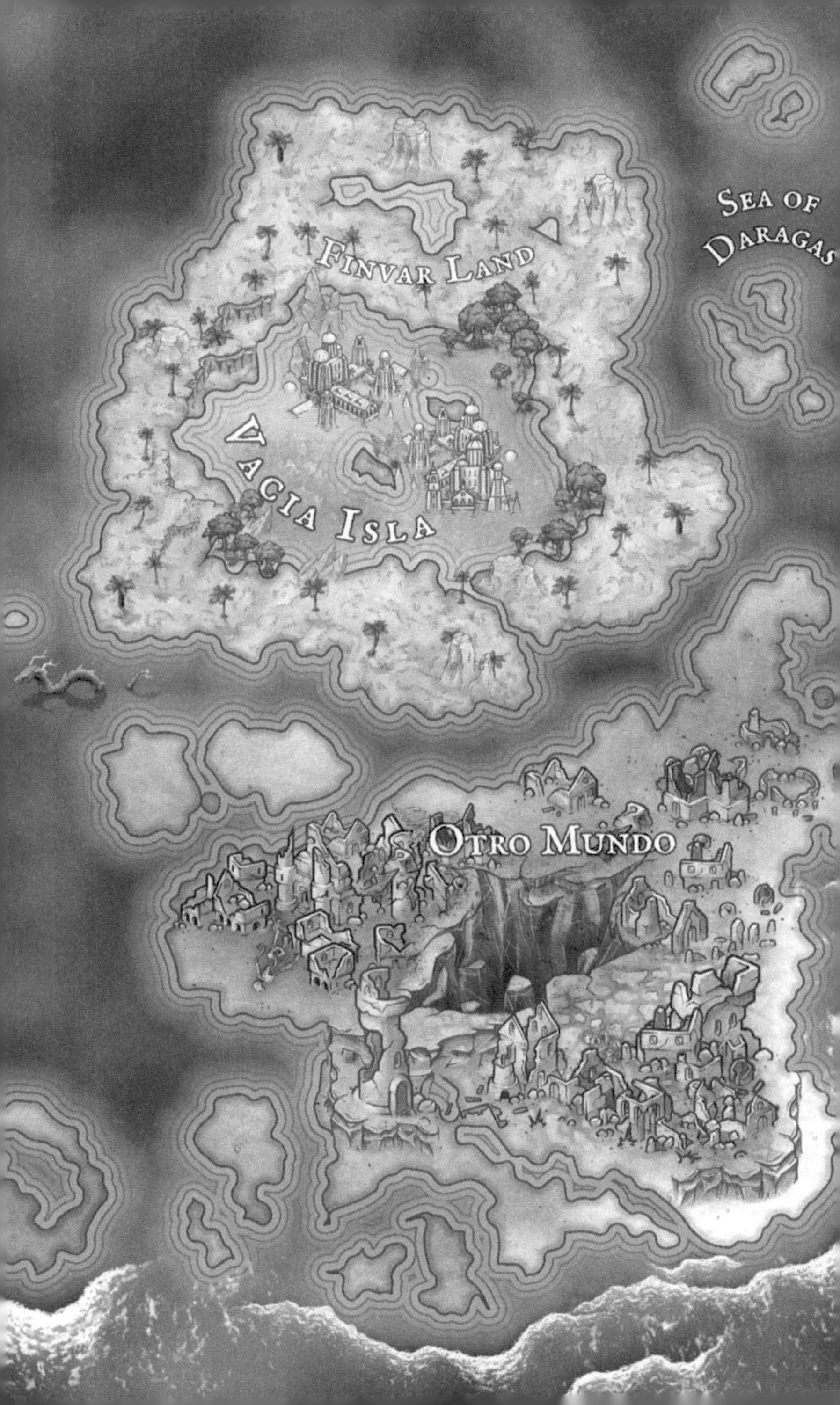

Sea of Daragas
Finvar Land
Vacia Isla
Otro Mundo

Sonsuz Forest
Antoli Realm
Lexia
Isle of Korsan
Orman

CHAPTER ONE

ALIERA

The wind beat against my body so violently that I thought the impact might pierce my chest. I was plummeting now, through almost complete darkness, dropping…dropping, and with no sign of stopping. I could see the outline of the Realm below me. The contrast between the still dark land and the rage of the waves crashing on the shores was stark. Still out of reach, but hurtling closer by the second, my eyes stung against the sharpness of the wind. Then I heard wings beating, gliding towards me, flapping against the assault of the gale, whistling ever so gently through the forceful gust. The bloodied, but still blue Dragon wings that belonged to Beau appeared as he sped towards me. Torin was pummeling behind him, heavier and with a greater force. He would hit the ground hard and never survive if he kept going, and he was only gaining speed.

I whirled a wind tunnel around him, suspending him in the air as I drifted towards him, using the obedience of the wind as my throne as I hovered forward. I fully submitted now, I let the power of my ancestors seep through me, guide me and empower me. Something inside me told me, I'd find it when I needed it most.

"Aliera?" Torin composed himself and froze as he stared at me, noting my presence and the power I held as he stared down with nothing below him. Terror appeared in his eyes as he floated, suspended before me.

"What? Did you think I was jumping to my death?" I smirked.

"But you're flying, kind of…" He gasped.

"Hovering? Draven said I had it, I just didn't know how, until now." I shrugged.

"Well can we start with getting us out of the sky?" Torin sucked in a breath as he shivered in the slight breeze I had wrapped around him. The sky grew darker as we descended, moving farther away from the glowing realm door and closer to the ground below us.

"What did you think was going to happen after you lunged through a realm door?" I questioned.

"Well, I expected to walk onto a field of grass, at the very least. I didn't think Beau was going to leap into nothing but air!" He huffed.

"Beau, has wings…" I reminded him as I raised an eyebrow.

"Noted! Next time…don't follow Beau." He rolled his eyes playfully.

Beau's eyes were watching us during our exchange. I wanted nothing more than to evaporate into the molecules that held me in the expanse of that dark sky. I didn't leap through the door in the hopes of being saved, I had hoped none of them would follow me, but I knew deep down that that wasn't who any of them were.

It was darker here, so much darker than I had seen through the realm door. The only light was coming from the doorway far above us now and that was quickly fading as we descended further into Tierra Hundida. Even with my power we were still falling. Beau flapped his wings harder, and he grasped Torin and then me. Together we glided through the unfamiliar sky into a world of perpetual night. The only source of light was fireflies that bounded through fields of long soft grass so tall it reached far over my head. There was a dull haze, almost like moonlight that hovered over the vast land as we came into landing.

Beau set us down as we reached a small clearing and Torin immediately began to sniff around, then he began snarling and he suddenly snapped upright.

"What is it?" Beau asked as his ears pricked up when rustling drew closer.

"There's movement, keep low." Torin whispered as softly as he could, his voice was horse and crackly.

We kept low and moved as one through the grass, but we had no idea where we were going or what we were moving away from. Whatever they were, their growls were deep. They belonged to something bigger, their feet thundering the earth with every step, their odor offending my nostrils, they were close now, too close.

"Two!" Beau said in his lowest voice to Torin.

Beau unsheathed his favorite blade. I felt the grass part as he stood upright. Torin did the same, his teeth growing visibly too big for his mouth now as he barely held his human form to prevent the sound of breaking bones alerting them to our position. I kept my distance as I moved behind them, they were following the odor of the beasts, the crunching of stones beneath the weight of their feet.

Torin stood upright first, his head just taller than the grass as he peered over the blades of dull green into the darkness. Beau followed his lead, his wings bobbing up before he could lock his eyes on them. I stood up, but I still couldn't see over the grass. I was at the mercy of Torin and Beau. I had to let them lead the way.

"You should stay here." Beau whispered to me.

I still didn't have words for him as my jaw gaped open and my eyes did all the talking, I was still numb towards him. I nodded as he and Torin raced off into the field. It didn't take them long to find their targets. Large brutish cyclops, two of them. One taller than the other, and that one fatter than the latter. Both had a singular, crusty eye and scaled, rough skin that appeared grey against the limited light provided by the insects, which quickly scattered as Torin leapt, mid morph, at the fatter cyclops.

His claws were gnarly, still chipped and broken from the war we just endured in Varsili. He impaled the collar of his enemy and Torin sat atop the beast snapping his fangs wildly in the cyclops face. The second cyclops didn't hesitate to swipe at Torin, but it barely moved him. Beau lunged into the air and battered him off with a single nudge of his wings before he dragged his sword across the neck of the scaled monster. The jagged blade tore through the scales, but Beau was still at a disadvantage, he had to saw that sword long and hard against the scales that were more like aetherium than skin.

"FUCK!" Beau growled. He was exhausted by the time he took the head of the cyclops clean off. The blade now dripping with a thick blood that Beau had to flick from his sword with big movements.

Torin growled violently at the fatter cyclops.

"Any last words?" Beau stood over them.

The cyclops darted his single eye between them both and winced in fear as Torin buried his claws in deeper, the blood pooling around his claws as he stood on the beasts chest. The cyclops shook his head from side to side as he resisted.

"Wait… shouldn't we get some information?" I stepped closer to them.

"You think it can talk?" Beau scrunched his face.

"I can…" The cyclops muttered in a voice that was low and gravelly.

I tilted my head to the side and glared at Beau as he grunted.

"How many are there of you?" I asked.

"Hundreds, if not thousands." He answered but kept his eye closed.

"If we let him go, they will all come after us!" Beau growled at me.

"Why are you even here?" I scowled at Beau. But it wasn't so much a question as pure outrage, it was what I had wanted to say since the moment I saw him pummeling after me.

"What the fuck do you think I'm doing here?" His shoulders dropped in defeat, and I fixed my eyes back on his shredded wings.

I knew why he was here, he was here to protect me. Even after all we had done to each other.

"Where are the cages with all the people and other beings?" I kicked the cyclops for answers.

"In the Harpy city, you'll never get through alive." He laughed.

"Maybe I'll let my friend here snack on your face then…" I hissed as I raised a brow at Torin.

Beau snatched my arm and pulled me to the side. "You're going to let that thing live?" His eyes stared with intent, his voice raspy.

I tore my arm away. "Let me do this my way!" I pushed past him.

"Trouble in paradise." The cyclops laughed through the pain of Torin scratching at his thighs with his hind legs.

"Where is the city?" I ignored his attempt to provoke me.

"North, but you'll never survive the Windreaper nests in the Cradle lands." He laughed.

"FEAST." I locked eyes with Torin.

Torin's eyes glowed yellow and he snapped, his jaws locking on the softest part of the cyclops, tearing his eye out and sending it to an immediate death, the body of the enormous beast became limp, and Torin morphed back into his natural form and spat the blood out.

"That tastes disgusting!" He wretched, his body forcing him to vomit.

"Gross." I covered my mouth as I stood back watching Torin vomit repeatedly.

But the vomiting didn't stop, he had ingested too much of the foul blood from the cyclops.

"We need to find shelter before any others find us." Beau pulled Torin to his feet and slung an arm around him for support.

I took the other side and held Torin up as best I could. We followed the tiny fireflies through the dark field of reeds. These lands were a maze, everything looked the same, fields, rocks, some trees, then more rocks and more trees.

"There, we can take cover between the large boulders and trees." I said as I peered into the darkness at a sheet of vines covering a stone wall.

We moved closer, slower with absolute care now. Beau's ears were on edge as he listened for the slightest of movements. The trees rustled in the gentle breeze as we found a somewhat sheltered area amidst the boulders and sat Torin down in the darkness where the insects didn't linger.

"He needs water." Beau sighed.

"He needs Ele…" I said softly.

"She's not here!" He growled.

"Well, whose fault is that?" I lowered my eyes on him and for the first time we made intentional eye contact.

"I was trying to save you!" He barked.

"I don't need saving, but now he might. You can fly him back up!" I said.

"No, I can't. The door's gone, that means they closed it." He answered.

"This isn't the same place I saw the last time I looked through the door." I sighed.

"Why did you jump?" Beau asked.

"There was a girl falling from the sky…" I answered. "I wanted to save her." I added. It wasn't a lie, but it wasn't the whole truth either and he knew that.

"Or you were running from me?" He sighed.

I glanced at him, his had the slightest flicker of blue in them as they watched me. I felt the weight in his gaze as he searched my face for something other than hostility, for forgiveness?

I scoffed. "Why were you even in Antoli?" I muttered.

"You and Zac agreed the Fae could have access to the magic there. I didn't expect you to hate me so much you would dive into another realm just to escape me." Sadness slackened his jaw now and regret swept over his eyes as a singular firefly floated atop the bridge of his nose, he swatted it away from his face.

Torin was asleep; finally the retching had stopped.

"I told you, I was trying to save that girl." I groaned.

"That girl is long dead. The only reason we survived is because we have powers." He huffed.

Beau looked to the sides of him now examining his wings with the light of the single firefly.

"You're bleeding…" I said softly.

"I'll live." His tone was harsh.

"You shouldn't have come after me, that's worse than it was in Varsili." I lowered my eyes to my fingers fidgeting in my lap.

"You forget there was a time I didn't have these at all." He muttered.

"I'll never forget that…" The memory of the hatched scars was etched into my mind.

"Let's find your girl and then find a way home!" Beau was firm now and I didn't argue.

"You think she survived?" I asked curiously.

"I hope you find evidence enough to bring you peace of mind." He muttered.

I rested my head on the cold stone as Beau pulled vines over the cavern to try and cover us from any roaming cyclops, and I shut my eyes to close him out. We were all still in our dragon-scaled armor, leathers that clung so tight to our skin it was just enough to warm us once we focused on sleep.

But sleep didn't come easy. The sounds of this world were different from the sounds of the Dunya: there were no howling wolves or people trading or laughing. This was a world cast into shadow, and so it lived as such. Morning never came, day never broke. Only the dull haze that lingered, bringing a small and fragile glow that barely illuminated the formations of the rocks and blades of the grass. But it wasn't enough to cast out the darkness.

The air was crisp and fresh, the oxygen clean and reviving. Dew formed atop the leaves from the large vines, pooling enough moisture for Torin to drink his fill. He was better now but needed sustenance before *we* became his target. Travelling with a Dread was always a risk, especially without Ele around to talk him down. Torin was a good man, but the beast inside him could very well be unpredictable.

There was no day nor night as we roamed through the notorious Cloplands for what felt like days. In the distance there was a beating of drums, an unwelcome reminder we were too close to harm. We'd pivot in the other direction only to hear the ominous, piercing cries of the Windreapers. Everything was a danger here, everything was hungry, and none of them would be afraid to strike if we crossed their paths.

Time was lost on us; the only true measure of it was how much our stomachs ached and growled as they yearned for sustenance. As exhaustion began to take over our weary bodies we stumbled upon the soft murmurs of running water. A small stream shimmered as the insects danced on its surface in the gloom of the haze.

I didn't hesitate to plunge my hands deep into the stream and cup the water to my face. Water had never tasted so good or felt so cold.

"Where did you see the prisoners?" Beau whispered through sips of water.

"It wasn't here. What I saw was just stone, and glowing crevices, some mountains in the distance, some rock, other greener lands nourished by a stream, rivers and lakes, but it was different to this." I explained.

What I had seen was a city built into a deep valley amongst towering stone cliffs where Harpies perched along the rocky edges while Windreaper's circled hungrily above the city— together they dominated the sky. A city that was alive with veins that ran from the spires of the mountain into the base of an arena. Above it hung aviaries of prisoners.

Talking to Beau was hard, but staying calm was even harder. Every moment in his presence was a sharp sting of betrayal dulled by the fact that I still loved him so deeply and by following me here he had denied me any chance to move forward. It was like I was being haunted by him, in the flesh. Zac had wanted him dead, but I gave him mercy on the terms we parted ways even though he had shattered my life, my trust, my family, and my heart.

I watched Beau from the opposite side of the small stream, observing as he washed his weary face. Sorrow lurked behind his gaze as our eyes latched and the pull between us felt different now. We were tethered together, whether I liked it or not— with something like a vine, with thorns that dug in deeper every time I tried to cut it loose. The harder I fought, the more it bled, because our love was still there, but it was twisted and painful, bruised and aching to be forgiven. Because when I had nobody, I had him.

The sadness escaped me as tears trailed down my cheeks and my shoulders trembled against my will as the grief of it all washed over me, heavy and suffocating like a titanic wave buckling me. Beau instinctually leant forward wanting to comfort me, but he stopped himself from reaching for me when I slumped back into the thick of the reeds and the long grass encapsulated me like the hug I so desperately needed. The feeling was bittersweet, the sting of his presence and just how lonely that made me feel—a reminder that I was so close to comfort, yet so far from trust.

"Please don't..." He was still hunched forward. My voice was fragile. I inhaled sharply, fighting for control. "I don't know how much tragedy I have left in me." The admission hung in the air between us.

"Aliera...I..." Beau faltered, his voice breaking softly. "I don't know what to say." He lowered his gaze, defeated and ashamed.

"He came after you, Aliera. Because the thought of you disappearing into another realm without so much as a goodbye would kill him." Torin interjected softly. He was trying so carefully to be a voice of reason.

"Do you think I don't feel the same way?" My voice hitched with sadness.

"Do you?" Beau's voice lifted with a sparkle of hope and his gaze became intense.

"It's going to take some time to stop loving you." I admitted, and a heavy silence fell between us.

"Then don't. Give me a chance to earn your love the way you deserve." His eyes were pleading and shimmering with unshed tears.

"It's not that simple." I sniffed as my voice trembled.

"I know, and if I could undo all the evil I've done, if I could give her back to you, I would." His face sunk into his palms, his shoulders quaking with anguish now as he referenced my mother.

That was the wound I couldn't heal—the lies. He had known most of the time we were together who I was, who my family was and still he lied, he kept things from me, he betrayed me. How could I forgive that?

"Let's just find that girl, she can't be too far away." I hoped aloud.

Chapter Two

DANI

Duncan and I had been in Ecuador for quite some time, and the cracks in our relationship were beginning to show. Our relationship tested by the complexity and isolation of travelling and by suddenly realizing that we had never had the experience of living together before this trip. We had only known the rhythm of weekend sleepovers that young couples had, not this side by side living we had taken up abruptly. The novelty of exploration and tight schedules began to wear thin on me, we had different ideas of what fun looked like and I immediately felt suffocated from my freedom when Duncan made it clear he wanted to drink his way through each city. I craved space, I wanted to explore something alone.

For the first time in weeks, I desperately needed distance, an escape from his incessant whining over the humidity. It wasn't even that hot for this time of year, but he had a way of making his discomforts known to all. Moaning seemed to be his go to now that we were struggling with regular conversations, complaining had become his default. Our relationship was hanging by a thread.

We had worked together for years at the 911 dispatch center—A flooded room with the constant buzzing of chaos and urgency. It was a place where stress never died. This vacation was meant to be an escape from panic and disorder, yet here I was babysitting the man who was meant to be my boyfriend, but he was acting more like a teenage boy on summer break.

Now all I wanted was solitude. It was time for me to embark on an adventure just on my own, somewhere quiet, with crisp fresh air and a silence so numbing I could hear my own heartbeat.

No hustle and bustle of a city's clamor seeping through the cracks of our hostel windows. I wanted to be miles away from the man I *thought* I knew.

My backpack was all I had. It was half packed with clothes and basic survival items and bare essentials. All I needed was some warmer layers to trek to the top of Chimborazo. It would be cold and icy at the summit; I would be staying up there for a few days. Any excuse to soak up a little more stolen solitude, and I wasn't upset that it might make him sweat a little.

I had booked a group hike without telling Duncan. It wasn't his typical directive anyway. He preferred bars over climbing extinct volcanoes and mountain trails, comfort over the hike.

This felt right, I'd slip away for a little while and collect myself without confrontation and drama.

He'd made quite a few friends now, fellow backpackers who were always ready for the next round. I could count on him not missing me for just a few days, I also banked on him not feeling sobriety for at least a week.

It had been dubbed the poor man's Everest, and poor I most certainly was, at least in comparison to what it would cost to venture up Everest. Two-hundred and fifty dollars for serene views, a possibility of altitude sickness, but no whining from Duncan. It was money well spent in my eyes.

I continued to fill my large pack with the remainder of my belongings. I was excited for some cooler weather even if it were just because we'd be at a higher altitude. As much as I had loved the warmth, I had to agree that even though it wasn't too hot, the humidity was beginning to get to me, even more so when I was being constantly reminded by Duncan grumbling about it.

So, I scribbled a quick note. . .

I won't be back for a few days. Gone to trek Chimborazo. You won't be able to call, but it's a guided tour. I'll be fine. Be safe, space your beers.

Dani

It was short and to the point. I wouldn't have to face an awkward conversation. It was four in the morning, and he was still out drinking with the locals and his new collection of worldly friends. Duncan was a people person who had a magnetic energy about him that strangers gravitated towards, that's how I fell for him too.

But being in my late-twenties I was well inclined to getting those occasional little niggling feelings that this wasn't right, not that he wasn't right, he just wasn't right for me—or at least not anymore.

I was after more in life than what street food, casual sightseeing, or the short sparkle an alcohol fueled night could bring me. All of that only filled a certain void until I was itching for more. The emptiness returned and it was louder than before.

I wanted excitement and adventure. To explore the unexpected not just the hot spots. Epic love stories right out of a book that would test me, burn me, and still keep me coming back for more. Tragedies that would rock me, friendships built on a real bond, something more than a likeness for craft beers and the best food stand within a mile's radius. I wanted to *feel,* to live. And maybe I was romanticizing it all a little too much, but if I didn't go looking for it, how would it find me? I wasn't meant for the life I found myself living. The noise wasn't for me, the shallow connections. I wanted something that stirred me and left me breathless. Once I found it, I planned to hold onto it, even if my nailbeds bled while grasping it. I was tired of floating for the sake of just existing.

In truth, I was no longer thriving…

I threw my heavy pack on my back and locked the door behind me, careful not to wake the other eight patrons we shared a room with in the dreary, musky hostel.

Outside the old building, the bustling street was filled with laughter, music, and drunken antics as I quickly hailed a cab. This city was alive, surging with partygoers, a tourists haven if you were into that lifestyle.

"Where are you going?" a voice asked. Shit, it was Duncan.

"Umm… I felt adventurous! I'm going on a trek for a few days up Chimborazo." I smiled anxiously as the cab driver glared at me to hurry and horns tooted from behind his vehicle.

"Oh, I would have come along." He sighed.

"It's not really your scene… It's ok, enjoy the city. I'll see you in a few days." I said as I pecked him on the cheek. A posse of his new friends slowly crowded behind him.

"Ok." his cheerfulness left him as he hugged me.

"Sorry." I whispered in his ear.

"I had a feeling…" he began.

"What feeling?" I questioned.

"The distance between us, from the beginning, I always loved you more than you loved me." He sulked drunkenly. I was cornered and sighed as I waved off the cab driver, I knew I couldn't leave Duncan like this. He had been a friend regardless of my feelings toward him.

I sat on the curb of the street, and he sat beside me, his friends drifted back to the nearest street vendor to wait for him.

"I don't know what to say…" I huffed guiltily.

"It's alright, really. At least we figured it out now and not in fifteen years when we had kids and a house." He said through a forced smile.

"If you want to come, I don't mind." I lied.

"No, I think I've held you back enough." He grunted.

"We'll talk, maybe it's just a rut." I squeezed his hand that rested on my thigh.

"Yeah, things might be different when we get back home." A glimmer of hope rejoiced in his eyes.

"I should get going, I have to be at the pickup point in an hour." I said with urgency.

"Be safe." He kissed my cheek. He smelled of beer and burritos, his new favorite combination.

"I will." I smiled as I hugged him tightly.

He wandered back up the street towards his new friends, mostly Americans with the odd European thrown in the mix, we had met most of them at bars and they shared a lot in common with Duncan. Eat and drink till you can't stand it anymore and with what daylight was left after sleeping off the tequila and empanadas, go see the Instagram worthy tourist locations. It wasn't a bad gig; they were having genuine fun—just not my type of fun.

Another cab stopped finally offering the quick escape I needed. I pulled my bag inside and gave the driver the instructions to the pickup point.

A chartered bus would then take the group most of the way up, then the hiking would begin. There was a comfortable lodge with hotel rooms, two restaurants, and a shop with rental equipment for mountaineering and overpriced clothing.

I stopped at the restaurant for breakfast and ordered a breakfast burrito with a strong black coffee and I sneakily stuffed single serve condiments into my bag for the late nights in my hotel room, a habit I had picked up from my frugal mother. I watched the restaurant and the people that filled it. I shouldn't have been surprised that I was the only loner here, a gush of regret filled my stomach as I second guessed my whimsical decision.

No, this will be good for me, I need to do this! I grumbled to myself—alone is what I wanted.

"We will depart in twenty minutes! Get sorted people!" Shouted a man from the doorway.

I already had everything I needed for the hike. My bag was packed, my boots laced, and I had layers upon layers to keep me warm. It was entertaining to watch the other hikers swarm around the buildings, skulling back hot espresso and energy drinks as I sat calmy against the bus with my second coffee for the morning, a caramel latte. They were like ants out of line. I waited patiently for the crowd to calm and reset in the parking lot. The guide stared at me curiously.

"Alone?" he raised a brow.

"Not really my boyfriend's thing." I smiled.

He sat down beside me in the snow and took a sip of his coffee.

"I'm Jeff." He offered his hand out and I shook it.

"I'm Dani." I replied.

"Well, Dani. I think you may be one of the few who will do this without a worry. The rest will probably head back here at halfway for more beer." He laughed.

"Oh?" I questioned.

"Happens all the time!" said a younger man who sat next to Jeff.

"Chris." He smiled as he shook my hand.

"She's got a boyfriend." Laughed Jeff. Chris and I shrugged off his playful tease.

"How many guides come up with us?" I asked.

"Depends on numbers, but at least three or four." Answered Chris.

"HAUL ASS!" shouted Jeff in his Texan twang.

Not exactly what I was expecting, but I knew it meant *'get on the damn bus.'* I couldn't help but let out a quiet giggle as the others scrambled to obey—shuffling bags and zipping up jackets with the urgency of schoolkids caught talking in class. There was something about the guide's tone, his stance, that carried just enough authority to make everyone a little nervous. It was almost charming, in a stern, mountain-man sort of way.

I picked up my pack and climbed into the bus. It would take us a little further up to the starting point. I sat in the front row and Chris sat beside me.

"Been doing this long?" I asked to be friendly.

"Since I was a kid. It's a family business. He's my dad." He said pointing to Jeff.

"Ahhh! You're American?" I asked.

"Born in Texas, raised here. My mom runs the restaurant." He replied.

"Delicious burritos!" I smiled.

"Well, I hope you make it up, not many do, and it's been a while since we went all the way." He smirked.

Chatter consumed the bus as it swarmed with more and more people and within a few minutes we were setting off up the road. It was a bumpy ride. On the way I spotted a small community of homes. Probably Jeff and Chris's family homes.

"Now everyone, be careful of landslides, the terrain isn't too steady in some parts, it's been marked but stick behind the person in front of you for safety!" grumbled Jeff.

He was a bit of a downer and Chris was giving me sleazy vibes, fair enough for a guy who only sees women for a total of five days I suppose.

The other guides were looking over an incredibly detailed map in the seats beside us.

Finally, we arrived, and I was the first off of the bus. The air was cold and crisp, even more so than what it was at the lodge. I pulled on my thick coat and everyone else began putting on their safety gear.

Chris helped me with my crampons as he saw me struggling to figure them out and gave me a gentle, but friendly knock on my helmet as he finished.

"Thanks." I said.

"Anytime." He smiled as he went to help some others.

Everyone was ready so we began to ascend up a well-used trail. It was a long journey, even longer with everyone stopping for photos every ten minutes.

"Can I go ahead?' I asked Chris.

"Only if I go with you." He smiled as we made our way past the group and other guides.

"Not a photo op kind of gal?" he asked.

"No." I replied.

"What do you do for work?" He asked as we bided our time trying not to wander too far ahead.

"I'm a dispatch officer." I replied.

"Wow! That sounds intense." He exclaimed.

"It is." I said through a tired breath.

"We are almost at the crater if you want to take a breather." He asked.

"Not yet." I said as I pressed on.

"You're the boss!" he smiled.

It was another fifteen minutes, and we made it to a beautiful peak, the views were spectacular. I took a seat on some rocks and pulled out my water bottle whilst taking in the epic views. A natural ravine sat just below us filled with melted snow making a clear natural lake in this majestic scene, infusing even more natural magic into the terrain. I pulled off my helmet and loosened my crampons so I could be more comfortable as we rested.

"So how long has the business been going?" I asked.

"Coming up to about twenty-five years." He answered.

"Wow! So how old does that make you?" I asked curiously.

"Twenty-seven." He replied.

"We moved up here when I was two, dad took over the business after a few accidents happened with the previous owners." He sighed.

"What sort of accidents?" I asked.

"About thirty years ago three kids went missing up here. The bodies never showed up. Nobody is really sure what happened." He explained.

"Happened with a few others too, but children's disappearances are always more unsettling, especially when they go missing in a tourist spot." He added.

"Oh, that's terrible." I sighed sadly.

"Yeah, the parents still come out every few years hoping for more answers. They never get any, but I think they feel some sort of comfort being up here. They are getting old and can't handle the tourist trek anymore, so they stay at the lodge." He said.

"I could never be a parent, the thought of being responsible for another person is terrifying. I hear too many horrible things at work." I said as I looked at him.

"Yep, it's a pretty scary world we live in, I'm grateful I live in a secluded place." He agreed.

"How long till they all get here?" I asked.

"Another twenty minutes, could be more." He replied.

"Well, I'm just going to take quick nap." I said as I took off my pack to make a pillow with a strap still hooked around one of my arms.

He laughed and did the same. We were head-to-head on the slope staring down at the ravine.

"It's so peaceful here." I smiled as I took in a deep breath and drank in the picturesque landscape.

"Yep, it's beautiful." He agreed.

I closed my eyes and soaked up the few rays of sun that kissed my cheeks, a welcome warmth without the humidity to accompany it. The snow beneath me was cold but somehow comforting. I had been up so early that morning; the short nap had been warmly welcomed.

Some time must have passed, I rubbed my eyes, and everyone was up on the hill near us eating their lunches. Chris was still snoring; I gave him a gentle nudge to wake him as I pulled myself up to start eating a banana. The bananas here seemed sweeter than back home, everything in America felt so fake, even the over production of food made nothing seem enjoyable. Here there was love in everything I consumed.

Chris finally sat up and pulled out an apple to devour.

"Where are you from anyway?" he asked with a yawn followed by a quick chomp into the vibrant apple.

"Indianapolis," I answered.

"Cool!" he smiled enthusiastically. I doubt he had any idea which state it was even in.

Suddenly a loud crack echoed throughout the summit, and I felt the ground beneath me become violent with rumbling. Snow began to cascade down the ravine into the pool of water, people who were eating were trying to stay closer to the ground. Nothing could fall on top of us up here, thankfully, but we could always tumble down.

"Was that an earthquake?" I asked Chris as I stood up throwing my pack on my shoulders. It hadn't lasted as long as I expected an earthquake to last.

"I think so, be careful." He urged with fear in his voice as he stood up.

But the rumbling hit again, this time with a bigger punch to it, people were thrown around from the shaking of the earth beneath their feet. I locked eyes with Chris, he grasped my hand as if he knew what was about to happen.

We were thrown viciously down the steep slopes of the ravine that we had sat too close to. The earth was still trembling, injuring us further as we collided with the sharp cold rocks. A crevice had opened up, and the water was sucked back into the depths of the earth leaving a soggy muddy field.

"CHRIS!" Jeff shouted from the top of the peak.

But he was unconscious.

I rushed to his side and applied pressure to a deep gash on his head.

"Get help!" I screamed.

The other two guides were already radioing for help. "Hang tight Dani, helps on the way!" Jeff shouted.

Chris's eyes flickered open, and I was relieved to see he was ok.

"Just try to stay awake, help is coming." I urged with panic in my voice. Blood was dripping down my own face, my cheek gashed and likely a broken nose from landing face first onto the hard terrain as I rolled like a raw egg down the slopes.

We were close to the crevice the quake had created, and steam was billowing out from the expanding cavity.

I moved closer to investigate. I had never seen or felt an earthquake before, this was just too good of an opportunity to pass up. I slowly moved towards it being careful of any loose ground.

But I was thrown to the ground once again. More jolts of violent earth thrust me toward the crevice. The earth opened up even further than before and with another shake I slipped into the hole and was swallowed by the ground. The fall went on for what felt like hours. I hit everything on the way down, roots, rocks, soil, even bones, water still flowed down from the ravine soaking me as I continued to tumble into the deep depths of the earth.

My landing was hard but surprisingly cushioned by a sea of long soft grass and my pack. Was I dead? It was dark, not intense, but what felt like moonlight. Although I saw no signs of the moon. I heard rustling throughout the grass and moaning coming from a few meters away.

"Ahhh!" groaned a man. I pulled my battered body up and followed the muffled sounds, my ears ringing, my sight fuzzy and my mouth tasting of my own blood. My only reliable senses were touch and smell. I could smell everything, dirt, fresh air, and things I was not yet familiar with. The air was effortless to breathe, I felt no need for deep or heavy breaths even though I'd had the wind knocked right out of me from the fall. The groans grew closer, and I began to smell it, blood, but not my own. It was Chris, he was in bad shape, and his wounds were clearly fatal. I could barely see him, but the smell was so intense, as if my face had been pressed into a bucket of blood.

"Chris? Can you hear me?" I begged as I wiped some blood from his face.

He didn't respond, but he grasped my hand. I rubbed my eyes trying to clear my vision some more and I saw it. He had been impaled by a large root, it was lodged beneath his rib cage and went upwards into his chest cavity. I had limited medical experience, but I knew pulling that root out would only put him in more pain and speed up the bleeding. There was no way of saving him. I offered what small amount of comfort I could by holding his hand and gently stroking his head. His eyelids were heavy, and he faded away quickly.

I was alone, unaware of my surroundings or what had really happened. There were large fireflies throughout the trees offering some small semblance of light, occasionally a few of them would land on Chris's body curious to inspect him, their facial expressions small and eccentric.

My arm was wounded, the muscle tissue exposed on my forearm. I wrapped it as best I could with the few resources I had, but my body was failing me. I collapsed in the grass beside Chris and closed my eyes.

Suddenly my body was shaking. "Wake up!" Nudged a whispering man.

My eyes slowly opened, and for a moment I thought it was Duncan. It had all felt like a very intense dream, but it wasn't. My body told me that the second I moved, it was riddled with aches and pains I couldn't yet identify.

"Can you walk?" Asked the man. But my body was unresponsive, not allowing me to speak from the shock of the events I'd endured.

He didn't wait for a reply; he picked me up and threw me over his shoulder. My eyes still adjusting to the darkness once more. Fireflies still lit up the grass and trees. Large shadows appeared behind me where I had laid with Chris and the man carrying me began to hasten his pace.

Large shadows dropped in the distance to where I once lay, and silhouettes of limbs and organs being strewn from shadow to shadow filled my eyes.

"What is happening?" I asked as the man rushed through the trees.

"They are feasting on his body." He whispered gently.

"Keep silent!" He grunted.

Shock filled me as tears began to cascade down my already bloodied face.

"Nearly there." He tried to assure me.

His voice was laced with fear as his head turned from every direction scouring the long grass for the illumination of eyes. There was nothing and his urgency began to settle.

The shadows had long since disappeared now, the fireflies too. All that remained was the scent of sweat and blood lingering on my skin. My damp clothing stuck to my body uncomfortably.

He set me onto the ground and pushed through a wall of unusually large vines, they were thick and coarse, but light to shift and carried on for a few meters until we reached a rocky wall with no obvious entry. He rolled aside a boulder which presented a hole no bigger than a crawl space that was tight for him to squeeze through. A small light was peeking out as he rushed me inside to conceal the brightness.

"Quickly, we can't expose this place." He ordered.

I struggled into the crawl space, trying not to put any pressure on my arm. He followed me and replaced the boulder behind him.

"Show me." He said.

"Where am I?" I asked.

"Good question." He replied but with no answer to follow.

I offered out my injured arm and he unwrapped it. His expression turned serious as he stared grimly at my flesh-torn arm. He was tall, had curly brown hair, tattered clothes, and a leanly built body. Probably in his mid-thirties.

"What is this place?" I asked.

"This? It's home." He sighed unenthusiastically.

"How did you end up here?" I questioned.

"Probably the same way you did." He said as he washed my arm with a natural sea sponge.

I looked around at my new environment curiously, it was little more than a large cave. To one side a fresh stream of water ran through and the other some beds were made up with animal hides. The middle of the cave was the lowest and some meat was hanging from ropes. Over the other side was what was meant to be a kitchen, some wood sat beside a permanent fire pit surrounded by stones and some seating.

He must have been here for quite some time. He had a kind face and was looking for a way to sew up my wounded arm.

"What's your name?" he asked.

"Dani." I answered.

"I'm Oliver." He smiled.

"Nice to meet you." I yawned.

"This is going to hurt." He warned.

He had some sort of small animal claws and used them to pull my wound closed. Eight pinching claws later and it was over. I'd never seen claws like that—they had a likeness to a crab's, but they were far smaller, stronger, and sharper. They punctured into the sides of my wound, but once in place they held the wound tightly together.

"That should do it." He smiled as he washed over it with some fresh water to rinse off the dried blood.

"Don't suppose you have painkillers?" I asked.

"Sorry, no. But these leaves could help, they dull the ache. We call them leafapain." He smiled as he handed me some large star shaped leaves.

"It's a dumb take on leaves and pain, don't have too many, it'll make you hallucinate," He chuckled to himself.

"It's clever!" I smiled as I took a leaf from him.

"You said *we?*" I asked through the gritty unpleasant chewing.

"My younger brother lives here also; he's out hunting at the moment." He answered.

"Get some sleep, you can take one of those beds over there." He pointed to the two large animal hides covering some makeshift beds.

"Thank you, for everything." I smiled.

"You're most welcome." He smiled back.

I walked over towards the beds and removed what remained of my jacket, the arm had been ripped off during my fall, probably the same way I got injured. Much of my body was bruised and covered in gashes and scratches, my eyes both swollen, my nose throbbed from a probable break, and my lip was split to one side. I got banged up rather badly during the fall, but I couldn't stop thinking about Chris. I laid down and closed my eyes as I drifted off into a deep sleep, eager to wake up and restart this whole day again.

It wasn't long before I was awoken by arguing, it was Oliver. I sat up to observe what was happening in the cave. He was arguing in the far corner with another man, slightly taller, about 6'3 with a muscular body, dark brown scruffy hair and blood covering his arms. On the kitchen table there was a fresh animal carcass. This must be his younger brother that he had spoken of.

"Get rid of her!" He yelled.

It was clear I wasn't welcome here. I pulled my shoes on trying not to draw any attention.

"She's injured Jake, badly! She won't last a day out there," Oliver protested.

"We did!" Jake growled.

"We had each other! She's alone..." Oliver snapped in my defense.

"One week Oli, then she goes!" He huffed as he cast me a dark look.

He was furious and went to carve up the carcass to relieve his frustrations. Oliver made his way over to me and urged me to rest as much as I could. The mood in the cave was dark, and I wasn't sure of what move to make next, but the exhaustion overcame me, the pain in my arm came in violent angry waves.

"I'll talk to him once he's calmed down." He tried to assure me.

"I don't want to put you out, if it's a problem that I'm here I'll leave." I said reluctantly.

"No! it's a miracle I found you when I did. You'll stay here and heal. Then we'll talk about somewhere for you to live." He smiled.

"Thank you." I sighed as I laid back on the bed.

Live? What did he mean by that? I wanted to go home. I wanted to get out of this place. I didn't know what it was that I saw feasting on Chris, but I wasn't interested in hanging around to find out. Oliver ignored my blank stare and removed my shoes then gently pushed my legs back onto the bed, subtly encouraging me to get some more sleep and I drifted off quickly.

I could hear a deep snoring beside me, it was somewhat of a comfort, it reminded me I wasn't alone and took me back to thinking I was still staying in a noise driven hostel. There were always snoring sleepers or even people having sex, something I had refrained from doing in public, even at all. It had been a long time since I was intimate with Duncan, but suddenly, I missed him if only for his presence, his bubbly outrageous personality would be a warmth in this mess.

When I woke the smell of food cooking hit me, Jake was asleep next to me, the culprit of the snoring that echoed in the cave. Oliver was frying some food on the open fire. I got up and went to investigate. My stomach growling and leading the way.

"That smells great!" I complimented him.

"Ever had a Windreaper egg?" He asked curiously.

"A what?" I asked with confusion.

"Well, they are colossal birds, enormous vicious creatures." He said.

"Gosh, anything else I should be watching out for?" I questioned as I sat down on a boulder.

He handed me a plate of omelet; the one egg had made more than enough for all of us and then seconds, even thirds. He cooked some of the meat Jake had brought home and dished that onto my plate also.

"What I wouldn't give for some salt and pepper." He sighed as he stared glumly at his boring plate of survival proteins.

"Oh, well you're in luck!" I smiled, excited that I had something to offer, perhaps Jake would let me stay if he shared Oliver's enthusiasm.

I grabbed my pack and pulled out my food supplies. I had two full mini bottles of salt and pepper, hot sauce, ketchup, some trail mix, and a sad squashed sandwich.

"Oh my! May I?" he smiled with wide gleamy eyes.

"Of course!" I smiled back.

Jake woke to the smell of food and made his way over to the log benches that surround the fire pit beside my boulder.

"LOOK! Condiments." Squealed Oliver in an excited tone.

Jake took his plate of food and sprinkled it with some hot sauce.

"Thanks." He said as if it pained him to speak to me.

"No trouble." I replied.

"Any more magic in that bag?" Oliver asked.

"Umm, I've got some thermals, shirts, soap, a knife, flashlight, matches, ice axe, socks, ohhh my phone!" I smiled as I pulled it out and tried to dial 911.

"Any good?" Oliver asked.

"Nothing, there's no signal." I sighed with defeat.

"Well, duhh!" Grunted Jake.

He was rude and unnecessarily so, it made me realize that my value here had increased, and it was about time he considered that regardless of not wanting to help me. I had something to offer that could be the difference between life and death and it wasn't just salt and pepper.

"Jake, have I done something to offend you?" I questioned.

His face twisted from stern to stunned and he let out a loud sigh, he hadn't expected me to question his motions.

"You're just another casualty waiting to happen. You don't know this world. You'll end up putting us all at risk." He sighed. "The fewer people the better off we are." He retorted.

"So, there are others?" I questioned eager to learn more.

"There was, once…" He answered.

"There still are others, they live far away in another part of the land," Oliver chimed in.

"Why don't you live there too?" I asked.

"Because you have to get there first." Jake interjected.

"What does that mean?" I asked curiously.

"It's quite a journey, some have tried, but we don't know if they made it." Oliver explained.

"We only know what we have heard, and people don't exactly come back to visit us." Jake growled.

"Why not?" I asked.

"Might be something to do with the Clops." Jake narrowed his eyes at me.

"What's a Clops?" I asked confused.

"A one eyed giant, with gnarly sharp teeth and a taste for anything with a heartbeat." Jake teased.

"Not funny." Oliver scolded.

"A Cyclops?" I questioned with wide eyes.

"Basically." Oliver answered.

"Is that what ate Chris?" I questioned.

"Yes, but those were younger kids. You got away thanks to their carelessness." Jake groaned some more.

"Yeah, absolutely nothing to do with me." Oliver scowled at Jake.

"You knew what I meant." Jake laughed.

"Well, how have you guys survived? How long have you been here?" I questioned as I looked between them both.

"It's really just a miracle! We lost track of the years, but we were kids when we fell through the earth. What year is it?" asked Oliver.

"Two thousand and twenty two." I replied.

"We fell through in two thousand and two," Jake said with a deep sigh.

"Twenty years," Oliver said slightly astonished.

"I'm twenty eight years old!" Jake said amused.

"Try thirty five!" Oliver laughed.

"All this time, you guys had no idea of your age?" I asked.

"Not exactly important down here princess." Jake scoffed.

"I just meant…. well, you're so primitive now I guess. You'd be surprised by everything that's going on up in the real world." I replied.

"You would be *primitive* too if you had lived here and had to fight for your life on a daily basis just to survive, and what for? To fight another day and probably die fighting just to get to *another* tomorrow." Jake growled at me with rage in his eyes.

The cave became silent as we all ate our food. I had *truly* offended him this time. It wasn't just my presence that was a nuisance to him now.

Jake's life had no meaning; he was stuck in a time-lapse that never moved forward. What purpose did either of them have?

Oliver was the brains, he was perkier than Jake, more hopeful, he had a spark to him that I couldn't quite put my finger on. Jake was the muscle, the hunter, the provider. I understood now that my being here put more pressure on his position to bring more food into the cave, and he didn't like it one bit.

Once my arm had healed, I would leave this place. I'd look for the other humans and hope they could help me find my way home or take me in. I wasn't getting anything but guilt here and I feared once the condiments ran dry the novelty of me would wear off of Oliver also. As friendly and charismatic as he was, it was only time that would show their true natures. Jake was already willing to cast me out into the unnatural world.

"When is daylight?" I asked.

Jake laughed at me mockingly.

"We don't have daylight exactly, maybe half a day of a light haze. What I'd give for sunlight!" Oliver answered with a longing look on his face.

"Get some rest Dani, that arm isn't going to heal without it." He added.

"What can I do to help?" I asked.

Jake turned to me and gave me a firm gaze then flicked his eyes to the boulder blocking the entry.

"JAKE!" Oliver growled.

"He's right! I'm a burden to you both. Once my arm is better, I will leave." I said nodding my head at Jake.

"You won't last a day out there!" Oliver protested.

"I won't last a month in here without causing problems either. It's for the best. I'll find the other humans and go from there." I said through a forced smile.

I was truly afraid. I'd heard about the monsters that haunted this place, and it occurred to me there would be more than Cyclops to worry about and giant flesh-eating birds, the waters would be different, the vegetation, the air was noticeably different upon arrival. I'd need to learn as much as I could from Oliver, even Jake, if I had any hope of surviving outside of this cave away from the protection it offered.

Jake was readying himself to go back outside to hunt and Oliver to go along with him.

"Wait!" I yelled across the cave.

I strode toward them with my pack.

"Take these, they may be of some use." I said handing the axe and knife to Jake. I knew he was the savage; I couldn't imagine Oliver harming anything. Jake's expression didn't change, but he took the weapons and proceeded to leave the cave. Oliver gave me a warm smile and waved goodbye.

"Back to bed!" He ordered with a friendly wink.

"Yes, sir!" I smiled back.

They rolled the boulder away and moments later rolled it back into place to conceal the cave. I was alone in their refuge and while a large part of me wanted desperately to sleep away the pain my arm was causing me, I couldn't fight the urge to snoop around.

The cave was unlike any I'd ever seen, the ground was mostly smooth with the exception of a slight elevation where they had placed the beds. From there you could see out over the entirety of the cave. Not that there was a lot to see, the kitchen, the stream and a nook behind a makeshift wall made of old leaves that I assumed was a toilet space of sorts and it linked up with where the water escaped. I walked around the kitchen and found only knives fashioned out of stone, bowls made from oversized coconuts and mountain of husks saved in a corner.

It dawned on me that what little clothing they wore they had owned for all the years they had been stuck down here, adjusting it over time to cover what they could. I had clothes in my bag, oversized shirts, thermals, and socks, it wasn't a lot but maybe they'd appreciate it. I knew Oliver would.

I wanted to do something for them, but I couldn't think of what. Perhaps I could make another bed, so they didn't have to push theirs together to accommodate me. There were enough husks saved which didn't appear to serve any particular purpose that could substitute as a base and several animal hides, I could lay on top.

It took longer than I had anticipated but after an hour of shuffling everything back and forth with my one good arm I had some substance of what I could only relate to a toddler's bed, or an oversized nest. It wasn't great, it wasn't as comfortable as my plush double cushioned king size mattress back home, but it would have to do.

At least the hides were soft and warm, one thing that came with the constant darkness was the painfully cold chill it brought, it was unescapable even with a roaring fire constantly going. This is what it would be like if the sun disappeared on earth—inherently cold for eternity.

The longer I was here, the colder I felt. I should have built my bed by the fire I thought with a wave of regret, but I had no energy to disassemble my laughable attempt at a cot and move it all over again.

I lay there in the firelit cave, the sound of water racing from the little stream which echoed throughout the large space, nothing to accompany it except my own breathing. No ticking clocks, no snoring from Duncan, no Netflix serving as background noise as I did laundry, no dishes slamming in the sink. Maybe I would never here those things again. My watch had stopped working and time felt so irrelevant now, I had taken so much for granted. What I wouldn't give for a cube of cheese. I had no idea if there were even animals here that lactated for me to try and make cheese. Not that I even knew *how*. Dairy goods and prosciutto were a thing of the past now. There would be no more cider or wine with my co-workers after a busy shift, just water, and I'd likely have to fight for that, eventually.

CHAPTER THREE

ELEANOR

I heard the screams, the howling and panic. Everything happened too fast and before I could react Zac was throwing me across the room and Draven had slammed the door shut and began barricading it with the help of Thane. They knew I'd likely jump in next.

"NOOO!" I fought against Zac, desperate to reach the door.

"You'll never survive the fall," Draven stood before me, towering over me with worried eyes.

"Where did they go?" Zac asked, his voice tight with concern as he watched Thane trace the Harpies' markings etched into the door's frame of ancient woodwork and runes.

"Tierra Hundida…" Thane replied softly, almost as if speaking to himself, eyes narrowed in deep thought as his fingers fell over the ridges of the door.

Draven released a weary sigh, his expression clouded with worry. "Of all the realms, why that one?" He punched a bookshelf, sending books flying across the floor.

I stepped closer, curiosity pushing me forward. "What's so bad about Tierra Hundida?" I asked.

"It's a realm of eternal darkness," Draven answered simply, exchanging uneasy glances with Zac, as though they shared an unspoken wealth of knowledge about this place.

"And?" I pressed, sensing more beneath their hesitation.

Zac turned toward me, his voice careful, but firm. "Ele, Tierra Hundida is the ancestral homeland of Dragons. They weren't born in bright skies or atop mountain peaks, they emerged deep underground, from the heart of the Pyre. When the stones heated so hot, they took on life, and from them Dragons were born." He explained.

I blinked, confused. "The Pyre?" I raised a brow.

Thane stepped forward slightly, his gaze distant but intense. "The Pyre is an ancient ground beneath the foundations of all the realms, ours is in Sonsuz, and they are all connected. Pulsing with energy hotter than magma or Dragonfire. Each is older than time itself, and they are the heart of their realm. Tierra Hundida's Pyre is where Dragons took their first breath."

I shook my head slightly, still unclear. "But why is that dangerous for Torin, Beau, and Aliera?" I was flustered, and my words came out demanding.

Thane hesitated, weighing his words carefully. "Because Tierra Hundida is not just ancient by even our regard—its land is scarred by war. Centuries ago, Dragons fought a devastating battle against creatures called Windreapers. The conflict was so catastrophic that it plunged the entire realm into an endless night, burying cities and leaving behind countless restless spirits. It's a place steeped in loss and lingering pain, haunted by echoes of the past." He explained. "Nobody chooses to go there." He pressed his lips together.

"Anything else?" I shrugged.

"Ele, it's a wasteland. It's also where the Titans sent the children…" Zac's voice was breathy as if he'd spent all this time piecing the facts together only to come up with that single truth.

"The giants? As in the kin to the Titans?" I gasped. Zac nodded.

"The cyclops…" He corrected me.

"After their banishment they were renamed, stripped of power and titles. Wiped from the history of the Dunya. Unless you ask the moles," Draven added.

"Okay, so there are Clops. We can handle them." I sucked in a breath of pride.

"There are Windreapers… and not to mention the Harpies." Draven's eyes lowered on me now as if he were trying to push my confidence back down.

"What is so terrifying about the Windreapers?" I asked.

Thane moved to the shelves in the room and pushed around the fallen books with his boot beneath the shelf housed even more books, not just any books, crumbling books, one of a kind history books. *Creatures and Beasts of the Titan Realms* was what was carved into the worn outer layer of leather that bound this one book together.

Draven stood with Thane now as they swept through page after page of the book until they came across a faded drawing of what look like a bird, but one so weaponized and volatile it truly could challenge anything else in the sky.

Compiled by the High Mole Thorley Hartwell.

The Windreaper is a formidable, extraordinary beast. They have been recorded since the parting of the lands and the crust of the earth shattered into its now known Realms.

Standing at a height of fifteen feet or more, this creature carries awe-inspiring dominance. Its feathers are described as sharp-edged, shaded in silver and cloud blue, granting the bird seamless camouflage amongst clouds and mist making it a terrifying opponent. The Windreaper is said to have a four foot long hooked beak with volatile sharp edges capable of piercing Dragon scales.

Elder Moles report that Windreaper's possess the unique ability to manipulate wind currents. Their expansive wingspan measuring upwards of thirty feet are capable of summoning storms of catastrophic intensity. These gales were known to uproot entire forests, with the razing of Underfoot Forest being the most catastrophic event recorded. This event was due to the sheer number of beasts more so than any individual power. A reckoning such as that can only be achieved by Windreapers in the thousands.

Their talons are curved and lethally sharp. Once documented in the only ever autopsy records as having split armored claws that open mid-flight.

In the historical records of warfare among mythical creatures, Windreaper's often appeared as strategic and cooperative predators. They were observed coordinating their assaults with meticulous timing and brutal efficiency, proving themselves capable of overpowering even fully grown Dragons. Due to their unparalleled prowess and destructive potential, Windreaper's were deeply feared and revered by civilizations across all known realms. As recorded in the Skywrit Annals, many early skyfaring empires considered Windreaper sightings to be omens of great change. Either divine ascension or cataclysmic loss.

Windreaper's are a particularly formidable enemy but have in recent times aligned themselves with the Harpies. The two species fought side by side during the Battle of Skyfall. Their combined aerial tactics shattered entire formations, turning the skies into a whirlwind of blood and storm.

One of the most haunting remnants of their ancient battles lies in a place now known as the Salted Sands. An abandoned graveyard to both Windreaper's and Dragons. Once a thriving jungle nestled near the Sea of Liolita, the land was poisoned by the sheer scale of death and destruction. Fallen Titans plunged into the lush canopies, the blood of all seeping into the roots, corrupting the soil beneath. Over time, the jungle succumbed, and salt from the storm-churned sea crept inland, whitening the land like bone dust. Today, the dunes shimmer with a quiet menace, concealing most of the shattered skeletons of sky giants, both feathered and scaled—a mute testimony to a war that scorched both sky and soil into oblivion.

May this entry serve future scholars with caution, and the understanding that even the skies can turn against us.

"So, we're fucked?" Zac sighed as he backed away from the book and Draven snapped it shut.

"I didn't realize how bad this was…" Draven gulped.

"I'm not leaving Torin in there! Or Aliera or even Beau!" I stormed for the door.

Draven grasped my shoulder and ripped me backwards. "You will die in there, Ele! We need to be smart." He growled.

"What can we do from here? We need to be down there." I pointed towards the realm door.

"We need to arm ourselves with information, we need to go to the archives in Lexia, there's got to be more in the histories, the mole's will help us find the information we need." Draven pressed.

"I'm not leaving." Zac scoffed.

"Zac…"Thane huffed.

"If they try to come back up someone has to be here!" He protested.

"He's right, someone should stay and he's the only Titan we have left. Zac belongs here in Antoli." I pressed.

"No going through the door!" Draven narrowed his eyes on Zac.

"I'll be right here, just hurry." Zac nodded submissively.

With that, Draven, Thane and I left Antoli. Thane swept me into his arms and before I had time to brace myself we were soaring above the treetops, climbing higher with every beat of his wings. The ground fell away beneath us to a place where there was no smell, no sense of time or direction. We cut swiftly through the sky, bound for Lexia and its pearlescent towers that shimmered in the sunlight and danced in the darkness against torchlight.

It wasn't far off at this speed, the tallest of the opal towers of Lexia shimmered on the horizon as sunset peaked in, daylight and moonlight clashing, calling us back to the bustling city.

Lexia was still in disarray. It was over-populated now, but the Fae worked tirelessly to build new homes on the beachside of the city, determined to shelter those in need. They worked well into the night, never tiring.

Thane set me down beside Draven at the steps of the main hall. My legs still wobbly from the flight, my skin still cold as a cloud. We walked briskly towards the doors that led down to the city archives, a library of a truly grand scale. The entrance was guarded by Fae, they stood down immediately once they saw Thane and Draven.

Starlette was already inside at the base of the stairs, her purple cloak trailing behind her, still beautiful as ever. Her eyes glistening against the sconces. Draven took her down before Thane and I as he explained the circumstances.

"Where's Zac?" She asked.

Draven cleared his throat, he was visibly tense as her steel gaze landed on him. "He's staying in Antoli, just in case they come back up." He swallowed hard.

I glanced at Thane, and he had the same awkward awareness I had, secondhand dread.

"Do you need a moment?" I offered, already taking four steps backwards and making eye contact with one of the Mole's for assistance. I wasn't waiting for an answer.

Draven shook his head, but we were already past the threshold. We spun on our heels and sat at the closest desk with all the grace of people fleeing a winter storm.

"What *was* that?" Thane murmured with a hushed laughter.

Thane was older, composed, but the glint in his eye betrayed him. He knew a relationship fight when he saw one. Even he wasn't above the petty drama; his wife, Teresina was a force of her own, a respected leader, sharp in every sense, and not one to let things slide easily.

Two moles landed at our desk, both with scrolls and leather bound books spilling over their arms.

"This will be a great start." I said with a grateful smile.

"Apologies, my dear, but this is all we have on Tierra Hundida." One replied as he adjusted his spectacles.

"What about the Harpies and Windreaper's?" Thane's brows furrowed as he unraveled a scroll that was so delicate it might crumble in his hands.

"Just what's in the scrolls, unfortunately much was lost after the battle of Skyfall, their histories weren't able to be brough back with the surviving Dragons." His response was tinged with regret.

"The battle of Skyfall? It's all in here?" I echoed.

"Yes, well…what little remains." He nodded solemnly.

Thane place the scrolls in front of us, opening it with weights on each corner so we could read together.

Entry by Melri The Pale

The Pyre is not a city, it is a living crucible. An open wound in the earth where heat and magic pulse as one, so fiercely that Dragon eggs formed without parentage. Dragon's revered it as sacred land. Titans, their ancient allies stood watch over the borderlands, Each Pyre was treated as the heart for all realm's. It became sacred ground, and their lush forests were treated as such. No kingdom dared encroach upon it, until the Harpies.

The Harpies have only ever claimed one single queen, a Crohn witch named Morog who has reigned since her inception. The Pyre was not sacred to Dragon's alone. It was a convergence point that called to all winged beings. The Harpies became spiteful, once tolerable became dark and decrepit. Morog began mixing magic to counter that of the Titan's and Dragons. The Windreaper's, too dangerous for the Harpian city were placed in the nesting grounds beyond the bog. In a land now known only as the Cradle. The Clops, the fallen children of the Titans live in close proximity to guard them.

Harpies believed the Windreapers were sky spirits, but they were demons.

At first they grew small, but with each new hatching they became colossal. Smarter, more organized. Sowing chaos over the land and Harpy flocks tried to ride and train them in the art of battle.

But they weren't a beast to be controlled, they were to be aligned with.

A golden-scaled egg, born on a stormy day, had not yet hardened for hatching when it was stolen. Cloaked by low storm clouds, a Windreaper and its Harpy rider snatched it from the nesting cavern of the Pyre. Mid-flight, the egg was shattered, intentionally. Its destruction was no accident.

There were whispers that the hatchling inside would have been unlike any dragon before it. Born of ancient flame, destined to rise as a power the realms had never seen.

To the Dragons and Titans, it was an atrocity...an act of war. To the Harpies, it was an opportunity for revenge.

The skies darkened as the Harpies rallied their armies and turned the Windreapers loose on the Pyre where the Dragons frolicked in their expansive jungle.

For three days, the heavens rained blood, scales and feathers.

The Pyre was once a sacred cradle, but it had become a charred battlefield. Trees were reduced to smoldering stumps. Titan warlords hurled boulders with the force of lightning. Harpies dove faster than arrows. Windreapers cut through the air with precision and merciless impact.

The surrounding lands were scorched into dust. The storms summoned by the Windreapers flattened the Extended Honey Hills, drowning them in fury. The elemental clash between Titans and Windreapers reshaped the world itself. What remained was no longer fertile.

What remained became known as the Salted Sands.

Some say it was the Windreapers who poisoned the land, dragging salt from the sea in their storm spirals. Others whisper of Sirens, rising *from the depths to extinguish the fires before they touched the lands of their kin.*

The heat of the battle was so intense, it could be felt all the way in Vacia Isla.

On the final day, the roots drowned. The skies fell silent. And there was no victor.

Now, only bones remain, bleached and crystalized by salt. Dragons. Titans. Harpies. Windreapers. All left to waste beneath the cursed sky.

In the aftermath of Skyfall, the Titans were fragmented and few, but they moved on. They crossed into the Dunya, a realm rich with sun and soil, where Fae and humans lived in peace.

There, the Titans tried to rebuild in distant lands. Antoli was not built for beauty. It was built for survival.

Forged of stone and magic, balanced on icy cliffs older than time, Antoli was designed as a fortress, a last bastion of order when all other realms frayed. A place where the threads of magic from every realm could unite in safety and be controlled by the Titans. Its purpose was singular: to protect the balance between worlds.

When Tierra Hundida was lost to shadow after Skyfall, it was Antoli that absorbed the burden of protection. The ancient barrier shattered by the fleeing Dragons and Titans was resealed, bound by the last surviving strands of wild Antoli magic. Now, it holds firm. No being may enter Tierra Hundida.

Only through earth can one accidentally reach it.

Long before Antoli rose. Before Skyfall scorched the skies. Before the realm of Tierra Hundida was swallowed in shadow, there were the Titans. And once, they were two.

The first were noble, wise, and grounded in elemental grace. They shaped mountains into sanctuaries and lived in harmony with the Farkli and other early races. These Titans passed knowledge through memory.

They would go on to help build Antoli into the mecca it is now. But not all Titans chose peace.

The second clan were larger, fiercer, giants, but fewer and untamed, they turned their power into terror. They roamed with cruelty, corrupting the land where they walked. They saw no value in peace, only in conquest.

The cultured Titans exiled them.

They cursed their kin as punishment. Their elemental powers were stripped. Their vision halved, now roaming the realms with one hideous eye. No longer Titans in form or name, they became something else entirely. The world forgot what they had once been.

The cursed were first driven into the northernmost reaches, into the sharpest mountains, where the snow never melts. And then... they were cast through realm doors, torn from the Dunya, scattered across the shadow realms with no way back. Their children were taken and cast into Tierra Hundida, the adults into Otro Mundo.

Their names are no longer spoken in Titan halls.

Draven and Starlette stood over the table now, the scroll curling across the floor like a coiled serpent as the Mole finished reading aloud.

"So, what's the weakness?" Starlette asked, arms crossed, eyes narrowed.

"Everything has to have one," I said. "It's a sharp hunter, but that also makes it sensitive. Doesn't it?" I asked.

Draven turned to me. "What are you thinking, Ele?"

"The bell!" I burst out, nearly shaking with the realization. "The Titans didn't hang that bell on Antoli for decoration. It's a warning beacon—*a sound weapon.*"

Excited, I grabbed Starlette by the arms and gave her a shake. "It disrupts the Windreaper's senses!"

"Okay," Thane said, ever the strategist. "So, we draw them through the door and trigger the bell?" He questioned me as he tried to keep up with me.

"Echobreaking…" the Mole muttered, eyes wide behind thick lenses. Then louder, "Yes! Echobreaking! It's odd… but it could work. It's never been done before, they've never penetrate the Dunya realm." He said.

"Hold on!" Thane snapped, his wings twitching with unease. "The Dunya has been safe for thousands of years *because* of the realm doors. You want to invite them in? We're barely recovering from Rael's onslaught." He argued.

Draven didn't flinch. "If we don't get Aliera back, we lose an air wielder. The *second-last* Titan in the Dunya. We don't even know if the others still exist, or where to find them if they do. And Beau, whether or not you agree with his past, he is valuable. He's unique. And if they find him in Tierra Hundida, he's in trouble." Draven sighed.

He paused. "Torin won't hold out forever. His instincts will turn on him. On *them*. They could tear each other apart." His words were harsh, but true.

"Please…" I murmured, the weight of it all crushing me as I sank into the nearest seat. "I don't think I can take it." A tear escaped my eye.

Starlette sat beside me without hesitation, sliding an arm around my shoulders.

"We're going to get them all back," Starlette whispered, fierce and certain. *"All of them."* She rubbed my back in slow, grounding circles.

"You have to stay here, Ele," Thane said suddenly.

"WHAT?" My voice cracked. It wasn't a question. My grief turned to fury in an instant. "You can't be serious." I pleaded now.

"He's right," Starlette said softly, though the words hurt her to say. "You're too emotionally connected. Aliera is your sister by marriage. Torin is your…" She hesitated, "…your heart. And Beau… he's your friend. You're a hearth, Ele. And it's already showing through." She sighed.

"I *can* help," I argued, standing to face them both. "I can *heal.*"

Starlette reached for my hands, holding them gently between hers. "Then let *me* go in your place. Let me do this *for you.*"

My voice dropped to a whisper. "What am I supposed to do here?"

Starlette didn't answer right away. She didn't need to. Her silence was steady, unwavering, like the calm before a storm she knew she could survive.

She was one of the few Farkli born with almost every elemental power. All the fire of Astrid burned in her veins. All my healing lived in her hands. And every potion my mother had ever whispered into the world, Starlette could conjure them without a second thought.

She was a force rarely unleashed. And right now, she was choosing to unleash it for *me*.

"You stay here," She said softly, brushing a strand of hair behind my ear. "Keep the hearth burning. Keep the door open. I will bring them back to you, Ele." Her hand warmed my cheek, catching my tears with the kind of tenderness that broke me.

"I'll be all alone…" I sobbed. "I've never been without Astrid." The grief finally cracked open inside me, sharp and childlike as I reflected on my beautiful scarlet haired sister. My body trembled. My voice broke and I wept hard, the kind that was healing but also soul destroying.

The room stilled. Scrolls stopped unrolling. Books snapped shut. The torch flames fluttered, shaken by the weight of my breath.

"Luna is still here," Draven said gently, crouching beside me. "She's with Cleo. She's waiting for you." He squeezed my hand. He was just as tall as Beau. Similar in looks but his wings were feathers. A seasoned warlord.

"Luna…" I whispered. The name was a joyful memory. My lips curved into a broken, wet smile at the thought of our precious family wolf. Loyal and fierce, fur like obsidian, always watching and waiting for us. She must be so confused, she wouldn't have seen any of us for weeks, maybe months. Time had meant nothing.

"Okay, but I'm waiting in Antoli." I wasn't asking, I was telling them now.

"Fine." Starlette agreed hesitantly.

The moles began to roll up the rest of the scrolls as the sound of boots echoed down the stone staircase. Cleo appeared first, two guards beside her.

"What have you learned?" Her voice was tired and crisp, it held no pause, she was all business, and who could blame her when her city had been burdened with the weight of restoring the Dunya and all its people.

Draven stood from where he sat. "More than we expected." He answered.

"Enough to act." Thane added with a firm nod.

Cleo's gaze lingered between me and Starlette, her expression softened for the briefest of moments. "Then let's move, we can't waste any time." She said.

CHAPTER FOUR

DANI

Days had passed, my only measure of time was that my arm was healing relatively well, and the pile of Windreaper eggshells was growing in size. My relationship with Jake was worsening day by day as the awkward avoidance continued. Oliver was caught in the rift between us. He was doing all he could to teach me as much as I could cram into my already exhausted brain about the plants, animals and threats that lingered outside the cave, but his knowledge was limited so we made do with what we could and explored together when it was safe to do so. He knew the day was coming when Jake would force me out.

Jake spent most of his time hunting, not because we needed it, but as a way to stay away from me. Oliver and I would spend most of our days prepping jerky or trying different plants and herbs. He showed me some form of mutated looking corn, although blue in color and pear like in shape, once dried and ground it made for an interesting flour and for the first time in years they had bread. It wasn't risen and fluffy, if anything it was the complete opposite, dense and chewy but still, a difference in diet was welcomed by at least Oli. Fortunately, we had an abundance of stone, so he had long ago engineered a mortar and pestle, making the grinding process far easier.

There were more plants similar to those on earth, meaty tomatoes, star shaped cucumbers, purple fleshed potatoes. Something more than meat protein from a Goafree. An animal that was as big as a donkey but had goatlike traits, extraordinarily fluffy which I learnt is where the hides were from. Oliver had wanted to trap one to keep in the cave for milk, but they were far too noisy once they got them anywhere near the vines and forcing them into the tiny crawl space proved to be a challenge, so they abandoned that idea.

They had spent so much of their time here hidden, only venturing out for the bare necessities and even at times they couldn't find them. I'd learnt that on several occasions both Jake and Oli had come close to death from starvation.

Oli had looked after Jake until he was old enough to learn to hunt, and then he took it upon himself to be the main provider, perhaps to repay Oli for caring for him as a young boy.

Oli was far different to Jake, more reasonable and willing to try new things. He liked hearing about life in the world and how things had changed. He especially enjoyed me recounting stories to him from television shows. I couldn't think of many. I used to spend so much of my time at work that I never really sat and watched a lot of TV. My house was more of a stopover, somewhere to eat and wash my clothes, get some rest, and kill time. This cave felt more homely than that pathetic existence I once knew, a life where I just lived for my job.

By now Duncan would know I was missing. They knew where I went missing and I could only hope they would find a way to get to me. An impossible dream, I knew Chris and I would have been assumed dead. I couldn't blame them, the fall alone should have killed me the way it did Chris. I knew I was out of reach, that where I was, was unlike anything most humans had ever seen or imagined.

"How many days will it take me to get to the others?" I asked Oliver.

"There's no telling, you'll have to sneak through The Bog, be careful not to disturb the water too much, travel to the right, ONLY THE RIGHT DANI!" Oli was firm with this direction.

"Okay, what else?" I asked.

"Once you're over the mountains, you'll see the bones that mark the Pyre, it's hot there and it glows red, walk through it, you'll see a hillside next to an old forest, go through it and keep to the mountainside. If you've kept to the mountains you'll see the small human settlement, Three Shadows. If you are on the wrong side of the mountain, you'll see fumes and vapors rising from a sharply cut valley, there's a whole other world down there." He explained further.

"What kind of world?" I asked.

"Couldn't tell you…" He shrugged.

"Comforting." I sighed.

"It might take you a week if you can get by unnoticed. You will have to pass through the rest of the Cloplands and the Cradle," He sighed.

"What's that?" I ask with a tired look on my face.

"The Cloplands is where we live, it's vast and known as the land where the Cyclops mainly dwell, they have several small villages throughout the land not far from here, it's quite widespread. There are some tunnels that other humans built long ago, that go around and under some of the villages, but I don't know where they begin or end, I'm sorry. They are most likely caved in by now." He sighed.

"And the Cradle?" I urged.

"Nesting grounds of the Windreaper's," He gritted his teeth.

"Any other deadly places I need to become an amazon warrior to pass through?" I huffed.

"Yes, there's The Bog," Said Jake as he replaced the boulder in the wall once he had squeezed himself through.

"Do I want to know what that is?" I asked.

"It's a dank wasteland of mud, luminescent puddles, oversized lily pads, giant insects, carnivorous fish and reptilians called the Talagata that linger in the deeper waters, they favor the stillness of the bog, it makes it easier for them to find their prey." Jake explained without any emotion on his face.

Oli scowled at him. "The Bog surrounds the base of the hills you will need to cross over. We are basically on another island, but it's only a few meters to the next one, you can swim it." Oliver informed.

"So, no way around it?" I queried.

"No, it goes for miles. The only way is through it," Jake added.

"Have you been through it?" I asked him.

"Once, I got bitten by a..." but Oliver cut him off before he could finish.

"let's not scare her! That could have been a one off," He smiled awkwardly.

It was hard to guess what Jake wanted to say. He was covered in scars, mostly bite marks from creatures with more teeth than I was accustomed to, creatures of a world I wasn't familiar with, he wasn't as forthcoming with information as Oliver had been until now, he probably didn't want to scare me in hopes I would leave sooner. I was still naive to the terrain and it's horror that that waited for me.

But I wanted to be scared, once I faced some fear maybe it wouldn't be as scary as my mind had made me believe it could be. Maybe I'd find safety in the danger by making myself think it was worse than it really was.

"How's your arm today?" Jake questioned.

"Better, I'll leave tomorrow," I answered.

His expression changed from stern to guilt, but I had hope now, a village with more than two people seemed far more appealing than just existing in a cave with a man who couldn't stand the sight of me and another who barely kept him in check. Although Oliver had become a good friend, I couldn't ask him to go against his own brother.

"Are you sure?" Jake asked hesitantly. "Let me see your arm." He ordered as he walked over to me without waiting for an answer.

He was tall, with broad shoulders and a muscular body, dark wavy hair and bright hazel eyes, the kind of eyes that when fixated on you, could reach into your soul. He wasn't a kind person; he was mean and crude. He looked over my bandaged healing arm and agreed that it would be fine for me to leave without so much as removing the bandage.

"You need more time!" Oliver protested; he knew beneath my bandage I was healing but any sudden blows to it would leave it worse than it began.

"She said she's fine, Oli!" Jake interjected.

Oli scowled in his face and turned to me, "I'll go with you till you reach The Bog, once you are over the hill you shouldn't have too much trouble finding the Three Shadows, just follow the instructions I gave you." Oliver grumbled, his heat all for Jake.

"NO!" scolded Jake.

"I'm not going to send her out there to die! If that's the person you want to be then stay here, but I'm getting her over that hill," He yelled as Jake looked on in disbelief.

Oliver began filling my pack with food and any other items we may need.

Jake was mad, he didn't expect this from Oli and he begun pacing the cave in an obvious rage.

"FINE! I'll go with you, but if anything happens it's on you," He pointed at me with the knife.

I knew what he meant, if Oliver were to be harmed because of me, he would kill me. He had it in him to do so, I assumed the only reason he hadn't already was because of Oli, we had bonded, we shared similar interests, and he had a friend for the first time in a long time that wasn't his own brother.

"We don't need you to come," Oliver scoffed with disgust.

"You are too soft for the world out there, without me you'll both be dead before a haze comes through," He growled back.

We looked at one another and knew he was right; Oliver turned to me awaiting approval.

"Come, but once I'm over The Bog come straight back here. You don't need to follow me all the way," I sighed.

I had this disgusting feeling in the pit of my stomach that something wasn't right. It could have been my unusual new diet of Windreaper eggs, jerky and Goafree steaks, but I was almost certain I sensed another being lurking somewhere in the shadows.

Oliver was muttering to himself in the kitchen as he carved up some meat to pack.

"Shhhhhh!" Jake huffed. I looked toward him; he pointed to the boulder. He had that same feeling I did.

It was moving…slowly. The crackling sound of the rocks moving against one another became louder and louder as the boulder moved from one side to the other. Oliver armed himself with the ice axe and tossed me a knife. I was closest to the entry, and I snuck up to side out of sight.

Laughter and giggling became clearer as the boulder was now shifted away. It sounded like children, but the sounds of their voices were louder and deeper, they came from larger beings and Jake rushed to my side.

"Clops!" He whispered.

What do we do?" I asked.

He didn't answer me, but one of the children tried to fit through the human sized hole headfirst and sliding in on its back. I could see their one eye staring upward towards the ceiling as it tried to shuffle further in. The child turned his head, saw us, and screamed, the force of its voice throwing me back like a harsh gust of wind. Jake pounced on him, dropped the small ice axe and pulled out a bigger knife, and with one heavy blow he plunged the stone carved knife into its eye, an immediately fatal blow. The Clops suddenly stopped struggling and went limp as it's black blood oozed from the wound.

The screaming worsened outside as the other children realized their friend was lifeless.

"Ga ta un mam gagda!" One shouted.

I didn't know what it meant, but I was sure it meant 'get help'. They could have taken us out if they were smart about it. They were twice my size even if they were only young children; I observed the body of the dead beast blocking our only exit, this was the only one I had seen up close. The only other memory I had of them was a silhouette of a pack of slightly larger Clops tearing Chris's body apart. This one's face was dirty, almost rough like a stone with cracks in the skin, callouses for eyebrows, a bald head with 2 small but prominent blunt horns in the corners of his forehead, dry chapped lips and a nose shaped more like a cow's snout. More black blood oozed from the eye at least the size of a soft ball. There were no eyelashes, but eyelids that closed from both top and bottom, only a small hint of the iris still visible, a vibrant orange.

Jake was covered in the black blood and handed me the knife as he walked towards the stream to clean himself off.

"Pack everything you can. We need to leave, NOW!" Oliver ordered as he threw the large pack to me.

"They will be back with more; they are bigger and move faster than us. Hurry!" He added with an anxious voice.

Jake didn't seem worried and took his time collecting some hides and weapons.

"Jake! Hurry," Oliver urged.

"Where do we go?" I asked.

"We all go now; we can't come back here," He sighed looking sadly at Jake.

"It was only a matter of time," Jake said as he rested his hand on Oli's shoulder.

"Help me," I begged as I tried to pull the clops body out the way.

"Not that way. Follow me," Oliver ordered.

Towards the back of the cave were more boulders, we used all our strength to move them exposing a path to the surface.

"Is this wise?" Jake asked Oli.

"We have an advantage if we don't go out that side, we can't use the caves now that they know we lived in one, they will expect use to use them as cover," Oliver said.

"But now we run the risk of Windreaper's *and* Clops," Jake protested.

I wasn't going to listen to them bicker, so I set off ahead and kept to the long grass with my head down following the sound of water.

They quickly hurried behind me so not to lose me in the menacing darkness, keeping as silent as possible. Hours passed and the haze began to drift in, it brought a poor amount of light but enough to see a tall collection of abysmally made homes.

"A Clop village! We need to get out of here!" Jake ordered.

"Wait, it's quiet?" Maybe there isn't anyone here? it could be abandoned," Oliver smiled with hope.

"So what? You want to bunk in their beds for a snooze," Jake sneered.

"Shut up!" I ordered as I pointed towards a Clop collecting a large bucket.

"Ugh, we need to find shelter," Oliver mumbled.

"The tunnels?" I asked.

Jake nodded and led the way towards an old dying tree, large thick roots buried deeply into the soil, it's base covered in long grass and large flowers. It seemed untouched for years and unstable with rotting bark and mold covering the base once exposed.

"You knew where this was and didn't tell me," Growled an angry Oliver to Jake.

"it's no use, it caved in years ago about a hundred meters in, but it should be safe enough for us to get some sleep for a while," He answered.

"I'll take first watch," I offered.

"Thanks Dani." smiled a tired Oliver.

Jake unrolled a hide and they both lay down on it and drifted off to sleep.

Several more hours passed, and I was awoken by Jake.

"you're a terrible lookout," He said nudging me with a disgruntled look.

"Sorry," I sighed as I stood up. He took my place and ordered me to go lay beside Oliver.

"Get some rest," He smiled softly.

"Was that a smile? Did it hurt?" I giggled quietly.

"Go!" He said slightly annoyed at my joke. I didn't argue and went to rest as ordered.

The sound of chewing woke me; it was Oliver munching on some dried meat next to my ear.

"Do you want some?" He asked politely.

"No," I yawned.

I was hungry, but I was sick of meat, the only thing worse was chewy dried meat. I needed vegetables and fruit. Something without the flavor of blood and death upon it.

Jake had gone to investigate the outer perimeter of the village as I slept and had been gone for some time.

"You guys must hate me; they would have been looking for me." I sighed.

"Not at all, you've been a breath of fresh air, and Jakee knows it, he just doesn't know how to say it without acting like a douche bag," Oliver smirked.

"who's a douchebag?" Asked Jake as he entered the tunnel.

"Keep your voices down! I could hear you a few meters away from here," He scolded.

"You're the douchebag," I whispered with a grin.

He threw an oversized apple and banana at me.

"Well, your resident douchebag just brought you some breakfast," He scoffed at my insult.

"Ohhh, thanks!" I smiled as I bit into the mutant sized juicy red apple.

"None for me!" Oliver smirked as he enjoyed chewing on his homemade jerky.

Jake pulled a massive loaf of bread out of the pack and my eyes lit up.

"Cheese? Tell me they had cheese?" I beamed with excitement at the fluffy loaf.

"Couldn't check, too many around," He sighed.

I tore a chunk of bread off of the enormous loaf and bit into it.

"Aww, it's so effortless to chew," I grinned from ear to ear.

"Shhhhhh!" Jake ordered as my mouth filled with euphoric explosions.

Oliver looked on as I stuffed my face with the bread and fruit, he finally put his jerky down to try some, he was in disbelief that clops would cook anything, their main diet was known to be raw meat, especially humans.

He took a mouthful of bread and was prepared to chew hard, but he was met with surprise. It was unchallenging to what he was accustomed to, a pleasant surprise, the loaf melted in our mouths as I remembered a buttery croissant would. Oh, how I missed croissants with ham, cream cheese and cheddar. I hadn't seen a pig here yet and my expectations weren't too high, my fondness of those delights were a pastime, a distant but beloved memory.

"We should leave soon," Oli whispered.

"I agree, we shouldn't linger in any one spot for too long," Jake nodded.

We continued our journey with the shelter from the constant darkness, keeping to the cover of the tree's. We had successfully evaded the Cloplands without being spotted and fortunately for us, the Clops wouldn't venture this far north towards the Cradle if they didn't have to, it was too open and exposed.

The trouble we would face with the Windreaper's was that they had exceptionally good vision and needed no help from the haze to see us in any form of lighting. We could be watched and hunted at any moment. We approached the barren dry desolate lands. The once long grass was torn up and shaped into colossal nests. The sight of them stretched far beyond what my eyes could see. The majority of Windreaper's seemed to lay their eggs here.

"Is this where you come to get the eggs?" I asked Jake quietly.

"No, the younger Windreaper's aren't allowed to nest here, they come to the outer Cloplands where our cave was," He explained.

"Why?" I questioned.

"The females fight for dominance out of boredom sometimes. The older the more vicious they are, the younger ones stay away till they are big enough to fight back. See all the blood one the ground? That's not from birthing eggs or hatching them," He pointed out the pools of blood and scattered feathers.

"We observed and learnt a lot out here as kids but were too afraid to venture much further after Ivy was taken by Harpies.

Being so small we could get by unnoticed, but she was caught, she was being too risky one day." Oliver said sadly.

"Ivy?" I asked.

"Our baby sister…she was really little when it happened, we weren't used to looking after her." Jake softened and his shoulders sunk at the thought of her.

"We don't really talk about her." Oliver sucked in a breathe and I cautioned on the topic.

"What happened to her?" I asked bravely.

"WE DON'T KNOW!" Jake hissed in a violent whisper.

I leant back as if the weight of his words had a physical impact.

"We shouldn't dawdle," Oliver muttered, eyes fixed on the distant Windreaper's.

They were shifting, restless, large, hulking birds with hooked beaks and claws that could slice bone like butter. One of them hissed, and in the next breath, a screech tore through the air as it lashed out at a smaller Windreaper, their claws raking the ground in a progressive rage, readying for attack.

"Now's our chance. Run!" Oliver shouted.

We didn't need to be told twice. We tore through the tall dry grass. Blades of hay scraping against our legs. My breath came ragged, heart pounding in my throat. Behind us, the Windreaper's shrieked again, distracted, but they wouldn't be for long.

We were running blind. Then my foot caught, and I fell, but I didn't hit the ground. A hand gripped my arm and slowed my fall, guiding me gently down. I looked up, blinking.

A woman crouched over me, breathless but composed. Her eyes were the color of storm clouds, but bright with something ancient. Her hair fell in wild waves streaked with auburn and violet. Armor clung to her like a second skin of scaled metal and leather.

"Shhh," She whispered.

I couldn't speak. Couldn't even think.

Oliver and Jake crashed in behind me, but they stopped short because suddenly we weren't alone.

Two men flanked her, crouched low in the grass.

The first had a primal presence. Not because of fangs or claws, but the *feeling* like if he lunged, it would be over in an instant. His muddy blonde hair was matted at the ends, a thick beard hiding a face that should've been rough, but somehow it wasn't. His eyes though were full of kindness and locked on Jake who stood sharp and cautious, but then the stranger flicked to me with something almost soft. Curious.

And then…him.

The last one stood half a step back, but he was impossible to ignore.

He was tall with broad shoulders, shoulder length dark hair, but he wasn't a man, not like one I'd ever known. Blood and dirt streaked across his bare chest. His skin shimmered faintly, like scales lived just beneath his skin. And behind him were wings.

Blue, tattered, enormous wings like a Dragons. They hung heavily behind him, dragging against the grass. Torn and bleeding in places. His golden eyes met mine and for a breath, I forgot how to breathe.

What the hell *was* he?

"Who are you?" The woman asked.

Her voice was calm, controlled, but not unkind. I could hear the strength in it, her power. She wasn't human, that much was obvious.

I opened my mouth, but nothing came out.

Jake stepped slightly in front of me, his first gesture of dominance and protection over me. Oliver's hand gripped mine, shaking. We weren't in the human world anymore. We'd just stepped into a story we weren't supposed to be part of.

"You're human," The woman said, her voice was low and sharp with disbelief. She stepped closer, her eyes scanning again, me, then Jake, then Oliver. "How?" She asked.

"There was... an earthquake," I said, still breathless. "Back on Earth. I don't even know how, but I fell. We all did...at some point," I answered.

She froze, just for a second.

Then her gaze locked on mine and stayed there.

Her breath hitched. I saw it. Just barely, her composure fell, her shoulders curled inward, and her guard went down.

"You..." She murmured. "You're the girl I saw falling." She gasped.

I blinked. "What?"

"I saw you," She repeated. "You dropped from the sky. I was watching from the Realm Door in Antoli... I jumped in after you." I felt the truth in her tone.

Something surged in her voice then, like a wave she was barely holding back. "I didn't think you'd survive the fall." She confessed.

I stared at her. Somehow, I knew she wasn't lying.

"You jumped for *me*?" I asked.

"I didn't know who you were. I just… saw you falling." Her voice became raspy.

Behind her, the winged man shifted. Watching me now too, less with hostility, more with curiosity. The way someone might stare at a glitch in the world.

Jake edged closer, protective again.

The other man broke the silence with a low voice. "She's Aliera," He said. "I'm Torin. That's Beau."

Aliera nodded once, recovering. "And you?" She smiled softly at me now.

I swallowed and straightened. "Dani. This is Oliver. And that's Jake." I tilted my head to him beside me.

Oli gave a small wave. "Nice to meet you, I think."

Torin smirked faintly. "Likewise." His voice was just as gritty as his appearance.

Beau said nothing, but his stare hadn't moved from Jake, who wasn't doing a great job of hiding his own scowl.

"I don't know how you made it through," Aliera said, still watching me with a strange intensity. "There's been no storm. No breach. But you…" Her voice faltered slightly. "You weren't supposed to survive that." A grin warmed her cheeks.

"Well," I muttered, "I'm not exactly thriving." I sighed.

Then it came.

A shrill cry, brutal, and close.

Aliera's face hardened. "Windreaper's..."

Beau was already turning. "We don't have time." He grasped Aliera's shoulder to move her. "Go between the bushes, stay away from the nests." He ordered.

"Then we cross the mountain," Aliera ordered, pointing to the jagged shadow rising on the horizon, half-sunken in mist. "Through the Bog." She added.

Jake frowned. "You sure you want to swim it." He glowered at Torin.

"Better that than losing your head out here," Torin muttered.

Another shriek. Closer this time.

Aliera raised her hand. "Stay close. Don't run ahead. That bog is alive." Her words lingered...*Alive*.

"Now," Aliera said. "Go."

We ran into the tall grassy bushes and rising mist, with monsters behind us and something worse waiting ahead, but for some reason, I kept hearing her voice in my head.

You weren't supposed to survive that.

And all I could think was...*Then why did she jump?*

We took rest by the stream that led to the bog. There was a small pool to bathe in. We would camp here for a short time before heading in further. Aliera, Beau, and Torin kept a slight distance, but close enough to react if something came upon us, far enough to offer space. Beau sat alone, mending what he could of his wings. Torin had started helping Jake with the fire, sharing a few quiet words.

"I'm sorry about the cave," I said to Oliver as I placed a hide down to sleep on.

"It wasn't going to last forever…not in this world," Smiled Oliver with his perpetual ray of positivity.

He was the more pragmatic force between the two. He and Jake were around the same height, but Oliver was leaner muscled, with a chiseled jaw, hazel eyes, and auburn hair. A handsome face with a scraggly beard, with specks of white hair poking through in some places. He oozed kindness, gentle mannerisms, and intelligence. He absorbed everything around him and learnt from it. Jake treated everything as an enemy. In truth, they balanced each other out rather well. I could see where force was of value in this world, but also where kindness would be held in high regard.

I glanced across the pool. Aliera was crouched at the water's edge, rinsing dried blood off her hands. She caught me watching and gave a quiet nod.

"What if we're not welcome? Jake always said, more people, more risk. I don't even know if he and you plan to stay." I said to Oliver.

Oliver's expression was thoughtful as Jake slipped away into the tall grass to keep watch.

"Oli… will you stay, if we find people who'll help?" My question pressed with more direction now.

"I'd like to," He said. "But my place is with Jake. If he doesn't wish to stay, then I'll go with him. We'll find somewhere else."

"What's his deal?" I asked gently.

Oli let out a troubled sigh and grabbed my hand.

"There used to be quite a few more of us. Then one by one, we started to drop off. The numbers drew too much attention. Restlessness. When it was just the two of us left, the Clops must've thought we were all gone. They stopped hunting for us. Two humans make less noise. Less impact. A missing Goafree or stolen Windreaper egg went unnoticed."

"So that's why he wants to keep the numbers down," I murmured.

"Exactly. Though you're small and don't eat much. Maybe we can persuade him," He smiled.

"Doubtful. In the time I've been here, he hasn't exactly taken a shining to me. Thanks for offering though," I sighed.

Beau shifted slightly across the camp, adjusting his ruined wings with quiet effort. Aliera turned her back to him. Whatever history sat between them, I could sense it was heavy. His eyes followed her longingly, like only a lover could.

"The fact that you came down with another helped gravely in your survival," Oli continued.

"How so?" I asked.

"The screams of the falling echo through the core. The Clops hear them too. Easy prey. I reached you first, but they found your friend." He explained.

My chest tightened. "The others who died… who were they?"

"My partner," He said softly. "Robin. He was hunting with Jake and one other when a Windreaper spotted him in the dull haze. His white-blonde hair was too easy a target." Oli sighed.

I hadn't realized his sexuality until that moment. The softness in his voice gave everything context.

"So… don't worry," He added with a grin. "I'm not going to try anything with you. Ever." His laugh was quiet.

I laughed, a genuine chuckle for the first time in days.

"The rest were a family of five. Mom, dad, three kids. And two older men who fell through like us and spent years traveling through the different lands. The family left after the men told them about the Three Shadows. They saw Robin die. Jake tried to guide them the long way, around the chaos, but the kids… they drew too much attention." He shook his head with sadness.

"What happened to them?" I asked. But I think I already knew.

Oli shook his head slowly. I took his hand.

"There's nothing you could've done." I comforted him.

"There's always something," He whispered.

"You can forgive yourselves. I'm seeing two tortured souls." I squeezed his forearm.

Oli gave a tight smile. "Tell me about your boyfriend?" He tried to lift the mood.

"Oh, well… it wasn't really going to last. I went on the trek alone because things weren't right anymore." I explained.

"You seem like the voice of reason." He added.

"I think he was clinging to the past. More parties. More drinking. Trying to recapture something that wasn't there anymore." I said.

"I'm sorry you didn't get to make peace with it." He sighed.

"So am I. The last thing I did was give him false hope." I sunk back.

"At least you weren't cruel." He said kindly.

The fireflies lit the pool in soft glimmers. I reached into my pack for my last little hotel soap.

"Think it's safe to bathe?" I asked.

"Cold as hell, but everything can kill you out here, might as well die clean," Oli laughed. But he quickly snapped a hand over his mouth to cover the sound.

I stripped off my pants and jacket and stepped into the freezing water.

"Christ! Leave something to the imagination," Oli joked.

"I'm not getting *butt* naked!" I splashed him.

"Care to join me?" I waved the bar of soap at him.

"Why not!" Oli followed, what little he wore left almost nothing to the imagination. The roman diaper look was hard to ignore.

"You should wash your diaper while you're in here," I giggled.

He doubled over in laughter. "Why are you like this?!" He snickered.

Torin's voice drifted from the fire. "She's not wrong." His laugh was a low growl.

Jake emerged through the grass just then.

"What are you two doing?" Jake grunted.

"Dani wanted to wash. I couldn't leave her alone," Oli answered.

"I'm getting out anyway, it's too cold for me. You on the other hand could use a bath, if you're nice she might share her soap." he added with a smirk.

Jake stared down at his own filthy skin. Then sighed. "Fine."

"Grab a shirt from my pack and make yourself a new diaper!" I teased Oli.

Jake cracked a rare laugh. "You wear one too!" Oli scowled at Jake.

Oli fought to rip the sleeves off a shirt. "You know you want one Dani." He teased.

Jake sank into the pool with a shiver.

"Here," I said, handing him the soap. "Scrub every nook."

"Bit hard with this diaper on." He shivered.

"Who said you had to keep it?" Oli said, flinging his own aside as he tied a new one on.

Fireflies danced. For a moment, things almost felt normal.

"I'm sorry I've been hard to live with," Jake said as I offered him the soap.

"It's okay. I understand now. About the others." I answered.

He didn't speak as I grabbed the soap and instinctively lathered his back. I touched his scars gently. Old wounds. Deep ones. Not all physical, it was the emotional and mental scars that hurt him most.

"Turn around," I whispered. He obeyed. No need for words.

"I'm sorry you wound up here," He said softly.

"And I'm sorry you had to grow up here." I added.

"I don't know how to let people in anymore." He admitted.

"You don't have to know that. It'll just happen when the times right." I whispered.

I lathered the soap in my hands and fisted a small amount of sand and mixed the two to help exfoliate his skin, I began scrubbing it up and down Jake's shoulders and arms, lifting what had to be years of dead-skin buildup. Jake raked the bar of soap through his hair and scrubbed hard, jaw flexing, and I couldn't help but watch as his biceps tightened beneath the sheen of water and moonlight.

The water carried clouds of brown away from his skin, exposing something deeper that lay beneath the surface. Emotion.

He caught me staring.

Of course he caught me staring.

His eyes flicked down to my hands on his shoulder, then back up to my face, slower this time. And suddenly the space between us wasn't just for washing grime…it was something else entirely.

"You don't have to do all that," He muttered. His voice was low, almost shy for a man built like a brick wall.

"I know," I said, but my hands didn't move away, the just kept going. "But you'd never scrub properly if I left you to it." I grinned.

He huffed a laugh, breath warm. "You think so little of me?"

"I think you haven't bathed since... ever."

I tried to play it off lightly, but my pulse betrayed me—beating too fast, my chest rose and fell heavily in the water.

Jake shifted, water trickling down the line of his throat, and something softened in his expression. "You've got dirt on your cheek," He said quietly.

Before I could react, his thumb was brushing it away. A small touch. But it felt like he'd reached right under my ribs.

Heat rushed through me, traitorous and uninvited as my breath hitched. I hated that he had noticed. He froze, his thumb still resting at the corner of my jaw, his brown eyes searching mine.

The world around us was silent except for dripping water and my heart betraying me like a drum.

"Dani..." He said my name like it meant something—like I wasn't just another person who fell through the realms and ruined his life.

I stepped back too quickly, pretending I needed more soap, pretending anything to break the moment I absolutely wasn't ready for.

Then the grass rustled sharply.

"There are Windreapers flying back south, from the Harpian city," came Aliera's warning.

We ducked. Then the screaming came, it was carnal and terrifying. His hand found mine beneath the water, and it should've been for safety—but it didn't feel like just safety. My breath caught as talons ripped through the sky. They were carrying humans.

Their screams, though distant, were all too real. When it passed, we surfaced one by one.

"They came from over the mountain," Jake growled.

"Or from the city?" Oli asked.

Jake didn't answer.

"It could have been anywhere," He said.

Oli nodded. "Let's keep moving. Maybe the colony on the outskirts can help. Someone might know how to get home." But Jake didn't reply.

I rinsed my hair of the soap and Jake helped me work through the knots.

The soap stung my wounded arm, and I shrieked as the suds licked across my arm.

"You're not healed," He said sharply.

"I didn't want to burden anyone." I whispered.

"You're not a burden." He sighed.

"That's not how you made me feel," I shouldn't have said it, but it came out like venom and I couldn't stop them.

Jake scowled, his wall went back up, and he stormed out of the water.

I followed eventually, bundled in my thermal. He lay beside me in silence until I felt the warmth of a hide being pulled over my shoulders.

"I'm sorry," He whispered. "Sorry I didn't give you a chance when it mattered." He added.

Warmth spread across my skin where the hide touched me, but the apology warmed me more. I wasn't ready for softness from him, not when it would be so much easier to keep him at arm's length.

I looked up at Jake. "It's okay, I understand why." I said.

Jake pressed his eyes closed as I stared up into the darkness; there was nothing. No stars, no moon, no clouds, just darkness. Under the shared hide our bodies didn't touch, but the few inches between us burned hotter than any flame. Maybe closeness was its own kind of torment.

Aliera sat beside me some time later, silent.

"You're brave," She said as she noticed me awake.

"So are you." I replied and pull myself to an upright position beside her and we sat together in the quiet of the night.

"Maybe we'll figure this out," I said.

"Maybe," she agreed. "And if not… we'll find our own way out."

The days here offered no warmth. No reprieve. Only a lingering cold that sank into your skin and stayed there.

There was no sun in Tierra Hundida. Just a muted, ash-blue sky that never brightened, never shifted. Even now, wrapped in a hide, I felt the worlds chill pressing through me. The moss beneath me was damp. The air unmoving. Around me, everyone slept or at least pretended to.

Jake's breath was steady beside me. Oliver was sleeping farther off, keeping watch with half-lidded eyes.

Aliera moved away now, she sat on a slanted rock, her frame still, her hands pressed to her knees with worry. I closed my eyes halfway as I laid back down facing Jake, enough to keep the illusion of sleep but still see her off in the short distance.

Then I heard him…Beau.

He didn't walk like Jake did, grounded and deliberate or like Torin, who moved more like a wild thing. Beau walked like the weight of the world dragged behind him. Or maybe it was just his wings. He stopped a few paces from Aliera, but she didn't look at him, she avoided him almost.

He sat, not beside her, but near enough that it said *I need to be close.* Far enough that it said *I know I hurt you.* Neither of them spoke for a long while.

The world around us was silent. No insects. No wind. No fire to crackle and fill the emptiness. Just the distant moan of the bog breathing off in the distance. The low rustle of trees that shouldn't have moved at all.

Then finally she spoke, "I thought you were asleep," Aliera said, her voice was quiet, it's intent was hollow.

Silence…

Something in her posture shifted. Not toward him. But not away either.

"You shouldn't have followed me." It was said as if she'd said it a thousand times before.

"I couldn't not." He sighed.

"I don't know how to exist near you," She whispered. "Not after everything. It's too hard!" Then her voice cracked with a sadness that was still broken. "You murdered my parents, Beau."

The words hung in the cold like breath you couldn't see.

"I know," He wasn't defensive. Just broken and defeated, it was exactly the way he carried himself.

"I replay it all the time," She said. "That moment I found out. The moment I realized the man I loved—" She cut herself off. "You knew how much they meant to me."

"I did," Beau said. "And that's why it haunts me. Because I still did it." He added.

Her hand balled into a fist on her knee. "You loved me…" She said it like she was trying to convince herself he didn't.

"I didn't know you existed back then," He said softly. "I didn't know the girl I'd fall in love with was the daughter of someone I was sent to kill." His voice broke.

A pause.

"I carry it with me every day," He murmured. "What I did. What I lost. What I ruined. And still, I would endure hell with you if that's where you walked next." He said it like a promise.

"I'm not something to follow," She whispered. "Not anymore, you followed the wrong Titan." She whispered.

"You always were more than you saw in yourself." He said.

"I'm not strong," She said. "I'm just what's left, I'm not like any of my brothers." She sighed.

"You're more than any of them! And you're still the only thing in this world that makes me feel anything." He sighed.

Another silence. Longer this time. I didn't breathe. *A Titan...like a real godly powered Titan?* I listened, hoping for more of the things I shouldn't be hearing, the words that weren't meant for me.

"You hurt me," She finally said. A long breath. Then, for the first time, her voice trembled with something raw and honest: "But I still love you. And I hate that I do."

Beau didn't move. He didn't speak, but his body relaxed in a way that granted him a small ounce of relief. But I could feel his angst, the way he craved her touch, the resistance to reach for her and the internal struggle he fought to let her be the first, if it ever came at all.

When he finally stood, his wings barely shifted. His body hunched with exhaustion and that same guilt.

He didn't touch her. Didn't try. He simply walked away in silence.

Aliera stayed still, but when she dropped her head into her hands after he walked away, I watched her shoulders shake as she cupped her face in her hands.

She didn't cry loudly. I closed my eyes again as I felt the weight of a grief I'd only just begun to understand wash over me. I wanted to cry for her, with her, I wanted to be her friend, but I doubted a Titan would know what it was to host a pity party with your girlfriends and cry over a break-up, especially one with that much weight to it.

Jake shifted closer to me, his eyes latching onto mine, he had heard it too and for the first time we shared a feeling, sadness, for them both. I moved closer to Jake, maybe for warmth, maybe for comfort, like her pain was my own. He gently held my hand and that's how we fell asleep.

Everyone else began to move now and without saying anything we packed up what we had and walked to the edge of the bog.

It was silent. The sort of silence that pressed against your ears like pressure under water. Even the trees above us didn't creak anymore. They just loomed with their big leaves and heavy branches.

"We climb over." Jake said as he pointed to the thick branches bowing across the water.

One by one we crept across the thick branches slowly, step by step, balanced between life and the black abyss below. I tried not to look down. Tried not to imagine the beast Jake warned us about, circling like death beneath the surface.

It had a name. The Talagata. He'd said it so calmly, like saying it aloud was safer than pretending it didn't exist.

Then came the snap, sharp and sudden.

I turned and saw Oliver drop. He had landed hard on a lower root, one hand gripping the edge. His legs dangled over the water. For a moment, everything stopped, then the water moved. It rippled, the shape of a serpent teasing us from below.

Jake froze; his face went white. "NO!" He cried.

"Hold on!" I yelled out.

But Oliver already knew.

He looked up, eyes wide, wild. "It's here." He said blankly.

Aliera surged forward, both arms lifting. I felt the wind before I saw it, rising up around her like a living being only she commanded, pulling it toward her chest, twisting at her fingertips. She threw her arms forward.

A blast of air shot across the bog, straight toward Oliver. It caught him just enough to lift his body from the slippery root. But the serpent was faster than her.

It rose like a massive wall, coiling into existence above the water. It was covered in rot and algae, black scales glinting dully in the lightless sky. Its mouth cracked open just slightly, wide and toothless at first glance, until the rows of curved fangs appeared as it stretched its hungry jaw wider now.

Beau launched off the branch, Jake with him. They didn't speak. Didn't even look at each other. They just *moved*, both diving from different angles, one with wings, one with instinct and a dull knife and not a care in the world.

Torin dove straight into the water with a guttural roar, cutting through the surface like a predator himself, his fangs were out now, and I suddenly realized he wasn't human either.

Aliera's wind struck again, a second pulse, harder, angrier, but the serpent didn't flinch. It was already wrapping Oliver in its long muscular body, his body vanishing beneath bands of thick, glistening muscle.

"Let him go!" She screamed, her voice cracking, it was loud now, reverberating like a gods.

Beau reached the serpent first. He slammed into it, a jagged blade drawn, driving it into the creature's side. Jake hit next, knife in hand, slicing across exposed flesh, both of them fighting together with terrifying, furious speed as they fought to stay above the water.

Torin surfaced beside them, arms grabbing at Oliver's shoulders, but the serpent jerked backward with supernatural strength, dragging them deeper into the thick water.

For a second, it looked like they might win…only for a second. The serpent wrapped tighter, then there was a sickening *crack*…bones breaking.

A scream…Oliver's. And then a choking silence.

The Talagata dove downward now, thrashing once before disappearing below, taking Oliver with it into the depths of the bog.

Beau erupted from the water, gasping, empty-handed. Jake surfaced seconds later, bleeding from the arm, eyes wide with helpless rage. Torin followed, chest heaving, eyes wild. None of them spoke and then the water was still again as if nothing had happened here.

Just like that, the bog erased him.

Beau was the first to climb back onto the rooted bridge, his soaked clothes clinging to him, blood and swamp water running down his jaw. He said nothing. His expression was blank. I could see the relief in Aliera's face as he sucked in a breath, but her grief as she looked down at her hands, they hadn't saved Oli.

Jake hauled himself up next, bleeding, his breath ragged. He looked over at Beau, just once. Beau met his gaze. Neither said a word. But then Jake did something I never thought I'd see. He reached out and gripped Beau's arm, not hard, not hesitant. Just real. Beau nodded and acknowledged his gesture, a silent thanks.

That was it...respect formed the shared devastation of trying and still losing.

I stood there, my heart in pieces, knowing I'd never hear Oli's humming again. That he'd never tease me, never smile at me again, he was gone.

Jake watched the water, still desperate for any movement, any sign of hope.

CHAPTER FIVE

BEAU

The bog had gone still, but not quiet. Silence had a weight about it, and this one hung too heavily. Oliver was gone. Dani hadn't moved, she sat frozen on the branch. Jake stood still clutching at the tree, his chest rising and falling, eyes lost in the water. Torin sat crouched, soaked, bloodied, breathing like he wanted the serpent to come back so he could tear it apart now that he was ready.

My wings burned. Every part of me ached. Muscle, bone, and guilt. But I didn't let myself collapse. I couldn't. Not when I felt it, a shift in the air.

The wind had changed, stale and dense only a moment ago it was fresh and crisp. Now it tightened. Drew inward like a breath. I turned to Aliera, and panic had set into her expression. Not the kind you find in fear, but the kind you find in the *knowing*. Her shoulders tensed, her neck tilted just slightly, her face unreadable as she listened to the air, like the wind had spoken to her in a language only she understood.

Her eyes locked on the sky a heartbeat before the screech came.

Harpies…

I didn't need to look up to know how many Harpies there were, the sound of their wings beating through the air painted a vivid picture. We were outnumbered.

Aliera spun, hands ready to act, but I stopped her. "No, they can't know what you are." I pulled her hands down beside her.

"They are going to take all of us." She panicked. My hand grazed her cheeks then a shriek cut through the air in a high pitch that meant one thing. It was a warning.

I didn't move as I felt it happening. That sound was meant for me. Aliera's eyes snapped to mine, wide and wild. "Beau…" She breathed.

They descended like shadows with one purpose, they were looking for something. This was coordinated, they had to of seen us coming through the realm door.

They saw the wings. Not Harpy wings. Not the feathered, bent things that came from their bloodlines.

Mine…A Fae, with Dragon wings. An abomination, a threat?

The first Harpy hit me mid-turn, claws slicing across my chest. I dropped to one knee but rose again, twisting, blade already in my hand. Jake pulled my straight blade from its sheath and whipped it around.

I caught sight of Aliera; her face was pure panic.

Not fear.

Not helplessness.

Panic for *me*.

"MOVE!" she shouted. I did as she said just as one Harpy lunged for me with its talons.

But it was all a distraction, a net dropped from above, heavy and metal, not rope. I felt the magic in it before it hit. It burned as I grappled against it.

It wrapped me tight, compressing around my chest, locking my wings in place, stealing the wind from my lungs and knocking my feet from under me until I stumbled.

Aliera surged forward, a violent gust screaming across the root bridge. It knocked one of the Harpies off balance, but the action not big enough for the others to notice that she controlled it.

I turned my head, trying to find her, but she was fast as she leapt from branch to branch trying to evade the attack.

She dropped in front of me suddenly and her mouth moved, but no words came out… *I'll find you.*

Then I was moving, the net lifted into the air, Harpies above me, more Harpies coming for the others, more nets to contain them.

The wind whipped around my face, the cold searing into my open wounds. My wings were trapped and twisted, fighting uselessly against the net. The Harpies beat upward, higher and higher, until the bog was no longer a place I could reach.

I saw her one last time, shrinking below me, her hair wild, hands still raised toward me like she could still call me back to her, but she couldn't.

The wind roared past my ears, carrying the memory of her words to my ears once more.

I couldn't feel it the way I used to. Not when my wings were pinned, crushed into the net, the sinew strained beyond pain.

My body was dragged through the sky behind three Harpies who flew like devils, each one silent, brutal, efficient.

But I didn't look at them.

I looked down.

Through the fog, through the branches below, I saw them again.

Aliera was already in the air. She had ignored my advice. Her wind curling beneath her like a storm building in real time. Her arms moved sharply, deliberately, cutting wind like a blade as she chased me through the sky.

Her eyes locked on mine, she was coming for me.

Not thinking. Not hesitating. Just rage fueling her decision.

Then Torin crashed through the underbrush like a beast unleashed, his long strides cutting through the bog, mud spraying behind him as he ran harder than I'd ever seen him run in his full form.

Jake was there too, vaulting branches, dragging Dani behind him. Her face was twisted in panic, her hand locked around his as they tore through the roots, trying to keep up. They were in pursuit of me, and they were trying to take me back.

Aliera pushed higher, wind lashing around her. She was so close I could see the dirt smeared across her cheek. She reached for me, our hands outstretched, but our fingers didn't meet.

A fourth Harpy dove from above and slammed into her shoulder.

I yelled as she spun out, her body twisting midair, her magic scattering. She caught herself just before she dropped below the tree line, but she couldn't climb again. Not fast enough.

I felt the shift as the Harpies carrying me angled sharply, banking toward the peak of the mountains. And others dropped to find her now.

I was slipping away out of sight.

Still, I looked down.

Torin was still running.

Jake was still fighting through the mud. Dani was crying, but she didn't stop.

And Aliera—bruised, bleeding, rose one last time, her voice lost to the wind, but her lips moved.

"I'm not done."

I held her gaze until the mountains swallowed her from view.

Then the sky turned red, and the world lit up as I set my eyes on the Harpian City. It was unlike anything I had ever seen before. A city built into the cracks of the earth itself. Each crevice was full of intrigue.

They hadn't knocked me out. Not yet. Maybe they wanted me to see it. To see how hopeless it was to struggle, to see how powerful they are and how impossible escape would be.

We crossed over the cracked earth that stretched in every direction, dry and broken. The Harpies dipped lower, following the veins of the land into deep crevices that pulsed like roads, winding and narrowing the closer we came to the city. But it wasn't a city built on the land, it was built *in* it.

It was carved into the mountain and the earth itself.

At first glance it looked like the mountain had bled open. Cavernous entries yawned in its sides, homes, tunnels, towers.

All stacked atop each other, misshapen and uneven, like a termite colony built in stone. Smoke drifted from the cracks. Lanterns burned in sconces hammered into the rock, casting sickly yellow and orange light that shimmered across the grey dust.

The streets weren't streets at all. They were the very cracks of the earth. Harpies moved in flocks, some on foot, others gliding overhead. Each one watched me as I was carried in. Some with curiosity. Others with open disdain.

But it was the cages that made my stomach turn.

They loomed along the outer lanes; iron monstrosities bolted into the stone walls or perched above entryways. Some were large enough to hold the bones of small Dragons. Others swayed with movement; they were too crowded. Creatures stirred in the shadows behind the bars: hunched Fauns, weeping Enfields, Fae with broken wings, and humans staring out with hollowed eyes.

A child clutched the bars of one cage and whispered something I couldn't hear.

The Harpies carrying me dipped down into one of the lower cracks closest to the mountain. Here, the lanterns swung lower, their flames flickering behind colored glass. Crimson, amber, a pale green that reminded me of bile.

I caught a glimpse of Torin, he'd been caught too. His arms were bound, blood was dripping down his cheek, he'd been dragged through the dust by a pair of shrieking Harpies. Then Jake, barely conscious, half-carried. Dani was limp between them but breathing.

Aliera…Where was she?

I struggled, but then I saw her as I whipped my neck around. Her head bowed low, her face turned just enough that I could see her eyes. She was the first to be stuffed into the enormous cage. They let me watch as they crowded the cage with Jake, Dani and Torin and a handful of other creatures with their hands bound.

Then they craned it into the sky with chains and Harpies clutching the bars to lighten the load as they suspended it on a giant hook on the outside of an arena that sat in the bosom of the south mountainside. Several other hooks already had full cages. Harpy children mocked the prisoners and threw stones at them.

There were other cages, dozens of them. They each hung like grotesque ornaments along the streets, some in the arena. Each packed with prisoners. Each rocking in the wind. Each full of eyes that had already given up.

Harpy children swarmed below, shrieking with laughter, throwing stones and bones and anything they could find. The impacts rattled through the bars, and Jake flinched with every hit, still dazed, barely conscious. Dani shielded her head with bound wrists. Torin snarled. Aliera didn't move at all. Her hair fell like a curtain across her face, hiding every emotion but panic.

The Harpies wanted me to watch it. Every second of it.

And as they carried me past the cages, toward the blackened mountains with spires like a castle, I realized the truth.

They weren't putting me in a cage. They were taking me somewhere cages couldn't hold what they wanted from me.

Chapter Six

IVY

The gates always thundered first, then they shrieked and groaned. A sound forged by rust grinding against the cold metal. The light flooded in more than usual and the oil lanterns lining the corridors were topped up during the walkthrough of the guards. But this time something was different. I knew the guards, their patterns, something was different this time.

I knew this dungeon well, I knew how it moved and who set the wheels in motion. There were four main guards, three who took singular shifts, one covered them for breaks.

Anyone who was caged down here wasn't getting out unless you were granted it. And in the years, decades that I'd been imprisoned in the Harpian City I had never seen anyone leave alive.

I heard the familiar scuffles, grumbles and then guttural cussing as another man was forced down the stairs, but he wasn't a man. I had never seen anyone like *him* before. He wasn't thrust into any regular cell either, he was brought into the Crohn's chamber. My blood ran cold for him. It was a cell where she would intimidate and interrogate her victims, Morog was evil itself. I felt my stomach sink for him, I knew his fate, I knew he didn't have long, he was already injured and covered in blood.

Hours passed as he sat in the silence with Me and Maxima. She was the female Faun down the hall closest to the Crohn's Chamber.

The guards changed sooner than usual and extras were brought in, guards I didn't know.

Footsteps tracked up my side of the hall, it was Roan. A sigh of relief escaped me, Roan was different, he was kind. For months now he'd become more than a guard. He stopped at my bars and looked in as I shuddered in the corner. He was young like me, the only guard who wore a mask, he was taller, he wasn't like *them*. There was a kindness about Roan. He was newer than the rest.

There was no way to measure time, but it felt like months, maybe a year. He would always drop extra food to me, he knew the other guards stole my rations.

"Ivy?" His hands were always gloved because he was different to the other Harpies. He reached into the cell with a package wrapped in cloth.

I crept forward and took the parcel with a shy nod.

"What's happening?" I stuttered, my voice smaller than a whisper.

"A new prisoner, everyone is talking about this one." He explained. "She'll be coming down here, stay calm." He said gently.

Morog, the Harpy Queen, the Crohn. She was all things hideous and cruel, always on a pursuit for power.

"Eat." Roan ordered as he waited for me to hand back the cloth.

I chewed the crusty bread and warm cheese as fast as I could. And to my surprise there was a sweet this time wrapped in waxy paper, it looked like a jewel, smooth and glistening against the torchlight, the color of amber. I tucked it away for later as I offered Roan a smile as my only way of thanks.

"Why do you help me?" I asked.

"Why do we all need to be cruel?" he answered my question with a question.

I passed the cloth through the bars as I crunched the crust of the bread and held the wedge of cheese.

"You're a Harpy...Isn't that your nature?" I said through crunches that spilled crumbs.

"Maybe it's time for a change." He shrugged.

He handed me a canteen of water, and I chugged it back greedily. "I'll see what I can do about getting you a bucket of water to wash. With all the distractions right now, it shouldn't be hard." He said as the water dripped down my chin onto my chest.

The smear of water left a trail of clean skin amidst the dust that had collected on my chest.

"See you later." Roan whispered as he walked away down the halls to patrol the other prisoners.

"Bye..." But my words didn't reach him, they just hung in the air as I looked after his big brown wings.

The torchlight dimmed in ragged movements against the weight of his movement, its shadows reclaiming the corners like they always did.

I curled back into myself, knees to my chest, the remaining bread crust still in one hand, the sweet tucked into a loose fold in my tunic. The cheese was gone. I had eaten it too quickly, and now I couldn't stop thinking about how soft and creamy it had been, how the sharpness lingered on my tongue long after it had passed.

I couldn't help but think how something like cheese didn't belong in a place like this. Was I too simple minded to believe the Harpies would eat seed? As a child I didn't understand the fear around them, we had pet birds as children. What could possibly be different?

The difference, they weren't herbivores, they were carnivores. But I knew Roan was different, half the guards were. They were taller, built more like humans than Harpies.

Roan's voice still echoed in my chest.

Maybe it's time for a change. The words rang in my ear.

No one down here talked about change. Down here, you were invisible, or you disappeared. You shrank so small you vanished into the cracks of your own mind.

I wasn't sure which one I was anymore.

The cell across from me was empty now. All the cells were well spread out. The one beside mine was filled with a creature who hadn't spoken in weeks. Faun, I think. His antlers had been cut, uneven and broken. The walls were mostly stone, so I couldn't see him, but I felt his presence, he was still with me, for now.

Farther down, a Foogal used to hum, she was cheerful and ignorant to the horrors of this place, but she was gone now. They took her weeks ago and never brought her back. The silence that replaced her was louder than the music she created ever was.

There were taller cages for the creatures with wings. Most housed Enfields, they were foxlike beings with feathered wings and narrow, intelligent faces. Even beaten and bound, they watched everything with a sharpness that made it clear they understood far more than the Harpies wanted them to. Their ears twitched with every cry, their feathers ruffled in agitation, and some pressed themselves against the bars to shield the smaller ones inside. They were cheeky by nature, playful and clever… but here, even their mischief had been smothered into silence.

Some days, I didn't know how much more of the cruelty I could endure.

My skin itched where the grime was thickest—behind my knees, under my arms, along my neck where hair clung to the cold sweat. There was no cool breeze down here, just stale air. Roan's mention of a wash bucket felt like a miracle. I closed my eyes and imagined clean water against my skin, maybe even a cloth.

The fantasy of it made me ache, but I was careful not to rely on it, a dream could be traitorous too.

I pulled out the amber candy from my tunic.

I rolled it between my fingers, catching the firelight. It shimmered like resin.

Maybe Roan didn't know what this meant. Or maybe he did. Maybe he knew that even the smallest sweetness in a place like this could remind someone they were still alive, and there was something to look forward to, even if it was just a sweet, there was a purpose.

I didn't eat it. Not yet. I wanted to save that feeling. For a moment when I needed it most.

Instead, I tucked it into the fold of cloth beneath the stone I used as a pillow. My only treasure. The one thing in this whole cell that hadn't been taken from me.

I closed my eyes and tried to steady my breath.

Down the hall, I heard the wind shift. The kind of shift that only happened when she was coming. Chains thrashed and I heard wings grating against the stone as soldiers hurried around.

Then there was a distant voice, sharp and echoing like the cry of a bird laced with that of a temptress.

Morog…she was coming.

Not to my cell. Not yet. But near enough that everyone, even her guards, felt the tension. The aura darkened now. And anyone who could hid as much as they could in their already tiny cells.

I pulled my knees tighter and shrank into the cold stone corner of my prison. I thought about Roan. About his eyes. His voice. The way he always passed the cloth through the bars gently, like he knew I hadn't been touched without violence in a very long time. He was careful with me, gentle and kind.

I let that thought warp around me as the Queen of the Harpies passed by my cell, her talons scrapping on the stone. Taunting each of us.

The air turned sour as Morog entered the Crohn's chamber.

I couldn't see her from here without moving, but I didn't need to. The sound of her arrival was unmistakable. Talons clicking in an unhurried rhythm, like she wanted the whole dungeon to *feel* her presence.

She moved like royalty. Her cruelty had a cadence, and she wore it like a crown.

The prisoner, the one who had been dragged in hours ago had gone quiet. Too quiet.

But then it began...the first sound wasn't a scream. It was a breath. One of those hollow exhales that gets pulled from the chest like it wasn't given permission to leave.

Then came her voice.

Soft. That was the worst part. Morog didn't bark or shout. She *whispered*. And somehow, it carried. It seeped through the stone with intent, she wanted everyone to hear her through the cracks in the cells, threading its way into my ears like oil.

I flinched. What was he?

I squeezed my eyes shut, willing the sound of her voice away, but her words hooked into you like a bad memory.

Then came his voice. Hoarse. Deep...angry. The kind of anger that had teeth, maybe even fangs. The kind of voice that told you he wouldn't give up easily.

They were too far for me to hear every exchange, but I heard one word.

Dragon.

My breath hitched… Dragons too?

That's why they brought more guards, that's why Roan said *everyone* was talking.

But then came the sound I dreaded most.

Pained grunts broke into a full sound. Guttural, raw, not quite a scream but the thing before it. Then the chains thrashed and then they came to a sudden halt, the weight of him stopping them mid clang.

Then, her laugh.

That shrill, jagged sound that always echoed long after she was gone.

The Faun in the next cell shifted. First movement in days. I heard his fingers curl around the bars, his hoofs trembling against the stone floors. He knew the sound too. We all did. The prison was electric with movement for the first time in months, we were all listening and waiting.

Morog liked to break people in layers. She never started with blades. She used words, history, and truths you didn't want to hear. And when that didn't work, then came the talons. She was an expert in interrogation, he would be in for more, if she kept to her regular pattern.

Morog taught me that sound only fed her. Silence was the only weapon I had left. A final crash echoed through the hallway, metal screeching against stone and then… silence. The kind of silence that makes you wonder if anyone was still breathing.

Roan was right. This prisoner wasn't like the others.

And if he died tonight, he'd be the first Dragon I ever heard scream. Even the mountain felt still in the wake of what might happen.

Then Morog's footsteps returned. There was no rush in her. She didn't slam doors. She glided and grated her talons tauntingly. When Morog was pleased, she moved like a queen after a feast. And this time, she was very, very pleased.

Her talons clicked all the way past my cell. I kept my face pressed into the crook of my elbow, pretending to sleep, barely breathing. The scent of her lingered long after. She smelt of scorched feathers and spoiled perfume.

I waited anxiously till not only she passed, but her odor. Ten heartbeats, then twenty. Then a muffled shuffle echoed from the Crohn's chamber. The sound of weight shifting from the Dragon.

He hadn't died, not yet. But if Morog wanted his death, she would have it.

The bars in dungeon weren't perfectly aligned. Years of moisture had warped the stone. But there was one small angle, a fracture in the wall's curve. Just enough to glimpse into the hallway if I leaned far enough into the bar.

My knees cracked against the uneven stone as I crawled forward, careful not to let out a sound. I pressed my cheek to the icy stone and peered through; I was able to catch only a fraction of a glimpse.

He was there, but he looked nothing like a Dragon. He looked human, but with dark blue wings, his shoulders glistened with scales, some were torn or completely plucked from their root of his skin.

He was slumped in the middle of the Crohn's cell, chained at the wrists and ankles, his body twisted like he'd tried to fight her to his last breath. His hair was long, tangled, soaked with sweat or blood, maybe both. I could see the streak of red trailing down his chest, staining his bare skin. His shoulders were massive but hunched. Unnatural. As if something inside him had been forced inward. His body was failing him.

There were bruises along his ribs, open cuts across his arms.

Dragon, Roan had said. I'd never seen one before. He didn't look like fire. He looked like ruin embodied. But there was something terrible in his silence.

He wasn't defeated; he was waiting.

My breath hitched and just as I shifted, his head turned…he saw me. Only for a second, but his golden eyes locked on mine, bloodshot and burning. And in them was something so fierce, so alive, it rattled me to my core.

Then a shadow passed before me. I spun quickly, my heart slamming against my ribs, but it was Roan. He crouched low and put a finger to his mask, a gesture of silence.

"I brought water," He whispered, pulling a small wooden bucket from beneath his cloak. "It's not warm. But it'll have to be enough for now." He said softly.

He pushed it between the bars. My composure relaxed as I received the bucket, and I had something to look forward to that wasn't food.

"I saw him," I murmured softly.

Roan didn't ask who he already knew.

"I thought he was going to die." I said softly.

"He still might," Roan sighed. "But not tonight."

I dipped a rag into the water and wiped the grime from my arms, from my face, from behind my ears. The first clean I'd had in weeks. The cloth turned brown almost immediately. Roan handed me another.

"I don't think she broke him," I said.

Roan was quiet for a long moment. "Good, if he breaks, what chance do the rest of us have." He whispered.

I looked up at him, the mask hiding his face but not the weight behind his words. There was something raw in his voice tonight. Something I hadn't heard before.

"Did she break *you*?" I asked before I could stop myself.

His shoulders stiffened.

Then, gently he whispered, "Not yet."

"I saved something," I said reaching behind me. I held out the amber candy. "For when I needed it most."

He tilted his head. "Why?"

"I think… I need it to remind me that kindness still exists. Even here." I explained.

Roan reached through the bars and closed my fingers around it again. "Then hold onto it. As long as you can."

He started to rise, but I caught the edge of his cloak. Just for a second. Just enough to anchor myself.

"Will he survive her?" I asked.

Roan paused. "I don't know," He said honestly. "But if he does, Morog will wish he hadn't. If he does, others will challenge her."

And with that, he disappeared into the torchlit halls.

The water felt like breath returning to my skin. I used every drop Roan left me. My rag was stained, my hands pink from scrubbing. I sat in the middle of my cell after, cross-legged, damp hair falling over my shoulders, the amber sweet still warm in my palm.

Down the corridor, the Crohn's chamber remained open. That door was always sealed like a tomb. But not tonight. Not with him, she was teasing him. I didn't know why I stood. I didn't plan it. My legs just moved. As if something in me, some long-dormant pull needed proof that someone else was still trying.

I crept to the edge of the cell, close to the bars, and leaned out just enough to see him again.

His eyes were watching me now, not like I was a prisoner, or a child, or something broken, but like my presence gave him hope, he couldn't see anyone else. He could barely see my whole face, but he clung to that.

I don't know how long I stood there, eyes fixed on the open Crohn's door. I waited for it to shut. For the cell to be sealed. For something to mark the end of it. But nothing happened.

Then came the soft sound of boots. Just careful steps on quiet stone.

Roan. I didn't move. I didn't want him to think I was waiting for him. But I was, he was all I had to look forward to.

He stopped in front of my cell and didn't speak right away. His wings shifted, broad and still cloaked in dust, feathers browner, earthier than the rest of the guards. I felt the weight of his gaze as he stood tall in front of the bars.

"You didn't sleep," He said finally.

"Neither did you," I whispered. He crouched down to my level.

He didn't reach for the bars this time. He just… sat. Like we were equals. Like this was a conversation worth staying for. We sat there for a while, the space between us full of things we didn't have words for.

Then I turned to him. "Why do you give me so much of your time?" I asked.

He didn't answer right away.

Then, softly: "Because you're the only one down here that hasn't stopped trying." He confessed.

His words broke something in me.

I looked away, blinking hard. I wasn't going to cry. I never cried. Not anymore, and Roan noticed.

He reached into his coat and pulled something out, something wrapped in soft cloth, not rations this time, but a bundle of herbs.

"For your hands," He said gently. "They're raw."

I stared at the bundle. My hands *were* raw from scrubbing, from clutching stone, from holding on too tightly to things that were never meant to last.

He passed the herbs through the bars, slower than usual. As if he wanted me to know this offering meant something.

Our fingers brushed, but nothing like before, this was tender, and Intentional. His hand was gloved, but I felt the tremor in his movement as he dared, then he pulled away quickly.

"I shouldn't…" He murmured.

"Why not?" I gasped.

"Because I'm still on the wrong side of the bars." His words landed hard. I wished in this moment I could see his expression.

I stared at him, puzzling his body language. He didn't mean physically. Not entirely.

And still, I asked, "Are you?" It had to mean something…

He didn't answer, instead his shoulders lowered.

"I could get in trouble for this," He whispered.

"I know." I mouthed as sound failed me.

"I'd do it anyway," His voice was firmer than mine, confident. "For you." He added.

There was something about the way he said it. It was soft, but steady. It excited me, igniting more than a flame, hope?

For so long, kindness had come in fleeting scraps. A crust of bread. A sip of water. A word spoken gently instead of harshly, I didn't know what true kindness really looked or felt like until Roan came along all those months ago.

But this was something else entirely, or if it wasn't I was happy to imagine it was anyway. Cause this set a fire in me. One I couldn't afford to extinguish, this fire was the difference between survival and perishing.

I tucked the herbs to my chest.

"I'm not used to people meaning things when they say them," I said quietly.

Roan leaned in just slightly, close enough for me to see the outline of his face beneath the mask.

"Then let this be the first."

And with that, he stood and walked back into the shadows, the edges of his wings brushing the stone behind him like a ghost leaving something behind.

And I was left holding more than herbs.

I was holding *hope* as I slept that day. I woke to the flicker of dying torchlight and the faint scent of pine. It was real. I blinked in the dim light and sat up, groggy and confused. There was something tucked beneath the edge of my pillow.

I pulled it out slowly, a small leather-bound object. A book.

I stared at it for a long time, stunned.

Books didn't exist down here. Not unless Morog was burning them. It was old, the leather cracked at the spine, the corners softened with time and handling. There was a simple braided band holding it closed, and when I slipped it free, the pages crackled. They were thin, hand-cut, and smudged in places.

The first page was a sketch of a tall tree standing alone on a hillside. In the corner was a single name, written in tiny script.

Roan.

I swallowed hard and turned the page.

There were more sketches. Mountains, cliffs, wings, feathers. Then a child's drawing, almost embarrassingly crude. A face with a beak. Another with a crown.

Then, writing. Small fragments of his memories.

She called me little crow when I was sick. Told me that the feathers in my back would grow stronger the more I listened to the wind.

I turned the page again.

I could never tell her I hated the wind after they took her away.

I pressed my hand to the paper.

Roan had drawn these. Roan had written this.

This was his. This was… him. He was sharing his life with me.

I flipped further through sketches of cages. One page had water damage, the ink running like tears.

I thought I'd stop feeling when I started wearing the mask, and maybe start feeling more like the others, maybe they wouldn't point so much. It didn't work. Sometimes, I still see her eyes. She was screaming when they made me watch.

The air left my lungs when I realized this wasn't a gift to pass the time, this was *trust*.

He hadn't given me food, or something stolen from the guards' stores this time, he had opened up his past. He'd given me a piece of his soul. Now it sat in my lap, full of weight. I closed the book carefully, my heart was pounding, and I pressed his memories against my chest.

For the first time in years, I whispered something to the darkness, a message for Roan. *"I'll keep it safe."*

I opened it back up again, I couldn't stop turning pages. The book was small; it had been made to be hidden. There was a drawing near the middle that stopped me longer than the other pages, a drawing of a woman, one that had been worked on, over and over.

Not perfect, his hand had trembled, or maybe he'd drawn it through tears, too painful to hold his hand steady. But the care was there. Long hair, swept back behind her ears. Strong shoulders. Eyes with sorrow etched into the wrinkled corners.

She looked kind, she must have been to raise someone like Roan. Her hands were drawn cradling a child with wide eyes and dark wings half-furled.

A note was scratched just beneath the image…

She named me Roan. She said the world would try to bleach or blacken me, but I would always be something in between both worlds.

I touched the name like it could warm me through the page.

The next entry was written differently. Smaller. Tighter.

She wasn't like the others. Her wings weren't sharp. Her voice wasn't cruel. She sang when she cooked, even when there was nothing much to eat. She said I had too much of him in my face to ever walk freely.

She meant my father.

I froze. My fingers paused on the edge of the paper, breath held in. I read on…I couldn't stop.

He was human. A hunter, wounded. She found him near the cliffs and nursed him back to life in the cave systems on the cliffs where no full Harpy would search. She said they spoke more with their hands than their tongues. He never returned to his people. Not because he couldn't, but because he chose her. They chose me. And they killed her for it.

There was no sketch on this page. Only ink. Pressed hard into the paper like his hand had shaken as he wrote it.

They killed him first, making her watch. She hid me for as long as she could. When they came back after giving her hope of survival, they burned her wings first. Said she'd broken nature's will by loving a human and birthing a mistake. That she had danced too close to the line as a half breed herself.

I didn't scream. She told me not to. She told me to listen instead. To survive. And if I ever had a chance to be anything else, anything kinder, then to do it.

I clutched the book to my chest once more as tears trailed down my cheeks.

Roan wasn't just different, he was like me. Half-hidden. Half-forgotten. Forced into this prison for one of two reasons.

I flipped to the last page. Only one line sat there:

Maybe she was wrong. Maybe I'm not meant for kindness. But I see it in her. In the girl with dust on her cheeks and eyes that won't stay dim.

He'd written about me. A smile spread across my cheeks. I pressed my forehead to the pages and closed my eyes. Butterflies exploded in my stomach. This wasn't just a prison anymore. It was a place where something real had begun to grow.

I traced the edges with my thumb and held it close, tucking it into the corner of my sleeping cloth where no one would find it but me. He had touched every page, and that part of him being here brought me comfort. He had bled into these words, sketching pieces of himself he clearly hadn't shared with anyone else. And now I held them.

All that day, I watched the hall from the shadowed curve of my cell.

The guards rotated like always. The same heavy walk, the same stale scent of armor and old feathers. None of them were him.

I tried not to look across the hall toward the Crohn's chamber, but I couldn't help it.

The Dragon prisoner was still here, still alive. His name was Beau.

I hadn't learned his name until I heard a guard muttering it under his breath in passing another guard. But now that I knew it, it felt like connection.

Roan didn't come that evening…or the next.

The ache in my chest grew tighter with each torch cycle. What if something had happened? What if someone noticed? What if he was caught? The thought made me sick.

I kept the book clutched to my chest at night and every so often, I'd open it to a sketch. I imagined the wind there, in those places, high above the cracks in the earth where this cursed city lived.

I imagined him standing there, younger and free.

Then, on the third night, I heard him. No footsteps just a breath. The quietest exhale just outside my cell. I jolted upright and scrambled toward the bars.

He was there kneeling low, cloak wrapped tight, mask still on, his wings dusted with ash. He looked tired, his eyes were full of something I hadn't seen in him before now.

He looked like he'd missed me.

"I was starting to think the worst," I whispered.

"I couldn't risk it," He said quickly, voice low. "There was a change in the rotations. They've posted a new warden near the Crohn's Hall. Someone more… loyal."

"I thought the worst when I found the book," I breathed.

His head tilted. "You read it?"

"I couldn't stop." I smiled.

Roan nodded, a breath of relief escaping him. "I meant for you to."

"Thank you for trusting me with this." I hesitated. "I just didn't know how much it would mean." I added sadly.

He was quiet for a long beat, then leaned forward slightly. "Do you think less of me?" He asked.

My eyes burned. "No," I said softly. "I think more of you."

Without thinking, I reached through the bars for him. Roan stared at my hand, then at his own. He slipped his hand through the bars. This time, no gloves, no leather, no barrier between us. Just skin. His hands were human. Big. Calloused. Rough in some places, but not from cruelty. From living. They dwarfed mine, and yet somehow he held them with such care that I forgot for a moment where we were.

He didn't just hold my fingers. He wrapped both of his hands around mine.

It had been so long since someone touched me with purpose, and gentleness. His thumbs began to move slowly, rubbing circles over the backs of my hands. His skin was warm from flight or fire or simply from being someone who hadn't frozen from the inside out like I had.

"You're freezing," He murmured, frowning beneath the edge of his mask.

"I'm always cold," I whispered.

His grip shifted, adjusting to cup my palms fully. He rubbed harder now, not harsh, just with intent. Warming the spaces between my fingers, cupping the bones of my knuckles like he could light me from the inside if he tried hard enough.

I felt my breath catch. Because of how quickly the tears wanted to come.

"You don't have to do this," I whispered, voice shaking more than I meant it to.

"I want to," He said.

I looked at our hands clasped together. Mine small, pale, chapped, scarred. They didn't look like they should belong together. And yet, they fit.

"You feel like fire," I murmured.

"You feel like something worth saving," he answered.

He let the silence hang there, not pulling back, not rushing away. It was as if time itself had paused to let us exist in this strange, beautiful stillness. Two people on opposite sides of the bars, warming each other with nothing but hands clasped together and a quiet, growing hope.

Roan exhaled slowly. His thumbs still moved, slower now, softer.

"You don't have to be alone in here anymore," He said quietly.

And somehow, I believed him. He didn't let go of my hands. Not even when the silence stretched. Not even when the torchlight flickered low, casting strange shadows across the stone. His fingers were still wrapped around mine, warmer now, less urgent. Like he wasn't trying to heat my skin anymore, just hold me.

I looked up at him through the bars, and in that fragile, flickering moment, I whispered…

"Can I see you?" I asked.

He froze.

His hands didn't leave mine, but his body tensed in that unmistakable way of uncertainty.

"I don't need you to," I added quickly. "It's just… I want to see you. You've seen every shade of me." I sighed.

His wings shifted behind him. Not in threat, but in thought.

"I haven't let anyone see me since…" He didn't finish. He didn't need to. I knew what he meant.

Slowly, he pulled a hand from mine and touched the edge of his mask. It wasn't like the others, not polished or feathered or adorned. It was plain, dirty, cracked near the temple, like it had taken a blow for him once or twice. Like he had fought for his right to live.

He hesitated. Then, without a word, he unhooked it from behind his head. And let it fall away.

My breath caught in my throat. He wasn't what I expected.

He was more like me. Lines of worry pulled faintly at the corners of his mouth, and a faint scar curved beneath his right eye. His skin was golden bronze beneath the torchlight, and his eyes, those eyes I'd seen through shadows were darker now, not cold, but deep and haunting, his jaw was strong. His lips pressed together like he was still bracing for something. Judgment, maybe.

I didn't speak. I just looked at him. *Really* looked.

There were faint traces of Harpy in him. The angles of his cheekbones. He was *beautiful*. Not in the perfect, effortless way. In the *true* way. In the way people were when they carried their grief openly.

"I thought you'd flinch," He said, voice quieter than before.

"I've only flinched at cruelty," I whispered. "Never at honesty."

His shoulders sagged, relief softening every line in his face as his forehead leant on the bars now.

"You're the first person to see me since I was a child," He said.

"And I like what I see, I see kindness."

He gave a breathless, broken laugh. Then reached through the bars again, this time not just to warm me, but to touch my cheek. His thumb brushed just below my eye, and I leaned into his touch before I could stop myself. That one touch made something in my chest break open.

"Don't put it back on, not yet." I said with squinted sleepy eyes.

"I won't," He whispered.

And in the hush of that dungeon, beneath stone and chain and shadow, two broken things held onto the beginning of something whole.

His dark hair curled slightly at the temples, a little messy from where the mask had pressed against it. His jaw was chiseled, sharp. His cheekbones were high, noble, the kind that might've belonged to some warrior in a story I'd long stopped believing in. But his eyes held me still.

I leaned further into the hand he'd cupped against my cheek. It was warm and solid, his thumb tracing lightly along my skin like he couldn't believe I was real. Maybe I couldn't either.

He drew a little closer, his wings rustling behind him as he shifted his weight, kneeling now fully at the bars.

I thought he might pull away. That he'd blink and remember who we were. What this place was. That he'd retreat behind caution and silence again. That he'd leave me and never return, and I'd just be here…

I didn't move.

Then he gently pulled me closer. Not forcefully. Just enough for our foreheads to touch, our lips barely apart.

"Ivy…" He breathed.

And in that one word, I heard everything.

Grief. Longing. Fear. Hope…Lust.

My lips parted just slightly, enough for the air between us to vanish. Then, slowly, he kissed me.

It wasn't desperate. It wasn't hurried. It was achingly careful. The kind of kiss you give when you think it might be your last, or your first, or both all at once. His lips brushed mine once, then again, firmer this time, like he needed to be sure he memorized our touch.

When we pulled apart, we didn't go far. He rested his forehead against mine again, our breaths mingling in the narrow space left between us. For once, there was no hunger in me. Only fullness, something about this moment completed me.

"I don't want this to be a moment," I whispered.

His hand smoothed down the back of my neck, slow and protective.

"Then let's make it more." He whispered.

CHAPTER SEVEN

BEAU

I'd been knocked unconscious and woke moments later and dragged down a flight of stone stairs. They were cold, uneven, and sharp enough to scrape my wings raw. Every jolt sent pain screaming through my spine, the damage to my right wing worsening with each step. The joint had gone. Splintered, if not shattered. The nerve endings were lit like wildfire, and the agony didn't fade—it bloomed.

The air changed the deeper we went from the castle and into the depths of its dungeon. It was damp, sour, and thick with rot. The smell of rusted metal had tainted everything, chains, blood, unwashed blades. Something underneath it reeked of open wounds left to fester. I hadn't seen the creatures down here, but I could smell them. Hear their breathing.

The torches along the corridor flickered, their flames choking on soot. The sconces were black, crusted in years of grime. Nothing down here had been cleaned. Not the cells, and definitely not the stains.

They shoved me into a chamber bigger than the rest, but not by much. There were chains already dangling from the walls. A stone bench slick with blood. Fresh or not, I couldn't tell. It could've been mine or might've been someone else's. Probably both.

I thrashed the second they tried to strap me in. Bucked, and gritted through the pain, fought with everything I had left.

"Save your energy," One of them muttered so only us two could hear it.

His voice wasn't cruel. It wasn't kind, either. Just flat. Like he'd seen what came next and figured I wouldn't make it that far.

He was taller than the rest, he had no talons, he wore boots. His gloves were thick leather, his face hidden beneath a dented mask. He didn't move like the others, he moved more like me.

I spat at him…He didn't flinch. Just shoved me back and pressed his elbow into my shoulder hard enough to pin me. Our eyes locked and his jaw slackened.

"This is the Crohn's Chamber," He said. "You'd be smart to keep your strength for *her*." His words dragged with a slight of pity.

The others chained me as he held me up. My wrists dragged above my head and became locked into the wall with chains. I could barely stand, couldn't sit. My feet hovered just enough to make every breath a strain, my wings crushing into the cold stone wall. The blood on me was still tacky.

The guards left. No threats. No final look. Just the echo of their footsteps disappearing down the corridor like they'd done this a hundred times before. Then the quiet settled in as they left the chamber.

I heard the drip of water. The shuffle of hooves. A Faun, maybe, stepping closer to her bars to get a better look at me. I couldn't lift my head enough to see her, but I could feel the weight of her gaze.

Further down, something clicked against the stone. Not footsteps. Not claws. Something stranger. Like it was testing the walls. Listening for a reply. A reverberation I didn't recognize. Then a flutter of curious little wings followed by the chirp of an Enfield.

And then further down the corridor, through a crack in the stone there was a human face.

Just a sliver of it. A flash of tangled hair, a glint of a dark eye as she peered out. She didn't move, didn't speak, but I felt the glance like it had been aimed with purpose.

And then she was gone again.

Hours passed by slowly. My body drifted toward sleep, but the pain wouldn't let me fall deeper beyond a thought. Every breath was a burn, every inch of my wing screamed out in pain. My arms were numb where they hung above me, my muscles shaking under their own weight. I might've slipped under if not for the sound she made, it was sharp and unmistakable.

The scrape of talons against stone.

My eyes snapped open, the exhaustion yanked back knowing I needed to be alert.

She came down the stairs with calculated grace. No guards. No fanfare. She didn't need it, she was the most lethal thing in this place, maybe even against me.

She was tall—almost my height, and far taller than the rest of her kind. Her form was slender but stretched in ways that made her seem otherworldly. Her hair wasn't hair at all, just fine, dark shreds of feathers that trailed around her shoulders like wisps of smoke. Her eyes were wide and slanted, more snake than bird. A hooked nose. Thin, scaled lips. Skin thick, like smoothed leather over bone. Her hands had fingers that were long and cruel, tipped in claws that curled slightly inward as if they were always prepared to strike.

And her gaze? It pinned me like prey. She didn't blink. Didn't waver. She reached the bars and tilted her head. Then pushed them open. They hadn't even been locked. Of course they hadn't.

She stepped into the chamber. The chamber she frequented, she knew this dungeon hell well— every inch of it. Her crown was a twisted ring of bone and metal, tall and jagged spears shaped like feathers, tarnished and sharpened at the tips, possibly made of Aetherium, not its usual use, but the shade of it was unmistakable. Her ears were pointed, with edges that shimmered like obsidian in the torchlight.

She was unlike any Harpy I had seen. And I had seen too many in my short time here.

There was something ancient in her face, something unnatural. Not born but made.

And the fact she was a Crohn made her worse. Much worse.

A bloodline whispered about even in the Dunya Realm. The Crohn's were rare. Touched by old magic, twisted by realm decay, it was a power that could mix with any species. She would wield powers no Dunya-born creature could ever harness. And whatever had given birth to her... it had never been meant to walk in daylight.

She smiled at me then. Her lips thin and crooked. Her eyes focused like she could read my thoughts. She moved closer. My eyes hung heavy, tired and desperate for respite.

Then she gripped my face like I was a naughty child, and her claws scraped just enough to get my full attention. "What are you?" She hissed. Her breath was a putrid stench, and my nostrils itched at the pungency.

I held her gaze, but I said nothing.

Her fingers tightened and her claws sunk just enough to break the skin.

Still, I didn't speak.

Then she hit me.

Not with her claws, not with magic. Just a simple, brutal backhand that sent my head snapping to the side. Pain flared across my jaw and teeth, but I bit back any sound.

"I asked you a question..." She said, cool and calm. I knew then she could do this for hours. Days, maybe. She didn't need to get angry. She *enjoyed* this.

My lips curled into a smirk despite the taste of blood in my mouth. "You're going to have to try harder than that." I mocked.

She struck me again, over and over again. I didn't give her anything.

Then she moved fast. One moment she was standing, the next her hand was against my chest, palm flat and fingers spread. I braced for pain, but instead, I felt warmth. Magic. Her magic.

I tensed, confused, as something shifted inside me. The pain in my ribs dulled. The fire along my spine receded. I could feel the fractures in my wing beginning to close. Bones and tendons began weaving back together with unnatural precision—she was healing me.

The bars down the corridor rattled suddenly, loud enough to snap my attention sideways. A Faun screamed from her cell, her voice shrill with panic, hooves slamming against the bars as she tried to warn me.

"No! No, don't let her—don't let her touch you!"

Morog laughed softly, her magic still working as the heat in my body rose.

"That's better," She said, her hand leaving my chest. "Now you're listening." Her smile was ugly, a line where her lips were.

I stared at her, breath coming hard and fast, every instinct screaming at me not to let her in. "What are you?" Her words were venom.

But I couldn't stop it. "Half-Fae," I gasped finally. "Half-human."

She raised a brow. "That's not all." She waited for more.

Something in me cracked, but not from pain.

"I was taken into the Eternal Tree," I said, the words slipping out before I could stop them. "Into the roots. Into the fire. I was... changed." My words were breathy, involuntary.

She said nothing. Just watched me. Waiting for the rest, knowing I would cough it up.

"Forged," I admitted. "With a Dragon. In the depths."

Her expression shifted subtly, but it was there. Curiosity. Excitement.

"Oh?…" She whispered. "Now we're getting somewhere!"

She moved beside me, and for a moment, I let myself hope she'd stop. That maybe, somehow, I'd intrigued her enough to buy time.

Then she grabbed my wing. Danced her fingers around the fourth finger in its wide span and snapped the bone.

The crack was so loud it stole the air from my lungs. I screamed, the sound ripped from my chest like it didn't belong to me. Pain burst across my vision, white-hot and furious, undoing everything she'd just healed. She was toying with me.

She stepped around again, unhurried, expression unbothered.

"There," She said with a hint of satisfaction. "Not as bad as before, you'll still fly with just one broken bone, it was much worse before! Now it's just enough to remind you who holds the power here." She scowled with pride.

I couldn't speak. I was barely breathing.

"You'll fly in the arena soon," She went on, brushing hair from my bloodied face with mock gentleness. "Not fully healed. Not fully broken. Just right to perform." She smiled.

She turned, her crown catching the light from the sconces, her voice trailing like silk dipped in poison.

"My people need to see strength again. It is time to reinvent the Blood Trials! And you… you'll give them a show. You'll bleed, burn, rise, fall. You'll be perfect!" She clapped to herself.

Then she left, just like that, with the confidence of a queen who knew she wouldn't be challenged.

The torches hissed in her wake. The corridor fell silent as she exited the cell. And I hung there in the dark, the words *Blood Trial* still fresh in the air, circling my thoughts. What was it?

Worse than that, I was separated from Aliera, Torin, Jake and Dani. The last time I saw them, they were being shoved into cages.

Almost everything went blank after that Morog left, but not completely. Suddenly there was movement.

Through the gap in the stone, I saw the girl again, the human girl in another cell. She was on her feet now. I could see her fingers curled around the bars. The tall guard with the dented mask stopped in front of her cell. Roan. I knew his name now; the others had said it several times.

He checked the corridor, then stepped closer to her. Too close for a guard and a prisoner.

"I thought the worst," She whispered. I could just make it out.

"So did I," He said. His voice was softer than it had been in the chamber. It was gentle for her.

He reached through the bars. This time, no gloves. His bare hands wrapped around hers like he'd done it before. Like he needed to. She didn't pull away. If anything, she leaned into his touch.

They stayed like that for a long moment. Just holding on.

Then he tugged her closer. Their foreheads touched first. A second later, he kissed her slow and careful, like he was afraid the world would end if he pressed any harder. It wasn't a guard comforting a prisoner. They were just two people in love in the worst place in the world.

My arms burned. My wing throbbed. The pain dragged me under again.

The last thing I saw before the darkness took me was Ivy's fingers still tangled with his, like she'd rather face the Crohn herself than let him go.

CHAPTER EIGHT

IVY

The bars to my cell rattled, and soon guards forced their way in. This was no normal shake down, they weren't looking for that singular piece of candy that I quickly grabbed and held tightly in my hand. One moment I was curled beneath the stone slab bench, hidden in the shadows of the lowest part of my cell, and the next I was choking on smoke as claws tore me from the darkness. I screamed for Roan, for anyone, but the sound vanished beneath the screech of Harpies and the iron slap of cell doors. There was no answer. Just a bag over my head, and now the sound of my own breath.

They forced me up the mismatched stairs, towards the surface. When they pulled the bag off my head I was suddenly standing in a large hall, just me and four guards. Four guards for one small girl. Two tore at my rags, stripping me naked, exposing me. Then a bucket of water as cold as ice was thrust over me and one of the guards scrubbed me roughly, just enough to get the first layer of filth off my back, the areas I hadn't reached before. Every scrape was rough and cruel.

They didn't dry me, but they dressed me in silence. Like they wanted me to sit with the shame of it all.

I didn't fight before, and I wouldn't fight now. They were shoving me into a gown. Black bodice, high collar, heavy with beads and feathers that scratched against my skin. The skirt was weightless but obscene, it flowed like blood, sheer ivory veiled in red embroidered roses that bloomed like bleeding wounds. It wasn't a dress. It was a message. I was the lamb for slaughter.

My wrists were chained, not tight, but tight enough. A whisper of rebellion still pulsed in my chest, but I wouldn't cry for them. They'd have to earn that; they'd have to beat me.

Then the doors to the hall burst open once more. Beau, he was forced onto his knees before me.

"Fail, and she dies." One of the guards chuckled.

They had him chained at the shoulders, blood crusted along his wings, one side of his face bruised so deeply it looked purple in the dim light. But even like that, even half-broken and stumbling, he looked like someone who could unleash hell.

His golden eyes locked on mine. They widened. And then he roared with rage as the Harpies shoved him to his knees.

"I'll kill you," Beau growled. "If you touch her again, I'll rip your throat out with my teeth." His voice was commanding.

"Shame you'll be too dead to try," Another said.

They marched us from the hall together, Beau still chained, me clutching the skirt of the awful dress to keep myself from tripping. The halls led us to the heart of the mountain to a door barely used. The Harpies of the city thundered with excitement and then the guards picked us up and flew us over the expansive chasm city of Harpia. The closer we got to the arena, the louder the sounds became. Cheers. Screeches. Roars. Thousands of them—This was the Blood Trial.

I'd never been this close. I'd only heard about the Blood Trials from whispers over the years, I'd never been chosen. A massive arena waited ahead, and filling it were Harpies, some Clops and Windreapers.

But before we reached it, we passed a line of Harpy guards. And at the center of them stood Roan, he was taller than the rest. Built like he belonged to another species entirely. Part Harpy, part human, masked once more. He didn't gravitate to the others; he was standing alone.

His body stiffened when he saw me, his fists clenched. His gaze flicked from the dress to my bare legs exposed by the thigh length slit right down the middle, then to the bruises on Beau's arms.

Beau met his eyes. Something passed between them. An understanding, something dangerous. Roan didn't speak. He didn't have to. But I saw it in the way he looked at me—not like a guard, not even like a prisoner. Like a man who had nothing left to lose. Like I was all that mattered to him.

He was planning who he was going to kill first.

My hair whipped across my face, the thin straps of the dress cutting into my shoulders as the Harpies lifted me by the arms, two on either side, claws curled too tight around my skin that they pierced my forearms and blood wrapped around them.

Below us, the chasm city stretched wide and endlessly. Cracks in the earth that split like veins through the doomed scorched land. Creatures moaned from their confines. Harpy children ran between shanty huts like none of this was unusual.

And then we reached the Arena. A gaping wound carved into the side of the mountain, ringed by obsidian spires and flaming braziers, already filled with thousands of screaming onlookers.

Ahead of me, Beau...One wing, half-healed and viciously re-broken, hung limp at his back. His chest was bare, scored with lashes. They weren't subtle with him. He was chained by the neck, suspended from a metal bar like some beast being offered up.

But his eyes...They never stopped moving, he was searching for something, or maybe someone.

He wasn't just watching the Harpies or me. He kept glancing towards the right flank.

He was looking at Roan again. So much about him was designed to disappear. No insignia. Dark leathers. His mask low, he was up to something. I couldn't make out Roan's expression. Not beneath the mask. But I saw the way his hand flexed around his weapon. The way his posture changed when Beau turned his head slightly. No words spoken, just the lock of two pairs of eyes that held a hidden promise.

Beau gave him the smallest nod. It was barely anything. Their eyes spoke a language of war I didn't understand. A blink of agreement. *Protect her, and I'll protect you.* Beau had worked out that I was important enough to Roan that he would kill for me.

We were flown over the edge of the arena, the crowd below erupting with bloodlust. Harpies screeched and hissed. The Queen's seat glimmered at the highest platform, surrounded by torchlight and crimson banners with a black harpy stained in ink on it.

And right below that was the center of the pit.

The place they would drop us. I could see the posts where they would chain me, on top of a circular stone platform. The sand around it was already dark in places where blood had been shed.

I couldn't breathe…They were going to make him fight, but fight what? And they were going to make me watch. Our lives were linked now.

I turned my head as the Harpies dipped lower, and from the side, I watched as Roan flexed his wings as he watched me. He was a fuse about to be lit.

We hit the ground hard, and the chains clanked louder than the crowd.

They snapped cold metal around my wrists and bolted them to a curved post at the center of the arena platform. The stand arched behind me, framing me for the monsters to see, I wasn't sure if I was bait, or a sacrifice.

The dress clung to my skin, already damp with sweat. The heat in the arena was worse than fire, it was hell. Harpies filled every ledge; every floating slab of obsidian or stone was carved out from the pit walls. Their screeches made the air vibrate, but I couldn't reach my ears to muffle their cries.

I tried not to cry. They wanted a trembling girl. They wanted my screams. Harpies pointed at me and laughed.

But I stared straight ahead with my chin lifted, I couldn't be a coward here, I had to face the Blood Trial with Beau. One Harpy leered and hissed, "Let's see what he can do."

Then the guards strapped Beau's swords onto him, and they pulled back as the ground shuddered. The Crohn made a speech

I was too dazed to hear what Morog said. Everything became a blur.

Across the arena, iron gates groaned open.

Beau was kicked forward by some of the hovering guards.

He hit the sand hard, shoulder-first, and rolled. The chains around his wrists had been removed. He was breathing heavily already. Not from fear. From pain. But even bruised, bleeding, he looked like he could break the whole mountain in half if he got mad enough.

He looked at me, his back turned to the gates that had just opened…then something moved behind him.

A creature all muscle and bone and too many eyes and joints. A Windreaper, but this one was bigger, deformed, vicious and starved.

The crowd exploded and I looked around the arena to distract myself from the horror of what was in front of me.

From the corner of my eye, one of the higher cages lit up, one of the holding cells carved into the arena walls.

A face was pressed to the bars. My heart knew it before my brain did. Jake, my big brother. He was different, he was older, but it was him. I almost cried out his name. But something stopped me.

A second pair of eyes tracked me and caught my attention. Roan, his eyes said more than words could as the seemed to beg me for caution.

He was stationed just behind the Queen's platform, his mask fixed on the fight, but his body wasn't still. His wings kept twitching. His fingers wouldn't let go of his blade hilt.

He was watching Beau now. Beau had just stepped between me and the creature.

And he didn't move, didn't strike…He waited.

The creature lunged and Beau took the blow straight to the chest. He flew back into the sand, blood pouring from his mouth as his body carved a trench with his weight.

The crowd screamed with roared with excitement, they were feral and delighted, but he wasn't done. He stood again. The beast lunged forward once more, striking Beau, this time to the ribs. I heard a crunch as he dust around his took air like smoke amidst his fall.

The beast locked it's eyes on me and raced heavy footed in my direction as it let out a low and guttural snarl that vibrated all through the arena. Suddenly, Beau cut it from beneath right across the intertarsal joint sending the beast tumbling forward and over itself.

He kept protecting me from every threat of attack, using his body as a barricade between me and the Windreaper.

Roan leaned forward now, mask tilted slightly. His wings stretched, like they wanted to fly down and rip someone apart.

Beau was swaying. His knees buckled, but he forced himself upright again.

This wasn't a trial, it was a death sentence. And the only thing more terrifying than watching Beau bleed, was realizing he *meant* to. Because he knew the crowd didn't want a monster slayer, they wanted a hero. And some even began crying for his mercy.

He was giving them what they wanted—entertainment.

Beau stumbled again.

The sand beneath him was streaked red, his blood soaking into the silt. His chest was heaving against his ragged breath and yet...He stood in front of me.

The crowd cheered louder each time he staggered upright, drunk on the violence, howling with delight at the spectacle of a Dragon blooded Fae, they had become ravenous for him.

I wanted to scream at him. Tell him to fight back. To burn the whole place down, but I couldn't. I was chained in a cursed dress, shackled in the middle of a nightmare.

And then, he looked up. His golden eyes found me as he prepared for his next move.

And I knew he was about to do something reckless. Something final. Something only meant for *me*.

CHAPTER NINE

ALIERA

We were separated from Beau now. Our prison flown and raised into the sky and suspended over an enormous arena with vines made of metal beside other cages carved into the arena itself, the stench of rust offending my nostrils while Harpy guards lurked closely, keeping watch on the exposed prison cages. Harpies were flying in from all around the city, perching on seats, taking rest on the higher perches, resting on logs or clinging to the outside of the prison aviaries. There were more now. I thought it was just us, but there were five more cages, full of more Sporlings, Fauns, Humans, Enfields, Pixies, and creatures I wasn't even familiar with.

The Arena was enormous, it sat at the far end of the city, where we came from. Nestled tightly against the cliffside, it looked over the expansive city. It was unlike any other. On the surface it was a desolate wasteland, but in the crevices, the chasms, it was alive, the glow of fire filled them like open veins of the city. From here I could clearly see the mountain, the one they had carved into a castle. It's towers were tall spears, it was where they had flown Beau. He was in there somewhere.

I looked down over the blood stained battlefield sprawling before us. The sand was browner in places where fighters had fallen. Below, beside and even above us were floating platforms, nicer than the rest… For their Queen.

The wind tore through the gaps in the aviaries. The cold air reminding us that there was no escaping, we were helpless, enslaved to this enclosure.

We'd been dragged here to witness what they were all calling the blood trial. The soldiers spoke loudly and excitedly about the event, about their latest capture, about Beau. Beau was a threat, an idea. Something new and Morog wouldn't be challenged in this way. The blending of a Fae and Dragon was an offense in her eyes.

Hours later, after we drifted in and out of chilling naps the city began to hum. Masses of wings battered now and suddenly I was upright as I leant my face between two bars and stared out over the flaming arteries that lit up the valley. They began to darken as the Harpies rose from their chasms and circled the mountain, cheering, roaring. Enthusiasm took hold and soon they were flocking to the arena. Thousands of them rushing for seats, many just hovered. And then a boom, a door rarely used cracked open, large enough that I could see it from the arena. Out flooded a small army of guards. Then—her. The Queen of the Harpies…Morog.

She flew to the arena. She was bigger than most of the Harpies here. She smiled and gestured kindness to the mob that gathered, warming the crowd to her. She flew to each cage and snarled, the masses demanded our deaths, sport for their entertainment.

Morog rested on the central pillar in the arena as she addressed the crowd.

"Children of the Chasms!" Her voice cracked across the arena, eerie and haunting. "Tonight, we feast not on flesh, but on *fear*." The word left her lips slowly.

The crowd erupted in howls, screeches, wings slapping wind.

"The skies have opened and emptied traitors into our lands. Filth born in fire and wrapped in stolen wings. A blending of Fae and Dragon… unnatural. Unholy." She was talking about Beau. She knew what he was.

She stood tall atop the central pillar, wings outstretched, her bone crown glinting in the arena torchlight.

"He walks among you now, caged like the beast he is. But not for long." She grinned, feral and wide. "Tonight, he earns the right to die *spectacularly*." A hush fell. Anticipation clung to the air.

"You will not see a clean death," She promised. "You will see pain. Defiance crushed. Power broken. And when he bleeds, remember… your Queen does not share her sky."

She raised a clawed hand.

"Let the blood trial begin!" Drums battered and the crowd ignited.

Dani grasped my arm hard, and Torin gasped and fell slightly into Jake as Beau was flown into the arena. He was weak, but still he stood tall. His one shredded wing tucked tight against his back. But he wouldn't show pain here. He couldn't.

He wasn't alone, a girl was being chained to the altar in the middle of the arena, but she wasn't facing us, we couldn't see her face. Beau's task was to protect her.

Across from them a large gate opened. The abomination crawling from the cavern beneath the arena. It wasn't a proper Windreaper, it was something once majestic, now warped. Its wings were too big to use, extra joints with no purpose that snapped in spasms as it began to pull itself upright and stalk Beau. Its beak wasn't the same shape as the Windreapers we'd seen in the Cradleland. This one had been sawn into something jagged, cruel, a weapon, not a feature. Its eyes glowed hollow red, like it wasn't even alive anymore, just rage embodied in flesh and feathers.

Harpies screeched in excitement, pounding their talons to a rhythm against stone.

A booming voice echoed across the arena. "LET THE BROKEN PRINCE EARN HIS FINAL BREATH!" A fat, bald Harpy barked to the crowd, and they cheered like animals.

The beast lunged without warning.

Its chains snapped taut as it whipped Beau from his stance—he went face-first into the sand. The mutated bird pecked the ground violently, trying to shred him, but Beau rolled, dodging each vicious strike by the skin of his teeth. He pulled his shredded wing in tighter, trying to make himself a smaller target. But he took every hit as best he could.

His swords were sheathed across his back. With shaking hands, he tore one free and faced the beast.

He didn't rush.

He moved slowly. Back and forth. Pacing like a predator. Confusing the bird. He played with it for a long time, tiring it out. Taking as much as he possibly could while the crowd roared for action.

It screamed an unholy, unnerving sound.

Beau whipped his sword through the air, striking the twisted beast with every ounce of force he could summon. The beast shrieked again.

The crowd roared louder.

He struck again—at the neck this time.

The creature reared back, howling in pain, preparing to impale him with its jagged beak, but Beau was faster.

He dove beneath it, sliding low, his blade slicing a brutal line from throat to gut as he ran under its towering frame.

I didn't realize I was squeezing Dani's hand until she whimpered. Her knuckles were white. I loosened my grip just barely, but neither of us looked away, because this was the moment where we'd learn if he lived or died.

The beast's wings lashed violently in its final breath. Fluids poured from its ruined gut, sizzling across the arena floor. But just as we thought he might escape with a clean fight, the monstrous talons tore down Beau's back, throwing him to the floor.

Beau stayed low, he mustered all of his strength for one final assault, his blade slamming into the Windreaper's neck over and over until he was drenched in blood.

The creature collapsed over him…Dead.

And the arena became ill with silence and then gasps, low chatter and confusion.

It wasn't the ending they'd wanted.

Morog's smile faltered. Her eyes narrowed as she leaned forward from her platform, waiting.

Guards rushed into the pit, shoving wings aside to search for Beau's body. And then Beau was revealed sitting in the sand beneath a wing of the beast.

His chest rose and fell in painful rhythm. One of his wings hung nearly torn from his back, blood pooled around his feet.

"GET UP!" Morog snapped.

Beau staggered upright, eyes flicking to the cage, right to me.

Blood leaked from his mouth. He could barely breathe, but he stayed composed.

And yet he looked at me like this was all fine. Like it had gone according to some twisted plan he had concocted. He wanted them to see him as a hero. He had a plan.

And then suddenly Jake moved. His face smashed against the bars, fists pounding.

"IVY!" He shouted.

My heart stopped.

I followed his gaze, he had seen his little sister...In the arena, chained. Her face lit in shock, she'd heard him. She saw him.

"Jake!" She cried.

The creature moved again. Even in death, its nerves twitched. And suddenly a guard bigger than the rest took flight and landed in the arena, sword drawn and ready to defend Beau.

"Who the fuck is that?" Torin growled.

"I have no idea…" Jake gasped as the soldier rushed to Ivy now and began trying to free her.

"TRAITOR!" Morog shrieked. "Roan, I should have killed you when I killed your pathetic mother, but I saw so much of myself in you. You could have been a son to me." She teased.

Roan didn't say a word, but he ripped the mask from his face and stomped it into the ground. He was more human than anything. Another half breed, maybe less. Morog glowered at him and waved her hand.

"DO NOT FEAR…THERE'S MORE WHERE THAT CAME FROM!" She spoke to the crowd, and they ate every word she fed them.

Another gate opened, a bigger one. And from the darkness a Clops emerged. Another monstrosity, not like a regular Clops, this one was a parent, from Otro Mundo, this one was more savage then the rest.

Torin growled now, his teeth barring, rage spilling from him as he gnashed recklessly at the bars as he tried to split them.

Jake pulled now as he tried to help Torin reach his friend and the tiny Foogals and Enfields even came to help, but their efforts were pointless.

"Aliera, can you? You know…" Jake whispered.

If they see her, they'll know she's a Titan." Dani said lightly.

"Each of you pull, we can mask this." I nodded.

As we were attempting to break the bars open, the Clops of gargantuan size was led into the heart of the arena by several guards with chains. It was bigger now…

"FUCK OFF!" Jake growled.

"Hold on everybody!" I said to the beings in the cage.

A whisp of wind was coming in and with all I had I pulled it directly at our cage, crashing us into the next, cracking the bottom open just enough for us to slip through.

Torin leapt over the crowds and into the arena like a bolt of fury, shifting mid-air into his formidable other self. His bones cracked, muscles stretched, and he landed with a snarl in his enormous Dreadwolf form, but even still, the Clops dwarfed him. The crowd erupted, and the chaos of screams and roars of excitement exploded as Torin, the Dread took his place beside his friend in the arena. Beau looked happy to see him, even beneath all the blood that lathered his face. Torin's presence gave Beau a much needed burst of energy as the two stood together.

Roan was trying to get Ivy free now, smashing his sword into the pillars, chipping away at the stone. She was almost free.

Beside me, Jake turned to Dani, grabbed her face, and kissed her like it might be their last, but it was their first. She blinked in surprise, a dazed smile blooming as he tore away and scaled the jagged stones that mimicked a staircase down into the pit of the arena.

"Whoa!" She smiled, touching her lips.

We'd all seen it coming. The tension, the looks, it had always been there. He was just too afraid to show it till now.

"Stay here! All of you!" I said to Dani, and the other prisoners as I jumped down from the ledge of the cage.

I raced into the arena and stood between Jake and Beau as the Clops eyed us, waiting for Morog's command.

"Mhmm." Was all she said when the Clops lashed for us.

The ground quaked under its weight. Each footfall was a sledgehammer to the arena. Pebbles lifted, vibrating in the air. Harpies rocked on their perches, wings flaring in alarm as they took flight and hovered instead.

The quake was all Roan needed to free Ivy now. He wrapped his arms around her and flew her up to the furthest corner of the arena.

Then the sky cracked open with a thunderous roar, the light of the Dunya world poured in from the sky illuminating the puddles of blood soaking the ground around Beau.

Draven descended like a specter, wings outstretched wide and gliding.

"Draven…" The words were a whisper on Beau's lips as Draven descended from the sky in a shadow of black, followed by swirls of purple haze, hair and robes twisting in the wind, Starlette. Finally, a fireball of heat gushed for the ground and landed on the arena floor—Zac. A shockwave thrust through the dust as he landed with an impact that surged a heat wave through the ground.

"Bit late." Beau panted as he spoke to Draven.

Draven smiled as he whipped his head to the Clops that Torin was keeping busy.

"See you brought your dog?" Draven smirked.

Beau rolled his eyes as a low growl came from Torin.

Starlette bolted for the aviaries, magic crackling as she shattered locks and lifted the cages. Prisoners screamed in hope. Fauns and Foogals celebrated and Enfields scrapped at the bars for her in desperation.

Zac was all flame and fury as he raised the arena to ash and smoke.

Beau collapsed to the ground now, his wounds weakening him. I rushed to his side. The Harpies began to scatter, shrieking from their perches as they realized this wasn't a part of the show.

Torin morphed back to his human state now as Zac and Roan took over the fight. "Look who finally showed up for the party." Torin smiled at Draven, dried blood crackling around his lips.

"Not the time!" I scowled at them.

Beau was down, and the battle around me continued as I froze and begged for the sound of his breath. His wings were in shreds, his scales torn from his shoulders. My breathing staggered as I tried to shake him back to consciousness.

"Please don't die!" I cried.

I hated him, but I loved him so much more. I could hate him later when I knew he would make it back to our own realm.

Roan and Ivy rushed to his side. Concern and sadness filling them.

My hands held the edges of his face, his skin was too cold, too still. "Come back to me, you can't leave me here." The words left me, and power pulsed between us as he pulled in a breath.

Relief tore through me as I faltered, collapsing onto him. My face pressed to his, our blood mixing in the dust. The rise and fall of his chest, however faint was the only thing I needed. The arena cracked and trembled beneath Zac's fury, but I didn't care if the whole world fell apart around us. He was alive.

"You're stuck with me," He murmured, voice rough like gravel. He lifted a bloodied hand to my cheek, brushing it with a single finger. "Still so beautiful… even when you cry." His voice cracked under the weight of his words.

His arms wrapped around me, and I let them. I melted into his warmth, clung to him like I could fuse us back together.

"Don't scare me like that again." I whispered.

I sat up just as Draven and Starlette dropped in front of us, the haze of battle still clinging to their cloaks.

"It's good to see you." Draven said with a knowing smile, silver eyes scanning Beau before flicking back to mine.

"Starlette, he needs healing." I said quickly, brushing the dirt from Beau's chest like it would make a difference.

"I don't know if I can." She breathed, her voice light, but I saw the worry flicker in her eyes.

Beau's hand caught mine and tugged me back down to him. And before I could speak, he kissed me. No warning. No hesitation.

It was wild and aching and full of every unsaid word. His mouth tasted like blood and heat and memories, and I let myself get lost in it. My fingers tangled into his hair, clinging to him like the wind to the sea. And for one second, there was no war, no pain, no past…just us.

"We gotta go.." Zac nudged me. "NOW!" His voice cut through like a whip. "They'll be back!"

He grabbed me by the arm and yanked me upright, pulling me away from Beau, urgency blazing in his eyes.

Draven and Torin were already hauling Beau to his feet between them, both steady and grim. Starlette stayed close, her magic finally gathering in a soft shimmer around her hands.

We stood in the shadow of the stairwell as an army of Harpies spilled into the arena.

Then she came, Morog, the Queen of the Harpies.

She descended like a shadow, her massive wings blending feathers the color of obsidian and bone. Her crown was made from the spines, teeth, and scales of Dragons, her armor forged from fallen stars and embedded with screaming faces, literal curses trapped in steel wrapped in Gloomstone, a signifier of battles won.

Her guards followed. Six of them, winged elite, each carrying twin-bladed spears and handles shaped like shrikes.

Morog landed at the center of the ruined arena. Her talons scraped across cracked stone. She surveyed the wreckage with cold disdain…silence reigned.

And then she spoke. "I WANT THAT TRAITOR AND HIS WHORE!" She hissed. Her voice low and echoing with unnatural reverb. "They spilled our blood in our own nest!" A Windreaper swooped low and dropped a burned Harpy helmet at her feet.

She looked at it. Then crushed it beneath her clawed foot.

From the shadows, one of the Clops stepped forward, armor rattling in fear. "We followed the scent. The rebels descended into the tunnels beneath the chasms. Should we pursue?"

Morog tilted her head slightly. Her feathers flared.

"No. Let them run. Let them cower in roots and filth. We will burn the forest after we burn their hope."

She turned slowly, wings lifting.

"Ready the Clops, ready the Windreaper's."

Another pause.

"Ready every Harpy that still remembers war." Her voice was piercing now.

She looked to the stairwell, like she knew we were waiting and listening in the shadow of the darkness.

Her smile was cruel. Her lips thin.

"Let the Realms know… *Morog is coming.*" Like she was speaking directly to us. Her voice reaching to find us.

The air in the tunnels was thick with moisture. The stone walls crumbling as the thundering of Clops feet pounded in the arena above us, raining dust from the ceiling.

We turned and ran through tight tunnels that stunk of waste.

Then we reached a fork in the tunnels. Roan paused and so did everyone else.

"If you go that way it will take you to the edge of Underfoot Forest, Pelk and Morel knows the way from there." He looked to the Faun woman who had escaped the cages with a few Foogals and an Enfield.

"I'll lead them." She nodded.

"I'll meet you in Faunmoor." Roan whispered to Ivy.

"WHAT?" She gasped.

"I have to go to my people. They don't live in the chasms, they aren't like the other Harpies, they live on the outer cliffs, they will have no warning." He explained.

"Why do they need a warning?" Jake interrupted as he pulled Ivy back by her shoulder.

"Cause most of them are like me, outcasts." Roan sighed.

"How many of you?" Draven asked.

"At least a thousand." He answered.

"Go." Beau said his hand as he leant between me and Draven.

"NO!" Ivy protested. "I'm not letting you go, it's suicide." She pulled away from Jake.

Roan took a step forward as he reached for her and stroked her cheek gently. "I have to do the right thing Ivy." He said sorrowfully.

"I'm coming then." She grabbed his hand.

"I can't lead you into danger." He shook his head.

"You saved me, more than once..." Her eyes pooled and his arms stretched around her body in a warm embrace.

"Please." She cried. "I just got you."

Tears clung to Roan's eyelashes as he rubbed her back.

He wasn't anything like a Harpy. He was kind and gentle, he loved her.

"I have to, Ivy." He leant down to kiss her. "But I will find you, I promise." She pressed up on her toes to reach his lips one more time.

He kissed the tears from her cheeks, and I watched everyone around us as we responded to their relationship is silence. Dani wept into Jake at the tension and sadness of it all.

"You gave me life, you didn't just keep me alive, you gave my darkness meaning, you taught me what love is." She cried.

"It's not over, not when we just started." They squeezed each other tightly and he wrapped his wings around them so they could share a private kiss.

"Go, I'll find you. They won't be far behind." He released her and before we knew it he was racing down the left tunnel.

"He seems nice." Jake sighed.

"Hi Jake." Ivy cried as she hugged him.

"I'm sorry to break this up, but we need to move." Starlette said.

We heard the screeches a moment later, the guards had entered the tunnel, they were hunting us. We fled through the darkness, to a place where the smell wasn't so wretched, through winding corners and puddles of waste.

One of the Fauns stumbled. I grabbed his arm and yanked him forward. "No stopping. If they catch us…"

"I know!" He rasped.

The tunnel narrowed ahead, the ceiling lower. I ducked as we slipped into the smaller crawlspace. At the end was a barred gate, but it wasn't locked.

The sound of wings was louder now and so was the screaming as they pursued us.

Draven dropped to his knees, pressing his weight against the rusted bars. They groaned in protest, years of disuse clinging to every joint until suddenly, with a piercing shriek, they gave way. We tumbled through, hitting the ground hard and gasping for clean air.

The field stretched before us, a wasteland of rough, sun-starved grass. It scraped against our legs like wire as we pushed forward, each step a fight to reach the distant edge of Underfoot Forest.

Finally, we reached the edge of the forest. It was unlike any forest I'd ever seen in the Dunya. It was a forest that had been tipped upside down. Roots coiled above us like the arms of giants, forming a dense canopy of earth. The Underfoot Forest was never truly above or below, it was something in between, a place where gravity seemed to forget itself, and the world turned inside out.

The survivors of the aviaries continued to pour out of the narrow stone stair, breathless and wounded, only to find the shadows waiting.

I held Beau steady as we stepped into the open space beneath the trees. Foogals, Enfields and Pixies crouched low, sniffing the dirt. Fauns clustered together, their ears twitching. Starlette's light flickered faintly as her spells scanned the surroundings, and Draven clung to her side.

Jake stared upward. "What the hell…".

Bodies were strung in the roots above us, dozens, maybe more. Wrapped in web-like silk, some *melted*, their bones dripping from the canopy. Others were half-intact, their eyes open, glassy, staring down in eternal warning.

A thick *buzzing* began. Low. Subtle. Then rising.

The Foogals recoiled. The Enfields growled.

From the far edge of the cavernous forest, shadows moved, not shaped like Harpies, nor Clops. Wasp-creatures.

Long-limbed, iridescent armor plating over skeletal forms. Their wings vibrated at speeds too fast for the eye. Their mandibles clicked, and fluid dripped from stingers the size of swords.

The first hissed and sprayed.

A jet of acidic fluid hit a tree beside them, it sizzled, hissed, and melted straight through the trunk.

A Faun screamed.

Zac was already moving, fire in both palms, hurling a burst toward the nearest hive cluster embedded in the unnatural trees.

"It's not safe!" Starlette shouted, her voice laced with panic. "This forest has been taken!"

Torin snarled in his Dreadwolf form now, he was protectively circling the group as more wasps began to emerge from hives in the canopy, from underground, from the cracks in the earth itself.

They weren't in a refuge. They were in a nest.

The forest writhed.

Wasps poured from hives in the earth, wings a blur of vibration, acid spraying from curved stingers like venomous rain. The survivors broke into chaos, spells crackling from Starlette, weapons drawn, children from the aviaries screaming.

Then, a voice rose above the madness.

The Faun woman Morel, the one with the infant still strapped to her chest turned on the stone ledge, eyes blazing, hooves scraping against the trembling roots.

"We can't stay here!" She screamed. "We must run to Lake Aravena!"

No one moved fast enough. So, she bellowed again, louder, this time with a voice that commanded.

"RUN! Lake Aravena lies beyond the far end of the forest, past the blackroot thickets and the crystal fissures. On the other side is Faunmoor. My village. Our only haven."

Zac shouted back, torching a wasp mid-air, "How far?!"

"As far northeast as the land will stretch." She called, turning and darting forward through a narrow path carved by root and erosion, glowing faintly under our feet. "MOVE!" She ordered.

Dani and Starlette locked eyes for just a second.

No words needed, they were told. Beau grunted as he pushed himself upright with Draven's help, wings dragging behind him. "Not the escape I imagined." He muttered.

"You'll live long enough to complain about it." He shot back, his grip tightened around me.

Draven flew overhead now in wide circles, eyes scanning for flankers, his shadow cast across the tangled canopy of strung corpses and bile-dripping nests.

Behind them, the forest screamed. Not a voice, but the sound of insects in fury.

The path through the Underfoot Forest was chaos. Roots clawed at our feet, the buzzing of wasp wings echoed like war drums, and acid hissed on leaves behind us.

Beau stumbled, knees buckling, his wings dragging through the dirt.

I caught him by the arm, only just.

"Hold on, dammit," I muttered. "Don't die now."

Beau gave me a painful, crooked smile. "You're a little too determined."

Before I could answer, Zac appeared, firelight in his veins, flickering like a storm about to break.

"I've got him." Zac said gruffly, already moving to Beau's other side.

I hesitated, then stepped back, letting them support each other with supervision.

For a moment, it was silence. Just the sound of leaves rustling and distant wasp shrieks as we safely evaded the nest with the group intact.

Then Zac muttered, "You're heavier than you look."

"Too much muscle," Beau rasped.

Zac's jaw tightened.

The silence between them stretched and burned.

"You shouldn't have followed her." Zac said. Not shouting. Just...honest.

Beau's response came after a beat. "I couldn't let her go alone."

"You're the reason she jumped." Zac retorted.

"I know." Beau sighed.

Zac stopped walking, dragging Beau to a halt beside him. I hung back, listening and watching at a safe distance that wasn't too obvious.

Beau looked at him. "Say it, Zac. Whatever you need to."

Zac's fists clenched, heat crackling around them. His voice was low, nearly shaking. "You murdered my parents."

Beau didn't flinch. "I did." He admitted.

"You left a trail of blood through every kingdom. Lied. You used her."

"I did that, too." He sighed.

Zac turned his face toward Beau, his eyes blazing, skin glowing from the fire coiling under his skin in rage.

And yet—He didn't strike.

He just exhaled a long, molten breath.

"But you jumped through the door." Zac finally said. "You didn't have to. You could've stayed in your broken little palace. But you went after her."

Beau met his eyes. "I always will."

Zac nodded, just once.

Then he reached out and clapped a firm hand on Beau's shoulder. Not forgiving but acknowledging.

"Good," Zac said. "Now don't you dare die before this is over. We still need to have this out, you owe me that much." Zac smirked as his flames dimmed to a crackling surge.

"Wouldn't dream of it." Beau said through the blood.

Together, they started moving again and I breathed a sigh of relief as Dani stopped my hands from shaking.

We moved through tangled roots and whispering branches, footsteps muffled by thick moss and the silence of shared fear. The buzzing behind us grew more distant with every mile, but no one relaxed—not yet.

Beau walked slower now, supported on one side by Draven, on the other by Zac. Their shoulders brushed with every step. The rhythm was unsteady, but it held.

The forest path curved through a bend of twisted trees glowing faintly with bioluminescent spores. The rest of the group was just ahead—Starlette leading with torches. Dani broke off to help Morel and Pelk with the children.

"She liked you." Zac said.

Beau glanced sideways. "Astrid?" He cautioned on her name.

Zac nodded. "She would've laughed at your brooding."

Beau gave a soft, tired chuckle. "That sounds… accurate."

They walked a few more paces before Zac spoke again.

"I blamed you." He said. "Not just for the war. For *her*. You robbed me of her last moment."

Beau didn't respond, because Zac wasn't finished.

"But you didn't kill her." His voice was steady now. Stronger. "You were following her orders. I know that now."

Beau swallowed hard. "But I didn't stop her either."

Zac turned to him. "No." He said, "But you crossed a realm door with shredded wings and nothing to gain to save my sister. That means something."

A long breath passed between them.

Zac looked ahead again. "I'm sorry, Beau. For blaming you. For needing someone to hate."

Beau's jaw tightened, and for the first time, he didn't have a sarcastic remark.

"Your hate wasn't misplaced, I have done you wrong more than once." He sighed.

Zac nodded, he didn't know what else to say. Zac nodded; he didn't know what else to say. He didn't have a smart remark left when Beau laid himself bare like that.

He glanced at him again, fire dimming under his skin. "We're both carrying things we shouldn't have to," He said quietly. "Maybe we figure it out on the other side."

Beau swallowed, nodding once. "I'd like that."

And that was its own kind of truce.

Lake Aravena was close. The light ahead shimmered faintly reflected water, we were nearly there.

CHAPTER TEN

ROAN

The tunnel narrowed behind me, swallowing the sounds of the others footsteps, the fading scuffle of bodies fleeing through the darkness. I turned left at the fork. Not because it was safer. Not because it was right. But because I knew where it led…Home, to the Screaming Cliffs.

The tunnel sloped downward quickly, the air shifting from damp and acrid to sharp and wild. The scent of rust and fire gave way to sea spray and stone as I found the exit, a gaping hole in the cliff, no bars, no security, just a steep drop off a long cliff. Every instinct in my body screamed to go back to her. To them. But instincts get people like me killed. Logic is what has kept me breathing. And logic says they'll die soon if I don't make it back to my own people in time.

Morog will retaliate. She always did, and without any hesitation, never a thought for mercy. She'd built an empire out of fear on the bones of those who dared to exist outside her own idea of perfection. Her flock was big enough to be used recklessly, and they were dumb enough to obey her. Harpies, true, full blooded

Harpies were mindless fighters at best, volatile and vicious at worst.

And those of us born wrong, born different, born *half* or quartered like me…we've always been first to perish.

She'll come for the Screaming Cliffs before rebellion even has a chance to whisper amongst us. She knows what's out here. She knows there is strength and command amongst the displaced and desperate.

She knows *what* we are…Not Harpies. Not humans. Not something new. But something she can't control because we were in between. We were mistakes in her eyes. Breeding accidents. War stains. Slaves with wings too large and hearts too stubborn. Exiled to the cliffs with clipped feathers and broken bones, told to rot quietly until death swallowed us whole. Toys for her to play with or weapons for her dungeons—like me.

But we didn't rot.

We survived.

We *changed*.

I reached the edge of the cliff and my breath caught. It always did, cause there it was. The sky…the sea…the edge of the world, all in one grasp, it should be peaceful, serene, but it was menace.

And perched along the black stone ridges lived my people. Winged silhouettes against the haze. Spikes were driven into the cliff face to support tattered tents fluttering in the wind. Shacks carved into the rock, suspended by ropes and beams. The Screaming Cliffs.

The wind howled loudly across the expanse, shrieking as it passed through the jagged teeth of the stone. That's how it got its name. It never stopped screaming. Some say it's the sound of the ones Morog threw over the edge after breaking their wings. Others say it's the cliffs themselves crying out for justice after generations of silence.

I stepped out onto the narrow ledge, my fingers brushing the wall beside me for balance. Below, the sea roared, white waves slamming against rocks like drums of war. Further along the cliffs, movement stirred, and shadows were rising, wings unfurling.

They'd seen me.

They didn't cheer in welcome.

Outcasts don't have kings, we have memories, and survival. But tonight, that might not be enough. Because Morog saw what I saw, what the arena made clear to everyone watching.

Beau didn't just survive that trial. He championed it, the loyalty he commands gave way to an uprising. A Dragon-blooded Fae in full power, breathing fury and fighting alongside others where there should've been surrender. They'll see him as a symbol…a possibility, an opportunity.

Morog will stamp it out. Before it grows legs. Before it takes flight, and she'll start with *us*.

The halfbloods. The ones who can't be trusted. We're too close to rebellion. Too desperate to stay silent any longer. She'd make an example out of us.

The first of them landed nearby, some with wings heavier than mine, eyes sharper, faces older and far less forgiving.

They wouldn't ask why I came back from the dungeons. Not yet, but I'd tell them anyway.

I came because war is coming. Because for the first time in our history, we have a reason to rise. A reason to *hope*. But if we don't prepare, if we don't unite, we'll be wiped out before we can even light our torches… we will be the first ones she'll burn.

I stood at the cusp of the cliff, the wind rushing against me like it had a message of its own. My boots bit into the rock, and my wings wavered behind me, steady against the gale.

My people had looked up and soon they filled with curiosity, I wasn't due back for days.

The low murmur of evening rituals, of fires crackling and rope bridges swaying, had stilled. One by one, figures rose from their ledges and hollowed homes, wings slicing the sky as they moved freely. The wind carried them into the open space before me. A suspended crowd of jagged silhouettes held aloft against the darkening clouds.

"War is coming," I called out, voice raw but sure, "And it will come here first." I announced.

No ripple of alarm, just silence. Suspicion as my kin looked between themselves with questions they didn't speak into existence, until one did…

"Why us?" Someone shouted. A female voice. I knew that voice, Thira, she was broad-winged, her left leg bound in splints from the Queen's punishment years ago. "We stay silent, we serve her. We do as we are told. We've always done what we're told." She exasperated.

Murmurs rose, some in agreement, others just breathing fear out loud.

"That silence," I said, my voice low but not soft, "Has kept us alive. But it won't keep us safe anymore. Not after what happened at the Blood Trials. Not after what they saw." I said.

A few heads tilted. Wings shuddered mid-air.

"You all saw it!" I continued. "Or you've heard by now. The Fae with Dragon wings. The one who stood in the Queen's arena and survived the beast she bred with her dark magic."

"Beau," Someone muttered. There were hisses. A few muttered prayers.

"Yes. Him." I nodded.

"He wasn't supposed to win or even exist. But he did. And he does. Now the Queen will move to erase the idea of him. Of power beyond her own. She will come for anyone who might see him and believe we can be more than what she's allowed." I said.

A young male—Cress, sharp and lean with mismatched wings spoke up, "But he's not one of us. He's Fae."

I took a step forward. "He's half-blooded. Like us. More powerful than most. We *are* same enough…" I growled.

I let that sit in the wind. Let them chew on it.

"This isn't a rebellion," I said after a long moment. "Not yet. This is a warning. I came because you deserve to choose how this ends. You deserve the right to decide whether we're hunted down one by one or whether we stand together and make her regret ever pushing us to the edge."

No one spoke. Even the wind steadied its gale.

Then Thira's voice again, this time quieter. "What are you asking us to do, Roan?" She said softly.

My wings spread wider, instinctively. Not in threat, but in strength.

"I'm asking you to be ready," I said. "To remember who we are. We are not discarded Harpies or broken humans; we are something more. I'm asking you to look at each other and finally see an army." My words softened at the end.

Eyes narrowed and the strongest straightened their spines. And slowly, one by one, wings tilted toward me. Not in submission, but in alignment.

Thira didn't speak again. Neither did the others. But the silence had changed. It wasn't the quiet of resignation anymore. It was the quiet before a storm.

A sharp gust snapped through the air between us, dragging cloaks and feathers, but no one moved to retreat. They just hovered—uncertain, waiting.

That's when I heard her, a soft whisper from the back of the crowd, a voice that hovered closer to the front, smaller than the rest. An older woman with weaker wings and mismatched feet.

"She fears us… because she is one of us." She spoke openly like she'd held this secret for too long.

"She's Crohn," Another voice murmured, just loud enough to be heard. "That's what they call it now. Born of two magics."

"She's bigger than the other Harpies, she doesn't age like them either." The old woman added.

"She knew how to wield the Fae relics." Another elderly yelled.

They were old suspicions that had been forcefully buried. Feared. And now resurfacing.

For years, there were whispers that Morog wasn't fully Harpy. That somewhere, somehow, Fae blood seeped into the veins of the throne. That her body's unnatural grace, her command over the Windreapers was no accident. That her elegance and violence were not born of training, but inheritance.

And if it was true… then everything we thought we knew about power, about purity, about worth was a fortified lie.

"She made a kingdom by outlawing the very blood that built her crown," I said softly, voice carrying through the high salt air.

Eyes snapped to me as I began to speak. "She made us into monsters, banished us from the chasms," I went on, "Because she couldn't let them look at her and see one of us too, so she kept us out of sight, out of idea or comparison." There was no cheer. No roar of agreement, just stillness.

Then Thira gave a slow, deliberate nod. "Then let the Queen face her mirror." And now whispers spread.

I stepped back from the edge, and the circle of wings slowly began to descend, breaking apart like a flock dispersing after a long sky-hold. But they didn't scatter in fear.

They landed in twos and threes, and began to prepare, not just because I warned them of war, but because, for the first time in years, they saw themselves not as the outliers, but as a threat.

And maybe, just maybe, as something divine that came with an odd sense of pride.

They say Morog keeps only the fiercest at her side. But that's not true. She keeps only the purest. The true-blood Harpies, the narrow-minded, sharp-taloned traditionalists who preach legacy and obedience like it's holy scripture. The ones who still believe wings must never touch the ground, that mixing blood is a betrayal worse than death. Those are the ones she feeds power to. Those are the ones she places on her high towers and lets perch near her throne.

Because they're predictable, because they're loyal, because they're afraid of change. And fear, to a Queen like Morog, is the easiest chain to forge.

I know her games, I've lived in her court long enough to understand the patterns. She keeps them close not out of kinship, but because pureblood Harpies, despite their violence are easy to control. They follow rules, they kneel to a legacy of power, they won't rise up unless told to.

But the rest of us have learnt to adapt to a different lifestyle, to fend for ourselves in unpredictable conditions, on the cusp of a dangerous sea. We learnt how to dive, how to fish and feed our own people in dark perilous conditions. She couldn't chain that, so she cast us out. That's the truth of it. Morog built her empire on the illusion of purity, while hiding from her own reflection. It's not Harpy, not fully, that magic, that grace, it's Fae.

No full-blooded Harpy can carry herself the way she does. Not with that stillness, that terrifying poise. Not with magic that sings when she speaks instead of snarling. Her power is fluid, not serrated. Controlled, not chaotic. And it terrifies, she can rip you limb from limb and put you back together just to feel it all over again, she makes a spectacle of this often.

Because she knows what they'd do if the full bloods found out. They'd turn on her the moment they realized they'd been kneeling to the very thing they were taught to hate. That's why she's always watching the cliffs so closely, we can't be seen too often, or they might put it together. It's why she keeps the city so heavily guarded at its edges. Why her soldiers have been shifting west, toward us. Toward the old bones of rebellion.

She doesn't fear invasion.

She fears revelation.

The moment someone like Beau survives the impossible or someone like me speaks out loud and sheds light on the lie, she's doomed. That's when the truth fractures a generation. And when it does, the purebloods will fall like anyone else.

By the next haze, we had an army forging weapons and readying for war on borrowed time, the halfbloods would rise, and not alone. With the survivor of the arena. The symbol we didn't ask for, but the one we need.

Beau.

They'd seen him fight. Heard the reports. Felt the shift in the air since the day his blood hit the sand and refused to stop bleeding.

Some still feared him. Power like that doesn't walk in quietly. But the fear no longer outweighed the need. And more importantly, they trusted me. That was its own kind of weight. One I wasn't sure I wanted. But I bore it anyway.

Before we dispersed to prepare, I gathered the core—Thira, Cress, the older winged brothers from the southern ridge, a few others who carried sense and had served in the dungeons also, but all on different rotations.

They needed to know what we were walking into.

"There are others," I said, my voice low as I traced a rough line in the ash-covered rock. "Not just Beau. There's a woman,

Aliera. She's… something else. Strong. Wields wind like it obeys her soul."

Thira frowned. "She's Fae?"

I hesitated. "Titan, I think. Or something like it. I've never seen anything like her."

Cress snorted. "What, wings of light and riddles? A Crohn?"

"No wings, not a Crohn," I said. "But you'll feel it when you're near her. The power around her bends like grass in a storm."

A few exchanged wary looks.

"There's another, Starlette," I continued. "Sharp. Clever, but dangerous. Carries magic in her hands like fire and frost."

"She's with Beau?" Thira asked.

"No," I said. "Not exactly. She travels with a man named Draven. Fae. Wings like knives. He looks a little like Beau, but silver eyes."

"And the other two?" Thira asked, brow raised.

"Zac," I said. "Fire-wielder. Mortal, but barely. He's the Titan woman's brother."

"And the last?"

"Torin," I said simply. "Dreadwolf."

Silence.

One of the older Harpies clicked his tongue in disgust. "They let one of them walk beside them?"

"He's different," I said firmly. "No wings. Loyal to Beau, to all of them."

"Still," Thira muttered, "It's a strange flock." She sniffed through her more beak like nose.

"That's why I'm telling you now," I said, voice sharpening. "There will be unknowns. Things that unsettle you. But none of them are our enemy. Not anymore, we have the same enemy now."

I met each gaze in turn.

"We fight together. We trust the chaos. We move toward the same goal."

"And where is that?" Cress asked.

"Lake Aravena," I said. "Beau's people are headed there. It's a haven. Hidden on the outskirt of the Underfoot Forest."

Thira squinted toward the north. "That's one day's flight if the winds hold, and we'll never get over the city unnoticed."

"Longer on foot," I said. "But we're safer as a group."

"We'll fly ahead," Thira offered. "Scout the air so the grounds are clear."

I nodded. "Good. Leave nothing behind. Morog's gaze will shift here soon enough."

The group dispersed. One by one, they took to the sky. Some with hesitation, others with hope. And I stood there a moment longer, staring after them, wondering if I'd just lit the first match in a fire we couldn't control. but maybe that was the point. Maybe the time for control had passed.

Now came the storm. They took to the skies like ghosts.

Not in formation. Not in silence. But in a surge of wind and rustling feathers and battle cries buried for years, now trembling loose from their throats. The Screaming Cliffs hadn't seen a migration like this since the Battle of Skyfall.

Back then, we fled. Wings torn. Families scattered. We bled across the sky in the name of survival, but this was not a retreat.

Dozens rose first. Then hundreds. Great, wide-winged halfbloods, those with talons glinting in the early light. Harpies with battle scars, with broken feathers grown back crooked, with eyes too wild for court life and hearts too stubborn to die in exile. We all looked different, the blood never flowed the same in any of us, maybe that was the common ground.

Some screamed. Others were silent, mouths closed against the wind. We weren't built to fly together. We were forced to endure. But still, we flew side by side, wingtip to wingtip, like something long buried was waking in us all.

I moved last, pausing on the edge as the wind built upward in gusts from the sea and from the sky. This cliff that held our shame, our punishment, was empty now and would likely never be filled again. We were no longer waiting for acceptance; we were taking it.

I stepped forward and let my wings open fully. The air caught me with a sudden, sharp pull, and for a moment I didn't flap. I just glided over the water in a peaceful private moment.

Below, the ocean roared. Above, the sky cracked open to greet us. I beat once. Then again. Then launched and the cliffs fell away beneath me. And the sound sent a soothing shudder down my spine. All those wings. The push and pulse of air moving around bodies that had always been told to stay hidden. It was thunder without lightning, a living rhythm of exiles reclaiming the sky.

Cress flew just ahead of me, fast and agile, weaving through the current like he was born for it. Thira was slower, but solid, her wingbeats steady, her eyes scanning the horizon for danger.

We didn't speak; we didn't need to. Lake Aravena was ahead, just in time as exhaustion set in.

Unknown creatures waited for us, but the only one I hoped to see was Ivy. Hope was dangerous and reckless. It made us bold…hope got you killed.

But today… I didn't care.

Because we were finally doing more than surviving.

We were rising, and I was loving, and finally being loved.

CHAPTER ELEVEN

ALIERA

We heard the flock approaching before we saw them. Wings slicing the air, the sound became a low thunder rolling over the lake as they flew closer. It could've been Harpies or it could've been Roan. Or could've been something worse altogether—Windreapers.

Torin's ears twitched as he crouched low to the ground, his wild eyes flicking to the sky, as his muscles tightened.

Draven was already in the air, hovering in the black night against the clouds, waiting for the shapes to breach the treeline that protected us.

Ivy gripped Dani's hand near the water's edge, both of them tense as the lake shimmered with unnatural light. The reeds glowed a pale gold, bending in a gentle north breeze. But I didn't care about the lake or the treeline or the sky, I cared about him, my attention moved back to the ground where Beau lay…he was dying.

The breaks in his wings were blackening, sticky and split. His skin had taken on a grey hue, sweat lining his brow. His breaths were shallow. One hand twitched as his jaw clenched like he was fighting the pain of an uncontrollable fever. He always fought, he was strong, even before he was half Dragon.

"Starlette!" I shouted, falling to my knees beside him. My voice cracked. "You need to heal him!" My eyes didn't shift from his body.

She didn't rush. She just walked over, slow, composed, her violet robes whispering around her legs with ease.

I wanted to scream at her, I wanted to make her care as much as I did.

She knelt down and placed a hand on Beau's chest and furrowed her brows into concentration. "His blood is turning, I don't know this magic," She murmured.

"I know!" I snapped. "So, fix it!" I demanded.

Starlette exhaled sharply. "I'll try." She sighed heavily.

I grabbed her wrist. "What do you mean, you'll try? You're a Hearth. You have the power to heal. I know you do! Ele wouldn't even flinch, she'd be doing it!" I screamed.

"HUMANS, FAE, FARKLI, YES!" Her voice cracked like a whip. "But he's not human anymore! He's not even fully Fae. He's Dragonborn, Aliera. His magic burns hotter than mine, he is stronger than me. I'd struggle with fatal wounds on a pure Fae, let alone something as unstable as what's in him. What he is has never existed before," She softened now as she tried to explain the complexity of it all.

Beau groaned beneath us. His head lolled, and his golden eyes fluttered open just long enough to find me.

And in them, I saw it.

Fear...not for himself, for me.

"Please," I whispered as tears trailed my cheeks, my voice trembled now without permission. "He followed me into this hell; this isn't how he redeems himself. We haven't had any time..." My lips shuddered.

Starlette looked at me for a long moment, then nodded, her lips tightening. She pressed both palms to his chest and shut her eyes. Her hands glowed faintly. The glow stuttered, then flickered as she fought against something.

She gasped as she was thrown back. "There's something inside him. Residual magic—Morog's. It's rotting him from the inside out. I...I can't reach it."

Behind us, wings filled the sky.

Draven landed hard beside us. "It's Roan. He brought the flock. Hundreds of them."

I didn't look up. I didn't care. I gripped Beau's hand, watching his face as Starlette tried to stitch him back together with trembling fingers and pointless spells, she exhausted herself with the efforts. If we'd come all this way just to lose him now, I'd burn this whole realm to ash.

A swarm of wings blotted out the clouds, sending ripples across Lake Aravena's glowing surface. Ivy flinched, stepping back into Jake, who instinctively reached for his little sister. The air trembled as one after another, Harpies descended. But not Harpies, not like the ones from the arena.

These ones were bigger, they moved differently. Wings that smelt of the sea, sleek armor glinting in streaks of bronze. Not Morog's soldiers, not anymore...now they were Roan's.

He landed first, boots crushing reeds as he folded his wings behind him. His expression was firm as he searched for Ivy. His mask was off, permanently.

His eyes darted to me, to Starlette, then to Beau as he lay in the grass. Ivy moved to Roan's side and grasped his hand.

"Are we too late?" He asked as he moved closer to Beau.

I didn't answer, I didn't know.

"Back up," Starlette muttered with stress and sweat trailing down her temple. Her hands trembled violently now, light flaring and stuttering beneath them. "Unless you know how we can save him, back up." She hissed under the stress. Draven looked concerned as he went to reach for her, but she flicked him away.

Roan stepped forward again. His soldiers stayed where they were, hundreds of them forming a crescent at the edge along the banks. Watchful and still.

"Beau fought for us," Roan said. Not to me, to the air, to his people maybe. "He fought that thing so we could run. So, Ivy could run." His gaze flicked toward her, softening just a little. "We owe him."

Ivy stepped closer. Her voice came quieter than a whisper. "Can he hear us?" She asked.

"I don't know," I said. "I don't think even he knows."

"I can," Beau rasped.

We all froze.

His voice was barely more than air, like it had to claw its way out from his throat. His eyes opened. They were glazed and distant. Then they locked on mine.

"Aliera…" He coughed, and blood painted his teeth. "I'm still here." His hand reached for me.

I crushed his hand in mine, trying not to cry. "You're going to *stay* here, do you hear me?" I couldn't muffle the sobs.

Starlette looked like she was breaking. "I can't stop it. Her magic is like poison. It was designed to undo him. Piece by piece."

Jake stepped forward now. "Then what do we do?"

No one answered.

For a second, the silence was so deep I could hear the lake hum.

"She can heal him…" Ivy said aloud.

"What did you say?" Draven asked.

"I heard them in the dungeon. She healed him and broke him all over again. Enough so he could perform in the arena but not take flight alone." She explained.

"You don't know what you're saying…" Starlette dismissed her.

"No, it's true. She's done it before." A tiny Foogal waddled forward and rested on Beau's forearm. "She's a Crohn! A wicked Fae." The Foogal's name was Lemmy from what I had heard during our travels. His voice was silky but echoed.

"They are telling the truth." Roan added.

"She's a witch!" Pelk snarled.

"Beau?" I waved my hand over his eyes trying to get him to communicate with us, but he didn't respond.

"FUCK!" Torin growled and barred his fangs.

"What do we do now?" Dani asked.

"We capture her..." Zac stepped forward. Hands flared as he leant beside me and rubbed my shoulder.

I darted my eyes to him, he held my gaze. "Are you sure?" I asked.

"She's coming for us, anyway. Let's flip it on her." He smiled. "He'd do it for me..." He said knowingly.

"Can it even be done?" Dani asked.

"She'll want me, I'll play the bait." Roan stepped forward too eagerly.

"Nooo..." Ivy whispered.

"He saved you, I owe him." Roan cupped her cheek. She closed her eyes as she leant into his caress.

I turned away, not out of discomfort, but because I couldn't bear to see any more sacrifice. Not when Beau was still slipping through my fingers.

"If this is the plan," Draven said darkly, "We need to move fast. Before she sends her first wave." He straightened as he looked over Roan's people.

Roan stood taller, and for a moment, I saw him not as a rebel or a half breed, but as a soldier. A leader of the Harpies damned, maybe, but a leader all the same.

"She'll come for me," He said. "She always does."

We gathered around Beau's still form like soldiers around a fallen king, because that's what he was, whether he ever claimed the title or not. Roan stood in the center, eyes scanning each of us. "We don't have time for second thoughts. We move tonight."

"Too soon," Draven growled. "We haven't rested, everyone's exhausted."

Roan raised a brow. "And how long do you think he has?" He pointed to Beau, whose breath came in ragged bursts. "Every second we wait is a second she has to prepare."

Zac paced, fire flickering along his knuckles. "We can't storm the city. Not yet. But we can draw her out. Somewhere she's blind. Somewhere she has no eyes, and nowhere to hide."

"The Salted Sands," Roan muttered, arms crossed. "No cover, but no shadows either. Just earth and bone."

"No escape routes either, it's a graveyard." Jake added.

"That's why it's perfect," Draven said grimly. "If she wants Roan, she'll come herself. She won't risk sending pawns."

"She won't be alone," Starlette warned. "She'll bring at least a dozen of her strongest. You've seen her wretches. Twisted Windreapers leashed to her call. She won't hesitate, she'll bring them to do her dirty work."

"We're not going in blind," Zac said. "Starlette, Torin, and I will take high ground. If anything moves outside of her, we burn it."

"I can distract her," Roan said.

Ivy turned sharply. "No! Please..." A tear escaped down her cheek.

"I'm not asking permission, Ivy. I'm giving my life back the only way I know how." He didn't look at her as he said it, but the tremor in her breath was answer enough. Their fingers tangled together, and Ivy rested her head on his chest, her eyes on me and Beau.

I spoke before anyone else could. "And what happens after we get her? Do we kill her? Force her to heal him? Threaten and pray she listens?"

"No," Lemmy piped up. "You bind her."

We all turned toward the Foogal.

He blinked innocently. "You didn't think Crohn magic had no leash, did you? If she's a true Crohn, she can be bound by relics older than her own bloodline."

"Relics we don't have," Starlette snapped.

"Relics the Dunya might have," He said, wagging a little paw. "You want to trap a creature like her? You'll need the bell. A Titan's weapon." Lemmy smiled.

"How do you know about the bell?" I asked.

"I have cousins in the Sonsuz, we aren't far removed from the pixies." He smiled.

Zac's fire dimmed. "Then we need to open the realm door. Lure her up into the sky. We open the door and ring the bell." He smiled.

"Zac, we broke the bell…" I screamed.

"Nooo we…did we? ohhh shit!" His words came out in stammers.

"What do you mean you broke the bell, Aliera?" Draven glowered at me.

"It fell, it's still intact, the clapper is still whole as is the bell but there aren't enough Titan's now to fix it. If my brothers were still here, we might have a shot, but…" I sighed at the thought of them.

"We can go back and try?" Torin asked.

"No, that bell can't be lifted by anyone other than Titan's." Zac answered.

"There are no other Titan's in the Dunya." I dropped my face into my palms.

"Maybe not in the Dunya, but we're in Tierra Hundida. Some of the Titan's stayed after the battle of Skyfall." Toggo added.

"You know of Titan's? Here?" Draven knelt as low as possible to match Toggo's height.

"It's only a rumor…" Lemmy elbowed Toggo.

"What is the rumor, Toggo?" Dani asked gently.

"He's a fisherman…I think! Or maybe there's two? I can't quite remember the story…" Toggo became excited. "They live in Vacia Isla." Lemmy finished his sentence. "They fish the sea's for the humans who take refuge on the Three shadows.

"Fisherman…this feels like a trend." I scoffed at my own past.

"You're sure?" Dani asked.

"That's what the Foogals say." He shrugged.

"Marcus also, he's more Faun, but his ancestors had the blood of the Titan." Morel stepped forward.

"Roan, can you send some of your wings for this Marcus? Bring Morel with you." Draven was plotting.

"Take us to these isles." Torin smiled.

"We meet on the biggest isle, move quickly everyone." Starlette ordered.

"Will that be enough?" Ivy asked as she and Dani came to sit with me. Jake quickly joined us.

"I hope so. If they are who we think they are, we better hope they have the power of Titan's." I sighed.

"You do, and you're no way full?" Jake asked.

"I'd be lucky if I were even half, but my mother was Farkli like Starlette, much of mine and Zac's Titan powers anchor from that." I explained.

"What are the Farkli?" Dani asked curiously.

"Just another race, one of sorceresses and sorcerers. Extremely powerful. Starlette is powerful, much more than most others. Zac's wife was Farkli, she was a fire sorceress, with some hearth magic. Her sister Eleanor is a Hearth, a healer." I smiled.

"Was?" Dani asked.

"That's a long story, she's not with us anymore." I sighed.

"I'm sorry," Dani squeezed my hand.

"You would have liked her, she was unstoppable. The only one who could handle my brother." I snickered.

"What was her name?" Ivy asked.

"Astrid…" Zac spoke as he sat on a log nearby.

"If Astrid was here, Morog would be dead already." He laughed.

Jake clung to Dani's hand a little tighter as she inched closer to him.

"How do we open the realm door?" Dani asked.

"We hope like hell Thane or Sina are peering through at just the right time?" I furrowed my brows.

Zac shrugged without answering.

"What is he?" Ivy asked. She was looking over Beau, his scaled shoulders.

"He was half human, half Fae. Then he became something more. I still don't know if he's all of that plus Dragon or just a recreation of a Dragon." I pondered.

"How?" Jake asked.

"He went into the earth's crust to hatch five dragon eggs, one sacrificed itself to be born within him." Draven wandered closer with pride across his face.

"That sounds like it would hurt…" Dani noted.

"When he's better you can ask him." I said with a faltering smile.

"He will get better, Aliera. We are going to fix this." She pressed.

I nodded lightly as I wiped a cloth over the bloodied scales on Beau's shoulders.

I wondered to myself for a long moment if there was anyway Azra's bond with Beau could communicate what was happening down here. Did she know? Would she help him? Could she do anything at all?

"I'm really missing Azra right now." I looked to Zac.

"She knows, she can feel everything her children feel. Kieran won't be far away from Antoli, nor with Ele." He assured me.

"TIME TO MOVE!" Roan appeared.

Ten of his soldiers were flying Morel, Maxima and another Faun to Faunmoor in hopes they could convince Marcus to join us. I'd even settle for just knowing his true parentage.

"Toggo!" I shouted.

"Yes…" He winced at my volume.

"Sorry, I didn't mean to startle you." I apologized. "You're leading the way to the Three Shadows." I pulled myself up.

He nodded approvingly, proud even as he poked his tongue at Lemmy.

Roan and Draven were pulling Beau upright. "Together." Draven said.

"I think we need some more help, he's a big boy." Roan grunted under Beau's weight.

Two of Roan's harpies raced over and picked up Beau's bottom limbs. Toggo and Lemmy sat on Beau's stomach for the flight and Pelk flew ahead to lead the way.

"Ok, I can take one…I think?" I said between the girls.

"You think?" Dani squared her eyes. "So, you could drop us?" She hesitated.

"Well, no, but flying is kind of new to me, I haven't had a passenger before, and to be honest I haven't really mastered it yet." I confessed.

"I can take one…" Zac laughed.

"Have you ever?" Ivy asked Zac.

"Ever what? Dropped someone?" Zac teased.

"Are *they* our only options?" Ivy said to Jake and Dani.

"Harpies?" Jake turned to a few remaining soldiers.

"No offense Aliera, but the wings kind of sell it." Dani giggled as she walked off towards the half breeds.

"Have it your way." I smiled at Zac.

"Race ya!" He winked and then suddenly shot into the darkness with a burst of flaming energy.

CHAPTER TWELVE

DANI

It was a sight to behold, watching Aliera and Zac shoot high into the sky, wingless but still soaring through the darkness defying nature itself. Zac was the easiest to track, he was lit by dull flickers of flame. Then suddenly the beat of wings thundered behind us, and I spun to find two half-bred Harpies cutting through the dark. The female dipped closer, her light brown eyes catching the minimal light as she grinned.

"Need a lift?" She asked, her voice was velvet and kind.

"I'm Thira," She added quickly, crouching low and extending a clawed hand toward me. Her smile was soft and warm, enough that I didn't hesitate before reaching towards her.

Beside her a broader figure landed with a hard gust of air. A male with wings that stretched wider than the others. "Cress," He introduced himself, his voice was calm but firm. His gaze flicked between Jake and Ivy. "I can take the two of you."

Cress and Thira wrapped their arms firmly around our waists, and in the next heartbeat we were climbing the sky, higher and higher, until the wind stung my face. From up here, the Harpian city revealed itself as heat steaming from the mountain, its glow rising like an inferno. The cries of Windreapers echoed through the night, and with a dip of their wings, Cress and Thira angled us lower. Their flock followed, gliding as one movement together toward a cliffside that dropped into a strange land alive with glowing vegetation and shifting creatures that ooo'd and ahhh'd in the dark caverns in the mounds as they watched us fly overhead.

"That's Stinkhorn," Thira said over the rush of air, a grin tugging at her lips. "Where the Foogals and Sporlings come from." She went on to explain.

"Lemmy and Toggo's home?" I asked, craning my neck to see more.

"Yes," She replied, sweeping lower so I could glimpse the shimmer of a protective film that veiled the valley. "They're well protected. Those enormous, colorful plants release a venom only they can endure. Anything else gets too close…" She laughed. "It'll melt your face off."

I shuddered. "How did they end up in the city?" I asked.

"Foogals are notorious for their mischief," Thira explained. "Always wandering where they shouldn't. The Sporlings are quieter, more reserved. They live north of Stinkhorn, away from the little troublemakers." She laughed.

"So, the Harpies don't go there?" I asked.

"Not unless they're stupid," She scoffed, wings tilting in a playful dip.

We broke out east over the ocean, the waves below colliding in bursts of light—luminescent, alive, as though the sea itself was readying for something.

We followed the ocean outward a little longer, the air growing cooler until two lonely but lively isles came into view. Their cliffs shimmered faintly, dotted with strange lights that danced like fireflies.

"I thought there were three?" I asked, frowning at the horizon.

"Three shadows," Cress corrected as he angled lower. "One of them rests on the mainland."

"Which one are we going to?" Ivy asked, her voice small against the wind.

"That one." Thira lifted her free hand, pointing toward the largest isle.

"Our welcome may not be too warm," Cress warned, his tone heavy. "So be ready for that."

"Who lives here?" Jake asked, eyes narrowed.

"Humans, I'm sure you've heard the stories." Cress answered after a pause. "Those who have fallen through from Earthside come here, if they can survive the journey. Morog doesn't know of it. She doesn't fly beyond Stinkhorn or the Pyre, and luckily for us, the Three Shadows are hidden behind both. The Cloplands give her more than enough sport with the humans she catches." He gulped, the sound lost in the wind but the tension clear.

"How often are people falling through?" I asked.

"Sometimes hundreds in a day..." Thira sighed, her wings dipping slightly under the weight of her words.

"And here I thought I was special," I muttered with a wince.

Jake's eyes flicked to mine, and a smile softened his face. "Ditto."

We hovered a little above the settlement, watching as Zac and Aliera touched down in the clearing. Draven, Roan, and two other half-breeds lowered Beau carefully to the ground, his weight carried with caution. Curious eyes turned toward us; people stalled where they stood, their gazes caught on the unfamiliar wings. Mothers pushed their children behind them. A few men lifted weapons, shoulders tight with fear. Their stances staunch as they waited for something more.

"We aren't here to harm anyone," Aliera said, stepping forward, her voice steady but commanding. "We only need a place to rest—and to heal."

"And the Harpies?" A man snarled. He lunged, dagger flashing.

Aliera raised her arms and the air around her snapped and he crashed into the sand at her feet, pinned by the sheer weight of her power. Gasps rippled through the crowd.

She strode toward him. "Do they look like your typical Harpy?" She demanded, thrusting a hand toward Roan.

We landed then, sand kicking up around us as Jake and Cress took their places beside Draven, Roan, and a wounded Beau.

"Look at him," Aliera ordered, her voice breaking like thunder. She pointed to Beau, then swept her gaze across the gathered faces. "Do they look like the monsters you fear? They are more like me—more like you. They live in fear too." Her voice softened on the last words, a sigh of truth that hung heavy in the tense silence.

"What are you?" A small child asked, voice barely above a whisper.

"I'm Aliera," She said gently, smiling as the child reached for her hand. She knelt, lowering herself to his height, but her gaze held firm on the wary crowd. "I'm here to help you—all of you."

"Aliera…" The child's father pulled him back, suspicion was heavy in his eyes. He jabbed a finger toward Zac, fists flickering with fire. "And what is he?" He asked hesitantly.

"We're Titans," Zac smiled. "And if the rumors are true, there's another one of us here. We need his help." He added.

A hush swept through the settlement. Then the whispers began—chattering full of wariness, disbelief and fear. One by one, the people sunk back into their doorways, becoming shadows, now vanishing into their homes rather than stepping forward with information.

"Well, that shut everyone up," Draven muttered, slapping Zac hard across the back.

"You could have helped… *Lord of Orman*," Zac shot back.

Draven smirked. "You were doing so well. If I knew a Titan, I'd definitely hand him over—just because you said so." Draven said with sarcasm.

"Okay," Zac growled, heat curling off his shoulders, "Maybe my delivery needs work, but we don't have time for pleasantries right now."

"WE DON'T HAVE TIME FOR ANY OF THIS!" Torin's voice rumbled low, more growl than words, as he strode forward from the next flight of half-breeds touching down.

Starlette was close behind, her sharp eyes scanning the group to make sure everyone had arrived.

"How's he doing?" She asked Roan, her gaze fixed on Beau.

"He's hanging in there," Roan answered, his jaw tight. "He's strong."

"Or…" Starlette cut in, her tone edged with grim logic, "She doesn't mean for him to die just yet. What kind of spectacle would it be for her flock if she couldn't prove *she* killed him? That would weaken her position—especially after the escape."

The weight of her words settled over us. None of us needed to say it aloud. We all knew she was right. My stomach twisted as we traded glances, the truth cutting deeper than silence.

"She's right," Roan finally said, nodding slowly. "Morog doesn't do anything without a purpose."

The village lights dulled as if swallowed by a shadow, and the sea turned restless. Waves slammed against the shore, spilling over into the narrow streets. Lanterns hissed and sputtered out under the spray, plunging everything into true darkness. Screams carried from inside shuttered homes, panic rising with the tide.

"What's happening?" I gasped, racing to Aliera's side.

"Take shelter. Get everyone inside," She barked, not sparing me a glance—her eyes were locked on Zac instead. She was focused and Zac's chest dropped as I looked between them.

"A fucking water wielder…" Zac groaned, fire flickering uselessly in his palms against the surge of brine.

Aliera's lip curled. "Ugh, I am not in the mood for this shit." She sighed.

"In the mood for *WHAT*?" I shouted, voice breaking as the tide rippled higher and the sound of water churned loudly along the shoreline like it was alive.

I couldn't move. I couldn't do what she said. My feet rooted to the sand as the sea began to boil, froth rising and bursting like the ocean was coming alive. Storm clouds tore through the night, lightning carving jagged scars across the darkness, thunder reverberating so deep it rattled the foundations of the stone homes around us.

Then the glow began. The sea glowed from within, two piercing beams of white light slicing up through the black expanse of water. For a heartbeat I thought the sky had cracked open—but no, it was the sea itself, illuminated as something gargantuan pushed closer, something beyond anything I had ever imagined. A far-off land flickered into view in that glow, alive with strange light, before vanishing again beneath the swell.

"We have company." Draven's voice was taut as he drew his sword, steel flashing.

Zac laughed under his breath, a low, playful growl. "And what are you planning to do with *that*?" He snickered.

"Torin!" Aliera's voice cut sharp through the storm. He was beside her in an instant.

"I don't know how this is going to go, but if I don't make it—"

"ALIERA!" Torin barked, cutting her off with a groan of frustration.

"Let me finish..." Her voice cracked, but her gaze didn't waver. "You have to get Beau and the others out of here. Zac and I can handle ourselves." She almost begged.

Torin's jaw clenched, but he gave no reply. His silence was answer enough, he would do as she asked.

"I don't like this," I whispered, every word sticking in my throat.

We all turned toward the shore just as the sea tore open. Water roared back, and from its maw surged two beasts of the deep. Serpents scaled and vexed. They crashed against the sand, their scutes dripping with seawater, eyes tracking us with horror as they teased the depth of water, not quite revealing themselves in full, yet.

Then the sea split wide and from the foaming surge, the two colossal sea-dragons heaved upward, scales glistening now like shards of obsidian. Lightning caught the curve of their horns, their wings were fins, hard as steel. And then the riders leapt down.

Titans.

But not like Zac and Aliera.

They landed hard upon the shore, the ground shuddering beneath their weight. Their forms were striking, every motion rippling with something both beautiful and terrible, I couldn't tear my eyes away from them, they were unlike anything I'd seen before.

"Just like Caxia..." Aliera whispered, her words breaking the silence.

One of them—male, broad-shouldered with eyes that gleamed like pearls grinned as he straightened. "Someone call for a Titan?" His words weren't spoken so much as sung, the sound lilting, sweet and violent in the same breath.

"I guess so..." Zac answered, his tone flat, though fire still flickered faintly in his veins that ran along his forearms.

"Not what you were expecting?" The female asked, her voice a melody, sultry and divine. Her white hair streamed wet behind her, every note of her words were laced with allure and threat. "You yourselves aren't whole." She remarked.

"There are no *whole* Titans left," Aliera hissed, her jaw tight.

The female only smiled, slow and knowing, her teeth too sharp in the dim light. "Calm yourself, wind-whisperer. You called us... remember?" The female smiled flashing her fangs.

The male scoffed at Zac, heat rippling along his arms, he was the only source of light right now. Zac squared against him, fire coiling at his fists, the two Titans facing each other with tension rising between them. The town seemed to hold its breath as faces peeked through torn cloth curtains and cracked shutters bringing candlelight into view now. Their eyes wide as they waited and Titans threatened to ignite in their streets.

"Put your dicks away!" Starlette snapped, striding forward with a scowl. The words cut the tension like a blade, though neither Titan flinched.

"Do your people not like each other?" I whispered to Aliera, keeping my voice low.

"We've never met a Titan we weren't related to," She murmured back, her gaze locked firmly on the female, wary and unblinking.

Meanwhile, Roan and Cress slipped past with Beau, hauling him carefully toward the tavern. Aliera's sharp nod of approval followed them, though her body never shifted from its ready stance.

"What do you want?" The female asked, her voice edged with disdain.

"We need your help…" Aliera's shoulders sagged with the weight of the confession, the words dragged out of her unwillingly, but necessary. A shadow of defeat loomed over Aliera in that moment, she was ready to beg.

"Why would we help you?" The female laughed, the sound whimsy and cruel.

"Then why come at all?" Aliera arched a brow, her patience thinning.

The two half-siren Titans glanced at each other, then back toward their sea-dragons. At their silent command, the beasts slithered back into the waves, vanishing beneath the froth.

"How do we know we can trust you?" The female pressed.

"Do you like the Harpies that control the skies?" Aliera shot back.

"Oh, you mean them?" The female gestured lazily toward Thira and the other half-breeds lingering at the edge.

"No!" Aliera's voice dropped to a growl, her eyes hard. "The full-blooded Harpies. The ones who terrorize these people. The ones who command Windreapers and drive Clops like their hounds." She spat the words out.

"Nobody likes them." The female's lips curved into a smug smile. "But I don't live here." She shrugged.

Aliera's temper cracked. "So, you turn a blind eye to the violence they unleash on innocents?" It came out more like an accusation.

"It's not our problem, wind-wielder," The Titaness purred, turning her back with a careless flick of her hand.

Something inside Aliera broke. "Well, now I *am* your problem!"

She hurled the woman into the side of a building. The crash shook the street, and before the half-siren Titan could recover, a gale roared to life around her. The wind stripped at her skin in thin, vicious strikes, peeling layer by layer with terrifying precision.

Zac's body flared hot, flames sparking at his fists. His eyes were pure fire, ready to burn anyone who threatened his sister.

"STOP THIS!" Starlette's voice cracked like a whip as ribbons of her magic lashed out, curling tight around Aliera's arms and chest. The gale howled, but Starlette's spell held fast, forcing the wind to stumble and fray just enough to stall her.

"LET HER GO!" Starlette scolded Aliera, her eyes blazing as the command thundered from her. The glow of her magic pulsed, straining against the cyclone Aliera had unleashed.

Aliera snarled, her hair whipping across her face, every line of her body still taut with rage. The female Titan writhed against the wall, skin raw where the gale had begun to strip her.

For a heartbeat, no one moved. Only the hiss of Zac's fire and the crackle of Starlette's restraint filled the air.

With a snarl, Aliera shattered Starlette's magic, the wind exploding outward in a burst that rattled shutters and sent sand whipping through the street. The female Titan hit the ground hard, but instead of fury, laughter spilled from her lips.

Her torn skin shimmered, glowing faintly before knitting itself back together. In moments, the raw patches smoothed, flesh reforming as if the wind had never touched her.

"Not bad," She drawled, brushing sand from her arms, her smile cruel and taunting. "More useful than him." Her chin jerked toward Zac, eyes glinting with challenge.

The male Titan chuckled, the sound low and teasing.

"Okay, we'll help you. What do you need?" The male asked at last, a grin tugging at his mouth as he leveled his gaze on Zac.

"SERIOUSLY?" I barked, heat flashing in my chest. "After *all of that*, now you want to help?" I growled.

"Dani." Jake's hand found mine, firm and tugging me back a step. "Let them deal with this." He whispered.

The street was still humming with tension. Eyes were peering from the shadows, the scent of sea clung to my nostrils. The half-siren Titans smiled like nothing had happened at all, as though the violence had been nothing more than a test.

"No, this affects all of us!" I yanked free of Jake's grip, storming forward until I was nose-to-nose with the male Titan. "Why? Why now? Are you suddenly ready to die with us?" I jabbed him.

"DANI!" Starlette shoved me back toward Jake, but the words were already tearing out of me.

"No! This isn't just about one life anymore!" My chest heaved as the fear twisted in my throat. "I want to go home! I don't even know *how* to do that, but you…" I swept my arm at all of them, the Titans, the Fae, the half-breeds "You sit on all this power and play with it like it's a toy. Jake, me, Ivy… we'll never get home, will we? We're stuck here. In this hell. Never seeing the sunlight again." Tears stung hot down my cheeks, blurring the faces around me.

But I fought through the tears. "She's spent most of her life in a dungeon." I pointed a finger toward Ivy.

"And he—" I turned to Jake, my voice breaking "—he watched their older brother die in the bog." Ivy's face went ghost white, her breath shuddering like I'd gutted her with the words. I'd said too much, but I couldn't stop.

"You have the power to stop this," I snapped, spinning to Draven. "You could *seal* the realm doors. End it all." I wept.

Silence hit heaviest now. Dozens of eyes burned into me as my voice frayed.

"So, when you *finally* decide to do something..." My voice dropped to a rasp, bitter and final. "...Make sure this place is decimated. Burn me with it but *BURN* it!" I screamed.

I turned, shoving past the weight of their stares, and walked away. The tavern loomed like a refuge and nothing more. Lemmy, Pelk and Toggo scurried after me, their quick steps were a run as they tried to keep my pace pattering at my heels as I pushed through the door where Beau had been left behind, slung onto a table in a cold room.

CHAPTER THIRTEEN

IVY

Oli was dead…The reality slammed through me harder than any blow I'd ever taken. I'd known it somewhere deep inside myself, that it was probable. But I hadn't had the courage to ask Jake. Not when everything else had been chaos. Now, watching him, I didn't need to. His eyes told me everything. They brimmed and broke a dam that wouldn't stop. A continuous flow of sadness, too heavy for words.

"You're in?" Aliera's voice cut through, sharp and unrelenting.

The male Titan answered without hesitation. "We're in." He didn't glance at the female, didn't wait for her approval. His eyes were fixed instead on the tavern door where Dani had vanished.

"We are?" The female demanded, her brows knitting with confusion.

He only smiled, soft but resolute. "We have eternity to do something worthwhile. Let it be getting that girl home." He sighed with pity.

Jake's tears dried into something harder. His jaw set, his gaze lifting to meet the Titan's with a steadiness that sent a shiver through me.

I trailed after Dani, Jake close at my side. The tavern air was thick with smoke and ale, the scent of wet stone and seawater seeping through the walls. Beau's body sprawled across one of the larger tables, his chest rising and falling in ragged waves. His wings, tattered and wide, hung heavily over the wood. Dani tugged a blanket over him with trembling hands before turning away, tracking up the stairs. A door slammed shut behind her.

"You should go after her," I whispered.

Jake blinked at me. "What?"

"It's kind of obvious," I murmured, lips quirking into a grin despite the weight pressing down on my chest. "If you don't, he will." I jolted my eyes out the door to the male Titan.

Jake's brow furrowed. "What do I say?"

"Tell her she isn't alone." I squeezed his hand, the way Oli used to with me when he offered me a small comfort. "She feels really lost right now, Jake. She needs someone who can help her through that loneliness."

"What if I say the wrong thing?" His voice cracked, the boy behind the man showing through. That thoughtful hesitation when you didn't want to screw something up.

"There's not much you can say that's wrong," I told him gently. "Not when all of that is already tearing through her head. Just… listen." I shrugged.

Jake drew in a long breath, pushing up from his chair. Without a word, he made his way up the stairs and knocked gently on the nearest door. Dani opened it, her eyes red, and let him slip inside. The door shut softly behind them.

"Ugh, finally… some quiet," I muttered to myself, sagging back against my chair.

I'd never thought I'd miss the silence of the dungeons, but I did. Outside, the world was relentless—so many voices, so many opinions, all of it loud. At least in the cells, silence was its own kind of company.

I slipped behind the empty bar, found a half-keg and poured myself a pint. The beer was flat, but I skulled it back in one go. The door creaked open just as I slammed the mug down.

"Beer?" Roan grinned at me, casually as if the world wasn't collapsing outside.

"It's curbing the hunger," I sighed.

"Let's try to find something better than that." He jerked his chin toward a side door and pushed through into the kitchen. Curiosity tugged at me, so I followed.

"Woah," I breathed.

The smell hit first—herbs and meat, rich and warm. Roan was already at the counter, ladling thick stew from a pot still steaming over the coals. He plated it up with chunks of bread, sliding one toward me with a grin.

For the first time in what felt like forever, the world didn't feel quite so sharp.

I hadn't had a full hot meal since Earthside. Down here, it was always scraps—meat charred on sticks with no seasoning, whatever could be foraged if you were lucky. Then in the dungeons… stale bread, moldy cheese, jerky so tough you could pick your teeth with it.

This plate in front of me was luxury. Steam curled into my face as I scooped mouthful after mouthful, the ache of starvation hitting all at once. Every bite filled the hollow in my stomach that I'd been carrying for years.

Roan ate beside me, slower, his eyes flicking up often as if to check I was still there, still real. Once, he passed me a cloth when stew smeared my cheek.

"This is delicious," I murmured through a grin I hadn't felt in months.

He smiled back, then he reached across the rough wooden counter, his hand brushing mine before settling around it. No words, no grand promise. Just a look, warm and certain, that said everything was going to be okay.

"What are they all doing out there? Still sizing each other up?" I muttered between bites.

"I think they're past that now," Roan chuckled, shaking his head.

"Good," I sighed, leaning back on the stool.

"I guess they'll wait for the others to bring Marcus," he said after a pause.

"Well, I hope he's nicer than these ones," I muttered. "I've had enough of Titans and their egos for one day."

He laughed softly. "Should we find somewhere to wash, or sleep?" his eyes landed on mine.

"Both?" I smiled, the word tugged at my lips.

Roan gathered our plates and set them on the bench, then reached for my hand. His palm was rough, warm, and steady. Together we climbed the stairs, passing the quiet of Dani and Jake's room, then up another flight where the air grew still. We searched door after door until, at the far end, the fourth and final room revealed itself, with two pails full of water waiting in the corner, a stack of folded rags beside them.

"This must be their washroom," Roan said, pointing to the hole that drained out through the stone wall.

The tension in his shoulders eased as he unclasped his armor. Piece by piece he set it aside, until he stood in only his shirt, the fabric clinging to sweat. His skin was streaked with soot and ash, reminders of everything we'd just survived.

For the first time, it felt like maybe we could breathe.

Roan pulled his shirt over his head, baring the length of his torso. His chest was marked with scars, muscles rippling under the lantern light, his frame so solid it made me feel small in comparison. The heat shifted between us, until he stepped closer and tilted my chin up with one calloused hand.

"You're safe with me, Ivy," He said quietly. His eyes held mine. "But if this makes you uncomfortable, I'll stop. I won't look at you, only protect you." His fingers began to loosen, to let me go.

"No." My hand reached up and pressed his gently into the warmth of my neck. My voice was barely a whisper, but I meant it. "I'm comfortable." My hands dropped to the bodice of the dress I was still strapped into. "Cut me out of this thing." I whispered.

He didn't hesitate. Roan drew his knife, the blade catching the faint light as he slid it carefully down the back seam. The fabric gave way with a soft rip, falling uselessly to the floorboards. I stood before him, bare at last, the chill of the room skimming over my skin.

But in his gaze, there was no judgment, no danger. Only warmth.

Roan dipped his shirt into one of the pails, scooped water over it, then worked a bar of soap into the fabric. He scrubbed it clean with steady strokes before hanging it on the line that ran across the beams. I turned back to my own task, cupping water into my hair and scrubbing hard, nails clawing at my scalp as if I could strip away years of filth in a single wash.

Then his hands closed gently over mine, stopping the violence of my movements. His touch wasn't forceful, only steady—enough to still me.

"Gently," He murmured.

My arms dropped uselessly to my sides, surrendering. He took over, fingers strong yet careful as he massaged the soap through my hair, lathering it into a thick foam. His thumbs pressed against my scalp, easing places I hadn't realized were aching.

The suds trailed down my back as he rinsed, and then his hands followed slower now as he moved to my shoulders. He took up a sea sponge, working it over my skin in long, even circular strokes, peeling away grime and the harsh, dead layers of time.

It was an intimacy I had never known. To be tended to, piece by piece, as though I was something worth preserving. His hands worked with a care that made me feel like I'd never known how to care for myself at all.

Maybe I didn't know. Maybe time had made me forget what it felt like to be touched without cruelty.

I turned to face him. His hands rose, cupping my chin, guiding me gently until I was looking into his eyes. My bare skin brushed his chest, the faintest graze of my nipples against him making my breath hitch. He leaned down, slow, unhurried, until our lips barely touched—just a brush, not a kiss. Not yet.

His hands slipped lower, firm against the small of my back, and he tugged me forward with a tenderness that undid me. I melted into him, pressed fully against the heat of his body. I was stripped bare, but Roan still wore his pants. He held the line, even now. It wasn't restraint out of rejection, it was respect. And for the first time, I didn't feel exposed. I felt *safe*.

"I know the others want to go home," I whispered, my voice trembling. "But I want to stay… with you." The words cracked something open inside me that was raw and fragile.

His eyes locked on mine, steady and unflinching. For a heartbeat I thought he wouldn't answer, but then I saw it. A glimmer of hope between us as a tear broke loose and traced down his cheek.

"I want that too," He said, his voice rough with truth. He pressed his lips into my forehead, lingering there, his smile warm against my skin.

"It isn't safe here," He added softly, regret woven through every syllable. His hands held me tighter, as if the strength of his arms could defy the danger, even if his words could not.

I knew he was right. What we wanted didn't matter in a place like this.

If Beau died, the world would tip with him. Morog would reign unchecked, her shadow stretching across lifetimes, her cruelty would break through every realm. Roan and his people would perish—snuffed out like the delicate flame of a candle.

But even if we won... what then? Victory wouldn't bind us together. Everyone would scatter, drawn back to their own realms, their own destinies. I would be left with memory, with longing, with the echo of something I had only just begun to touch. I didn't know how old I was when I fell into this earth. I didn't know how old I was when they captured me. But I knew I was a woman now.

"Ivy..." Roan's voice was gravel, low and certain. "I will choose you every time. But I won't put you in danger." He saw the thoughts unraveling in me, the weight I carried even in silence.

"Could we go somewhere else?" I asked, my voice barely more than breath. "If we survive... could we live in their realm?" I asked.

His hand slipped into my hair, fingers stroking softly as though he could calm the chaos of thoughts inside me. "We can always ask," He nodded.

Fists pounded against the door, rattling the frame.

"IVY!" Jake's voice thundered from the other side.

"I'm washing!" I shouted back, heat rushing into my cheeks.

A pause—then sharper, edged with suspicion. "Who's in there with you?" His tone was accusing.

"I am," Roan answered without hesitation, he was unbothered. He wasn't afraid of Jake. They hadn't spoken much, but I knew Jake would never stop seeing me as his baby sister.

"Come out. Now!" Jake's growl shook through the wood.

"Leave me alone, Jake—I'm a grown woman!" I snapped back, fury prickling my skin.

"If you don't come out, I'm coming in," He threatened.

"Leave her alone!" Dani's voice cut through, muffled but sharp from the other side. "She's allowed to have a boyfriend!" Dani protested.

"I'm coming in! Cover up!" Jake ignored her, his temper boiling over.

The door shuddered under his kick. Roan grabbed his damp shirt and tugged it quickly over my head, the fabric clinging cold to my skin.

"Jake, STOP IT!" Dani shouted, but the wood splintered as he threw his weight into it.

Roan glanced at me, a wry grin curving his mouth. "Do you want me to kick his ass?" He snickered.

I couldn't help but giggle. "Yes—but no. Let me handle him." I tugged the sleeves down over my arms, bracing myself.

The door gave way with a crack and Jake stumbled through, landing hard on the floorboards. Dani stood behind him, arms folded, unimpressed.

"Sorry, I tried," She sighed, rolling her eyes. "He's had this tough guy attitude since the day I met him." She laughed.

"Yep. Nothing's changed." I smiled at her, warmth flooding through me despite the chaos.

I liked Dani. She was fierce yet calm, the kind of presence that steadied the others when they needed it most. She felt like the instant friend I hadn't realized I'd needed.

Jake's mouth fell open, his eyes darting to the shredded remains of my dress on the floor between us.

"You could have found your own clothes before you came up here," He muttered, dragging a hand over his face. Roan's white shirt clung damp to me, nearly see-through, and all three of us noticed at once.

"GET OUT!" I hissed, my cheeks burning.

"FINE… but no funny business!" Jake jabbed a finger at Roan.

Roan's glare was sharp, unflinching. "You're afraid I'll hurt her?" His voice cut like stone. "I'd *die* for her. I'm the last person you need to worry about with your sister." Roan snapped.

Jake faltered, but before he could snap back, Dani stepped in with a groan. "Jake knows that. He saw everything unfold in the arena. Stop being an ass. Can we please go and find some food?" Her stomach rumbled in protest.

"There's a kitchen downstairs," Roan said glancing at her. "There was a pot of stew that was still warm." He added.

"Jake…now, before the others eat everything." Dani muttered as she tugged him out into the hall, already angling for the stairs.

But Jake lingered a moment, his eyes cutting back to me. "You really like him?" His voice was quieter now, more serious than macho.

"I love him, Jake… and he loves me." Roan's arms came around me, firm, certain, sealing the words. His warmth was instant and soothing.

Jake's shoulders slumped as he exhaled. "Then I'll leave you alone… to be a woman. But I'm always here if you need me." He sighed.

"You don't need to worry about me anymore," I said gently, though my eyes flicked toward the stairwell. "But *she* could use your attention." I nodded toward Dani.

For the first time in a long while, Jake's gaze softened.

"Sorry, Ivy," Jake said, his voice rough. "I just didn't get to see you grow up… and now you're standing here, a woman, and I missed everything in between." His gaze flicked to Roan, softening just a fraction. "Oli would be proud of you. And he would've liked you too, Roan. Maybe… just *maybe* we can be friends one day. When all this shit is over."

He extended his hand, awkward but genuine.

Roan looked at it for a moment before clasping it firmly, his grip steady. "I'd like that," He said simply.

For the first time, Jake's jaw eased, the sharp edge of his protectiveness gave way to something gentler.

Jake left the room at last, his footsteps fading down the hall. Roan moved to the back wall, striking a flame until the fireplace crackled to life, chasing the damp chill from the air.

In the corner, a pile of old sheets lay heaped, yellowed with age. Beside them, an ancient sewing kit rested—its needle worn nearly blunt, the kind of tool that had been used and loved into retirement.

Roan knelt and tore one of the beige sheets into strips, working with slow determination. "Something simple," He muttered. "At least until we find you proper clothes."

"I can sew," I said, a small smile tugging at my lips as I reached for the fabric.

His gaze flicked to me, the corner of his mouth curved up too. He pressed the sheet into my hands. "Then I'll leave it to you." He kissed my forehead sweetly.

I smoothed the cloth across my lap, fingers already finding a rhythm with the old kit.

"Let's go check on Beau when you're done," Roan added.

I nodded, setting the needle and thread to work.

CHAPTER FOURTEEN

ELEANOR

I had been sleeping in Antoli for what felt like weeks. Every day began the same. I'd wake from the small bed I'd made in the same room. I'd press my cheek against the cold frame of the realm door and listen for voices, but there was nothing, not even a gust of wind dared thrashed against the door. I'd read through ancient texts, desperate to learn something that might help when the time finally came. I'd take multiple walks around the grounds when I heard the Dragons coming and going.

Azra and Irmak were restless without Aliera, Beau, and Zac. Azra's cries often echoed from the highest tower, her keening so sharp it rattled through the stone, begging for a reassurance that would not come. Irmak was quieter, though no less troubled. He often vanished into the icy mountains, wings carving through the frost and clouds, cooling his fire the only way he could now that Zac wasn't there to ground him.

The castle itself fought me. The walls whispered in the night, twisting into voices that were not mine, trying to drive me out with threats and nightmares. Sometimes, it was Astrid's ghost I saw—her shadow haunting the corridors, her name clawing against the inside of my skull. Antoli pulsed with magic, and too much grief. There were days I thought I'd break. Days I almost gave in and left for Farkli, but there was nothing left for me in Farkli, I'd be walking into empty homes, so I stayed.

I had to be here when they returned.

Sina and Thane allowed me to crack the door once a day, in the deepest hours of night when no light would bleed into Tierra Hundida. Each time I pressed my palms to it, I wondered if they could feel me on the other side.

Thane or Cleo would bring food when they remembered, though they rarely lingered. Cleo busied herself rallying what was left of her army, convinced that the darkness of Tierra Hundida would one day spill through into the Dunya. Thane scoffed at the idea—said it was impossible. But Cleo had once thought Dreadwolves impossible too.

And through it all, I missed Torin. Fiercely.

Each morning, I forced myself into motion, a brisk walk through Antoli's shattered doors into the cold that never lifted. Antoli was ever icy, a kingdom of perpetual winter. Frost hung like breath in the air, snow clung to the broken stones.

Some mornings, Azra shadowed me, her scaled body moving silently at my side as if she were waiting for news, for answers, for me to speak the words she longed to hear. I spoke anyway, because I knew she understood, even if her bond belonged to Aliera and Beau, not me.

"I wish I could tell you something good," I whispered, tossing a rock across the frozen lake at Antoli's edge. It skipped twice before vanishing with a hollow crack. "But I have no news...again." I sighed.

Overhead, Irmak cut through the clouds, but he didn't land as he often did. Instead, he swooped low, skimming the frozen lake until his wings flung up a shower of ice shavings that drenched me. I sputtered but couldn't help the ghost of a smile—he was Zac in Dragon's form, playful even here, but always steady when it mattered.

Then Azra froze, her head lifting sharply, golden eyes narrowing on something I couldn't yet see.

"What is it?" I asked, following her gaze.

But she didn't respond. With one massive beat of her wings, she leapt skyward, the air cracking with the force of her ascent. Irmak wheeled to meet her, and within a heartbeat, they were racing. Azra streaking ahead, Irmak falling into place behind her.

I stood breathless as their shapes shrank against the pale horizon, then vanished entirely, swallowed by the mountains that divided Antoli from Sonsuz.

Something had called them. And whatever it was, it was stronger than me. I climbed back up the hill toward the castle, boots crunching over the frosted stone. Thane sat perched on top of the broken bell, antlers haloed in the mornings light.

"Beautiful morning," He greeted, his tone lighter than the bags of sleepiness under his eyes.

"It is," I agreed, though the words felt hollow.

"No word?" He asked.

"Nothing." I shook my head.

His gaze drifted toward the horizon. "Where are the Dragons off to?" He asked.

"Something's caught their attention." I shrugged, pulling my cloak tighter around me. "Maybe a lone Dreadwolf. Or something else to keep them busy." I shrugged.

"Draven's men will be here soon," Thane said, shifting his weight. "They'll begin working on restoring the bell."

"They can't." My words came sharper than I intended, but I held his gaze.

"We have to try, Ele," His voice firm now. "It's the only weapon the Dunya has against those dark beasts."

I exhaled, bitter frost curling from my lips. "Can't hurt to try, I guess. But even with a thousand Fae, you won't get that thing off the ground." I added.

Thane shook his head, jaw tight. He knew I wasn't wrong. Titans were the only ones who could restore that bell. And we were fresh out of Titans.

Hours later, Cleo arrived with Draven's men—hundreds of them fanning out across the snow under Thane's command. I sat on the frozen wall and watched their efforts, every pull of rope and shouted order ending the same way, in failure. The bell refused to budge.

It wasn't long before the sky split with thunder. Azra and Irmak swept over the mountains, their roars shaking the stone beneath my feet. But they weren't alone. My breath caught—more shadows followed.

To my surprise, Keiran was astride the largest of them. The babies. Only… they weren't babies anymore. They had grown monstrous in size, wings cutting the sky like blades. They were big enough to ride.

"What the hell…" Cleo groaned, her voice carrying across the courtyard.

"They aren't supposed to be joyriding around the realm," Thane snapped, his antlers glinting as he glared skyward.

"They needed to stretch their wings!" Sina's voice called from above. She leaned against the neck of another Dragon, grinning wildly.

"You're missing all the fun, husband." She leapt, wings flaring as she descended in a glittering arc, landing lightly in the snow before us.

"They're huge!" I gasped, unable to hold back the awe as Keiran guided his mount down, the Dragon's talons carving furrows into the ice.

Keiran slid down, his face flushed from the cold air. "The Drake Hoca's got them on some herbal breakfast—once a day, every day. She says if they get enough exercise, they'll outgrow Azra in no time. The Dunya's safe now, so Sina thought we'd… take them for a flight." He grinned sheepishly.

"Safe," Thane repeated, narrowing his eyes at Sina, the word dripping with disbelief.

"Relax," She laughed, bumping his shoulder. "They could fight better than either of us if it came to it."

I shook my head, still marveling. That's why Azra and Irmak had vanished so suddenly. They'd sensed the others—drawn to the little ones they'd once guarded.

Only now, the little ones weren't little anymore.

The Dragons tumbled into the forest before the castle, their massive bodies shaking the ground with every step. Trees snapped like twigs beneath their feet, branches splintering as if the woods themselves bowed to their play. Their roars echoed like thunderclaps, but there was no malice in them—only joy.

Azra stood at the treeline, her great head lowered, eyes half-lidded in contentment. For the first time in weeks, she looked at peace. No restless pacing, no cries that rattled the castle walls. Just a mother watching her brood, her chest rising with something close to pride.

The sound of their laughter—if Dragons could laugh—rolled through the icy air, and for a heartbeat, Antoli felt alive again.

This was how Antoli must have felt hundreds of years ago, when Titans reigned and Dragons stood as their equals. For a fleeting moment, the castle almost breathed again.

Keiran stayed outside with the others, their efforts with the bell relentless. They even harnessed the Dragons, straining every scaled muscle against the ropes, but the bell refused to budge. Not even an inch.

By the time night fell, I was back at the realm door, cracking it open just enough to let the faintest sliver of air pass through. I lingered in the frame longer than I should have, peering down into the abyss. Searching. Hoping. But it was too far. Too dark. The only light came from the Pyre, pulsing red against the dark sky.

"BOO!"

I jolted, clutching the door harder as Keiran pretended to shove me forward.

"DICK!" I snapped and my heart hammered.

He only smirked. "What exactly are you waiting for? Someone to come knocking? They won't know where to knock, Ele. The door doesn't just float in the sky. It's only visible when you open it." He said.

I clenched my jaw, but he wasn't wrong. It made sense—too much sense. Nobody was going to come knocking for help. And even if they did, the timing would have to be perfect.

"So, what do we do then?" I asked, my voice thinner than I wanted.

"It's been weeks," Keiran shrugged, leaning against the frame. "We gotta go in after them."

"I promised Starlette I'd stay here," I admitted, guilt gnawing at me.

"I'm sure she'll forgive you—when you save her from being pecked to death by Harpies," Keiran snickered.

"What if… what if that's it? What if they're already dead?" I whispered, my face draining cold.

"NO!" Keiran shook my shoulders until I met his eyes. "Don't go there! They're fine—but they might need some backup." His voice softened. "We go together." He held me steadily. "You're my best friend, Ele. I won't let Draven or Starlette hurt you." He winked, as though that settled everything.

"We go," I breathed. "But we need the door open so we can get back." My eyes darted around, desperate for something, anything. My gaze snagged on a candle.

"A candle?" Keiran arched a brow.

"Anyone who sees it from down there will just think it's a star, right?" I pressed, trying to convince him and myself.

"…Sure," he nodded, lips twitching.

"Grab a weapon." I darted across the gargantuan hallway to the chamber where Antoli's ancient swords lay. Dust coated their hilts, but they were still sharp. I picked one up, the steel biting cold into my palms.

"Do you even know how to use that?" Keiran asked, following close.

"Poke… dead?" I shrugged.

"Good enough. We're wasting time." He seized my arm and tugged me back toward the realm door.

"You can levitate, right?" He asked, too casually.

"Most Farkli can… but I haven't done it in a while. Give me a— moment!" I shook my body out and then I screamed as he grabbed me.

"No time. Just do it!" And with that, he grasped my hand and hurled us both through the door.

"WHAT THE FUCKKK!" I screamed, air tearing from my lungs as the ground rushed up to meet us. I wasn't hovering. I wasn't anything. I was falling.

"Flap! Or—whatever you do!!" Keiran begged, his voice breaking into a cocktail of laughter and terror.

"Bright idea, idiot!" I snarled, squeezing my eyes shut and trying desperately to focus.

And then—salvation. A shadow rose beneath us, scales glinting a molten bronze. Keiran's Dragon swept in, catching our fall smoothly, as if it had always been planned. We landed hard on its back, both of us grabbing a horn to steady ourselves.

"OH SHIT!" I laughed, half hysterical, the sound ripped from my chest.

"We're going to be in sooo much trouble," Keiran yelled back, grinning like a maniac.

But before I could reply, three more Dragons swooped in, wings blotting out the light from the door. And then came Azra. Irmak. The sky above Tierra Hundida belonged to us now.

We skimmed low over the Pyre when I suddenly caught sight of movement above us. Thane was plummeting down toward us, his antlers cutting the sky, his wings spread wide as he angled into a hard dive.

"Well, that was short-lived," I muttered, jabbing my finger upward so Keiran would see. Thane's shadow grew larger, closing in faster.

And then Draven appeared from below, sweeping in with effortless control. "THIS WAY!" He ordered, turning sharp and banking toward a cluster of dark isles below.

We followed, and the Dragons thundered after us. Their landings were less than graceful, claws tearing up the soil and sand as wings folded tight against their flanks. Aliera burst from a tavern door, racing across the sand. She threw herself against Azra's neck, clinging tight. Azra lowered her head, eyes sliding shut as she leaned into Aliera, both of them trembling in the reunion.

"What the fuck was that?" Thane's roar broke the moment. He slammed Keiran to the ground, boot crushing into his chest. "The next Drake Hoca, and you put them *all* in danger?" Spit flew with his curse, rage making his antlers look like weapons in the dim light of the tiny village.

"STOP!" I stepped between them, standing over Keiran as he gasped for breath. "They weren't meant to follow us, I swear it. We were only coming to see if they needed us!" My voice shook, but I held Thane's glare. Out of the corner of my eye, I caught Torin—silent in the shadows, his eyes dark, following every twitch of Thane's hand as though weighing whether to strike in my defense.

"WHERE IS BEAU?" Thane snarled, finally dragging his boot back and scoffing at me as he turned on Aliera.

She didn't answer. Her eyes glossed with tears as she stared toward the tavern door.

Thane's expression hardened. He stormed inside, and I followed.

Beau lay sprawled across several tables, his massive frame sagging beneath the weight of his wounds. His wings—once divine, were shredded, their edges dulled to a shade of ashen grey. His skin was pale, his chest rising shallowly, each breath an effort.

"What happened?" Thane demanded, his voice barely more than a growl.

"Morog," Draven answered grimly. "She got her magic into him."

Thane's head snapped up, his antlers catching the low firelight, cruel in their silhouette. His voice seethed, venom in every word. "Where is the witch?" His voice was deep and gnarly.

My stomach dropped at the sight of Beau. Each ragged breath was a whisper against the tavern's silence. His wings were ruined, his veins blackened like rot were crawling under his skin.

"No…" The word broke from me as I stumbled forward. "No, no, no."

"Ele—" Thane's voice followed, but I was already on my knees at Beau's side, pressing my hands to his chest.

Light flickered under my palms, weak at first, then brighter, sinking into his skin. Beau arched, a groan tearing from him as the black in his veins recoiled. I pushed harder, forcing the magic into him, tears spilling hot down my face.

"You're going to be fine," I whispered through clenched teeth and my body pressed me upward to stand. "You have to be. Aliera needs you, we all need you."

Beau's body trembled, wings twitching as patches of color tried to bleed back into him. But every pulse of healing ripped something from me, the magic eating at my strength, at my breath. My hands shook.

"Eleanor, stop," Thane warned, voice rough.

"I *can't!*" I snapped, sobs breaking in my throat. "If I stop—he dies!"

Aliera dropped to her knees beside me, grabbing Beau's hand in both of hers, her face streaked with tears. "Please, Ele. Please save him."

The veins fought back, black magic snarling under my touch. My body screamed, but I held on, every shred of me pouring into him.

The air around Beau crackled, the veins in his chest shrinking back under my palms. I was sobbing, begging the magic to stay with me, when the tavern door slammed open.

"ENOUGH!" Starlette's power hit me like a wave. My body lifted from the ground, and she slammed me hard into the tavern wall, the breath crushed out of my lungs. Splinters rained over me as the wall cracked under the force.

"STOP THIS, ELE!" Starlette's voice rang in my ears, her eyes blazing with silver light. Her magic tightened around me, pinning me in place like a snared animal. "If you keep forcing it, you'll kill him. You'll kill *yourself.* You'll kill the *both of you.*" She approached me slowly.

"I can save him!" I croaked, straining against the invisible grip.

"You can't!" She snapped, the word rattling the air. "Not like this." Her gaze cut to Beau, then back to me. "Do you think I'd risk him for your desperation? Do you think I'd let you burn out everything we have left?" Her power crushed tighter until spots danced in my eyes.

"Starlette!" Aliera shouted, her voice breaking. "Don't hurt her..." Aliera leapt to my side.

"She's already hurting *him*!" Starlette snarled, silencing the room. "One more push and there won't be anything left to heal."

Her hand flicked, and I crashed to the floor, gasping, my hands trembling uselessly.

Beau groaned faintly, his body twitching, the darkness returning to his veins. I pressed my forehead to the floor, tears blurring the world. "I was only trying to help."

"And you almost killed him," Starlette hissed, her magic finally withdrawing. Her face softened a fraction, but her voice stayed sharp. "If you want to save him, Eleanor, you listen. You obey. Or you'll bury him with your stubbornness."

I lay gasping on the floor, my hands trembling, my whole body humming with what I'd tried to force through me. Beau's shallow breaths rasped in the silence.

Starlette's glow dimmed, the silver bleeding from her eyes until only the woman was left behind. She crouched beside me, her hand hovering uncertainly before settling on my shoulder.

"I know you want to save him," She whispered, her voice no longer harsh. "But you can't do it alone, Ele. None of us can. Don't make me lose you too." Tears burned down my cheeks. I nodded, unable to speak as she pulled me upright.

The ground shook before I could draw my next breath. Heavy steps thundered through the tavern, rattling mugs and knocking dust from the rafters. The doorframe filled with two massive silhouettes. Sea-born Titans, their presence smothering the air.

Thane jerked around, his antlers nearly clipping the ceiling as he flared his wings. His hand went instinctively to his blade. "What in the hells…" He gasped.

Before anyone could answer, a rush of wings came from outside. Three half-breed Harpies swept in. Behind them, taller, broader, strode a man I didn't recognize. His eyes gleamed, sharp and assessing.

"Marcus," One of the Harpies announced, their voice carrying as if they wanted the whole tavern to hear.

The room froze. Aliera's hand stilled on Beau's, Thane's blade half-drawn, Draven was tense as he looked between Thane and Marcus. Even Starlette's touch lingered on me, her eyes snapping to the newcomers.

Everything we'd been holding back grief, rage, and hope seemed to hang in the air, waiting for the right moment to break.

CHAPTER FIFTEEN

ALIERA

The air was thick with tension, but as if sensing the storm had passed, the inhabitants of the isle began to emerge again. They drifted back into the streets, dispersing into their routines, no longer cowering in doorways or hiding behind shutters.

Draven handed the innkeeper a heavy pouch of coin. "For the food we've all eaten," He said, his tone steady and kind.

The man nodded, but it was a woman who stepped forward, her face pale and lined with worry. "Will you save us from this dark hole?" She asked.

Draven held her gaze. "We're going to try."

Thane and Marcus were speaking, but their words flowed with a surprising ease, as if they had known each other a lifetime. I exchanged a glance with Draven, and then with Ele. None of us understood it, but neither man seemed willing to explain as they became caught up in talks of life not war.

Outside, Starlette lingered with Keiran and the Dragons, their laughter carried faintly into the tavern. Azra paced around her children. Her sharp eyes never left them. Her tail whipped protectively whenever one strayed too close to the edge of the square. Through the window, I saw Irmak resting at the shoreline, his great body stretched against the sand. Zac sat beside him, He was an ant in comparison to Irmak. Zac's hand trailed over Irmak's scales that glowed faintly in the firelight. It was the calmest I had seen him since Astrid's death, Irmak brought him a sense of peace and together they were finally able to rest.

Inside, the other two half-siren Titans had joined us. Titus and Vara. Their presence felt heavy in the room, their standoffishness apparent, but they lingered. They believed in the cause enough not to leave. That, at least, was something.

Thane called us to the shoreline. Rarely did anyone disobey Thane. Marcus was still with him, they were similar in height and build, though his face carried more human lines than Faun like Marcus. Marcus's hands were calloused, his feet were hooves, and he had a commanding presence—eyes restless, jittering, but full of intention.

As we gathered, Titus and Vara's serpents broke the surface of the water, their dark heads gleaming, their long bodies coiling far back into the sea like Caxia's once did. Irmak roared fire in warning until Zac laid a hand to his flank, steadying him.

"They're friendly," Zac muttered, though his jaw was tight. He saw what I did—their resemblance to Caxia was unmistakable, a pale sea serpent so similar to the Dragons—but not, these ones were blackened like the sky they lived beneath.

Irmak stepped back, nearly trampling Ele as she scrambled from his path.

Finally, everyone sat along the sand, the waves snapping at the shore as Thane stood to speak.

"Marcus is a distant cousin," Thane announced, his voice carrying across the group. "He carries threads of Titan blood in his line. He will go with you, Aliera—and with Zac—to restore the bell of Antoli. Titus and Vara will join you. The more hands, the better."

Vara crossed her arms. "How do you know it can be done?" She asked.

"Antoli was built by Titans," Thane said simply. "Only Titans can restore it."

Titus scowled. "How do you *know* that?"

"Because we tried," Thane snapped. "Hundreds of Fae spent the day breaking themselves against the bell. It didn't move, not an inch."

"He's not lying," Keiran cut in.

"Even the Dragons couldn't shift it," Ele added, stepping forward. "I saw it with my own eyes."

My eyes strayed to Beau, broken and pale in the tavern. "I can't leave him," I whispered to Draven.

"You have to," Draven said firmly, his gaze like steel. "That bell is our last line of defense if the realm door is found."

"Why don't we all just go back through the damn door and forget this place exists?" Zac snapped, his fire flickering in his fists.

"Beau is being poisoned as we speak," Torin roared back, his voice shaking with fury. "The only cure is in that Crohn—or did you forget him already?" Torin snarled.

"It's always bloody Beau," Zac muttered, low and bitter.

"Like it or not, he's become the figure of hope here," Roan said, his voice hard. "The Harpies saw him beat her beasts, saw him stand against her. Then they saw Starlette, Draven, and Zac fall from the sky. They're not sitting idle anymore. They'll be preparing to strike."

The silence that followed was heavy. My gaze drifted to Jake, Ivy, and Dani—their faces pale, full of uncertainty.

"Humans stay here," I ordered, my tone leaving no room for argument. "Jake, Ivy, Dani. Stay put." I ordered.

Then I rose, taking Zac's hand. He reached for Vara's, and together with Titus and Marcus we lifted into the air, our ancient power driving us skyward.

"Follow the orange star—if the Dragons haven't moved it," Ele called softly after us.

Her voice fluttered across the shore. "You should be able to find it. Cleo will be waiting with Sina."

We rose slowly into the sky, the Dragons shifting uneasily below as their eyes followed us. Their rumbling growls carried on the wind, unsettled by our departure.

Vara surged upward like a jetstream, her body carving through the air with liquid grace. She belonged to both sky and sea, magnificent in her ease. Titus followed her with raw force, every beat of his power a reminder that they were something much more unique. They weren't like Zac or me. Their magic stretched further back, into something not entirely human, not entirely Titan, something more.

The clouds thickened, black and churning. We thundered through them hard and fast until the flicker of orange came into view. The star Eleanor had left to guide us.

We were only feet away when the shrill cries split the night.

Harpies. Dozens of them. Their wings beat the air violently.

And then came the roar.

"IRMAK!" Zac's voice cracked like fire itself. He tore from our line, a bolt of fury streaking back toward the Three Shadows. His flames lit the darkness below us as flashes of war sparked with violence through the haze.

From where we hovered, the battle unfolded, a storm of terrifying Harpies tearing into the village.

"What do we do?" Vara's voice, sharp with panic.

"Go through the door!" I barked. "Take Marcus with you. Sina will know him—Cleo will know what to do. I have to help my brother." My throat tightened, but I didn't hesitate.

"I hope you know what you're doing, *Wind*," Titus growled at me.

"So do I. Stay with me..." I forced a breath, then let the storm inside me burst free.

The sky howled at my command as I dove for the isles, cyclonic winds rippling downward. Harpies screamed as the gale hurled them from the sky, Windreapers flailing in the chaos. The villages below were under attack, but I wouldn't let them fall without a fight.

The sky whirled around me. My terror ripping through the first wave of Harpies, flinging their twisted bodies into the black sea below. Their shrieks cut through the wind, drowned out by the thunder of more wings behind me.

Thane came streaking past, antlers ablaze with light, his sword humming as he carved through a Windreaper's throat. The beast spiraled, its rider screaming into the storm I commanded.

Behind him came Roan's people, their war cries fierce, wings flared. They weren't graceful like Vara, but they were relentless. Talons ripped through feathers and bone as they met their full-blooded kin in the air, claw for claw, tooth for tooth.

Draven's wings snapped wide as he vaulted higher, a flash of silver in the sky. Lightning cracked along his blade as he drove it down into a Harpy matron, splitting her chest with a roar that made even the Windreapers scatter.

The air was chaos, a whirl of claws, fire, blood and steel. I called the storm harder, spinning funnels of wind that shredded formations, scattering their ranks. Each Harpy I flung down only made room for two more to rise.

Below, the villages perished. I saw roofs split, trees collapsing under the weight of screaming wings. And through it all—Zac. My brother was a comet of fire, carving through the sky with Irmak at his side. His flames lit the battlefield, turning every shadow into ash, his roar and Irmak's blending until it was impossible to tell them apart.

"Hold the line!" Thane bellowed as three Windreapers dove for me. He intercepted, slamming one back with his blade while I whipped the air into a wall that crushed the other two together in a storm against each other.

The Harpies shrieked in fury, circling like vultures. But they weren't the only ones watching.

Far below, I glimpsed Starlette and Ele. Their magic shimmered in shields that cocooned the tavern where Beau lay broken. Dani and Ivy braced at the doorway, blades flashing. Jake stood like a wall before them, his blade sparking with each strike that came too close. They couldn't join us up here, but they were holding the only thing that mattered.

And still, more shadows rose. The Harpies poured from the mainland, Windreapers flocking in tighter swarms. The air rained with blood. It was a war we couldn't afford to lose.

I drew in the wind until it burned in my lungs, until it felt like the whole sky belonged to me. "Push them back!" I roared, hurling everything I had into the gale.

And for one blinding moment, we did.

The shrieks grew deafening, and my lungs burned with the sting of smoke, every strike from Thane and Draven carving only brief reprieves.

And then the sky changed.

A roar split the heavens, young, raw, and unbroken. Four shadows rose from the isles now, the young Dragons, their wings clumsy but wide, their cries sharp with the thrill of first blood.

Irmak and Azra flanked them, their bodies vast and shielding, guiding them like generals on a field. Irmak's fire streaked across the night, catching a Windreaper mid-dive and snapping its rider into cinders. Azra's voice thundered in a draconic scream that rattled my bones, her tail lashing a Windreaper into pieces.

The young ones followed, eager, reckless. One dove too steep, nearly clipped by a spear of black magic launched by a Harpy, until Irmak slammed his shoulder into it, rolling the creature away till it lost balance to fly. Another young Dragon snapped too soon at a Harpy, missing by feet, but Azra corrected it, her body curling around the youngling to shield it before sending her own blast of flame into the swarm.

And then the sea answered too.

From below, Titus commanded the serpents to rise, obsidian-scaled bodies slicing the waves. They lashed upward, wrapping around Windreapers and Harpies, dragging them screaming into the depths. The water churned red as wings thrashed and vanished beneath the surface. One serpent breached like a nightmare, jaws snapping with thin razor sharp teeth.

Harpies shrieked in panic as the tide turned. Their perfect formations shattered, their momentum breaking under the chaos. For the first time since the battle began, I felt the weight lift…I felt the chance of victory.

"Push them back!" Thane's roar mingled with my own as I summoned another gale. The Dragons answered in flame and fury, their cries vibrating through the skies.

For the first time, Tierra Hundida burned with hope.

The sky lit with fire, Dragons screaming as they tore through the Harpies. For a heartbeat, it felt like we had them. For a heartbeat, I let myself believe, and then the scream came.

One of the younglings, the boldest of the four dived too fast, he was too eager. A Windreaper rider caught him mid-turn, a spear sliced across his wing. The Dragon's cry spread through the sky, high and piercing, a sound that curdled my blood.

Irmak's growl thundered like the earth itself were breaking. He dove, flame trailing like a comet, scattering the Windreapers that pressed in for the kill. Azra swept in from the other side, her massive wings shielding the wounded Dragon as he faltered, tumbling sideways through the storm as he plummeted downward.

The Dragon's blood glittered against the night, spraying like sparks as he fought to steady himself. His wing bent awkwardly, but he stayed aloft, clinging to Azra now as she carried him away from the heart of the fight.

"Hold the line!" Thane bellowed, rage turning his voice to steel as he cleaved another Harpy from the air.

I clenched my fists, pulling the storm tighter. My winds wrapped around the struggling Dragon, steadying him long enough for Azra to guide him toward the sea's edge. Titus's serpents rose like sentinels, coiling protectively as they dragged Harpies down into the depths, buying Azra time.

The dragon was hurt—but he wasn't broken. Not mortally. His cries were painful, but still fierce, he was still alive.

Zac's flames streaked past me, his voice raw with fury. "No one touches them again!"

The tide surged in our favor once more. The Harpies weakened their stance, Windreapers began scattering. But the taste of victory was bitter on my tongue, laced with the sound of that Dragon's scream. They were still inexperienced, we had been lucky.

The Harpies broke first. Their shrill cries wavered into panic, wings pulling back as they spiraled toward the west. The Windreapers followed, their monstrous shapes shrinking into the haze as they fled back toward the Harpian city.

The sky was left reeking of smoke, wings littered the sand, feathers scorched, the sea still thrashing where Titus's serpents had dragged bodies below. The air stank of fire, blood, and salt.

Thane descended beside me, his antlers covered with ash. He was breathing hard, but there was a steadiness in his gaze, his voice carrying the weight of command.

"You did well," He said, eyes flicking between Zac and me. "Both of you. Without your fire and your storm, this would have ended differently."

Zac let out a grunt, fire still curling at his fists, but he gave a sharp nod.

Thane's expression hardened. "But this isn't over. Not even close. We can't afford to linger." He pointed toward to the sky, where the faint orange star still pulsed against the clouds. "The bell is waiting. Restore it. That is the only way we stand a chance when the Harpies strike again. They were just testing us…" He groaned.

His gaze met mine, steady and unflinching. "Aliera. Zac. Back to the door. Now." He ordered.

My heart twisted—I wanted to argue, to beg for a moment to check on Beau, to see the Dragon's wound for myself. But Thane's tone left no room.

I glanced at Zac, and he gave me the barest shrug. For once, he wasn't fighting the order.

"Fine," I murmured. "Let's move."

Chapter Sixteen

ALIERA

We carved through the sky, breaking through clouds of residual smoke that clung to our skin like oil. The others shrank below us, their shapes fading like shadows in the haze, and I couldn't stop my eyes from lingering. We didn't have long. We couldn't be gone longer than needed. Our position was exposed now.

"Faster!" Zac grasped my arm, and together we blazed forward, the orange flicker of the flame pulling us towards it like a beacon.

Vara, Marcus, and Titus had already slipped through the crack in the realm door. It was small and subtle, the only orange star in the sky.

Night had draped itself over the Dunya when we emerged through the realm door. The halls of Antoli were the same as always, cold, haunting, full of whispers, but no bodies. Outside was different, torches blazed, hundreds if not thousands of Fae filled the square, watching in silence as Marcus, Titus, and Vara strained, dragging the bell meter by meter across the stones—in awe that it was moving at all.

"They need help," I said, arms folded.

"I got this." Zac cracked a grin and bounded down the stairs. He took his place beside Marcus and Titus, fire lighting in his veins as he pushed shoulder to shoulder with them.

I stayed where I was, walking instead to the edge of the stairs, watching patiently. Cleo and Sina stood there, tired and weathered, their faces drawn but unbroken.

"Not your scene?" I murmured, resting my head briefly against Sina's shoulder.

"Are you really going to watch them struggle?" Cleo smirked playfully.

"Just catching my breath, we were delayed by an attack." I said.

Cleo's humor faded. "We heard there was an attack?" Her expression became curious.

"Yes. But we came out of it better than I thought. One of the young Dragons was seared through the wing, though." My voice dipped.

"I fear there will be more casualties before this is over," Sina sighed.

Below, the bell lurched again, rolling grudgingly across the stone, the four Titans straining against its weight. I gritted my teeth.

"They aren't doing it right," I muttered.

"You know what to do?" Cleo asked, arching a brow.

"Isn't it obvious? If it isn't fire, water or earth who can move it enough…" I straightened and winked at Sina. A grin tugging at my lips teasingly.

Sina smiled back and flicked her hands at me to move.

I leaned over the railing, cupping my hands to my mouth. "NOT MUSCLE...POWER!" I shouted, my voice cutting through the night.

Marcus was red-faced, his eyes bulging, exhausted from digging his hooves into the dirt, he was an earth Titan like Mason had been. He had strength in spades, but when he released the bell, it slammed back, nearly bowling Titus into the stones. The crowd of Fae gasped.

The clapper of the bell shuddered, its deep toll still vibrating through my bones. The others pushed harder, straining until their veins bulged, but it wasn't enough. It would never be enough with muscle alone.

I closed my eyes and felt the air, the way it curled and bent through the corridors of Antoli. The way it remembered us. Titans. This place had been built from our hands, for our people, by our people.

"Stand back," I called out, stepping down into the square. Zac frowned at me but obeyed, dragging Marcus back by the arm, his hooves covered in mud and soil.

The bell was enormous, it loomed above me from sheer size alone, a mountain of iron and memories, a weapon in disguise. My chest tightened. I spread my arms wide, summoning the wind until it howled, until the stones themselves began to rattle beneath my feet. The bell lifted slowly, groaning against the weight of centuries—its chains snapping taut as I forced it skyward.

My knees buckled. The storm burned through me, but it was too heavy. My hair stood on end, my fingers sprawled as I fought against the weight of not the metal, but the magic. I wasn't sure now if I'd be enough.

Then Titus stepped forward, his arms outstretched, his power like a tide pushing beneath mine. Vara joined him, her strength a current that steadied the air, made it less jagged, less wild. Together we lifted, the bell rising higher, inch by inch, its shadow spilling across the crowd.

"Almost there!" Zac shouted, fire curling around his hands as he poured his heat into the wind, lightening the pull.

Marcus's eyes gleamed, his body trembling as he reached for his own power. Chains of silver light flared into existence, wrapping around the bell. They clinked and groaned as Marcus heaved them, fixing the bell into place in the tower's frame.

The moment the last chain locked, the storm inside me broke. I dropped to my knees, gasping, my hands pressed to the cold stones.

Above us, the bell settled into its cradle. It rang once, a deep, resonant sound that rolled through Antoli, echoing into the night sky. The crowd erupted, voices rising like a flood. The Fae cheered at the spectacle.

I lifted my head as my chest heaved and sweat plastered my hair to my face. My arms still shook, but finally the bell was hanging where it should be, it was ours once again.

The chime still rolled through Antoli, shaking the stones, rattling the glass in the windows. It carried far beyond the walls, over the mountains, across the icy lake, down into valleys where the air had not heard such a sound in centuries. It wasn't just a bell, it was a declaration.

The crowd celebrated and the Fae fell to their knees. For the first time since this war had begun, hope rang louder than fear.

I leaned against Zac, my body still trembling, sweat cold against my skin. He was grinning, as if he'd just set the sky alight. Marcus's smile still glimmered faintly, Titus and Vara both panting, their eyes wide with something close to awe.

We had done it.

The bell of Antoli had been restored.

The echo of the bell faded into the night, but the tremor it left behind hummed in my bones. For a heartbeat, it was only a small victory—the people cheering, Zac laughing breathless at my side, Vara and Titus staring up in awe, Marcus sagging against the stairs with pride. We knew more was to come.

But Cleo's voice cut through the celebration.

"Enough…" She said aloud.

The crowd fell to murmurs, turning as she stepped forward, her silver braid caught the firelight of the sconces Zac had lit around the castle. Her gaze was hard, her tone sharp, every word commanding and respected.

"The bell will not save us on its own. It is not the only weapon in this war, and it will not kill them all." Her eyes swept the gathered armies of Fae, then the five of us Titans. "But it *will* help. And now every Harpy, every Windreaper, and every beast in Tierra Hundida knows we are preparing to strike back." She announced.

The cheer withered into a heavy silence. Torches crackled. The bell hung above us, gleaming like a frosted white star that sat in Antoli's heart.

Cleo turned to her generals. "Rally the legions. Every blade, every bow, every shard of magic, emberleaf, glass arrows, eclipse thorns! I want all of it, and I want them armed and ready before dawn. This won't be the same as Rael and his Dreadwolves…" She sighed as she whispered the words to him.

She turned to Sina now, "Send riders to the villages. Warn them—the Harpies will strike hardest here."

Her eyes found me last. "And you, Aliera…do not think this is done. You Titan's may have restored the bell, but this is only the first stone in the wall. If we falter now, all we've done is tell the enemy where to aim." I nodded.

"But we stand a chance…don't we?" I asked blindly.

"Our armies are still battered from the war at Varsili," She sighed. "Unless you have something else up your sleeve— a hundred more Titans perhaps?" she fumbled over the words.

"What can we do?" I looked from Cleo and Sina to the other Titans.

"Call on everyone." She looked to Marcus.

"The Sporlings won't fight, the Foogals and Enfields are tricksters. My people are fewer and fewer." Marcus shook his head. "I can't ask them to fight." He sighed.

"Then they die. Everyone dies…" Cleo said sharply.

Her words bit, but I couldn't deny the truth in them. The bell was no victory on its own. It was a beginning. And wars always demanded blood, and that blood would come from every side.

The bell's victorious hum still echoed in my chest when I pressed my hand to the realm door again. The frame rippled with vibrations beneath my touch, resisting as though it wanted me to stay, but I pushed harder. Zac relit the candle and left it in the tiny crevice of the dark room.

The air of Tierra Hundida hit me like a fist. Heavy. Damp. Stained with smoke and death. I emerged over the Three Shadows, the sea still boiling where Azra and Irmak circled protectively above the sea serpents. But the moment I looked to the shore, my stomach sank as I sensed something was off as I landed.

Roan was gone.

Draven too.

"What…" My words faltered as I spun, searching for their wings among the darkness. Nothing.

Ivy's cry split the silence. She was crumpled against the tavern doorframe, Jake holding her shoulders as she shook. "They left us!" She sobbed, her voice breaking into jagged pieces. "They left us, they've gone after her!" She wept.

Torin's face was stone, his jaw clenched so tight his teeth could have cracked. "Roan knows the castle," He said reluctantly. "Every hall, every guard's watch. He thinks he can slip in and take her." Torin growled.

"Abduct Morog?" The words felt like poison in my mouth.

Torin nodded once, rage simmering in his eyes. "With Draven at his side, he might even try to kill her outright."

"That's suicide," I hissed, my chest tightening. My gaze flicked back to Ivy. She buried her face in her hands, her whole body trembling, the sound of her grief ripping me rawer than any battlefield scream.

"Why?" She choked, looking up at me through tears that streaked her face. "Why would he do this without us? Without *me*?" Her sadness cut me down the middle and I dropped to cradle her in my arms. Ivy felt like everyone's little sister, she was sweetness itself, innocence and kindness when there wasn't much of it around.

I didn't have an answer for her question. Only the truth. That if Roan and Draven failed, we'd all pay the price for their actions.

CHAPTER

SEVENTEEN

ROAN

The sky was quiet after the battle, too quiet. Smoke still clung to my wings, the stench of blood and sea spray was still thick in my nostrils. For a long while I didn't say anything. I didn't have to. Draven was there, his silver eyes watching the sky like he could see what came next.

Finally, I broke the silence. "This doesn't have to end in fire and corpses. If we take Morog alive, we can end it before it begins." I said hesitantly.

Draven tilted his head, feathers shifting as he sheathed his blade. "You really think the Harpy Queen will surrender?" He asked.

I shook my head. "I know her," I said. My voice was low, steady. "She thrives on power and fear. Strip that from her, chain her down where her flock can see it, and the rest will scatter. No war. No rivers of blood. Just an end." I said.

He studied me for a long moment, then gave the faintest smile. "You almost sound like me." He chuckled.

I held out my hand. "We do this together." I tilted a brow.

His palm clasped mine, firmly. "Together." He agreed.

We gathered Cress and Thira in the shadows, both half-breeds eager but wary. "Fly low," I warned them. "Keep to the cliffs. Don't draw eyes unless we need to." I ordered.

The four of us slipped into the night, wings beating against the stillness. The land was black and red beneath us, chasms alive with fire.

The Harpian city burned bright, every spire and ledge bristling with movement. Harpies lined the ridges, their wings sprawled as they readied for war. The arena lay cracked and broken, but still the Clops moved there, hulking silhouettes sharpening weapons, training for slaughter.

Along the Bog's edge, Windreapers gathered and perched on the mountainside, their eyes gleaming in the dark. Columns of them began to shift, moving on foot through the valleys and up the dark hills.

The whole realm was preparing for war.

Draven drew closer, his voice pitched low against the rush of wind. "So, tell me again, Roan… how do we walk into the fire and pull the Queen out without losing our heads?" He asked.

I scanned the chasms ahead, the firelight turning the city into a living wound across the mountainside. My wings twitched, restless, but I forced them still. Flying would paint us as targets and would get us killed before we even saw her face.

"We go in quiet," I said, folding my wings tight against my back. I dipped lower, toward the dark gullies and broken ridges at the city's edge. "On foot. The Harpies are watching the skies, not the ground." I answered.

Cress landed first, his talons scraping stone, Thira just behind him. Draven and I followed, boots crunching against the shale. The air down here stank of rot and rust.

The four of us melted into the shadows, moving along the narrow cliffs. Above, Harpies screeched and rallied. Ahead, the city seethed, torches blazing as though the mountain itself were burning from within.

I tightened my grip on the blade at my hip. "Keep close. Keep silent." Draven sighed.

And for the first time, the idea of ending this war without rivers of blood didn't feel like a dream. It felt like a knife I could reach out and take.

We scaled the mountain in silence. The higher we climbed, the thicker the smoke and steam, the harsher the cries that echoed from the city. By the time we reached the second-tallest peak, my lungs burned from the smell of the forges and decay.

From there we could see two paths.

One path narrow and dark, the entrance Harpies rarely bothered to guard. The other opened wide, carved straight into the mountain's eye, the road to the throne room.

Even from here, her voice carried. Morog's screeches echoed as she dished out commands.

Her voice carried fury. The shrillness of a queen denied what she believed to be hers. And then came the reports—shouted by commanders as she snarled.

"The Dragons."

Their return had shaken her to the core. She called it blasphemy and destiny all in the same breath, and I heard her promise to awaken the Pyre. To call life back into the bones of her fallen beasts, to *'heal'* them, twist them back to life, and march them into war.

"That's not all," Draven murmured, silver eyes narrowed as he tilted his head, listening closer.

And then we heard them.

The Clops scattered across the plains, gathering. Rallying. Preparing to march on Faunmoor.

Two fronts…

I clenched my jaw, staring at the two entrances opened before us. The quiet path would get us in. But we were walking into an open jaw.

And all the while, her laughter echoed through the stone, the sound of war blooming in every shadow. Her voice was so loud it was like a chorus with the doors flung open for all to hear. She knew she had the upper hand.

"How do we get her out of there quietly?" Cress asked, his voice low, feathers trembling in the updraft.

I didn't answer right away. My eyes stayed fixed on the throne room entrance, where the glow of firelight flickered against the black stone. Morog's shadow loomed across the wall inside, her voice rising sharp and cruel. Quiet wasn't in her nature, and neither was surrender.

"We don't," Draven said flatly, his silver eyes catching the light. "Not if we walk straight into her nest."

Thira's wings twitched. "Then we take the side path. Wait for her to leave the chamber, strike when she's alone."

I shook my head. "She'll never leave her throne, not willingly." My hand curled tighter around the hilt at my hip. "If we want her alive, we need to cut her out of it. Pull her from her flock before she can summon half the city to her aid." I said.

Cress swallowed hard. "You mean drag her out. Through *that*." He gestured outward to the outstretched city, flumes of steam rising from the veinous chasms, alive with thousands of Harpies and the glow of fire preparing for war.

"Better dragged than dead," I muttered. "If we kill her, we might risk killing Beau. But if we take her… if we show the flock their queen on her knees—" I met Draven's gaze.

Draven's lips curved, humorless. "This is feeling like a suicide mission. I don't know whether you're brave or insane."

"Both," I said. My voice was steady.

"So, what now?" Cress asked.

"We wait until she's alone," I said. "I go in first, draw her eye. The moment she turns her back, you two hit her with those chains. Hard. No hesitation." I pointed to a stack on chains I knew where kept in a side keep.

Cress swallowed. "And then?"

"Then," I breathed, "We drag her out of her own throne room and give every Harpy in this cursed city something to fear."

Draven snorted. "So, we're definitely going to die."

"Not if we're fast," I said. "And not if Beau is still fighting."

Silence fell thick between us, until finally Draven nodded. "Alright. We take the Queen."

The throne room was a furnace even from where we spied. Its walls dripped with heat and shadows of Harpies lurking in the shadows. Flames coiled in iron braziers, casting Morog's silhouette high against the stone. She was waiting for us—perched on her throne of bone, her crown of Dragon bones glinting with a hunger that hadn't been fed in a long time.

Her wings unfurled lazily in a welcome as I walked in first after watching the Harpies leave.

"I wondered when you'd come," She purred, her voice carrying to every corner of the chamber. "Little traitor. Little prince of the half-blooded…" Her eyes looked around for me, even in the stairwell, her pupils bright and venomous.

Cress hissed under his breath, shifting closer to Thira, but I raised a hand to silence him.

"You don't look surprised," Draven said coldly, his hand already resting on his blade as he stepped into the open.

"Why should I be?" Morog leaned forward, resting her chin on her hand as though we were children who had come to beg. "You want me alive. But I want something too. And I don't mind telling you what that is." Her smile sharpened, hatred gleaming in her teeth.

"I want the Dragon-born...Beau!" Her gaze glittered as she spoke Beau's name like a caress. "Healed. And then..." She rose, her talons clicking against the stone, her shadow swelling behind her. "...I will slaughter him. I will slaughter *you,* Roan, beside him, and the skies will run red as my flock feasts on your bones." Her cackle was hoarse and cruel.

Cress bristled, feathers rising, but Morog's laughter cut him off.

"Do you think I fear telling you this? No. You'll deliver yourselves to me in time. Your friends can't keep him breathing forever. And when he stands again, you'll all die together. Why else would you come for me?"

She spread her wings wide, her crown gleaming in the firelight. "The Dragons' return only makes it sweeter. Imagine the flock, watching me break him while you filthy half breeds scream in the sky. Those pesky little Titans forget themselves." She muttered.

Draven's jaw clenched, his blade trembling against its hilt, but I held still. I let her speak, but every word was like a knife.

She wasn't afraid. She was *thrilled.*

Her laughter slithered around the chamber, high and excited, until something in me snapped. My teeth bared, the sound that left me was half growl, maybe half words.

"You think you'll touch him?" I stepped forward. "You think you'll break *me* in front of your rabid flock? You'll never get the chance." I growled.

Morog's eyes narrowed, and for a heartbeat the hall went quiet. Then she tilted her head back and cackled, the sound cracking like a whip.

"There it is," She crooned. "The wolf bares his teeth at last." He lips thinned into an ugly smile.

Draven's hand clamped onto my forearm, but I shrugged him off, my rage boiling hot. "I've seen your cages. I've seen what you did to Ivy. To every soul locked beneath your city. I'll tear your throne apart bone by bone before I let you touch him again." I growled.

Morog's smile only widened. She stepped down from her dais, her talons scraping the stone stairs, her crown catching the firelight like a halo of bones. "You burn so bright, half-blood. But a flame can quickly become smoke." She leaned close enough I could smell the iron of blood on her breath. "And smoke always fades." She whispered.

I tightened my grip on my blade, every instinct screaming to strike. Draven moved closer, his silver eyes sharp, a warning in them, *'She wants this.'*

"Go ahead," Morog whispered, her voice sweetness and a threat all at once. "Make me bleed. Let them watch you try." She teased.

Behind her, shadows stirred, and Harpies bristled on the ledges above, claws clicking, wings ready. She had her whole flock waiting for this moment.

And still, I took another step forward.

"All I'm asking for is a fair fight," I said, but Morog laughed, the sound as sharp as broken glass. She turned her gaze on Draven, her lips curling. "One for the Moles of *grand* Lexia to write about in their scrolls?" She scowled.

Draven stiffened, his eyes flashing. "How do you know about Lexia?" His voice was a snarl, raw, too close to breaking.

Morog's smirk deepened. "Secrets travel on wings, little Fae. You of all people should know that."

Something clicked in my chest, jagged and raw. I stepped forward, pointing a clawed finger at her, my voice rising until it shook the chamber.

"She's half Fae!" I spat, the words echoing up to the rafters. "And what do all your little Harpies think of that? Of their glorious queen perched on a bed of *LIES!*" I Yelled.

The words ripped out of me, an accusation more than speech. My wings flared, feathers rattling in the tension, and for the first time, the flock above shifted uneasily. Murmurs ran through the Harpies, wings twitching, eyes darting between me and their queen.

Morog's smile faltered for a fraction of a second, then hardened again. "Careful, half-blood..." She scowled, though her voice was sharper now, forced. "They will tear you apart for those words."

But I saw it. The fracture. The doubt I had planted in their eyes.

And it fueled me like blood in the vein, the flicker, the twitch of unease in their wings. That was all I needed, the seed of doubt.

"Look at her!" I roared, throwing my arms wide to the ledges above. My voice carried, cutting through the heat and smoke. "Your queen, so proud, so merciless... yet she hides the truth of her own blood. Half Fae! The very people she swore were your enemies." I said as I watched the Harpies simper into doubt.

Harpies strode along the stone, eyes flashing, wings restless. The murmurs grew louder, sharper.

"She tells you you're pure, chosen, born pure. But she's no different than me!" My chest heaved, fury rattling in my throat. "She's a half-blood. A lie perched on a throne of bones."

Morog's jaw tightened, her wings snapping wide in warning. "Silence!" she screeched, her voice strained. But the stutter in her voice carried desperation now, not command.

I pressed harder, stepping toward her, forcing her back against her own dais. "She would have you die for her lies! She would have you march to Faunmoor, bleed for her vanity, starve in her wars. And all the while, her blood runs Fae. The very thing she spits on." I forced the words out.

Cress shifted beside me, his eyes on the flock. Thira leaned forward, voice low but firm: "They're listening, Roan." She said at my side.

The Harpies muttered, some glaring down at Morog, others glancing at one another in doubt. The unity in their lines had splintered.

Morog's talons sprawled and clicked as she walked about the room, her smile strained. "You think words will save you? You think this matters to Harpies? They crave slaughter. And I will give them yours." But her eyes flicked to her flock—and for the first time, I saw her afraid.

The throne room buzzed with wings and whispers, the flock unsettled, their eyes darting between me and their queen. The air was tilting, and the power slipping from her grip.

Morog hissed, her hand dipping behind the throne. Something small and leatherbound struck me hard in the chest, tumbling to the floor at my feet. I stared down—my blood turned to ice.

The journal.

My journal. The one I had left with Ivy. The one I had sworn no Harpy hand would ever touch.

"Poor little Roan," Morog crooned, her voice sweet like syrup. "He likes to make up stories. Fairy tales for little girls in cages. Just read this filth!" She laughed.

She circled me now. "His mother was like him," She spat, "A Harpy in her own right. But she mated with a human and bred *this*." Her talon traced the air in front of my chest, eyes raking over me like I was nothing more than a carcass to be picked clean. "This *thing* who dares to call me a liar."

My teeth ground together, fire in my throat. "Shut your mouth—" Her strike came faster than thought.

Claws cracked across my jaw, pain blooming hot as my vision tilted. Blood filled my mouth as I staggered back, wings snapping wide to steady me. Gasps rippled through the Harpies above, their chatter swelling, some laughing, some shrieking, some cheering.

Morog leaned close, her crown lurching over me like a weapon, her eyes full of cruel delight. "They'll believe me before they ever believe you, half-blood. And when you bleed, they'll cheer again." She whispered so only I could hear her.

Blood dripped from my chin, warm against the cold stone. My jaw ached, but her words cut deeper than the strike.

Morog spread her wings wide, filling the throne room with her shadow. Her voice rolling over her flock like a disease.

"NOW BRING ME THE DRAGON," She shrieked, her talons raised high. The walls shook with the force of it. "So, I can *sew his wounds...*" She dragged out the words, savoring them, her tongue sharp with mockery. "…and kill him all over again." She smirked.

She threw her head back and cackled, the sound scraping raw through the chamber, echoing off every stone.

The Harpies above howled in answer, some jeering, some laughing, others watching with eyes wide and uncertain. The throne room pulsed with the heat of their frenzy, the air thick with their bloodlust.

And in that moment, I felt the journal heavy at my feet. The life I'd tried to protect. The truth I'd tried to carry.

If she touched Beau and made a spectacle of him—I knew there would be no end to this war or to her reign.

I forced myself upright, wings trembling, vision blurred with anger and worry. My voice came low, hoarse, but steady enough to carry.

"You'll never have him." My voice came out like gravel.

Morog's laughter thinned into a hiss as she leaned close, her talons grazing the edge of my jaw. Her eyes were molten, her grin cruel and ugly.

"If you don't," She whispered, loud enough for every Harpy in the chamber to hear, "he'll die anyway." She smiled.

The words reached every being in the room, sinking into every shadow, every watching eye. Gasps rippled through the flock, their chatter swelling like a tide—some thrilled, all of them hungry for what came next as they hung onto every word she spat.

She straightened, spreading her wings. "You see? It doesn't matter what you do, Roan. He is already mine. Your Dragon born champion, your precious spark of hope—rotting in a tavern bed, he's just waiting for my hand to finish him." She sighed dramatically.

She wanted to parade Beau before her armies. She wanted me broken at her feet. She wanted a spectacle—one that would seal her power forever.

And every second I stood here, she came closer to getting it.

"Leave me this..." Morog's claw extended, sharp as a blade, pointing straight at Draven.

"*You three,*" She purred, eyes sliding over me, Cress, and Thira, "bring me the Dragon, and I'll let him go. Unharmed. *If you don't...*" Her wings snapped open, the chamber rattling with the sound. "I'll feed him to my Windreapers. Bye now." It took one movement of her hands to throw us out the doors.

The flock shrieked and surged all at once, wings and talons slamming into us. I fought to stand my ground, but they were too strong. More Harpies swooped and slammed Draven to the ground, their claws pinning his arms.

"*DO AS SHE SAYS!*" Draven shouted, his voice ragged over the frenzy, his eyes locking with mine. "Go! Don't waste time—just *go!*"

Cress hissed, feathers flying as he shoved a Harpy off of my back. Thira dragged me toward the shadows, her voice a desperate rasp in my ear. "If we stay, they'll tear him apart!"

My chest heaved, every instinct screaming to cut him free, to fight till the last Harpy fell. But Morog's laughter drowned me, her shadow sprawling over us all, her talons poised above Draven's throat.

I tasted blood in my mouth as I choked back a roar, forcing my wings tight. We were being driven out—herded away.

"GO!" Draven yelled again, a grim smile on his bloodied face.

And then the Harpies' wings closed in, shoving us through the side passage, their shrieks a cage all on its own.

We didn't fly—we fell. Driven on by Harpy wings, they snapping at our backs until the smoke of the city thinned and the cold sea opened beneath us. Only then did they scatter, leaving us tumbling into the safety of the isles.

I hit the sand hard, feathers bent and bloodied. Cress and Thira crouched low beside me, both shaking with fury. But there was no time to curse or grieve, Aliera and Zac were already there.

Starlette came next, eyes blazing as she stormed across the shore. Her gaze raked over the three of us and then stopped. Empty.

"Where is he?" She demanded, her voice low, deadly and commanding.

None of us answered quickly enough. Her magic surged, slamming into my chest like a hammer. "WHERE IS DRAVEN?" She yelled.

"They kept him," I rasped, shoving myself upright. "Morog wants Beau in exchange."

Her scream cracked like lightning, raw and violent. She spun on Aliera, anger framing her expression. "You're the one who told us to hope! To fight! And now what? You'll give her Beau and let Draven be her trophy?"

Aliera's face was ashen, her eyes hollow. "If I surrender Beau, she kills him. If I don't... she kills Draven. Either way—Beau doesn't survive." She went ghost white.

The words silenced even Zac.

Starlette's fists shook, her voice breaking. "Then what the fuck are we fighting for?"

"We need another way," I said, the words rough in my throat. "A backup plan. Let her do it. Let her heal him. If she wants Beau whole, then he *lives.* For now. But we'll need to steal him back before she makes her move."

Cress exhaled sharply, nodding. "A heist."

"Not just us," I added, eyes lifting to the dark sky where wings still wheeled faintly in the distance. "The Dragons. If we're going to take him back, we'll need everyone we can get." Zac said.

Aliera finally looked up, her jaw set. "Then we plan for war in her own house."

CHAPTER EIGHTEEN

DANI

The sky was bleeding fire. Harpies and Windreapers poured out of the dark mountains like a plague, their wings blotting out the stars as they streamed toward the Isles. I could feel the beat of their wings in my ribs, the ground trembling like it wanted to split open beneath me like it had on earth.

Everyone was arguing again. Ivy was pacing and crying for Roan. Starlette spitting venom over Draven. Aliera and Zac snapping back and forth about the bell, the Dragons, who should go where. It was chaos.

And Beau—he just lay there, pale and broken, each shallow breath louder than all of them put together.

I couldn't take it anymore.

"Enough!" The word ripped out of me before I realized I'd shouted it. All their eyes swung to me—Titans, Fae, half-breeds, Dragons peering from the shore in shock. And me. Just Dani.

I swallowed, but I didn't back down. "While her army is out there ready to burn the Isles, we can slip into the city. We need a diversion!"

Silence. Then a scoff from Zac, fire sparking between his fingers. "Slip into the city? Like it's that easy?" He mocked me.

"It *is* that easy," I shot back, my hands shaking but my voice steady. "She'll empty her nest if we give her a reason. Which means we can walk right in."

Aliera frowned. "Walk in and do what, Dani? Let her tear us apart?" She raised a brow.

"No," I said. My gaze drifted to Beau, still clinging to life. "We bring her what she wants. We bring Beau."

Starlette's eyes blazed silver. "Over my dead body."

"She already has Draven," I snapped, anger shaking my chest. "If we do nothing, we lose them both. If we give her what she wants, we can at the very least buy our own defenses some time."

Cress shifted his wings uneasily. "And then what?"

"Then," I said, my throat dry but my heart steady, "The rest of us walk straight in with Beau. She'll think she's already won. And when she's healed him for her to play her games… we take him back. All of us."

The words hung there, mad and heavy, but no one spoke against them. Because they knew I was right.

If we were going to gamble, we had to gamble in her house.

"And how do you propose we just take them both back?" Thane's voice cut across the circle, heavy as stone. His tone more mockery than question.

Every instinct in me screamed to look away, to shut my mouth and let the Titans and Fae figure it out. But I was past caring what they thought of me.

"Same way we've done everything else," I said, staring straight at him. "With whatever scraps of luck we can wring out of this cursed place." I shrugged.

A ripple went through the group. Ivy's eyes widened, Jake shifted closer to me like he was ready to back me even if no one else would. Starlette's mouth pressed into a thin line, unreadable as she thought to herself.

I pressed on, because if I stopped I'd never start again. "You want details? Fine. We retreat to through the realm door, we make it look like we are *all* fleeing. Then whoever choses to remain walks Beau in and you let her think it's surrender. She'll heal him like she bragged, because she wants him strong enough to kill in front of her flock. That's her mistake. While she's busy gloating, we get Draven out. Then we hit her with everything we've got. She doesn't know how many of us there are, how many Dragons we have."

I turned, pointing toward the shore where Azra and Irmak loomed, the baby Dragons crouched in the dark like restless shadows. "Aliera, Zac, Dragons, and every bit of magic that's left. If Morog thinks she's putting on a show for her flock, then let's make it one *she* doesn't survive."

The silence that followed was sharp, stretched thin. My heart hammered so loud I thought they'd all hear it.

Thane studied me, expression unreadable, then finally gave a low hum. "Bold. Reckless..." His eyes narrowed. "But not impossible. You do know there is every chance we'll all die? We are outnumbered by thousands."

"All we have to do is get airborne, get through the realm door, ring that fucking bell you all keep talking about and *boom!* We just need Beau well enough to fly, we just need that tiny moment of vulnerability." I shrugged, trying to make it sound simple even though my insides were shaking and knew damn well it was a suicide mission.

"Get in, get healed, get out…Her Harpies will react to a mass movement if we follow Dani's plan, we just have to be faster, and the first through the realm door, I think this can work," Aliera nodded slowly.

"Cleo was readying the armies," Zac added. His voice was flat, but his confidence was building.

"There were already hundreds if not thousands of Fae at Antoli when we left, and they were armed and ready for anything," Aliera reminded him.

Jake's hand brushed mine, his smile soft, nothing but pride in his eyes. For once, it felt like maybe I wasn't just the powerless human in the room.

"You were *stupid* to go there alone, and to leave Draven!" Starlette snapped, her voice like steel drawn from its sheath.

"What choice did we have?" Roan growled back before I could answer. His wings twitched, his eyes dark. "Wait here for another attack? They know where we are now. Next time, they'll come back with more. Stronger." He jabbed a finger toward the shoreline.

Azra crouched there, her great big body curling around one of her young. The young Dragon was almost the same size as her now, still shuddering from its wounded wing. Her tail lashed, protective, a mother on edge.

"I wasn't risking another Dragon," Roan finished, his voice thick with defiance.

The silence that followed was heavier than the sea air. Even the waves sounded muted, like the whole shore was holding its breath.

The silence stretched, tight as a bowstring. I thought Starlette might rip into Roan again, but Aliera lifted her hand, her face carved with exhaustion.

"Enough," She said, her voice quiet but sharp. "We can stand here blaming each other until Morog swoops in and finishes the job, or we can put our rage to work. I know which one I choose."

Zac folded his arms, embers crackling between his knuckles. "So, it's settled. We go through the realm door, we make sure that bell stays rung, and we don't give her the chance to rebuild. Not this time." He said.

Roan nodded stiffly, wings flexing. "She wants Beau alive? Fine. Let her play healer. But the moment he's strong enough to stand, we take him back. Her own ego will be her undoing."

Cress's feathers rattled as he exhaled. "And the rest of us?"

"Walk in with him," I said before anyone else could speak. My throat felt raw, but I pushed on. "Half of us go up to lure the armies out of Harpia. Aliera, go with Roan and Cress and Beau, the rest will wait on the spires with the Dragons."

"Dragons, the young need to leave..." Zac added, nodding toward the shoreline. "Azra and Irmak can circle the skies until we need them. They'll come down when the signal's given."

Starlette's eyes narrowed. "And Draven?"

"We get him out too," Aliera said, firm enough to sound like a vow. "We don't leave anyone behind again." She looked between us all.

The plan hung there, fragile, dangerous, but alive. For the first time since the retreat, the despair cracked. It wasn't hope yet— but it was something close.

Jake squeezed my hand, his smile small but certain. "Guess we've got ourselves a suicide mission."

Aliera's shoulders lifted with a long, heavy breath. She looked at each of us in turn—Roan still bristling, Starlette's eyes like knives, Zac still uncertain, Ivy pale with grief, me and Jake clinging to scraps of courage. Even the Dragons stirred uneasily, the sea restless behind them.

"Go," Aliera said at last, her voice cutting through the silence. "All of you. Rest while you can. We leave in an hour."

Nobody argued. Not this time.

Cress dipped his head and led Thira toward the far rocks, their wings folding tight as they settled into the shadows. Zac stalked down the beach, Irmak rising to follow him like a blazing sentinel. Roan lingered a moment, but even he finally turned away, his broad shoulders hunched against the weight of what was coming.

Starlette didn't move, not right away. Her eyes were fixed on the sky, silver light rippling faintly as though she could see Draven's chains through the dark. Then, without a word, she swept toward the tavern, her steps sharp and furious.

Ivy sat down hard in the sand, her face buried in her hands. Jake lowered beside her, wrapping an arm around her shoulders.

I just stood there, staring at the sea. One hour. That was all the time we had left before we walked into Morog's city with nothing but a dicey plan and a lot of anger to hold us together.

One hour before the end began.

Chapter Nineteen

ALIERA

Beau's breaths came shallow, ragged, slipping in and out like the tide of the sea. His skin was almost completely gray, his wings dry and cracking where the injuries festered into something more, his strength dwindling with every moment.

I sat by his side, my hand resting against his. My fingers tracing the rough calluses I knew better than my own. His golden eyes fluttered open for a second, unfocused, then closed again.

"You remember the first time we met?" My voice cracked, but I kept talking because silence felt too much like surrender. "You were meant to capture me for your father." I huffed out a laugh, bitter and sweet all at once. "But instead, you followed me. Always following, always chasing."

The memory pulled me back to that inn, that night burned into me like fire on my skin. "I saw you through the sheet. Just a silhouette, tall with every line of you outlined by lantern light. I thought I was imagining things, but no… you caught me glancing, didn't you?" I smiled faintly, brushing hair from his damp forehead. "I fell for you right then. I knew you'd ruin me. I didn't care…but I was right."

The smile broke, my chest tightening. "I'll forgive you, Beau. For all of it. For the lies, for what you did to my parents. I know it wasn't your choice—it was orders. My father's orders, not yours. And my mother…" My throat closed, but I forced the words. "I know you were following orders once again when it came to her…if we make it out of this alive, you don't take orders from anyone anymore,"

His fingers twitched faintly against mine, and I held on tighter.

"No one blames you for Astrid. Not really. That was war, and war changes all of us, Astrid was willing to die to give us all a chance. Even Zac knows that."

I bent closer, my forehead against his temple, my breath uneven. "So, hear me now, even if you can't answer. I'll fight for you. Right up until the very end. I want a world where we can live without rulers drunk on greed, without ridicule and chains, without blood in every sunrise. I want a world where you and I are free to live the way we want to live."

His chest rose, shallow but steady, and I clung to that rhythm as though it was the only thing tethering me to hope.

"Stay with me, Beau. Just a little longer."

"I do love you," I whispered, my voice breaking as the tears finally won. "I always will. I know you can fight this—you're the strongest person I know. Use the fire inside you. You have Dragon's blood in your veins. Find it. Use it. Come back to me."

The words crumbled into sobs. I wept hard, clutching his arm like it was the only thing keeping me upright. He shifted barely, but his arm slipped weakly around my neck, the faintest echo of the strength he used to hold me with.

It was a small comfort, so slight, but it burned through me like sunlight in the dark.

He was weak. He was *so* weak. His breath rattled against my shoulder, his pulse faint beneath my fingers. I pressed my face into his chest, inhaling the fading scent that was his, and for one desperate moment I imagined him whole again—standing tall, golden eyes bright, wings unbroken, laughing at me the way he used to when I pretended I wasn't staring.

I held him tighter, as though my strength could pour into his veins and wake the fire slumbering there.

"Don't leave me, Beau," I begged, the words muffled in his skin. "Not like this."

His head turned slightly, just enough that I felt the faint brush of his breath against my hair. A tremor ran through his chest—too weak to be words, but enough to tell me he heard.

Enough to tell me he was still here.

I hadn't even noticed the door open, too lost in Beau's shallow breaths, until the boards creaked softly. Ivy slipped in, quiet as a shadow, her steps hesitant at first. She didn't say anything, just sank down beside me on the bench, her small frame pressing against my shoulder. Her hand found mine where it clutched Beau's arm, and she squeezed gently.

I let out a shaky breath, resting my cheek against Beau's chest. "I don't know how much more he can take," I whispered. "But I won't stop fighting for him."

Ivy nodded, her eyes red from crying.

"You care for him, don't you?" I asked softly.

Her head jerked up. "Roan?" She asked.

I managed to make the faintest smile, brushing my thumb over Beau's knuckles. "You don't have to say it. It's written all over you. The way you look at him… I know that look. It's the same one I have when Beau breathes too hard and I think I'm going to lose him." I sighed.

Ivy's lips trembled. "He went into that city knowing she was waiting for him. Knowing what Morog would do."

"Because that's Roan," I said. My voice cracked, but I forced myself on. "Reckless. Stubborn. Brave in the most foolish way. He thinks if he can put himself between the people he loves and the villain, it'll be enough."

Ivy sniffed, wiping her face with the back of her hand. "And you think he'll come back?"

I glanced down at Beau, then back at her, meeting her wide, frightened eyes. "I think men like Roan always come back. They may be broken and bloody when they do, but they're alive. Because they're too damn stubborn to give death the satisfaction." I smiled.

For a moment, neither of us spoke. Just two women clinging to broken men who'd thrown themselves into storms for us.

"Then we'll bring him back," Ivy whispered fiercely, her small hand gripping mine tighter.

"Yes," I said, squeezing back. "We will."

Ivy's eyes shimmered, and for a moment I thought she'd hold it all in like she always did. But then the words spilled out in a whisper, fragile and desperate.

"He was the only one who ever looked at me like I wasn't broken," She said. "In that dungeon… everyone else saw me as a weakness, a burden. Roan never did. He risked food, sleep, everything just to keep me breathing. He made me laugh when there was nothing left to laugh about."

Her voice wavered. "I think…" She faltered, her hands tightening in her lap. "I think I started loving him the moment he told me I was more than what they'd done to me."

My throat tightened. I thought of the first time Beau had let me see through the assassin who should have been my enemy but instead showed me the man who lingered underneath it all. I reached out and touched Ivy's shoulder, pulling her closer until her head rested lightly against me.

"That's not weakness," I told her softly. "That's strength. You survived because you held on, and he survived because he saw someone worth holding on for. That's what love does."

Her breath hitched. "But what if he doesn't feel the same after all of this?" She glanced toward the door, where Roan's shadow moved faintly outside, pacing the sand.

I brushed a tear from her cheek, my own eyes burning. "Then you'll know when it's time. Men like Roan… they don't say it easy, but they show it. He's still here, isn't he? He's brought a thousand of his people to fight because he fell in love with you."

For the first time, Ivy smiled through her tears. She nodded and whispered, "Thank you, Aliera." But she hesitated to chase the shadow outside the door.

"He's just distracted right now," I said, brushing Ivy's hair back from her damp cheeks. "By all the things he wants to do to keep you safe, like he did in the dungeon." I gave her a faint, tired smile. "Go to him. You don't know when you'll get another moment alone."

Her breath caught, eyes flicking again to the doorway where Roan's shadow passed, restless and watchful. For a heartbeat she stayed frozen, torn between fear and hope. Then she nodded, quick and sharp.

"I'll try," She whispered, squeezing my hand one last time before rising to her feet.

I watched her slip out into the night, my chest aching with something that was not entirely my own grief. If Beau and I were running out of time, maybe she still had a chance to claim hers.

And I wanted her to take it.

CHAPTER TWENTY

IVY

Roan stood in the street with Jake, Cress, and Thane, their voices low, the kind of talk men shared before walking into the unexpected. My feet moved before I could stop them and suddenly I pressed gently to Roan's side.

"Can I steal you away?" My fingers laced with his.

He turned to me, and the hardness in his eyes melted. His smile was quiet but sure. "Always."

He didn't spare another word for the others, he just squeezed my hand in his gentle way and let me lead him away. Down the narrow path toward the shoreline, away from the fires and the restless wings above. Dani caught my eye as we passed and she pressed a folded blanket into my arms with a knowing look, another tucked under hers for herself and Jake. It seemed we all understood without saying anything at all. Tonight was for last words, last touches, and last breaths before whatever came next.

Torin and Ele had already vanished into a room in the tavern, their laughter and low murmurs drifting faintly. The world was burning, and yet here we all were, clinging to what was left of the people we loved.

I spread the blanket on the sand in a quiet corner where the waves crashed a little gentler. Roan sank down beside me, his hand never leaving mine.

"Are you sure this will work?" I asked, searching his face in the dim light.

He exhaled slowly, almost defeated. "I think it will… I hope it will." His shoulders slumped as he looked out at the sea where the serpents splashed playfully in waiting.

I curled against him, needing to feel the solidness of his body, the steady heat of his skin. "That's enough for me," I whispered.

I leaned into his warmth, the rhythm of his breath grounding me. For this moment, *our* moment, there was no shouting, no battle plans, no fear pressing in from every direction, just the two of us in the quiet corner of the isle, the sea folding in and out before us seductively.

"Do you remember this?" I whispered, reaching into the fold of my dress. My fingers brushed against the hidden pocket I had stitched there myself, tugging out the small, crinkled sweet. The wrapper was worn soft from being handled too many times, but the candy inside was still whole.

Roan blinked, then his eyes softened in recognition.

"You kept it?" His expression softened into a smile.

"I thought I'd save it for a time when we could share it. No time like the present." I said as I snapped the candy into two.

"You sure?" He asked. "You don't want to save it a little longer, you might need it." He stammered over the words, but I knew what he meant—this war meant any of us could end up back in one of those cells again.

I nodded my head. "It wasn't food to me. It was a promise. A reminder that someone out there saw me as more," My voice wavered, but I pressed on, my eyes locked on his. "That someone was you."

He swallowed hard, and for the first time his walls cracked. He lifted my hand, the one still clutching the candy, and he pressed his lips against my knuckles. "I gave it to you because I didn't know how else to give you hope," He said gently. "But you made it into something more. You always do."

We both took a piece of the candy as we watched the lanterns burn in the small town and listened to the waves crashing on beach as we savored the sweet.

I leaned over Roan, brushing my forehead against his. "Let's make tonight into something more too. Not war. Not loss. Just... us."

His arm came around me, drawing me close until his lips found mine, soft and searching, tasting of all the things we hadn't said but had always known.

And for that moment, with the sweetness of the candy still painting our lips, we weren't prisoners of this world or pawns of war. We were just Roan and Ivy...two broken souls who had found each other in the dark of that dungeon.

The kiss lingered, slow and aching, his lips brushing mine like he was afraid I'd vanish if he pressed too hard. But I leaned into him, my hands curling into the rough fabric of his shirt, pulling him closer until there was no space left between us.

The blanket rustled and he gripped me gently and turned me over and lowered me gently down, his body hovering over mine, careful, he was always careful, as though I were something fragile. But I wasn't—I didn't want to be. Not with him.

"Don't hold back," I whispered against his mouth as I lay beneath him. My fingers slid up into his hair. "Not tonight." I pleaded.

His breath caught, his forehead resting against mine. "Ivy…" My name on his lips was ecstasy, and a promise all at once. His hands trembled as they traced the curve of my waist, settling at my hip. "I don't want to break you." He stalled.

"You won't," I whispered, pulling him down until his chest pressed firmly against mine, the warmth of him seeping into me, grounding me. "You've never hurt me, Roan." The words came our breathy.

The fear in his eyes flickered, then softened, replaced by something raw and unguarded. He kissed me again, deeper this time, his weight settling over me as the blanket tangled around us. His hands explored me, and that made my heart ache, every touch from him was both discovery and confirmation that he was memorizing me in case this was the last night we had.

I clung to him just as fiercely, tasting salt and fire on his skin as I trailed my lips down his neck, breathing him in like I could stitch this moment into my soul and keep it forever.

There was no war here, no queen, no chains or cages. Only Roan and me, giving each other what pieces of ourselves we still had left.

The world fell away until there was only the steady press of his body against mine. Roan kissed me like every second mattered, and I answered with everything I had left to give. My hands explored the ripples of muscle along his back, the ridges carved from conflicts he should never have had to fight, every scar telling me he'd survived for this—*for us.*

The blanket tangled around us as I shifted beneath him, my dress yielding under his touch. His fingers hesitated at first, trembling against my skin, but when I guided him with my hand, the hesitation broke. His touch was warm, hesitant, as though he were afraid to take too much, but I wanted to give him all of me. I wanted to feel alive in his arms, to burn in the only fire this world had ever given me that didn't destroy me, the fire the raged between us.

He whispered my name against my throat, the sound low, rough, and desperate. My breathing became heavy as I arched into him, letting him know without words that I trusted him, that I needed him closer—deeper. His weight settled fully over me then, and I gasped into his mouth as our bodies aligned, heat sparking where we fit together.

The rhythm we found was slow at first, careful as though we were still learning each other, but it built quickly, urgency clawing at the edges. Every movement carried the weight of desperation and fear of what might come tomorrow, the fear that this could be the last time. And so, we clung to each other, giving everything to this moment, and holding nothing back.

The waves whispered just beyond us, the night air cool on our skin, but under the blanket it was all heat and heart and breathlessness. His forehead pressed to mine as we moved together, his eyes locked on mine even through the haze of it, like he wanted me to see the truth he couldn't put into words.

When I finally cried out as he moved inside me, making me ache in all the right places, he muffled the sound with his mouth, kissing me fiercely, as though silence could keep this moment safe from the world waiting beyond the isles.

And when it was over, when we were both trembling, spent, and clinging to one another beneath the sky, he didn't let go of me. His arms wrapped around me tightly.

"I'll choose you," He whispered hoarsely, as though he feared I might not believe it. "Every time. No matter what."

I buried my face against his chest, holding him just as tight. "Then don't let this be the last time." I kissed him.

We lay there tangled together, my body curled into the solid strength of him. Roan's wings stretched over us, folding down like a shelter, sealing us away from the night air and the troubles of war. The steady thrum of his heartbeat lulled me, a rhythm I wanted to memorize forever.

For the first time since I'd fallen into this realm, I wasn't cold. I wasn't afraid. I was at peace, I was right where I wanted to be.

His hand traced slow circles over my arm, his lips brushing the crown of my head every so often, wordless promises in every touch. I whispered nothing in return, only breathed him in, because there were no words for what it meant to be safe in his arms.

We stayed like that until the silence was broken by a voice calling down from the tavern.

"Everyone back!" Thane's command rolled over the shoreline, he was ready for blood. "It's time."

Roan groaned softly, tightening his hold on me for just one more heartbeat, as though refusing to surrender. I clutched at him in return, burying my face against his chest.

Then, slowly, he pulled back, his eyes searching mine. "One hour was too short." He sighed.

I smiled faintly through the ache in my chest. "Then let's make sure we get more."

He kissed me once more, before gathering the blanket around us both. And together, hand in hand, we rose to meet the others, our hearts still burning with the warmth we'd stirred in the dark.

We walked back along the sand, fingers laced together, the blanket draped over my shoulders like a cape. The air was crisp with a chill. Ahead, there was a small cluster of firelight glowing where everyone had gathered again.

Dani and Jake were the first to spot us. Dani elbowed Jake, a smirk tugging at her lips. "About time," She murmured, just loud enough for me to hear. Jake tried to keep his face straight but failed miserably, his grin giving him away.

Roan's fingers squeezed mine once in silent amusement before he let go, the soldier in him already returning as we neared the others.

Torin and Ele stepped out from the tavern just then, Ele's hair tousled, Torin looking more relaxed than I'd seen him in days. She was smiling at something he'd said, and for a moment the sight almost made the night feel normal—like this wasn't the calm before the storm, but I knew none of us would walk away from this unchanged.

The rest of the group had gathered near the shoreline, lit by the flicker of lanterns and the low orange glow from Zac's fire. Aliera stood between him, Vara, and Titus— Titans shoulder to shoulder, the sheer power of them humming in the air. Behind them, Cress and Thira listened intently, their wings twitching. Even the Dragons were part of the conversation—Azra's serpentine head lowered close, Irmak's tail sweeping the sand in slow, rhythmic motions, the younger Dragons crouched nearby with an obvious restlessness.

Thane stood beside Marcus at the center, both of them looking like they could have been carved from the same stonework.

"We've decided," Thane announced as Roan and I drew near. "Marcus and I will fly to Faunmoor. We'll meet the Fauns and lead them to Aravena. If Morog's army turns north, they'll be ready to meet her there."

Marcus nodded, his voice calm but resolute. "The Fauns of Aravena are skilled fighters, and their kin in Faunmoor will follow their lead. It's time we unite them." Thane added.

The news rippled through the group, a mixture of tension and cautious hope.

Aliera's eyes flicked over us as Roan, and I joined the edge of the circle. Her gaze lingered on me for a heartbeat, a knowing look that was soft but unspoken. I felt like everyone's little sister in that moment, and then she turned back to Thane.

"Then we move fast," She said.

The Dragons rumbled low in agreement, their wings stirring the sand.

And just like that, the air shifted again. The hour of rest was over.

War was breathing down our necks.

CHAPTER TWENTY

ONE

ALIERA

The night was alive with motion as wings stretched, and the talk of plans were set into movement. Roan was already striding toward the tavern with Cress and two of his soldiers at his back. Their boots thudded softly against the wooden planks. Inside, Beau waited there, the faint glow of his veins was pulsing weakly under his skin. Roan would carry him with his men. He'd insisted on it. *No one else touches him,* he'd said, and no one had argued.

Outside, Thane and Marcus spread a map across the sand, the parchment glowed under the torchlight.

"Once we're airborne, Marcus and I will head west over the ocean—past Sula Mound and the Cliffs of Gideon. We'll reach Faunmoor by dawn."

Marcus traced the line with his finger. "The Fauns will rally, and Aravena will open its borders. When what's left of Morog's army turns north, we'll be ready to catch them between us." He said.

I nodded, my throat tight. It wasn't a perfect plan, but it was one of the few we had left. "Go," I told them.

With a sharp nod, Thane unfurled his wings as he grabbed hold of Marcus. Together, they launched into the night, vanishing beyond the isles and into the endless black of the ocean that stretched far north.

Zac moved to my side, firelight dancing in his eyes. "The army's ready. The Fae, the half-breeds, and the Dragons. They'll fly through the realm door and draw her attention. If we're lucky, most of her forces will follow." That was the main plan, distraction. We needed her alone, we needed to lure out the majority of Harpia if we were to have any sort of chance.

"Our luck's running thin," I murmured. "But I'll take it."

Behind us, Ivy, Dani, and Jake were already mounting up with the flight teams—riders pairing with Dragons, soldiers adjusting their harnesses. Ivy met my gaze for a moment across the sand, her small frame dwarfed by the massive wings beside her. I gave her a nod, and she returned it with quiet resolve.

They would lead the army toward the realm door—our diversion, our last hope. This plan couldn't fail, we didn't have a backup.

And me, Zac, Roan, Cress, Thira, the strongest of our ranks would stay behind to make the *trade*. Beau for Draven.

Except it wouldn't be a trade at all.

It would be the trap Morog never saw coming.

I turned toward the tavern as Roan re-emerged, Beau cradled between his arms and the others, the faint shimmer of Dragonlight flickering under his skin and over his scaled shoulders. Cress and Thira followed close behind, faces set, wings already stretching for flight.

"Positions!" Zac shouted, his voice carrying across the beach. Humans gathered out of their homes now to watch us depart.

The Dragons roared in answer, wings beating the air and summoning a gust that stirred the sand beneath our feet.

I for the storm whispering through my veins, sharp and ready. "This is it," I said quietly. "One last gamble." I whispered to myself as I sucked in a deep breath.

Roan met my eyes as he adjusted Beau's weight between himself and the others. "Then let's make it count." He smirked at my personal pep talk.

Kieran sat astride the injured Dragon, his posture defiant despite the worry creasing his brow. The creature's torn wing was wrapped tight in linen and herbs, but its eyes still burned bright. He wasn't supposed to come, yet no one had the heart or the authority to stop him.

Azra had already sent him ahead with the other younger Dragons, insisting she and Irmak would hold their ground behind the blackened hills on the outskirts of Harpia. Their role was clear, wait for the signal, strike when the sky itself rumbled with threats of Harpies.

Every creak and clang of armor felt louder in the stillness before we launched.

I turned to face them all, each one marked by exhaustion, scars, and a stubborn hope that wouldn't falter. Faces I'd grown to trust, maybe even love in some strange way.

"Good luck, everybody," I said, my voice louder than I expected, carried on the wind. "I hope I see you all again." I sighed.

A few heads bowed. Others raised their weapons or wings in silent salute. I caught Zac's eyes, and he gave a single nod that said everything words couldn't…it was a look of sadness, but also pride. He knew I wasn't this person a year ago. I was a shell of whom I once had been. I didn't feel like the same person, I still felt like I was stumbling through this role I had been forced into, everyone expected me to be wise and strong, because I carried this exceptional blood in my veins. In my head I was still a woman who didn't get it right every time, I fell in love with the wrong man, and I was still ready to wage war for him, just so we could co-exist, that maybe one day I could forgive him just enough.

Roan glanced at me once more steadily, unflinching. There were questions in his eyes, he had caught me deep in thought. Dani gripped Jake's hand; Ivy saddled onto a Dragon. Thira looked back at me, her feathers rippling silver and brown. "You good, Aliera?" She asked.

"Just wondering how the hell I got myself in this position." I confessed.

"Simple, you didn't have a choice." Zac smiled.

"Let's get this over with!" I said as I tightened my boots.

Above us, Kieran lifted his hand in farewell from the injured Dragon's back, his voice cutting through the roar of wind. "We'll be waiting for you!"

And then, with a shudder that rippled across the sand and through our bones, the sky came alive. Wings flared open. The Dragons screamed, and suddenly everyone was airborne.

The army of half breeds rose with the others toward the realm door in a torrent of color and power, lighting the clouds in streaks of gold and flame.

I watched them disappear into the darkness with torches of fire before I watched toward the dark mountains where Harpia waited.

"Let's move," I said quietly, summoning the wind. "It's our turn." I strode forward.

The ground trembled beneath us as the larger Dragons drew breath, their roars swelling into the night until it felt like the world itself was a part of the war. The sound tore through the air, low and guttural, then we climbed higher into the sky.

I lifted my arms, the air answering my command. Wind surged, spiraling upward, catching their cries and carrying them through the heavens until the roar of Dragons became something more—*thunder.*

The sky lit in flashes of white and violet as Starlette lit the way to the door, the echo rolling from one horizon to the next. Zac caught my glance, fire glinting at the corners of his grin.

"Your turn," I said.

He clenched his fists, and fire leapt from his palms in a twisting arc that seared across the clouds. Irmak mirrored him from above, great wings spanning the length of the valley, his flame joining Zac's until the sky itself blazed in shockwaves of violet, gold and crimson. The air crackled with power, and the fire of Dragons. Our bait for the monsters that dwelled below us.

And then came the answering cry.

Screams that were sharp, shrill, furious. The Harpies. Their wails tore through the darkness, a thousand cries rising in rage with a yearning for violence lurching in their call. From the cliffs to the cracks in the mountains, from every shadowy perch, they poured into the sky as black shapes against the lightning that lit the sky, their wings were slicing the air, waiting to be challenged.

"FASTER!" I shouted, my voice carrying on the wind.

The Dragons launched first. The army followed in their wake— Roan's half-breeds, the Fae and humans were all swept upward. The realm door shimmered faintly above, the dim orange candle we'd left burning a flicker against the storm.

It was waiting.

The Dragons reached it first, vanishing into the glow, their roars echoing through the breach. The army followed, silhouettes swallowed by light until only their shadows remained on the clouds.

I hovered for a breath, watching as they were swallowed by the burning star. The sky was alive with chaos, lightning dancing across my fingertips. Then I turned to Zac, Roan, Cress, and the others still grounded with me.

"They've got their distraction, they'll keep looking for the door." Zac said, his voice low but steady.

"Then let's make sure it counts," I answered.

We turned toward the blackened peaks where Harpia waited. Morog's fires burning deep in the mountain's veins. The storm roared at our backs, the last of the Dragons' thunder still shook the air.

And together, we flew toward the city.

"Let's just hope they shut the door in time," Zac muttered, glancing back toward the fading glow in the clouds.

"They will," I said, though the words felt thin against the weight pressing on my chest. I didn't dare imagine what would happen if they didn't.

"Time for us to go." I said as I pushed the thought to the back of my mind.

I leapt onto Azra's back, feeling the ripple of her muscles beneath me as her enormous wings battered. Zac vaulted onto Irmak with ease, the Dragon's scales flaring hot beneath his hands. Behind us, Cress and Roan lifted Beau together, his head lolling weakly between them, his wings dragging limp behind him. Thira followed close, her eyes never leaving them as she played scout.

We flew low and silent over the isles, over the vaporous fueled shield of the Honey Hills and finally into the dark spires of Harpia. The city loomed above us, jagged and grim. The fires that usually burned along its walls were faint, dying embers in the dark. The sound of distant movement carried from every direction: the groan of Clops dragging chains, the shrieking cries of Windreapers sweeping the outer cliffs.

We'd just flown straight into the heart of danger...

Vara and Titus flew ahead, gliding easily through the thin mountain air. When the stronghold of Harpia finally opened before us, I felt the familiar pull in my chest—the air was heavy with the stink of decay and iron.

The throne room's great doors gaped open with intent, the carvings along their edges glimmered faintly in the torchlight. Vara landed first, Titus beside her. The rest of us followed, wings beating dust into the air as we touched down on the grey marble floor.

And there was nothing but silence. No guards. No screeching sentries. No Harpies clinging to the walls or circling the rafters. Only the echo of our own breathing.

The chamber stretched before us, vast and hollow, the great bone dais sat empty at the end of the hall.

"Where is Draven?" The words tore from my throat before I realized I'd spoken aloud. My voice bounced off the stone walls, unanswered.

Zac stepped forward, fire rippling through his fists. He slammed them into the dais, a surge of flame rushing across its surface— only to be smothered instantly. The fire vanished into a dull haze, swallowed whole by the bones that build it.

He stepped back, eyes narrowing. "It choked it out. Like it's alive." He gasped.

A chill ran through me, crawling down my spine. "I don't like this…" I whispered, moving closer to Beau. His head hung low, his skin gray in the dim light. Even with Roan and Cress holding him upright, his knees were trembling, wings twitching weakly against his back.

The air around us shifted slightly, like a breath drawn in the dark right beside your ear, the touch of a lover. It sent chills down my spine and the hairs on my arms stood upright.

Somewhere deep within the mountain, something *moved.*

A small, frail Harpy hobbled from another shadowed hall, her feathers brittle and her skin like parchment. Her voice came out cracked and trembling. "You're late," She stuttered.

"Late?" I asked as I stepped forward.

"Morog has taken the Fae to the Pyre," She croaked, a crooked grin pulling at her lips. "She'll hatch her own Dragon hero."

"There's one in every realm," Cress explained grimly before I could answer. "It's the birthplace of Dragons, a land that burns so hot it birthed life itself. Dragons came from *this* Pyre. It's forbidden to go near it, even for Harpies." He explained.

The old woman chuckled, the sound low and rasping. "Forbidden," She echoed. "But your queen does not care for rules."

I crossed the space between us in two strides, fury burning in my chest. I grabbed the creature by the throat and slammed her against the wall. The impact sent dust and feathers scattering. "Where's the rest of your army?" I demanded.

Her cloudy eyes gleamed with defiance. "Everywhere!" She hissed. "You won't win."

"Kill her, Aliera!" Zac growled, his fists blazing at his sides ready to strike her down.

She only laughed, her voice wheezing through the pain. "Ahh, the Titaness herself," She mocked. "Morog is looking forward to you."

I pressed harder, my temper fraying. "And once she kills us all, once she has all this power—what's left for her to gain?" I asked.

The Harpy's smile twisted wider. "With Morog at the helm, we'll conquer not just Tierra Hundida or the Dunya. We'll seize

Otro Mundo and Vacia Isla too. We'll wipe the Fae from existence." She spat the last words like venom.

I turned sharply to Zac, my stomach twisting. "What the hell did the Fae do to be so hated?" I asked.

The old Harpy chuckled darkly. "Makes you wonder, doesn't it? Maybe your precious Moles should dig a little deeper in their libraries…"

The word *deeper* struck me like a blade. The libraries of Lexia ran for miles beneath the city, like catacombs of forgotten history and sealed scrolls. No one could read everything in a lifetime, it would be easy to miss something significant. *What secrets are buried down there?* I wondered.

"Still," I snapped, shaking her once more, "Draven and Beau are innocent!"

The Harpy wheezed out a thin laugh. "Innocence doesn't matter anymore, Titaness. Not when gods start to wake."

"You know Morog is *half Fae!*" Roan growled, wings flaring slightly.

The old Harpy's laugh was dry and brittle. "And how do you think this castle still stands, boy?" She bared her yellowed teeth, grinding them together. "It's *Fae-built.*"

"Fae?" I echoed, the word tasting strange on my tongue.

She tilted her head, feathers rustling, a cruel glint flashing in her sunken eyes. "We Harpies were a slave race to the Fae, once bound in their wars, chained to their skies. But when the Rising came… when the Battle of Skyfall turned daylight to black, they fled." Her voice trembled with equal parts of hatred and pride. "The Fae abandoned Tierra Hundida, left us crawling in the ashes while they escaped into their shining Dunya. You think your precious cities are divine? The spires of Harpia were *Fae once*. Aren't they resonant with Lexia?" She splayed her hands and circled the room.

She furrowed her brows, her expression twisting into something close to amusement. "You can still feel it, can't you? The hum in the stone, the whispers of magic under your feet. This place remembers its masters, Titaness… and it's not you."

"That throne," The old Harpy hissed, her eyes flashing toward the dais. "It's made of *Bastion* and bone."

"So what?" Zac growled, stepping forward, his hands sparking with fire.

Her cracked lips peeled into a grin. "Morog is the key, the first half-breed, the first *example* of what equality could have been. And they snuffed her out for it. But the Harpies now are young and wild, they don't remember the truth. They only remember the *hate* that was fed into their veins."

"Is that why she hates us?" Roan asked, voice low, eyes narrowing.

The Harpy tilted her head, feathers whispering. "Crossbreeding is a dangerous idea, boy. You risk the whole chain of command—no more masters, no more slaves. And it just so happened that when the Titans and Dragons fought the Windreapers, the Fae forced an alliance between Harpy and Windreaper, an alliance they couldn't control."

Her laughter rasped through the hall like claws on stone. "And so, you had your great tragedy—the *Battle of Skyfall*."

She leaned closer, voice dropping to a hiss. "You think the world burned by chance? No. It burned because the realms tried to mix what was never meant to blend. And now… history repeats, with Dragons, and ironically…Fae."

"What is she going to do?" I asked, my voice barely a whisper.

The old woman's eyes flicked toward Beau, her lips curling into something cruel. "Exact revenge," She rasped. "Breed the most *elite* half-breed she can. He was just an idea…the human weakens him," Her gaze lingered on Beau's broken form, and the meaning hit me like a blade.

"We need to go—before she changes Draven." I turned to Roan and Zac. They both nodded without hesitation.

"You're welcome…" The Harpy wheezed, laughter following us as we raced out of the throne room.

The night air hit hard and cold. We leapt into the sky—Zac vaulting high as Irmak swooped under him, catching his weight mid-air. Azra dipped low to cradle Beau, her vast wings shimmering with firelight. I climbed up behind him, wrapping my arms tight around his waist, feeling the faint flicker of warmth still pulsing through his veins.

Roan flew beside us, his voice carried on the wind. "Do you believe her?" He called out.

"I don't know," I called back, the toxic air burning my lungs. "But there's only one way to find out."

"Starlette will know," Zac shouted over the roar of the wind, the fire from his hands streaking as a torch across the dark sky.

"If we ever get the chance to ask her," I answered. "We'll look for ourselves. Until then, we keep this conversation between us."

My gaze swept across the others—Roan, Zac, Cress, Thira. One by one, they nodded. No words. No argument. Just a shared understanding that this information could be dangerous, even for us.

The wind howled around us as the peaks fell away below, the horizon burning faintly ahead where the Pyre waited. It was glowing like a heartbeat at the end of the world, it was bigger than I had expected, easily the size of a small isle.

And whatever truth waited for us there, I knew it would change everything.

The earth was moving slowly, rumbling, like it was breathing and alive. Heat rippled through the rocky terrain, waves of molten air shimmering like the ground itself had veins of lava that would sting a humans face. The smell of burning stone filled my nostrils.

Ahead, bones jutted from the earth in massive arches, forming a grotesque cage. And within that cage was Draven. He hung suspended, bound in tendrils of charred root, his head low, his wings spread wide like a dark crucifix and nailed into place.

"You're just in time for the show!"

Morog's voice rang out across the valley of salt, an echo that seemed to crawl through the ground itself. The air trembled with it, the sky pulsing red overhead.

For as far as I could see the earth cracked open beyond the boneyard of wings. And there at the heart of it all was the Pyre.

It blazed hotter than any sun could, it was hotter than the roots of the eternal tree in Sonsuz. Resting atop the Pyre were Dragon eggs—*hundreds* of them. But these were not like Azra's. They were colossal, each one the size of a small Clops, their shells gleaming and pulsing against the heat of the Pyre.

I followed the light upward and froze. Beyond the green hills, an army was gathering—Harpy wings glinted in the shadows, their silhouettes stretching as far as I could see.

"We've got company," I said tightly, turning toward Zac.

He gave a sharp nod, his jaw set. Together, we leapt from the Dragons, landing hard on the scorched ground. The air stinging with heat as it clawed at our skin, the warmth radiating through our boots.

Behind us, Azra and Irmak roared. Their massive wings beating the smoke into a spiral dust storm. Roan and Cress landed beside me, their weapons drawn, eyes fixed on the army rising over the hills.

And then, through the rising heat, Morog's laughter echoed again. Low, terrible, and triumphant, like she had already won.

"Now…" Morog drawled, her voice dripping with venomous amusement, "I just can't quite figure out how to give him *dragon form* when he already has those pretty little *Fae* wings, got any ideas? Or would you like to hear mine?" She sneered.

Her sarcasm slithered through the air, twisting around us like smoke. She spread her own dark wings that were vast and sharp. She hovered above the bones where Draven hung suspended.

Then she turned her gaze toward Beau on the back of Azra.

Her smile widened, cruel and curious all at once. "Tell me," She purred, rising higher into the heat. "How did *you* do it?" She extended her clawed hand towards Beau.

Beau barely stirred, his skin was wet with sweat, his breath ragged. Azra growled in response.

"Don't touch him!" I shouted, stepping forward, wind beginning to gather around me.

Morog tilted her head, her wings folding slightly as she regarded me. "Ah, the Titaness," She said, her voice echoing through the valley. "Protective, aren't we? You should be proud, Aliera. Your little monster survived what none of mine could. He's magnificent."

"Let Draven go," I hissed.

Her eyes gleamed like embers. "Oh, I will… once he's *useful*."

Without warning, Azra reared back with a roar that split the air. Her throat flared gold, and she unleashed a torrent of flame straight at Morog.

The blast struck her dead on—an explosion of fire and smoke that lit the entire Pyre into a storm flames. The shockwave rippled through the valley. I threw my arm up to shield my face, the heat biting through my skin.

When the flames finally cleared, my stomach turned cold.

There were no ashes.

Morog hovered there, wings outstretched, her skin unburned. The fire danced harmlessly across her body like silk on glass. She smiled—a terrible, knowing smile.

"You think I'd leap into war with Dragons if I weren't *immune* to their fire?" She snarled. Her voice was layered now, like more than one being was speaking through her.

"HEAL HIM!" I shouted, stepping forward. My power cracked through the air in violent gusts, shaking the ground at her feet. "We did as you asked!"

She turned her head slowly, her gaze sliding down to Beau, limp and trembling in Roan's hold as he and Cress pulled him down from Azra. A cruel smirk curved her lips.

"If I heal him…" She drawled, voice laced with false sweetness, "…can I keep him?" She smirked.

My hands curled into fists. "He's not yours to keep." I scowled.

Morog tilted her head, mocking. "He's not yours either, Titaness. You think LOVE changes what he *is?*" Her grin widened as she floated closer, her eyes wide and locked on me. "You're both experiments of the same sin—creation that should never have been."

Azra growled again, smoke flaring from her nostrils, but I raised my hand to hold her back. My heart hammered, every nerve alive with anger.

"If you're so desperate to play god," I said, my voice steady despite the quake in my chest, "then heal him. *Prove* you can."

Morog's smile deepened. "Oh, I can."

And the air around us began to burn.

CHAPTER

TWENTY TWO

THANE

The mist over Faunmoor shimmered pale green as Marcus and I descended through the canopy of trees. The forest was alive with sounds, the hum of insects, the hiss of spores rising from the ground, and beneath it all, the rhythmic pulse of an army breathing as one.

We landed in a clearing where the trees had been stripped back, and the roots braided into walls. It wasn't what I expected.

An army was waiting for us.

The Fauns stood at the front, they were tall and ready, their horns were polished, their armor made of woven vines and gifts from the earth. But what struck me most were the ranks behind them...*Sporlings*.

They were tall, bark-skinned creatures, their bodies streaked with moss and lichen. Along their collarbones, glowing venom sacs pulsed faintly like fireflies under their skin, they were biological weapons ready to burst into a spray of poison if provoked. Their eyes glowed amber, sharp and unwavering.

And fluttering among their ranks were the little *Foogals.*

Tiny, delicate creatures that were versed better in trickery than sword fights. They were no taller than a child's forearm, their caps smooth and round like button mushrooms. They weren't fighters, not really. They hummed and sang songs, their faint bioluminescence casting warm pools of light on the ground as they darted between the warriors, straightening straps and whispering small charms of luck. Where the Sporlings were fierce, the Foogals were the calm.

Marcus exhaled beside me. "They're ready," He said. "Fauns, Sporlings, Foogals and Enfields who had ventured far from Heluva Village and even as far as Elgar's Rest. I didn't think Faunmoor could muster this much unity." He smiled proudly.

Before I could answer, a pair of small figures came barreling through the ranks, one glowing faintly green, the other trailing a spore cloud that sparkled blue.

"Lemmy? Toggo?" I blinked, startled.

Lemmy straightened, saluting with a hand that was mostly velvet covered in tiny spores. "Reporting for duty, Lord Thane! We heard the call and couldn't just sit around waiting to be saved again!" He smiled.

Toggo nodded eagerly, his cap bouncing as he puffed up his chest. "We brought venom!" He said proudly. "And snacks." He shrugged as he patted his tiny satchel bursting with things *I* myself didn't consider appetizing… insects.

Marcus laughed softly, shaking his head. "You shouldn't have come, but… I can't say I'm disappointed."

Around us, the clearing pulsed with Fauns chanting in low tones, Sporlings testing the charge in their glands, Foogals spinning in small circles of light, humming what sounded like lullabies.

I looked upwards where the sky glowed faintly orange. The Pyre's light was visible even from here, a bleeding wound against the clouds.

"We march now," I said. "Morog's already begun. We can't let her finish."

Marcus nodded, his voice steady. "Then let's make sure Faunmoor isn't remembered for how it burned… but for how it fought back." He agreed.

As the first horns sounded and the army began to move, I looked once more at the Foogals drifting between their towering kin, their tiny lights reflecting off the venom sacs of the Sporlings.

War and wonder, side by side. The strangest allies the realms had ever known.

Faunmoor trembled under the weight of thousands moving as one. Fauns with spears of polished eclipse thorn and arrows of emberleaf. Sporlings bristling with toxic vapors, and the soft hum of Foogals lighting the path ahead like drifting lanterns. The forest was commanded, and it complied and parted for the armies, vines curling back and roots sinking deeper into the soil. It was as if the realm itself had decided to join the cause.

The air was thick with tension. And then came a bloodcurdling scream.

The shadows over the tree line shifted. "Windreapers!" A faun shouted.

They came fast, as dark shapes slicing down from the sky, wings stretched wide, talons outstretched. A small flock of them, hunting low, their shrieks sending the little Foogals scattering in terror.

One dove, snatching a Foogal midair. The tiny creature screamed, its glow blinking out. Another Windreaper dived toward the second line.

"Down!" I bellowed, wings flaring as I leapt from the ridge. Marcus was already at the front line, his spear blazing as he thrashed it above himself.

But before either of us could strike, the Sporlings moved.

They stepped forward in eerie unison, their chests swelling, their collar glands pulsing with venom. The first one let out a guttural hiss. Jets of green mist erupted from their sacs, coating the air in a shimmering toxic haze. The Windreapers dove into it, screeching in agony as the venom seared through their wings. One crashed into the trees; another fell to the ground twitching.

A Foogal fluttered toward the fallen creature, touching its scorched feathers gently and for a strange heartbeat, the war paused—Then the valley exploded.

A shockwave rippled through the air and the ground crackled in threat, it was the feeling of old magic awakening. I turned toward the south ridge — and my stomach dropped.

The barrier around Stinkhorn was receding. The great shimmering shield that had once sealed its venomous jungle was peeling apart, releasing clouds of bright, toxic vapor that had once spread through the valley as it's protective layer was vanishing before our eyes.

Hundreds of new figures surged forward. Sporlings larger and darker than the ones beside us. More Foogals rode their shoulders, their little bodies trembling from the motion of the footsteps of the Sporlings.

Marcus's jaw fell open as he took in the sight. "They've lifted the barrier."

"Then this is it," I said, drawing my blade. "The whole of Stinkhorn are marching." It was filled with both admiration and sadness.

Foogals and Sporlings were an ancient race, older than Fae or Dragons, they had lived in seclusion for countless millennials. Stinkhorn was a realm of its own, one so guarded and magical nothing could penetrate it.

The valley roared in excitement. A sound that was part song, part war cry. Sporlings slammed their fists against the earth, releasing bursts of venom that erupted like a light storm. Enfields circled overhead in excitement. Fauns cheered and danced on their hooves in excitement.

We had become a single, impossible army of thousands.

And as the Windreapers broke formation and fled, I realized Morog would feel this tremor in the Pyre. The populace of the realms were rising against her.

We marched for hours, the forest falling away behind us, the scent of sap and soil replaced by the tang of smoke as we passed the dark spires carved from the dead mountains of Harpia. The horizon burned faintly orange against the Pyre's glow. Every step took us closer.

The army stretched for miles now. Fauns, Sporlings, Foogals, all moving in rhythm. The ground quaked beneath their march, a steady drumbeat that rolled through the valleys. And then, softly at first, came a sound that didn't belong to war.

A song sadder than the rest.

It began with the Foogals small voices, high and bright, weaving through the ranks like the ringing of glass chimes in the breeze. The melody carried strange notes, not quite words but something that was a thousand years old, or a thousand more than that, it was a song that lived only at a time of war, etched in their bones rather than their memories.

If the dark comes, we will bend,

If the claws fall, we will end.

Break our caps and spill our glow,

From our dust, new foogals grow.

The Sporlings slowed, their venom sacs pulsing softly to the rhythm. Even the Fauns lifted their heads, ears twitching toward the sound that soothed the ache of battle.

Marcus looked back at me. "Do you hear it?"

I nodded. "Ancient magic." I smiled.

One of the Faun captains was a grey-haired veteran with scarred horns. He began to hum under his breath, deep and low, matching the tone. Another joined. Then another.

Roots will rally, seeds will wake,

Earth remembers what they take.

If the Harpies scorch the skies,

We will answer— we will rise.

The tune spread, rippling through the armies.

Soon all the troops were singing — a harmony of light and dark, of high Foogal voices like birdsong and the low baritone of the Fauns. Even the Sporlings, their harsh, rasping tones, joined in, beating their fists against their chests to keep time. The forest itself seemed to answer. The wind shifted, carrying the song ahead of us. For the first time since leaving Antoli, I felt something that wasn't anger or dread. I felt *hope* as the Sporlings sang.

> *Kin to Foogal, kin to Faun,*
>
> *We rise rooted, we march on.*
>
> *Realm by realm, through ash and rain,*
>
> *We fight so peace may bloom again.*

Marcus smiled faintly as we crested the next ridge. "It's been generations since any race sang that song," He said. "We used to sing it to the Dragons before battle." I said softly.

"Now they'll hear it again," I murmured, gazing toward the rising smoke and the howl of Enfields completed the song.

Below us, the path widened into a rocky plain. The final stretch before the Pyre. The heat was already reaching us, rippling through the air. The little Foogals took to the shoulders of Sporlings now or rid with Enfields, drifting ahead on the wind, their voices carrying far into the distance became drained out by the gust of hot air.

And as the Pyre came into view, the earth cracked open in fire and light, but our army didn't falter. They sang again, this time louder. The world was burning again, but this time, it was singing, too.

Chapter Twenty Three

ALIERA

The first tremors reached us like a heartbeat beneath the ground. They were deep, rhythmic, and growing faster. At first, I thought it was the Pyre itself, but then the sound changed. It became organized, and steady.

Footsteps, marching. There had to be thousands of them.

And then, distantly through the smoke, came the sound of a shattering hum, the unmistakable crack of magic breaking. My pulse spiked. The barrier over Stinkhorn surged and then it went down.

Morog lifted her head from where she'd been circling the flames of the Pyre, her dark eyes narrowing.

"Ah," She hissed, the air vibrating around her wings. "The ants are marching." She snickered.

Before I could move, she lunged.

Her claws closed around me with a crushing force, the world tilting as she yanked me off my feet and into the air. Her strength was immense — greater than anything I'd felt since the wars in Dunya. She was bigger than me, her wings a dark explosion of feathers.

"Let me go!" I shouted, thrashing as wind surged around us, my power sparking in thin bursts against her grip. But she only laughed, dragging me higher through the smoke.

"Why would I?" She taunted, her voice echoing through the storm. "You're my audience, Titaness. Watch me burn your realms to ash."

Below us, the Pyre blazed like an evil sun, fire pouring from it like lava.

Azra's scream ripped through the air. Her Dragon's fury so fierce it moved the clouds. Irmak followed, his flame sweeping across the valley. They'd seen me in her grasp.

"NO!" I shouted, but it was too late.

Azra surged upward, colliding with Morog midair. The impact was deafening, and my ears rang from the impact. I wrenched free as their bodies slammed together again, fire erupting around us in violent spirals. I dropped through the smoke, catching myself mid-fall with a burst of air, the shockwave scattering ash across the Pyre.

But there was no pause, no breath only chaos as the Windreapers came to her aid.

Dozens of them. Hundreds. Their screams tore through the sky as they descended in flocks, wings slicing so sharply it made the air whistle. The land around the Pyre turned black with their shadows.

And then, cutting through the madness, came a sound that froze the realm for one impossible second.

"ATTACK!"

Thane's voice boomed across the battlefield, echoing from mountain to sea. The armies of Faunmoor and Stinkhorn surged forward. Fauns, Sporlings, Enfields and Foogals alike, their battle cries filling the air. The ground shook as the Clops arrived from the east, each step a quake that split the Salted Sands. The Pyre's light reflected off their skin as they waded through the chaos, swinging their clubs with terrifying strength.

Roan's voice cut through the noise from below. "Now!"

He and Cress were at the base of the Pyre, Thira beside them, all three working to free Draven from the bone cage. Above us, Morog rose again from the flames.

My body was aching from the clash, but we were only just getting started.

"Come on then," I hissed, the wind spiraling around me, blades of air forming at my fingertips as I forced myself back to my feet. "Let's finish this."

Morog smiled, all teeth and fury.

"Gladly."

The Pyre burned between us like the heart of the realm, and the war for Tierra Hundida began in full.

The sky was chaos — fire and feathers, Dragons and death. The air burned against my skin as I surged higher into the sky so I could see every army on every front.

Morog's laughter cut through it all, sharp as steel. She circled me high above the Pyre, her black wings still dripping embers as she healed her burns, her claws slick with soot. She was faster than I'd expected, too fast. Every beat of her wings sending shockwaves through the air that rattled my bones. But I couldn't fight her the way I wanted to. Not here. Not now. Every instinct screamed at me to tear her apart, to split the air and drop the sky on her head. But Beau was down there. And if she truly was the only one who could heal him…

I couldn't kill her yet.

She darted in close, talons grazing my shoulder. The sting was sharp, the smell of my own blood sharp in my nose.

"You're still holding back?" She taunted. "Pity. You Titans used to be magnificent." She teased.

I flung out my arm and sent a burst of wind into her chest. She reeled, wings flaring, but she only laughed harder.

"Stop playing with me," I hissed.

"Oh, but this is the fun part," She purred, twisting through the smoke. "The part where you hope your monster survives long enough for me to finish him or heal him."

My jaw clenched. *She's baiting you*. Don't give her what she wants.

Below us, Azra and Irmak were in full fury, sweeping through waves of Windreapers, cutting them from the sky with fire and claws. Below us the ground was shaking from the onslaught. Thane's army had reached the Pyre's edge. The Clops smashed through ranks, while Fauns and Sporlings advanced through the smoke, their battle cries a roar that echoed into the heavens.

And still Morog hovered there, watching me, wings shimmering with stolen magic.

"Why are you hesitating, Titaness?" She called out, smiling as if she already knew. "You could end me. But you won't, will you?"

Her words hit too close.

"I need you," I said quietly, the truth bitter on my tongue. "You're the only one who can save him."

Her smile sharpened. "Exactly." She pulled in a deep relaxing breath.

For a fleeting moment, her attention flicked downward toward Beau's still form. Roan and Cress had freed Draven from the cage, Thira was shouting something I couldn't hear over the noise. The Pyre flared beneath them, flames licking at the air like a living organism, like something would erupt from it.

Morog saw it too. Her smile faltered, and she dove — fast.

"NO!" I roared, plunging after her. Wind tore at my hair, the air around me screaming as I flew on the back of the storm downward. My thoughts were white-hot panic.

The Pyre grew closer, the heat unbearable now. My lungs burned, my vision flickered, but I couldn't stop.

Not until I had her.

Not until I had Beau.

The air cracked as Morog and I collided midflight. Her claws raked across my ribs, her laughter echoing like thunder. I struck back with wind sharp enough to split stone, but it wasn't enough to put her down.

"Why fight me, little Titan?" She sneered, spinning through the air, her wings fanning flames into cyclones below. "You need me! You begged me to save him."

I steadied myself, my chest heaving, blood dripping down my arm. "I said heal him, not own him."

Morog grinned, her teeth catching the firelight. "Ownership is relative."

Before I could answer, a column of flame split the sky between us.

"Get the hell away from my sister!" It was Zac.

He came in from below, wreathed in fire, Irmak soaring beside him in a blaze of red and gold. The Dragon's roar shook the heavens as molten breath rained upward in a fury, forcing Morog to recoil midflight.

"Zac!" I shouted, the wind carrying my voice across the battlefield.

"I've got you," He called back, sweeping closer, fire wrapping his arms like armor. "We end this together!"

Morog hissed, her eyes narrowing. "Ah, the Fireborn. The loyal brother. How quaint."

But in that moment the ground below cracked open, releasing a blinding surge of light. Bone that once lay dormant over the Salted Sands rose and spiraled upward as if drawn by invisible strings. The very earth screamed as the bones began to move like a living being.

"Zac—!" I gasped.

The dead were rising.

Carcasses of Dragons and Windreapers burst from the shimmering sand, blackened bones reforming, charred talons glinting in the infernal light. Magic awoke in them once more. They screeched a hollow sound that didn't belong to life or death as they took to the sky, skeletal wings spreading wide.

Below, Thane's army collided with the Harpies pouring from the cliffs. Fauns met them with horns and weapons, Sporlings released clouds of venom that shimmered in the air, and the Foogals dove between them like streaks of light, singing war songs that trembled with fear and courage as the Enfields tore their enemies from the skies in packs.

The sky itself was filled with fire and beasts.

Zac rose higher, his flames burning hotter with every breath. Irmak roared beside him, incinerating one of the reanimated Windreapers midair, but three more took its place.

"Aliera, she's drawing power from the Pyre!" Zac yelled. "We've got to cut her off from it!"

"I know!" I shouted back, my wings of air flaring wide. But how? Every surge of power from the Pyre made her stronger, and I could feel my own strength bleeding away into the wind.

Morog hovered above the inferno now, her voice carrying like a spell. "Do you see it, Titaness? This is the balance restored—life reborn in death's image. My army will not die, they will not fade. They will serve until the realms are ash!"

"Not if I can help it," I whispered.

I reached deep, calling the wind from the highest peaks and the lowest caverns. The storm screamed to life, spiraling around me, shaking the Pyre's flames until even Morog faltered against it.

Zac caught the cue, he raised his hands high, and Irmak poured a pillar of fire into my cyclone. Wind and flame twisted together, roaring into a storm so fierce that the entire battlefield turned red with fire and blood.

Morog shielded herself, her wings cracking under the force. "You think you can break me?" She spat. "You are nothing without your Dragons and flames!"

"Then it's a good thing," Zac growled, "We brought both."

The storm hit her like a hammer. She shrieked, her form fracturing in the air. For a heartbeat, I thought it was over.

But Morog was laughing.

Even as she bled, even as her wings burnt, she reached for the Pyre again and the dead answered her call once more.

Hundreds of Windreaper skeletons rose from the sands. The bones of Dragons turned their skulls toward us, jaws snapping open as if remembering what it meant to hunger.

And through it all, her eyes burned into mine.

"You can't win, Titaness," She whispered, her voice echoing in my skull. "You need me alive. You need me to save him."

I hesitated. Just for a second.

It was all she needed.

Morog shot upward through the smoke, disappearing into the blaze above the Pyre, her laughter trailing behind her with echoes.

Below us, the world was unraveling. Out of the smoke, Thane rose, wings blazing, his voice yelling over the battlefield like the toll of a war bell. Vara and Titus flanked him, their power rippling through the air in waves that sent Windreapers tumbling from the clouds.

"She's lying!" Thane roared, his voice echoing across the inferno. "It's not healing, she's feeding!"

The words hit me like ice.

I turned where Draven stood at the edge of the Pyre, his eyes hollow, his body trembling under the pull of Morog's magic. He was shaking his head, muttering something I couldn't hear through the storm and the screams.

And then he moved.

He grabbed Beau's limp body from where Roan and Cress were shielding him, dragging him to the edge.

"Draven—DON'T!" I screamed, my voice tearing through the chaos.

But it was too late, I wasn't fast enough to reach them.

He hurled Beau into the fire.

The Pyre erupted, a blinding surge of red and gold swallowing the sky in a shockwave. The sound was rage, pure and alive, the roar of creation and death collided. The flames reached for me like hands, clawing through the air as if they knew exactly who to take next.

"NOOO!"

My scream broke apart as my power failed me. The wind I'd gathered faltered, turning against me in violent gusts. I plummeted through the smoke, the world spinning, my vision swimming with blood.

I hit the ground hard.

The breath left my body in a violent gasp, and for a moment, I couldn't move. All I could see was the Pyre burning hotter than before, swallowing Beau whole.

This isn't happening. This isn't happening.

Azra shrieked above me, her cries shaking the mountains, and even Irmak's flame faltered, dimming with grief. The Dragons knew. They felt it.

Through the haze of sound and fire, I saw Roan's face twist in horror, Thira screaming as she tried to hold him back. The armies of Faunmoor faltered. Even the Sporlings stopped, venom glowing dull under their skin.

Everything stopped.

I couldn't hear the battle anymore. Couldn't breathe. My ears pulsed loudly as everything begun to move in slow motion.

The Pyre burned brighter, reaching upward, higher, until something shifted inside it.

My tears blurred the light and cooled my burning eyes. My hands clawed into the earth, my nails breaking against the stone.

"Beau…" I whispered, my voice gone. "Please don't leave me."

And then the Pyre roared again—louder than before, as if answering me.

"Draven—WHAT THE FUCK DID YOU DO?!"

My throat tore with the scream.

He didn't even flinch. His eyes were locked on the inferno, his jaw set hard.

"Just wait! Remember what she said…there's one in every realm! The one in our realm healed him once. Let it work its magic on him once more!"

He didn't move to comfort me; there was no softness left in him. A Harpy swooped low, claws flashing, but Draven spun, his sword slicing through its throat in one brutal motion.

"I need you to fight! Get up, Aliera!" he shouted at me as he tried to pull me up from the ground.

I forced myself to look around, but the sight hollowed me.

Tiny Foogal bodies littered the sand, their faint glow dimming into lifeless bodies. Harpies sprawled among them, their feathers tangled with moss and spore. Windreapers hissed and bubbled where Sporling venom had burned through their hides, the air thick with the scent of acid and rot.

Above us, Azra and Irmak roared through the storm, locked in aerial combat with skeletal Windreapers. Shattered bones fell from the sky like hail, but for every creature destroyed, another rose from Morog's magic.

And then through the smoke, I saw it. The Dragons. All of them.

Not just Azra and Irmak, but others, younger Dragons were emerging from the clouds of smoke that rose from the Pyre. The were emerging from broken shells, and they were fighting the living Windreapers. They were fighting beside the other Dragons.

"Draven!" I pointed upward, my voice breaking. "The Dragons—look!"

He risked a glance and exhaled sharply. "They aren't exactly known for liking Harpies."

"They remember…Beau being thrown in must have surged the heat enough to hatch them," Roan shouted from below, voice hoarse but alive. "THEY REMEMBER!!" He cheered.

Draven nodded grimly. "Then you and yours better keep your heads down, or they'll remember you next!"

The Pyre erupted again. Once, twice, over and over again, each explosion a boom of wild, uncontrollable magic.

The Fauns fought the clops with their horns lowered and their amber-tipped spears cutting through their thick skin with ease. The darker, larger Sporlings fought beside them, releasing clouds of venom that turned the battlefield into a glowing mist. Clops fell to their knees, their flesh dissolving beneath the toxic rain.

The world was ending—and it was beautiful.

Then a voice shuddered through the heavens.

"She's heading for the door!" Zac yelled out.

I looked up, my heart hammering as Morog and her Windreapers rose higher and higher through the flames, their wings cutting through the smoke. Above them, the faint orange light shimmered in the sky like a dying star.

The realm door.

"She's going for it," Draven said, his voice rough with exhaustion. "If she gets through…"

"She won't," I whispered, my body trembling as I forced the wind back into my lungs.

The Pyre roared again, it was alive. And somewhere inside that fire, something had answered my prayers.

CHAPTER TWENTY FOUR

BEAU

Fire…That was all there was.

It wasn't burning me anymore, at least, not in the way it should. The flames were healing me, coiling through my veins like they'd been waiting for the chance to come home. Every breath felt like I was inhaling broken glass, every heartbeat cracked my chest and reshaped my broken bones.

I tried to move, but I didn't know where my body ended and the Pyre began. The heat had become a life source, steady and deep, and I realized it wasn't just mine. The Pyre was alive. Breathing with me. Watching me.

"You were never meant to die here." A whisper.

The voice came from everywhere and nowhere all at once. It was ancient, masculine, feminine, something beyond both, completely ethereal.

"Who are you?" I whispered, though the sound was smoke.

"The first flame," It answered in wispy notes. The beginning and the end of your kind. "The Pyre remembers its blood." It finished.

And then I saw them—shapes in the fire. Dragons, dozens of them, their skeletons glowing. They weren't dead. Not truly. They were waiting, within the inferno like embers biding their time.

"Why am I here? I should be dead." I said.

"To remember what you are." It answered again.

The flames shifted, showing me flashes of the past. Azra as a hatchling, Irmak roaring against the Harpies, the Battle of Skyfall. Titans falling. Fae running. Fire raining as Fae fled to the Dunya while thousands of Windreapers twisted the forest into a storm of uprooted trees and whirling dust.

And then, Aliera.

Her face cut through the chaos like wind snuffing out smoke. The memory of her hand in mine, her voice soft as air.

I reached for her, but my fingers weren't fingers anymore. They'd hardened into talons, black as ash, the familiar shape of my hand swallowed beneath dark, creeping scales. I tried to hold on to her—to anything human, but the monster in me reached first.

"No..." I whispered, panic twisted through me. "No, no, no!" I growled.

"Yes," The voice murmured. "You carry our blood. You carry my blood. You were never just Fae. Never just man. You were the bridge that linked us all," The voice said.

My chest heaved. I could feel my wings, the pain of them, their torn membranes knitting themselves back together, bone and muscle reforming. But they were different. Heavier. Stronger. Draconic.

"Stop this!" I begged. "I don't want this, I just want…her." I gasped.

The word was a whisper in my head, and it wasn't the Pyre's voice this time. It was mine.

The fire pulsed again, the color deepening from orange to white. And then it burst outward—through my chest, through the ground, through the sky itself.

The Pyre roared as I screamed, every part of me coming apart and together in the same heartbeat. Wings exploding around me, vast and dark blue. My eyes burned as my veins glowed.

The voice spoke once more, quiet but undeniable.

"Rise, Dragonborn. The war is not done." It said.

Images flickered through the flames. Fragments of another life, another man. I saw Aliera the first day I met her, wind in her hair, defiance in her eyes. I was supposed to capture her. Deliver her to my father. Instead, I followed her into exile. Into war. Into ruin.

And I fell in love.

Her laughter rippled through the fire like music carried by wind, soft and haunting. I saw her running through the fields outside Lexia, her bare feet touching the grass as if the world itself bent for her. I saw her face the night I told her the truth. the betrayal, the hurt, the grief. I saw her look at me as if I was both the weapon and the wound.

"Sadness with her…"

The whisper came through the flames, gentle, patient, but not mocking, just ancient and true.

"Sadness without her."

The fire shifted again, showing me every version of her I'd known. The fury in her stance, the compassion in her silence, the wild, unrelenting heart that never stopped fighting even when the world burned around her.

I wanted to see her again, just one more time. Not as a monster or a Dragon. Not as the killer of her past…As me, the me before I wrecked her.

But the flames were merciless. They coiled tighter, pressing into my chest, branding my bones with fire. My breath caught, it wasn't air anymore, it was power. Each exhale came as a rumble. My heart pounded, heavy and unfamiliar.

Scales shimmered across my skin. My spine cracked and stretched, wings unfurling from the fire like banners of flame. The pain was unbearable — until it wasn't.

Because beneath it all, I could feel her.

Aliera.

Her grief reached me through the inferno, her scream echoing in my chest, pulling me back from the abyss. The voice returned, closer this time.

"Let your sorrow become fury. Let it become flight."

Then the ground split apart. The Pyre erupted again, flames spiraling outward, carving light into the storm.

And I rose, spilling out from the Pyre.

Fire poured off me in rivers. The earth around me shrank. The battlefield, once vast, now felt small beneath my wings. Dragons both living and undead faltered midair at the sight of me. Even Morog's laughter broke off into silence.

I towered over them all.

The wind screamed as I beat my wings once and I surged into the sky.

Below, I saw her…Aliera.

Kneeling on the scorched earth, her face lifted toward me, eyes full of shock and awe. And though my body was no longer human, though the Pyre had burned away my form and remade my flesh into scales and flames, she still knew me.

Our bond snapped tight across the distance, not of words, but of recognition. Her lips moved, a whisper lost in the thunder, but I felt it in my chest.

Beau.

And for the first time since dying, I could breathe again.

Morog was flying faster now, her wings cutting through the smoke like blades without any hesitation. She was almost upon the door to the Dunya, the light of it glimmering faintly above the storm.

Thane was right behind her, his wings cleaving the air in furious pursuit. Draven followed just breaths behind, his sword drawn ready to strike her down.

Below, Aliera rose into the sky as if drawn by instinct alone, the wind wrapping around her like armor. And when she rose, every being below us followed.

The Dragons, the Half breeds, the Sporlings and Fauns all the others worked together to get everyone airborne.

Even the wounded and the dying.

Carried by wings, the armies of Tierra Hundida surged into the sky together, good and evil alike were all chasing the same fleeing figure.

Far below, Vara and Titus called to the sea.

The oceans responded.

Their serpents were colossal. They were ordered to flood the coasts, washing across the Salted Sands and the blackened valleys of the Pyre. They came in waves, thrashing and coiling, their bodies breaking through the coast like living storms. I'd seen serpents before, but not like these. Not this many. They moved as one, a single tide of ancient wrath.

Then the world shook. A low tremor at first, then a roar. The earth itself rebelled, the ground splitting as the quake rumbled across the horizon.

Dragons paused midflight at the sound. Windreapers screamed in fear. The realm froze under the threat of the sound.

Aliera's voice rose above it all.

"VARA!"

I turned just in time to see the sea split in half as towers of water rose as the serpents dove, their bodies vanishing into the abyss of dark vast oceans. Vara and Titus lunged upward into the storm, their power flaring bright as the Salted Sands below began to crumble.

And then, the land broke. The crystal white plain that had once been the grave of Dragons and Windreapers split and sank. The ocean swallowed it whole, pulling the bones, the sand, and the history of war into its depths.

For one brief, horrifying heartbeat, everything went still.

Then Thane's voice cut through the silence like a blade. "THE DOOR!"

I looked up and saw Morog slam her hand against the air itself.

The realm door burst open in a blinding explosion of light, its carvings glowing to life. Ancient power spiraled outward in a scream that felt like rejection, but it was helpless to stop her.

And through that widening crack the Dunya spilled its light into Tierra Hundida.

It was beautiful and terrible all at once, like the sun was bleeding into twilight. It was glorious, and impossible to look away from.

The war had its gateway, and she had just stepped through it.

CHAPTER TWENTY FIVE

ALIERA

The air was burning as we pushed upwards. The ground wasn't ground anymore, it was splitting open into caverns of molten fire crawling through the earth as the land swallowed itself, the sea claiming its victim.

"Everyone! TAKE FLIGHT!" I screamed, my voice raw, torn from my throat.

No one hesitated. The armies of Faunmoor and Stinkhorn moved as one. Enfields lifted Foogals onto their shoulders before leaping into the air, Fauns and Sporlings clung to the legs of Dragons or half breeds—whatever wings they could find. The world below was no longer safe.

"Grab a Foogal, a Faun, ANYONE who can't fly!" I shouted again, pulling a Sporling up with my wind as he slipped into the collapsing earth. His eyes glowed bright green as I set him onto Azra's back with me, Lemmy and Toggo already nestled tightly between Azra's horns with six other Foogals, they all clung to horns or each other.

The sky was chaos, beasts and wings and ash.

And then the Pyre screamed.

It wasn't a sound. It was a feeling, a deep guttural, roaring tremor that hit me square in the chest, knocking the air from my lungs. The flames didn't burn upward anymore, they exploded outward.

"Beau…" I whispered, my heart stuttering.

The Pyre burst open.

Fire tore through the battlefield in waves. The earth cracked apart, the sky glowed red, and for a single blinding heartbeat, I thought the realms were ending.

And then he rose.

The explosion shattered everything. Dragons faltered midflight, Harpies screamed as they were flung backward, and even the Windreapers stilled in terror.

He emerged from the inferno, like he had once before. Massive wings unfurling through fire and smoke, scales and wings the same blackish blue. His roar wasn't a sound, it was an answer. Every creature on the battlefield froze at the sheer force of it.

"By the gods…" Thane whispered somewhere behind me.

It was him.

Even through the fire, even through the change, I knew.

The tilt of his head. The light in his eyes. The bond thrumming through the air between us.

"Beau…" I breathed, my hand trembling as the wind gathered around me again.

He was magnificent, terrifying and holy all at once. The Pyre's light rippled across his wings, each beat scattering embers like falling stars. He rose higher and higher, his shadow sweeping across the armies below like nightfall.

And somehow, through the roar of the fire and the chaos of the quake, I felt him, his heart, his grief, his love, it was all still there. Still Beau.

Morog hesitated midair. For the first time, her laughter died.

I lifted my hand, the wind circling my wrist like it recognized his return. "End this," I whispered, as if my words could reach him.

Beau turned toward her, his wings stretching wide enough to eclipse the door's light.

And as the sky burned gold, I knew the war wasn't over, but the realms had just met their reckoning.

The realm of the Dunya came spilling through the door.

The realm magic stretched and bent, its frame widening to whatever size it needed. Dragons folding their wings to pass through, Harpies dragged screaming by the pull of its power. Antoli was bursting with war.

I ran hard and fast down the stairs of Antoli, the door had opened onto the rooftop of the castle this time. My boots were slamming against marble slick with frost. The air outside was thick with wings. Dragons and Windreapers collided over the battlements, their roars shaking the icy mountains.

"Hold the line!" Cleo's voice cut through the chaos. She was on the front steps, silver armor that shined bright, her sword in her hand. Beside her was Sina, her hair whipping in the wind. Behind them stood the armies of the Fae. Starlette and Ele, among them, their faces hard with panic and Torin morphed into his beast and dove into the field of Harpies.

Kieran was at their center, the Dragons' fire glinting off his eyes, his hands glowing with the blue heat of drake magic.

And through the smoke and light, I saw Roan's soldiers, battered but alive, their weapons slick with Harpy blood. Dani, Jake, and Ivy stood at the front, armored and ready, each one carrying more courage than they should have left.

"RING THE FUCKING BELL!!" Cleo bellowed.

Titus didn't hesitate. He charged up the spiral stairs. At the top, he planted both fists against the side of the ancient bell and struck.

The sound wasn't a note, it was a force.

It tore through the air like lightning, rippling through Antoli, echoing down the mountains, and crashing into every living thing. The Harpies froze midair, their wings twitching, their eyes rolling white. They screamed a hideous, shrill sound, clutching their heads as the bell's tone sliced through their skulls.

"LET IT FINISH!" I screamed over the roar. "THEN AGAIN!"

The first chime faded, leaving a hum that seemed to hold them still. Titus drew back his fists, veins glowing with blue sea light, and he struck again.

The second ring split the sky open.

The sound rolled over the castle, down into the valleys, through the realm door itself, reaching everywhere. Dragons roared in unison as Windreapers fell from the air.

Cleo's hair whipped across her face, eyes alight with victory. "That's it!" She shouted. "Keep it ringing! Break the cursed creatures!"

It didn't just ring, it resonated. It spread like a shockwave through the air, the kind of sound you didn't just hear, but felt in your bones. The Windreapers screamed.

They dropped from the sky in clusters, their wings convulsing. The bell's tone carried an ancient frequency of Titan magic, something older that the world had forgotten. It struck them where they were weakest.

"Look!" Ele shouted, pointing upward.

The creatures spiraled in confusion, crashing into one another midair. Some simply froze and fell, hitting the icy ground with sickening thuds. The Fae lines surged forward.

Titus struck the bell again.

The next wave rolled outward, visible this time, as a pulse in the air like ripples across a lake. Wherever it passed, the Windreapers faltered, their cries exploding into chaos.

"They can't withstand it!" Starlette yelled, her voice half a sob of relief.

"THEN DON'T STOP!" Cleo barked back.

Fauns charged beneath us, spears raised. The Sporlings followed, releasing clouds of glowing venom that mingled with the bell's sound until the battlefield busied with the fallen Harpies, grounded but still alive. Harpies fought on the fringes, but the Windreapers, Morog's greatest beasts were losing control, thrashing wildly in blind retreat.

And overhead, Beau roared.

His voice rose with the bell, a second, deeper note that shook the heavens. Dragons across Antoli lifted their heads and echoed him.

It was working, the Windreapers scattered, colliding in panic. For every beat of the bell, they grew weaker, they were grounded.

Cleo turned to me. "This is our chance, Aliera. Tell your brother—tell everyone. The Windreapers are breaking!"

I looked to the skies, where Zac and Irmak blazed in combat, chasing the Harpies closer to the bell. "They already know," I whispered.

The bell rang one final time. The sound washed through Antoli, through the mountains, through the heart of the realm door itself.

And when it faded, the only things left flying were Dragons, for now.

The bell's tone rolled across the battlefield like thunder in a cathedral. It wasn't death it brought, not yet, but it invited disarray.

They weren't dead, but they couldn't think or fly. The bell had stripped the sky bare of our enemies.

"THEY'RE GROUNDED!" Cleo shouted. She raised her sword in celebration.

That was all the Fae needed to hear.

The armies surged forward with a roar. Fauns struck harder, their spears flaring with amber fire as they charged the dazed Windreapers and Harpies. Sporlings followed close behind, unleashing clouds of glowing venom that hissed and burned wherever it landed. The Harpies fought back, wild and vicious, but disoriented. Their screams filled the air, desperate, furious, and fading.

The bell tolled again, its pulse shivering through every creature on the field. Even the Dragons wheeled lower, drawn by its rhythm, their wings brushing the storm as they circled overhead.

Through it all, Beau was gone.

I looked up just in time to see him, the colossal Dragon he'd become, sweeping through the air. His wings cutting the clouds apart as he rose toward the light spilling through the realm door. Morog was a streak ahead of him, her form blurring as she fled.

He was chasing her.

"Beau!" I screamed, my voice lost to the roar of wind and war.

He didn't turn, he didn't need to. I felt him. The bond between us thrummed in my chest like a second heartbeat. His anger. His pain. His need to end this once and for all.

Cleo's voice reached me through the storm. "ALIERA! LET HIM GO!"

I shook my head. "I can't!"

The air around me gathered, wild and fierce, drawn by the storm inside me. I rose from the ground, the wind curling beneath my feet like invisible wings.

Thane saw me take off. "Don't you dare!" He snapped.

"Tell Zac to hold the line!" I shouted back ignoring his command.

And then I was gone, thrown upward into the cloudbank, chasing the trail Beau had carved through the smog. The air grew thinner, colder, sharper.

I saw him.

Beau.

A comet of flame and fury ascending toward the door.

And Morog flying just ahead of him.

The wind burst beneath me, hurling me upward, through the smoke, through the broken air after him.

After them.

After the end.

Chapter Twenty Six

DANI

The battlefield didn't sound like anything human anymore, there were no humans here, just me, Ivy and Jake as we stood ready to fight alongside those who had fought for us.

Harpies were shrieking, the bell still tolling somewhere above it all like the drums of war. The ground was riddled with blood and bodies, so much so that the snow had turned red.

I swung my blade through a Harpies neck as it raced at me, the shock jolting up my arm. The body dropped at my feet, wings twitching. I didn't think, I couldn't. I turned and drove my sword into the next one before it could claw Ivy.

She moved beside me like she'd been born to this, her knife flashing, her hair braided back, her face hard but alive.

"Left!" I shouted.

She ducked, and I sliced the Harpy that lunged from the shadows, my blade glancing off its ribs before cutting deep. Blood sprayed my face, hot and slick, but I didn't care.

Then a shrill voice cut through the noise that was small, familiar.

"Oi! Dani!"

I turned.

Lemmy.

The little Sporling was bounding across the field, glowing venom was dripping from his collar glands. Toggo was behind him, swinging what looked like a broken Harpy spear twice his size.

"Couldn't let you have all the fun!" Toggo grinned, his voice almost lost to the chaos.

"Not the time!" I shouted back. But it was good to see them, and thankfully alive.

Lemmy vaulted onto a fallen Harpy's chest, plunged his hand into the creature's feathers, and spat venom straight into its open wound. The Harpy shrieked, its body steamed from the inside out.

"Works every time!" He yelled proudly.

Ivy laughed. Even as another Harpy dropped between us. She and I lunged together, our blades crossing in the creature's throat.

Around us, the battle raged. Jake was fighting back-to-back with Roan. A Windreaper swooped low, skeletal. Its claws scraping the ice as it tried to lift them both. Roan's sword carved into its leg while Jake drove his blade into its chest, the creature howling before it collapsed.

"Jake!" I called out, my voice hoarse.

He looked up long enough to flash me a grin — wild, alive, bloody.

And then another wave of Harpies hit us.

Thira and Cress tore through them from above, their wings soaked crimson, their faces pale with exhaustion. They'd been fighting for hours, days maybe. I saw Thira's talons crack as she raked a Windreaper's skull; Cress's eyes were mad as he smashed another with his bare hands.

The bell rang again. The sound made the Harpies clutch their heads and stumble, shrieking.

"Now!" I yelled. "Finish them!"

We pushed forward, all of us. Fauns, Sporlings, humans — hacking and stabbing as the enemy faltered. Lemmy's venom sizzled in the snow, Toggo screamed. "For Stinkhorn!" and Ivy and I kept cutting until our arms ached from the weight of the swords and our blades dulled to blunt objects from colliding with too many bones and stones.

Through it all, I couldn't help but look up.

The sky was tearing itself apart.

Morog was rising, wings ablaze, her Windreapers clawing after her like shadows trying to catch the sun. And behind her was Beau in pursuit.

He was no longer the man we'd known. He was all flame and fury, his skin now scales, wings bigger than before. He was a Dragon, a menacing enormous Dragon.

And behind him, smaller but unrelenting, was Aliera — the wind bending to her will, her eyes locked on him like nothing else existed.

"They're going after her," Ivy whispered, staring up beside me.

I nodded, too breathless to speak.

Above us, the Dragons broke through the clouds, following Beau into battle.

The sky was full of wings again as the Harpies and Windreapers fought off their confusion and disorientation.

"They need help!" I screamed as the sky thrashed with movement I couldn't always see behind the clouds.

The Windreapers were fighting back. Shuddering, screeching, their skulls vibrating from the bell's magic, but they weren't falling anymore. One by one, their wings steadied. Their shrieks turned from pain to fury as they forced themselves upward, breaking free of the sound, desperate to protect their queen.

"They're shaking it off!" Ivy shouted, cutting down a Harpy that lunged from the side. "They're going after her!"

Kieran whistled — one sharp, piercing note that cut through the chaos. The air rumbled in response.

A shadow passed over us, then another. The younger Dragons came roaring down through the storm. They hit the ground hard, crushing Harpies under their claws and splitting their bodies wide open with the force of their landing.

"Get on!" Kieran yelled, sliding down a Dragon's wing to grab a Faun by the arm.

"Are you out of your mind?!" Ivy glowered, ducking as a Harpy's talon missed her by inches. "They'll burn us alive!"

"Better burned than buried!" Kieran barked back, shoving her toward the Dragon's leg.

Before I could argue, a blast of fire scorched the air behind us and Zac landed hard beside us atop Irmak. The Dragon's claws dug into the ground, his flame still dripping from his teeth.

"LET'S GO!" Zac roared, his eyes blazed with fire. "She's trying to escape — we end this now!"

The heat coming off him made the snow steam. His gaze cut between us, then up toward the light pouring from the realm door where it had risen higher into the sky out of reach of all of us.

"She's already in the air," He growled. "Morog's halfway there. We can't let her make it."

Irmak rumbled beneath him, the ground cracking from the pressure of his claws.

Kieran vaulted onto the nearest Dragon, gripping a saddle strap. "Then what are we waiting for?!"

I met Ivy's eyes, wide, terrified, but ready. " Ready?" I asked, forcing a grin.

"I'm scared…" She whispered.

"Then you have to do it scared, but as long as you do it!" I urged.

She sighed and began climbing the Dragon.

"You'll thank me later." I followed her up.

"If we don't die…" She huffed.

The Dragons roared, spreading their wings, shaking the snow and ash from their scales. The ground dropped away beneath us as the Dragon's took to the air together, their flight tearing through the blizzard like knives through butter.

The bell tolled again behind us, its sound rolling across the mountains as the Windreapers gathered, shrieking in fury, the sound only enraging them now.

We rose into the sky, searching for the chaos above — chasing after Titan's, monsters, and the end of everything.

A few Fae soldiers flew up beside the Dragons, breath steaming in the cold. Their hands were full of bows, spears, and quivers of strange, gleaming arrows.

"Take these!" One shouted, shoving a handful of them toward us.

Ivy blinked at the weapon in her hands. The arrows were clear glass-tipped and shimmering faintly with a blue surge inside them. "I don't even know how to use this," She said, eyes wide.

"You only need one shot," The Fae soldier replied, his tone clipped, urgent. "Don't shoot yourself. They explode on impact, kills instantly."

He grabbed another bundle, and another Fae passed the same weapons to Jake on the next Dragon at the same time as me, his fingers were shaking. "These are poisonous once they hit the bloodstream," The Fae explained, motioning to a darker set of shafts. "And these…" He held up a handful of amber-colored arrows "These ignite once they reach speed. They'll catch fire in flight."

"Fantastic," I muttered. "Flying grenades and venom sticks. Love that for us." I looked to Jake over on another Dragon.

Before I could ask how the hell we were supposed to survive this, Cleo flew up past us. Even in the chaos, she moved like a queen. Her armor glinting that of shade of silvery blue. Her wings tucked splayed so reverently.

"And this," She said, handing me a small round shield, "Is made of Bastion. It will protect you."

The shield was almost weightless, enough that I knew it was there, but not enough to tire me out.

"Why us?" I groaned, gripping the Dragon's horns as he shifted restlessly beneath me. "There are literally thousands of you with wings and training!"

"Because you're lighter than a Fae or Faun," Roan called from the next Dragon over. "They can't carry a Faun and a Fae together, and the rest of us already have wings." He flashed Ivy a grin. "You'll balance it out."

Ivy rolled her eyes. "You mean I'm luggage."

"Luggage with good aim," He teased.

"Don't miss, then," Jake said, slinging the quiver across his back.

Kieran shouted from his Dragon, "Everyone ready? We don't get a second pass!"

Dragons began wheeling as Windreapers began clawing their way back into the air. The world was ripping itself open.

I tightened my grip on the shield, feeling it's strength against my skin, and I looked at Ivy who sat behind me.

"If we die," I said, "I'm haunting you."

"Fair," She said, and then smiled, that small, reckless smile that made me believe we might actually survive this.

The Dragons spread their wings, the air vibrating with power.

And then we launched fire and fury tearing through the sky, chasing the queen of ruin into the light.

Fire streaked across the heavens where Beau and the Dragons clashed with the Windreapers over the frozen sea. The flames reflected off the ice, turning the world hot and red. Steam was rising in columns as every burst of fire met snow. From where I stood, it looked like the ocean itself was bleeding light.

Draven was already moving through the ranks ahead of us, his sword drawn, his eyes locked on the far horizon, on *her*. Morog. He would lead the strike.

Aliera and Zac rose into the air beside him, two storms in a tandem of flame and wind spiraling together.

"She's not running," Ivy whispered beside me.

I shook my head, wiping blood from my cheek. "No. She's waiting."

Morog hovered above, her wings stretched wide, her voice carrying across the clouds like the crack of thunder as she gave her beasts orders we couldn't hear clearly.

"She can't die yet," Draven shouted over his shoulder, his tone sharp and commanding. "We capture her. That's the order!"

The Fae around him nodded, spreading out to form a circle, their weapons drawn. Every strike they made now was calculated.

Cress and Thira soared overhead, rallying the half-breeds, their shrieks echoing. Roan stayed close to the front, his blade stained with blood, his eyes darting constantly toward the sea where Beau's fire lit up the horizon, he was fighting Windreapers, they had pulled him away from his original target.

"Push them back!" Torin's order carried high into the wind, and the Fauns surged forward with renewed force as we watched from above.

But nothing, *nothing...* matched the chaos over the sea.

The water there wasn't water anymore — it was glass and steam as the icecaps melted away. The Dragons raised infernos, their fire reflecting in the mirrored surface below. Beau was at the center, his enormous form a threat in itself. Every strike of his claws sent shockwaves across the ice, Windreapers dropping into the icy water below.

And yet, even with all that power, Morog's presence dominated everything. She turned her gaze toward the sea, her wings beating once, twice, the light around her darkening like an eclipse as she dove for Beau.

"She's got her target," I said under my breath. "She wants him still."

Draven heard me. His jaw tightened. "Then let's not give her what she wants."

He raised his sword, a flare of blue light bursting along its edge. "Now!"

The Fae advanced as one, bolts of magic and steel flashing in unison. Aliera's wind stormed across the sky, while Zac's fire followed, an inferno rolling forward in waves of heat and now lightning crackled as a storm rolled in.

Morog laughed, the sound low and terrible. "You think you can bind me?" She laughed.

Beau was already answering her. With a roar so deep, it shook the frozen sea into plates, his scales breaking through the ice as he surged upward.

The other Dragons rallied behind him, and for the first time, I saw fear in Morog's face.

Draven met my eyes as he charged. "We end this now."

And then the battle truly began.

Every Dragon on the field reared back at once, their wings snapping wide as if some unspoken command had rippled through them. The Windreapers were regrouping, and the sky above the frozen sea had become a riot of flame and shadow.

"Get ready!" Kieran shouted over the chaos. "We're going in!"

The younger Dragons swooped low. They were ready to back Beau.

Ivy grabbed my arm. "Are we really doing this?"

"Yes," I said, more breath than sound.

Roan vaulted up first, his movements practiced and clean. His gaze locked on the horizon where Beau's fire tore holes through the clouds. Jake was still beside me, the Dragon's shuddering beneath us, alive with energy.

"Hold tight!" Roan barked.

The wind struck first. Cold and sharp, and then we were rising. And then the sound hit, the scream of a Windreaper cutting through the clouds.

"Left!" Ivy yelled, and our Dragon banked hard, the world tilting sideways. The creature's tail whipped through the air, clipping the Windreaper's skull and sending it spiraling into the sea.

"Eyes up!" Jake called as he noticed I couldn't help but watch as the beast fell out of the sky below us.

Ahead of us, Beau was a storm of his own, the other Dragons circled. They were smaller but relentless, diving and slashing through the Windreapers that tried to close in on him.

"Stick close to Irmak!" Kieran's voice carried from another Dragon just above us. "The heat's worse near Beau!"

"Worse?" I coughed as the air shimmered with flame. "How are we not already charcoal?!"

To the west, I could see Aliera and Zac as two streaks of gold and blue hurtling toward Morog. Draven's forces fanned out beneath them, the glow of their magic flaring brighter with every strike.

We were part of it now, not just witnesses.

"Ready your arrows!" Roan shouted.

I fumbled one from the quiver. The clear glass shaft trembling in my hand. Ivy already had hers notched, her expression steady.

"Wait for my call," Roan ordered. "We only get one chance."

The Dragons banked together, lining up in formation as the Windreapers swarmed ahead. My heart hammered so hard it felt like it might break.

"Dani," Ivy whispered.

"Yeah?"

"Don't miss." She whispered.

"Wouldn't dream of it." I smiled.

Roan lifted his sword —that was the signal.

And the Dragons dove.

Chapter Twenty Seven

IVY

The wind tore at my face, cold and sharp, and the world was nothing but wings and fire. I didn't dare look down, heights had always terrified me, but the sudden realization that I was hovering in the air on a Dragon no less, had me feeling green with sickness. Dragons didn't fly smoothly; they were a rough and tumble ride that often forgot when something or someone was riding on their backs. I'd endured at least three nose dives at this point, surges through the air that had me tilted so far back I thought I might fall off his tail end. I was thankful Roan had pushed his body to keep pace, I knew he'd never let me fall if he could help it.

"Ready your arrows!" Roan called over the roars as he came to a standstill that hovered so high in the sky I could no longer tell the difference between the land beneath me. I didn't even have to look down, the flames that were visible were off in the distance, it looked no bigger than a freshly struck match.

My hands shook as I notched the glass arrow, its tip glowing faintly. It hummed like it *wanted* to fly.

The Dragons banked in unison, cutting through the clouds, steam curling from their scales, their bodies hot with fire. I could barely see through the smoke, but I didn't need to, the Windreapers screamed ahead of us, black silhouettes twisting against the sky.

"Now!" Roan shouted.

I exhaled one clean breath and then released the glass arrow.

The arrow cut through the air so fast it disappeared.

For a heartbeat, nothing happened. Then a Windreaper's head *burst.*

The explosion threw everyone back and shards of glass and bone and flesh rained down, scattering like jewels through the sky. The creature's scream died instantly, its wings folding as it plummeted into the frozen sea.

"Oh my god," I gasped as I ducked and clung to the raised scales on the Dragons back, Dani gripped my hand and together we narrowly missed the falling corpse of what remained.

"That's one way to do it!" Dani yelled. Her hair whipping around her face.

The air was filled with chaos — Windreapers shrieking, Dragons roaring, bursts of fire lighting up the clouds into ghostly orange plumes. The smell of blood and ash clung to everything. Another Windreaper came up from below, jaws snapping, and Roan leapt onto our Dragon forcing us to bank sideways just as its claws sliced through the space where we had been.

"Get another shot off!" He barked as he then flew off but remained just above us.

"I'm trying!" My fingers fumbled for the next arrow, they were trembling with sweat and fear. These weren't ordinary weapons, they had minds of their own, or so it seemed.

I notched another, aiming for the largest shadow ahead. The Windreaper dove straight for us, mouth wide, the inside of its throat glowing with a sickly smelling saliva.

"Not this time,"...I fired.

The arrow hit its tongue and the whole body began to convulse. The explosion was deafening, the creature disintegrating into a storm of burning feathers as it died from the inside out.

The shockwave sent our Dragon reeling, wings flaring to catch balance. My stomach dropped, and for a second, the only sound was the wind screaming past us.

"Woah! What was that one?" Dani asked as we watched the beast ignite in flames as it fell to the ground.

"I don't know, it was bronze with green markings all over it." I shrugged.
"EMBERLEAF!" Roan shouted. "They ignite on impact." He added.

"Perfect shot," He smiled at me.

My heart hammered so hard I couldn't even answer. I was still in shock.

Below us, the sea boiled where the body fell. And beyond the chaos, Beau's fire burned brighter than the sun.

"Come on," I whispered, gripping the next arrow. "Let's finish this."

The smoke was alive. It coiled around us in thick ribbons, hot and wet against my face, stinging my eyes. The higher we climbed, the harder it was to breathe. Ash and cloud had merged into one choking blur. The world above and below the same color of death.

"Can you see her?" Dani shouted.

I wiped the soot from my cheek and peered through the haze. Nothing but flashes of orange flame, wings, then gone again. "No! I don't see anything anymore."

"Then she's *up there!*" Dani yelled, leaning forward over the dragon's neck. "We're going rogue — hold on!"

"Rogue?! Dani, what does that mean?" I growled.

The Dragon surged upward before I could finish. The world tilted, the wind slamming against us so hard I thought my lungs would split. The roar of the battle below us faded as we rose higher again.

The clouds thickened into walls, then swirling in shapes that looked like faces. It was impossible to tell where we were anymore.

And then we heard it.

A voice.

Not a scream, not a shout…a *whisper.* It slipped through the fog like smoke in our ears, curling around our thoughts.

"Come closer…" It was Morog.

Her voice wasn't angry. It was sweet, low, threaded with something that made my stomach twist.

"Do you hear that?" I whispered.

"Yeah," Dani said through clenched teeth. "And I don't like it."

We climbed higher, cutting through pockets of cloud so thick the Dragon had to beat its wings just to stay upright. Sparks danced around us and lightning cracked in the distance, flashing through the haze.

"Aliera!" Dani shouted, her voice swallowed by the wind.

No answer.

"ALIERA!" I joined in, screaming until my throat burned.

The clouds moved like they were listening. They parted for a moment, just long enough for me to see something glinting ahead. The shape of a woman suspended in the air.

"There!" I pointed.

We dove toward her, but the wind shifted, the smoke wrapped around her figure and swallowed it whole.

"She's gone!" Dani cursed.

And then Morog's voice came again, closer this time.

"Hide and seek, little darlings…" A laugh followed.

The Dragon shuddered beneath us, the sound vibrating through its chest.

"Keep him steady!" I yelled. The Dragon was nervous too.

Dani's knuckles were white around the reins. "I'm trying! She's playing with us!"

The voice came again, this time behind us. "You shouldn't have come here alone." She whispered, it felt like she was right behind me.

I twisted around, bow ready, but there was nothing. Only the faint glimmer of something moving fast through it.

A wingtip brushed our Dragon's flank. The creature roared, jerking violently in horror and fear.

"She's toying with us," I said, fear curling cold in my gut. "We can't see her, but she can see us."

"Then let's make it loud." Dani drew one of the fire arrows, her expression set.

"If she wants to play…we'll burn her out," I finished. I notched an arrow also.

Our Dragon levelled its wings. We rose together into the storm, two humans against a queen of monsters. But the clouds had turned on us. They weren't sky anymore, just smoke and shadow and the faint glow of red from the fire below.

We'd lost sight of everyone.

"Where the fuck are they?" Dani shouted, her voice raw, breaking against the wind.

"I don't like this," I muttered, gripping the spear tighter. The shaft vibrated faintly, alive with the hum of Bastion metal.

"We're alone…" Dani's voice was quiet this time, almost swallowed by the clouds. "We're powerless against her."

Before I could answer, something shifted in the air — heavy, sharp, *wrong*.

"DOWN! NOW!" Jake roared as he flew up alongside us suddenly.

Both Dragons dropped like stones, wings folding tight, slicing through the smoke in a spiral. I could barely breathe as the pressure crushed against my ribs and the wind screamed past.

And then…she came.

Morog dove from the clouds like lightning, her wings black , her eyes wild and luminous. She was faster, too fast.

Her claws tore through the air and found *me.*

Pain shot through my chest as she wrenched me from the back of the Dragon, her filthy talons digging into my collarbone. I screamed as the spear slipped from my grip, spinning away into the void of endless sky. Dani latched onto my legs, but she wasn't strong enough to fight Morog's pull.

"IVY!!!" Jake's voice shattered through the chaos, terrified for me.

Morog's laughter was poison in my ear. "You wretched little human… your sweet romance with Roan almost cost me *everything!*" She shook me violently. Her grip tightened, claws piercing deeper. I could feel the blood as it ran down my chest and dripped off my feet.

"JAKE!!!" I screamed again, but the wind ripped the sound away.

And then everything changed.

The clouds moved., and the wind swirled as a shadow tore through the storm like a blade of light — and Draven appeared.

He hit her like thunder itself.

The impact sent us spinning. Morog shrieked, her claws ripping free of my flesh as she reeled back. The world flipped upside down. And all I saw on the fall down was sky, smoke, flames and before I could even process the fall, strong arms caught me midair.

Roan.

He held me tight against his chest, his voice breaking. "I've got you! I've got you, Ivy!" His voice was both anger and sadness.

I could barely breathe through the pain, the cold struck me hardest, the rush of wind freezing the blood I was drenched in.

Morog's screech echoed above us, furious and unearthly, as she clashed with Draven through the storm.

And I knew, even before Roan's wings flared wide to steady us, this wasn't over. She wasn't done, and neither were we.

Chapter Twenty Eight

ROAN

I saw her falling. Just a streak of red and white and brown hair against the storm. Her body was twisting in any direction the wind sent it, limp, her blood spraying like rain.

"IVY!" Her name tore from my throat, lost in the chaos. My wings flared wide, every muscle in my back screaming as I dove as fast as I could to catch her. The air cut like blades across my skin, the wind howling in my ears, the heat from the Dragons' fire searing the air.

Below, the battle was collapsing into madness. Dragons and Windreapers crashing into one another through the chaos. I didn't care. I didn't even see them. There was only *her*.

She was spinning fast, too fast. Morog's shadow still loomed above her, her claws dripping blood as she thrashed against Draven.

"I'm coming," I breathed.

I folded my wings tighter and let gravity take me as I plummeted to match her descent. The wind screamed. My stomach lurched. My vision blurred from the sheer velocity.

For a heartbeat, she was almost within reach, the light in her eyes barely flickering. She was unconscious and then the current of the wind shifted, pulling her sideways through the clouds.

"NO!" I yelled.

I threw my shoulders hard into the downdraft, forcing my wings to pivot.

Another second, one more second…finally I had her.

My arms wrapped around her body, pulling her against me just before we hit the next gust. Her blood was hot through my shirt, her breath shallow against my neck.

"I've got you. I've got you, Ivy," I said, but my voice was shaking.

She whimpered, the sound barely there. Her skin was pale, her collarbones punctured deep, blood running down her arms, she was drenched in it.

"Stay with me," I whispered.

She tried to speak, but it came out as a wet gasp.

Above us, lightning split the sky. Draven and Morog collided again, a shockwave of force rippling through the clouds. Morog shrieked, the sound tearing through my skull.

"Hold on," I told her, even though she couldn't answer. I beat my wings hard, gaining altitude, trying to get clear of the fight. The air was thick with soot — too dangerous to fly blind.

"I can't lose you," I murmured, tightening my grip around her.

Through the smoke, I caught a glimmer of scales— the faint golden shimmer of Dani's Dragon looping around, Jake right behind her on his.

"Roan!" Dani's voice carried faintly, muffled by distance.

"I've got her!" I yelled back, though I doubted she could hear.

I looked down at Ivy again. Her lashes were dusted with ash, her pulse weak beneath my fingers. Her blood soaked through my tunic, dark and warm.

Every instinct in me screamed to turn back. To tear Morog apart, to end her for what she'd done — but Ivy's heartbeat kept me here. Kept me flying.

"Breathe, Ivy," I said through gritted teeth. "Just breathe."

And for the first time since the war began, I didn't care who saw the tears streaking through the dirt on my face.

Because if I lost her now, if I lost *us*... there would be no war left worth fighting for.

The lower air was a storm of wings and screams, more fire that above. Starlette and Cleo shot past me, twin flashes of light slicing through the haze as they climbed toward the clouds where Draven fought. Sparks trailed from Cleo's blade; Starlette's magic spiraled in violet arcs that cracked against the smoke. They were heading straight for Draven and Morog.

Above them, Beau's fire torched the sky. He was everywhere at once. The great Dragon twisting, claws raking through Windreapers both living and skeletal.

Below us, the Fae and Fauns fought back-to-back, their ranks surged beneath Beau's shadow, spears flashing in the light of his flame. Sporlings tore through the Harpies that still swarmed the ground, venom splattering across the snow. The Foogals were there too. Some riding the Enfield's, the rest darting between the Sporlings' legs, their songs turning sharp and fast, a kind of battle rhythm that carried through the smoke.

I held Ivy tighter. She was still bleeding, her body limp against mine, her head lolling with the motion of every wingbeat.

"I'm getting you to Ele," I said, voice low and tight. "Just hang in there a little longer, all right?"

Her eyelids fluttered but she didn't answer. Her skin was pale, almost translucent, and every time I blinked, I thought she'd gone still.

I beat my wings harder, pushing through the downdrafts that rolled off Beau's firestorms. The heat burned the edges of my torn feathers, the air crackling with raw magic.

"Come on, come on…" I muttered through clenched teeth.

The castle spires of Antoli were rising ahead now — glowing in flashes of the Sporlings vapor. I could see Ele on the terrace, surrounded by healers, her hands already glowing white with power.

She looked up just as I descended, her eyes widening when she saw the blood.

"Hold on, Ivy," I whispered again, voice breaking. "Almost there."

And with that, I folded my wings and dove — straight toward the terrace, praying to anything that would listen that I wouldn't be too late.

I hit the terrace hard, the stone cracking under my boots as I ran.

"Ele!" I shouted, my voice breaking with every footfall.

The patios of Antoli were unrecognizable. Once a garden of marble and frost light, now it was a hospital, rows upon rows of makeshift beds, blood staining bed sheets, Fae, Farklian and Faun healers bent over bodies that barely breathed. The air reeked of death.

"Ele, you have to heal her!" I dropped to my knees, Ivy still in my arms. Her skin was pale. Her blood coloring my hands.

Ele was already moving. She rushed to us with two other healers, their magic lights flaring brighter.

"Get her on a bed!" Ele barked, her voice sharp and commanding. Two Fae stepped forward, lifting Ivy gently from my arms. My fingers trembled when they left her skin.

"I'll do everything I can," Ele said, placing a hand on my shoulder. Her touch was steady, but her eyes were worried for me.

"I can't lose her," I whispered.

"You won't," She said softly, though even she didn't sound sure.

I dragged in a breath, forcing myself to stand. "How many dead?"

Ele's face shifted, a flicker of pain, exhaustion. "Thousands. We can't keep up with the injuries. There aren't enough of us." Her voice cracked on the last word.

Behind her, a healer cried out for more light, a Foogal, barely the size of my arm was carried past us, limp and motionless.

I turned my head away, blinking the sting from my eyes. "Have you seen Kieran or Torin?" I asked.

"Torin's grounded," She said, wiping her hands on a rag already soaked in blood. "He's been fighting alongside the Sporlings in the lower valley. I haven't seen him in hours." She answered.

"And Kieran?" I asked.

"Still in the air, last I heard. Riding one of the young Dragons. He's holding the western ridge, backing Beau."

I nodded, but my body was shaking. "I'll see if I can find Torin." I rubbed her shoulder as worry raked her face.

Ele caught my wrist before I could move. "No," She said firmly. "You have more important things to do right now. He's strong. He'll hold."

She looked back toward the triage, where healers were shouting orders, dragging more wounded through the doorways. "I'll see that Ivy is cared for. You can wait here if you wish. You look like you could take a break,"

And with that, she turned and disappeared into the chaos of the halls of Antoli, where the air reeked of death and it clung to every breath. Every bed held someone else's last hope.

I stood there a long time, staring after her, the world still burning outside the walls.

Cress landed hard beside me, the flagstones cracking under his boots. Thira hung limp in his arms, her wing torn nearly in two, blood streaking down her back in ribbons.

"I need help!" He bellowed, voice cutting through the chaos.

The nearest Farkli healers raced forward, their hands already glowing. They took Thira gently from him, laying her onto one of the stone benches that had been turned into makeshift cots. Her eyes fluttered once before she passed out completely.

Cress's chest was heaving; his face streaked with gashes and blood. He looked like he hadn't taken a breath since the sky fell.

He turned to me, grabbed my shoulder, his grip like iron. "There's something you need to see."

My stomach tightened. "What is it?" I asked.

"Draven," He rasped. "He wants revenge. Starlette went after him, he's alone."

For a moment, everything around us seemed to fade.

Alone. That didn't sound good.

Cress's eyes burned into mine.

"I can't leave her," I said again, my voice raw.

Cress's jaw flexed. "Roan… you have to. Something's wrong with Draven."

I turned on him. "He's not the enemy." I growled.

"I didn't say he was," Cress snapped back. "But he's not himself. He hasn't been since the Pyre."

The words hit me like a slap.

I looked down the marble hallway, the sounds of healers and wounded echoing like ghosts through the once-holy walls of Antoli. "What do you mean?"

"Like she's still in there," Cress said. "Like she left a piece of herself behind."

Before I could respond, a scream tore through the hall — Ivy's scream.

I ran, crashing through the triage doors. Ele was already there, her magic flooding the room in silver light. Ivy was awake, trembling, her hands pressed over her chest as she tried to catch her breath.

"She's stable," Ele said between breaths. "She's going to be fine."

I dropped to my knees beside the bed. Ivy's eyes found mine, frightened, but alive.

"You're okay," I whispered, brushing her hair back.

She shook her head faintly. "You have to go," She coughed. "It's not over yet."

"I can't leave you…"

"Roan," She said, firmer now, the light of the healer's magic dancing across her skin. "I'll be here when you come back. But if Draven's still out there and she's inside his head—"

She didn't finish, but she didn't have to.

Ele's voice broke through the hum of magic. "She's right. If Morog planted something in him, it's spreading. We better hope he's just angry. I heard she crucified him at the Pyre…"

"Yeah, she did," I nodded. My chest felt hollow at the reminder of how we had found him, a storm building behind my ribs. "I'll find him."

I pressed my lips to Ivy's forehead and stood. "Don't move from this room. Promise me."

She gave me a small nod, her breath shallow but even.

By the time I reached the terrace again, Cress was waiting with his sword drawn, the night sky behind him alight with Dragonfire. "He's heading north, toward the ruins beyond the frozen sea."

I spread my wings. "If she's in his head, she'll use him to open the next door."

"Then we stop her before she can."

Together we took off, the cold Dunya wind cutting through the smoke, the bell of Antoli tolling once more behind us, a grim reminder that even in this realm, the war wasn't over.

"WAIT!" Ele's voice cut through the chaos.

Cress and I stopped mid-stride and turned back.

"If he's really sick with her magic, this will tell you." She reached into her pocket and pulled out a thin silver chain. A dark crystal hung from it, glowing faintly like lightning caught in glass. "It's Gloomstone. It'll burn his flesh if his essence has been altered. Don't let it touch Beau or Torin." Her eyes flicked between us with sharp warning.

"Thanks, Ele. For everything."

Without another word, we launched into the night. The wind cut cold against my face as Antoli shrank beneath us. From above, the Sporlings glowed faintly, their bodies luminescent as they marched the frozen plains. Thane and Marcus fought back-to-back, their figures haloed as the last of the Harpies fell around them.

Above them, Beau soared, commanding Dragons that had risen from the Pyre and followed us through the realm door. Some were hatchlings, newborn yet already the size of Azra's grown children. Others were older Dragons forged only for war, their scales cracked and dulled by centuries. And then there were the *undead ones*… not skeletal, but hollow, their eyes vacant of flame or soul.

"None of the Windreapers she raised are dying," Cress said, his voice carried thin on the wind.

I looked down across the frozen sea where their shadows moved like ghosts beneath the ice. "Of course not," I murmured. "You can't kill what's already dead."

"What do we do?" he asked.

"I think," I exhaled, "we find someone older and wiser."

Cress barked a short laugh. "Then we'd better find Cleo. She and Starlette should be easy enough to spot."

We rose higher, splitting the clouds apart in our search. The sky was filled with smoke and lightning, but then—there. Two silhouettes hovering above the battlefield. Cleo and Starlette floated in the storm's heart; their eyes fixed on the duel raging just below them. Morog and Draven locked in combat, while Aliera, Zac, Vara, and Titus tore through the Harpies surrounding them.

"We have a problem," I said as we hovered near them. "The Windreapers she raised from the dead—they're not dying."

Starlette didn't turn. Her gaze stayed on the chaos in front of us. "Then they're not meant to," She said quietly. "They're her army now."

Cress bristled, voice sharp. "So, we're just going to watch them fight?" He raised a brow.

Cleo's eyes cut sideways toward him, cool and assessing. "If we interfere now, we'll lose more than we save. Draven's the only one who can reach her, he's the strongest Fae warrior. But if she gets inside him—"

"She'll use him to end us all," Starlette finished, her expression hard.

The silence that followed was heavy, broken only by the shrieks of Windreapers in the far-off distance. Then I stepped forward, the Gloomstone clutched tight in my hand. "Ele gave us this," I said. "If Morog's magic has touched him, this stone will burn his skin. If it doesn't—then he's still himself."

Cleo gave a slow nod. "Then go. But if it does burn him… don't hesitate."

I didn't answer, I knew what she meant. I launched into the sky.

Draven was wild. Furious. Every swing of his blade sent sparks through the storm. His wings were shredded at the tips; one bent at a brutal angle where Morog's talons had clipped him.

"Draven!" I shouted.

He turned, breath harsh, eyes half lost to rage. "Stay back, Roan!"

I raised the Gloomstone. "We need to know if she's in you!"

He stared at me for a long moment, then, slowly he extended his arm once Morog was distracted.

I pressed the stone to his wrist. Nothing. No smoke. No burn. Just a faint pulse, a deep vibration that rolled through the air between us.

"She didn't infect you," I said, relief breaking through my chest.

Draven's mouth twitched. "No. But she *almost* took my wings." His voice cracked with raw anger. "She won't get the chance again." He was full of rage, but not rage born of her magic, born of the desire for revenge. She had almost taken his wings, and she would still try.

Above us, Morog's laughter rippled through the storm. She hovered in the air, the queen of the Harpies, the Crohn blazing with unnatural light.

I looked at Draven. His wings splayed, battered but unbroken. "Let's finish this," I said.

He met my gaze—fire for fire. "Together."

And with a single beat of our wings, we rose through the storm toward her.

Fae soldiers rose with us into the smoke-choked sky, more than twenty of them, each holding a length of glinting chain.

"Aetherium." Cleo's lips curved into a grim smile as they flew up from Antoli.

"It's the only thing that'll bind her," Starlette added, eyes cold with purpose.

Aliera's face was raw with exhaustion; she spat the question like a blade. "And where exactly do we keep a monster like Morog?" She asked.

Cleo's voice lowered, grave. "Otro Mundo. Deep in the chasm world. It's a darkness worse than Tierra Hundida. A candle wouldn't burn there; the air itself is starved of light." She explained.

The Fae looped the aetherium around Morog's throat, cinched it tight, then lashed her legs and wings. Fingers of chains locked her talons and scaled flesh, until her hands, too, were bound. She thrashed, but it was useless.

"This won't hold me," She hissed between teeth.

"Got one for her mouth?" Aliera spat.

"We could kill her now," I growled, rage hot at my throat.

"No, you heard Cleo. We let her rot, Her mind will be her own prison." Zac said without mercy. "Starve her in the darkness she worships." He growled.

"How do we get her in there?" Vara asked.

"Simple," Starlette replied. "The Clops don't live in the chasm itself; they only occupy the outer surface. We can lower her in."

Zac swallowed "What else is down there?" He asked.

Cleo shook her head like a woman turning away from a bad omen. "Don't ask that."

The chains hummed faintly with aetherium's chill. Around us, the battlefield still smoked and roared, but for a brief, hollow second the sky felt like it had exhaled. We had her. We had a plan.

Chapter Twenty

Nine

ALIERA

They rode home like a thunderhead, Dragons and Titans and battered wings cutting through the smoke with the last of their strength. The sky trembled around them. Between Draven and Roan, Morog hung in her chains, not a Queen anymore but the grim proof of what it had cost to get here.

Below us, Antoli rose out of the haze like a beacon. Torches blazed along the walkways. Balconies overflowed with people reaching for us, shouting names into the night as if calling the living back from the dead. A roar rose from the city and shook the air, a sound of triumph cracked open by grief.

People cheered until their voices broke. Some cried. Some simply fell to their knees. It was victory.

For a breath, the world sounded almost like joy.

Draven held Morog pinned against his shoulder, the aetherium swallowing her power until her crown of Crohn magic flickered like a dying star. Roan gripped her arms with bruised, unyielding hands, his stare menacing. Even chained, she thrashed and spat, refusing stillness, rage boiling through every bone as the last shreds of her reign bled out into the night.

I turned to Zac as we descended, wind whipping the ash from my hair. He looked at me, smudges of war covering his clothes and body, fire in his palms. I didn't waste words.

"Ring the bell one last time, Zac," I said. "We take out anything that remains."

He nodded.

Starlette's voice cut through the commotion, sharp and practical. "We need to lure the Windreapers back through the door." Her eyes flicked to the widening gold of the realm crack now lowering from the sky, the door knew. "Make them cross back into Tierra Hundida."

"Go to Beau, Draven," Cleo ordered, voice steel. "Tell him the plan." Her glance was a command. Draven moved without hesitation, racing toward Beau's war-formation where the Dragons circled tirelessly.

Vara and Titus moved toward the realm door, their heavy steps shaking grit loose from the stone. Even exhausted, they carried that unmistakable Titan presence — the kind that made soldiers part instinctively, clearing a path without a word spoken. The glow of the door washed over them in pulses, casting light across their armor.

Cleo stepped forward, shoulders squared, her voice steady despite the tremor of fury running beneath it. "Vara. Titus.

You'll go with the others." She pointed to Morog, chained and writhing between Draven and Roan. "Take her to the door."

Her eyes burned as she spoke the next command. "And drop the bitch into the abyss." She spat the last word like it was poison, like just saying Morog's name left a foul taste on her tongue. Her anger wasn't loud; it was sharp and contained.

Vara gave a grim nod, jaw clenched. Titus rolled his shoulders once, the tension crackling off him like distant thunder. Together, they moved in to take Morog's weight, two Titans escorting a fallen Queen to a place where even her twisted power would not claw its way free.

Vara's face was unreadable. Titus' hovered with the gravity of the moment. Around us the Fae readied chains and lines. The plan was brutal and simple: render the sky safe, push the restless dead back through the door or into the dark, and bury the source so deep that no wind could ever carry it home again.

I felt the bell like a pulse in my bones before I saw it, the weight of what we were about to do settling in my gut. Below, the streets of Antoli were a blur of motion of Fae, Fauns, Sporlings, Enfields and Foogals pressing forward to watch. Healers were bracing at the gates, soldiers stood wide-eyed and stunned. The silhouettes of the Dragons rallying everything focused into one terrible, hopeful hinge.

"Make it count," Cleo murmured close enough for me to hear.

I swallowed. "We will."

We dragged Morog toward the plaza. The bell waited while the door to Tierra Hundida opened all on its own, big enough for every beast like a looking glass into another realm.

The bell chimed one last time as Zac struck it harder and louder than ever before. The sound split the air like lightning, pure and terrible. The remaining Harpies dropped to the ground mid-screech, blood pouring from their mouths and ears. The Fae wasted no time. Fires were lit to incinerate the bodies. The stench of burning flesh filled the air.

Above us, Draven and Beau drove the last of the Windreapers toward Antoli, their dark wings swallowed by the light of the realm door as the castle's ancient magic pulled them through.

"Let's go," Roan said, his grip tightening on the chains wrapped around Morog. "Our turn." He pushed her forward.

Vara and Titus flanked me as Zac bounded into the air above the bell, his flames illuminating the storm the realm revealed, Tierra Hundida was in complete anarchy, the earthquakes leaving most of the lands displaced and ruined.

I rose to join him, the others close behind, and together we dove through the door that Antoli had manifested across its rooftop spires. The castle shuddered as its walls flared with Titan light — its own magic now echoing through the sky.

The air changed instantly. The warmth of Antoli bled away as the stale grip of Tierra Hundida took hold. The clouds here were heavier, darker and beneath us sprawled the broken lands of Otro Mundo.

We hovered in silence, wings beating slowly and steadily as we looked down.

The chasm was enormous — a wound in the earth that seemed to swallow light itself, completely unforgiving. The air was rank with decay and death. It groaned faintly, like the realm itself was alive and hungry.

"So… we just toss her in?" Zac's smirk was humorless, more tension than jest.

"Shouldn't we make sure she actually hits the bottom?" I asked, squinting down into the endless dark. Columns of jagged stone jutted like fangs, wet with some kind of black tar or oil.

"I don't like the look of those Clops," I murmured, spotting faint movement along the rim as giant silhouettes crawled across the barren surface.

"They're too far away," Vara said calmly. "They can't reach us from here."

Zac's flames dimmed slightly. "I don't trust it," He admitted.

"Then we all go down together," Titus decided. His voice was resolute, grave. "We can protect each other. Zac, us your flames to light the way."

"Gladly." My brother's palms flared, his fire spilling across the cliff face in molten ribbons. Shadows leapt and danced along the walls of the abyss, revealing just how deep the descent would be, it appeared to be bottomless, and the light never landed.

Vara coughed, pressing a sleeve to her face. "Aliera, if you could do something about that *awful* smell…" She exclaimed.

I breathed deep and raised my hands. The wind obeyed, swirling downward into the pit, carrying the rot and the heat away. The air cleared just enough for us to see — and what we saw made my stomach turn.

Bones.
Thousands of bones. And something *moving* beneath them, this wasn't an abyss, this was a tomb.

We dropped like stones.

The wind shoved at us, clawing through feathers and robes as the chasm became wider the deeper we went. Zac's fire burned like a sun in the dark; his light threw monstrous shadows along the jagged stones. The aetherium chains clinked at Morog's wrists, dull and metallic in the gloom, while the rest of us clung to one another, lowering into a throat of land that smelled of old iron and decay.

At first it was only bones—ribs and vertebrae half-buried in the black silt, the shapes of great beasts half-mulched into the earth. Then the bones moved.

It unfolded with the slow, horrible logic of something that had never needed a name before we gave it one. Scales like rusted armor, feather-splinters along its flanks, a maw rimmed with cracked beaks and teeth, and eyes, too many eyes, ringed along its neck like lanterns. Limbs ended not in claws alone, but in the padded, blunt fingers of a Clops and the hooked talons of a Windreaper all at once. A shattered wing lifted, not one wing but a dozen ragged membranes. Steam rolled from its mouth where some internal fire still smoldered.

Vara swore. Titus tightened his hold on the chain. I tasted bile as I gagged at the smell of the beast.

"Gods," Roan breathed beside me. "What the hell is that?"

Cress's voice was flat. "A thing made from everything we fought and lost. It's… a hybrid. A Chasmwyrm."

It was the wrong word and the right one at the same time. A creature like this had never known loyalty. It was born from Pyre heat, Harpy talons, and Clop hide, fused together into something the world never meant to exist. What came out of that fusion wasn't a beast with sides or purpose. It was hunger embodied. A primal instinct older than any war being fought above it. It didn't choose. It didn't follow. It didn't recognize the difference between friend and enemy. It bit, it fed, it survived. And it would keep doing so long after every banner of the known realms was dust.

Something in the chasm answered. A groan, an answering rumble that rolled up the walls and into our chests. The wyrm's lantern-eyes focused, and then the whole thing rose, scraping stones and sending out a wave of dust that stung like sand in the lungs.

It struck without hesitation. The first sweep sent us all ducking, it missed. It lashed again, a wing large and heavy like a falling tower, folding half the lowering party into a whirl of stone and flame.

"Get back!" Zac roared, pitching his fire like a spear into the beast's flank. Fire light sizzled across its hide, but the Chasmwyrm's skin didn't burn the way a normal beasts would. The wound it gave bled out black ichor that smoked and hissed like acid lived and thrived in its veins.

Titus slammed his shoulder into the creature's ribs and did what a Titan does—pushed. We counted on raw force, on the weight of muscle and the old, ugly power that made mountains move. For a second the wyrm staggered; its dozen eyes rolled, narrowing in a slitted crown of hate.

It was then that the sound rolled over us: not flame, not a roar, but a cry of recognition…Beau.

He dropped from the ragged sky above, larger than any Dragon I'd seen, scales that were deep blue, fire like a furnace blasting from his throat. Beau hit the air between us and the Chasmwyrm and everything changed.

Where his flame licked, the black ichor steamed and pulled back. Where his wings beat, gusts tore the beast's stitched membranes into ragged sails. Beau came with one goal in mind, destroy and shred every enemy. His claws found the weakness of the beast and his teeth clamped down hard. The Chasmwyrm twisted, a living mountain of pain, and for the first time the thing that had grown out of dead things bled like something alive this time.

"Hold her!" Roan yelped as Morog struggled.

 Morog was pulling free in the confusion. The chains tightened, the Aetherium screamed softly, but the creature's thrash tore at everything.

The Chasmwyrm met Beau with hate and hunger. It favored neither side, true enough, but Beau, the great Dragon rolled and drove his weight against the creature, and the pit echoed with the smash of their bodies like thunder on stone.

We fought then. Only to survive the thing that had no quarrel beyond its appetite. Titus and Vara hammered at the beast's neck and Roan's sword beat against the monsters hide. I felt the weight of the world around me, closing in inside this narrow chasm. Someone, something had created this monster. A monster so colossal and monstrous it could only be contained. The unblinking eyes of the Chasmwyrm flicked to Morog before it turned to face me.

Beau moved like a meteor.

He threw himself at the Chasmwyrm with a violence that made the stones shudder. His jaws closed on that terrible throat, and for a heartbeat the world was only the sound of tearing. The wyrm's eyes flared wide and then shattered into wet sparks as Beau's teeth ground through tendon and bone. He ripped, again and again, claws raking up and down the length of the beasts body until he broke through the thick hide, and the great body convulsed and fell in on itself. Black ichor sprayed into the pit and steamed where it struck the air; the smell of rot was swallowed by the roar of his triumph.

He didn't stop.

Before any of us could breathe a sigh of relief, Beau whirled, sight sliding to Morog. Beau snapped forward and then suddenly, impossibly, monstrously…he snatched her up in that cavernous Dragon maw. Beau's jaw locked on her as he bit down. He tore. The queen's scream was all sound and no pity, a high, frantic pitch that somehow silenced everything else.

Blood painted Beau as he worked. Morog's blood and the Chasmwyrm's and his own drenched his scales and dripped from his mouth. The muscles under his scales quivered; his wings beat in ragged, furious arcs. Then something savage and ancient unspooled inside him. His body began to falter.

His body shrunk slowly, the Dragon was gone, he was back to his old form. His shoulders hunched, his scales bled and flaked from injuries. His flesh tore, a chest heaving with a human rhythm, ribs black with burns and bruises. He looked like my old memories again. His eyes that once seared like a furnace, fluttered between draconic and human depth now. His wings splayed as he fought to suspend himself and I lunged to his side.

He staggered, Morog still in his arms. The fire in him spent. A great, aching silence fell for the length of a breath as if time had frozen still. Then blood oozed from every wound he had collected. Beau's huge arms slipped from around Morog's broken form and the Harpy Queen's body rolled from his maw and slid into the blackness, lifeless and small against the scale of what we had all fought to stop.

He dropped. For a second I saw him looking at us, the man inside the beast trying to find the faces he loved.

"Beau!" Roan roared, and the name pulled something raw out of me. I didn't think. I dove.

Zac was already beside me. Roan dove harder, wings folding and pushing the air into a protective tunnel. We fell together. The chasm hit us like a wall, trying to pry us apart. I felt Beau's heat like a furnace beat against my chest as I closed my body around his.

I caught him first—my arms snaking under the weight of his shoulder and rib. Zac came in beneath, taking the other side, and Roan latched to his waist. We held him as we rose upwards finally. He was unconscious.

He didn't wake. His breathing was thin once more; every rise of his chest was a fight. Our only objective now was to get back to the Dunya realm.

For now, the monsters were dead, Morog was gone, and Beau, who had become a beast of flame and then bled himself into a man, lay in our arms like something fragile.

I pressed my forehead to his blood-slicked shoulder and let the world tilt as Zac's fire warmed our hands, Roan's breath fogged in the pit air. We had saved him just in time. We had taken a monster into the dark and almost paid for it with everything.

"Hold him," I whispered, getting him out would take every hand we had left.

We climbed together, slow enough to breathe and check each shadow, the air colder the higher we went. Vara and Zac led. Titus and Roan bore Beau's weight between them, his body slack but still warm against the chill. Morog was gone, and the pit smelled of death.

"Move quickly," Roan said, his voice the steady drum that kept us from shaking apart. "The Clops will be waiting. Stay in the middle."

I nodded, forcing myself to steady. Around us the chasm narrowed.

"When I say, use all the speed you have." Zac's voice was taut, eyes flicking upward. I followed his gaze and saw them: the giants, pale with their single eyes, lining the perimeter like statues, waiting to lash out and grab any one of us.

"Now!"

We shot upward in a blur of flame and wind. The rush tore the breath from my lungs, the sound of our flight echoing off the stone like thunder. Clops lunged from the ledges, their arms outstretched, claws raking empty air as we passed. One brushed my boot and missed. Ten more leapt after us and fell into the endless chasm, their screams fading into the darkness below. There would be no climbing out. Otro Mundo kept what it claimed.

The faint light of the realm door was bleeding down. We broke through the clouds together, and for the first time in what felt like lifetimes, I drew a clean breath.

We rose higher still until the smoke of the pit became a blur beneath us. Beau's weight between us was heavy, but he was alive. None of us spoke. The war, the monsters, the endless dark—all of it drifted below like a nightmare losing its hold. We were still bleeding, still broken, but we were flying home.

The door was open above us. It was like looking straight into the heavens. The halls of Antoli glared down, gold and blinding, the glow of torches and stained glass spilling through the realm's light like a warm hug welcoming us home. The magic of Antoli's door shuddered as we passed through, dragging the warmth of the sun over our frozen skin.

"Seal that door!" I ordered, my voice breaking the stunned silence.

Fae soldiers were already waiting in the secluded chamber, their faces drawn and pale. They moved fast to ensure the massive door slammed shut, locking Tierra Hundida away for good.

"Nobody goes through any realm door without mine or Zac's permission." I glowered at each of them, the exhaustion shaking my hands. "Is that understood?"

For a heartbeat, only the sound of heavy breathing answered me. Then a familiar voice rasped from behind.

"Rich," Beau coughed, blood still streaking his lips, "Coming from the girl who jumped through that same door."

Zac barked a laugh and helped prop him upright. "He doesn't know how to fucking die."

Beau grinned weakly, clutching his ribs. "I tried. It's inconveniently overrated."

I exhaled, the tension finally breaking, and for the first time the room was filled with the sound of laughter.

I didn't laugh. Not yet.

Relief and fury burned in equal measure as I spun on him, my voice sharp enough to crack stone. "You think this is funny? You nearly died — again!" I yelled at Beau.

Beau blinked up at me, still grinning through split lips. "You're welcome."

"Don't you start." I jabbed a finger toward him as I turned to Zac and Roan. "Get him to Ele, NOW. Farklian healers, all of them. I want him breathing and upright before I finish this sentence." I ordered.

Zac raised an eyebrow, smirking. "You heard the lady."

Roan didn't bother to argue. He ducked under Beau's arm and hauled him up, Zac grabbing the other side. Beau grunted, half protest, half laughter.

"I can walk," He groaned against the pain.

"You can shut up," I snapped, stalking ahead of them. The Fae soldiers stepped aside as I passed, none daring to speak.

The corridor leading to the healing quarters glowed with lanternlight, warm and steady. The scent of herbs and blood and fire filled the ancient halls that were once empty, now they were filled with beds. I could already hear Ele barking orders, her voice fierce and fast as ever.

"Ele!" I called.

She turned, her hands still glowing from another patient's bedside. When she saw who Zac and Roan carried, her expression darkened. "What did he do this time?" She snickered.

"Died. Mostly," Zac answered dryly.

"Don't encourage him!" I barked, then softened as I met Ele's gaze. "Please… just fix him." I sighed.

Ele nodded, her tone shifting instantly from sarcasm to focus. "Get him on the table. Farkli healers, now!"

Beau was lowered gently, his breath shallow but steady. I hovered by his side, fingers brushing the blood on his collarbone. He was warm and alive. I was so thankful he was alive.

"I'll yell later," I muttered.

He smiled faintly without opening his eyes. "Looking forward to it."

I turned to walk away when his hand caught mine.

"We did it…" He said softly, a faint smile tugging at his mouth though I could see the pain behind it.

"*You* did it," I murmured, letting out a breath I hadn't realized I'd been holding. "I've had enough war for a lifetime." I sighed.

He chuckled weakly. "I know that feeling." He strained against himself in pain.

For a moment, the chaos outside the healing halls faded. No shouting, no fire, no blood. Just us, standing in the echo of everything we'd survived.

"I'm glad you're alive, Beau." I squeezed his hand, meaning it more than I ever could say aloud.

He looked up at me, gold still flickering faintly in his eyes. "I love you too."

His grip loosened, as though he was giving me a choice whether to stay, to return his sentiment, or to walk away.

And of all the pain I'd borne thus far, the cuts, the loss, the endless ache and exhaustion of battle. This single moment hurt the most. Because choosing him, or choosing to walk away from him, felt like tearing myself in half either way.

Morog had been right about one thing, and her words were burned into me forever... *sadness with him, sadness without him.*

Both truths, and neither easy.

I had a decision to make, but not tonight. Not yet.

First, I needed to see that everyone else had survived — that this war hadn't taken more than it already had.

"I'm going to find Ivy, Dani, and Jake," I said quietly, and his hand slipped from mine.

He smiled faintly, eyes closing as the healers moved around him again.

And I walked away, carrying both the weight of the world and the shards of my heart.

HOME OF THE HARPIES

CHAPTER THIRTY

BEAU

I watched her walk away, the sway of her hair catching what little light filtered through the shattered windows. Ivy and Dani ran to her, and she dropped to her knees as she met them. The three of them folding together in an embrace that said more than I could ever name. Relief. Love. Survival. All the things I wasn't sure I was built to feel anymore.

Torin appeared at my side, limping, his face a patchwork of scratches and dried blood. He was missing chunks of hair, a tooth gone from his grin, but still standing and stubborn as ever.

"You didn't fare too well," I said, my voice rough, but smiling despite it.

He snorted and nudged my shoulder. "Speak for yourself."

I let out a small laugh, then winced as it caught in my ribs. "Glad you're alive, friend."

Torin rolled his eyes. "Yeah, yeah, don't get all gooey on me now."

He said it with a smirk, but there was something heavier behind it — the same thing that was sitting in my chest. We'd both seen too much, lost too much. But in that moment, bruised and bloodied and breathing, we were both still here.

I leaned back against the cold stone wall and let my eyes drift shut, the sounds of laughter and quiet crying filling the corridor. For the first time in what felt like forever, the war didn't feel endless.

Torin sank down beside me, leaning against the wall with a grunt. His skin on one forearm was charred, his knuckles split open. We sat there like two ruins among the many — held together by nothing but the fact that we hadn't fallen into the arms of death.

"Close one," He muttered with his eyes shut.

"Which part?" I asked.

He chuckled, then winced and touched the corner of his mouth where his broken tooth had been. "Take your pick. I thought we were done for the minute the Windreapers flooded through the door."

"Yeah," I breathed, staring out across the hall. "Didn't think we'd be walking out of that one either."

Silence settled for a bit. The kind that follows too much noise. You could still hear the healers working, the occasional sob, the soft drag of bodies being carried past.

Torin rubbed a hand over his face. "You ever think about what it costs? All of it?"

I nodded. "Every second." I sighed as my eyes fluttered open and closed.

He tilted his head, waiting.

"I've killed things I didn't even have names for," I said quietly. "Watched people I swore to protect burn, fall, disappear. And for what? A realm that's broken beyond repair? A peace that won't last a year before someone else tries to take it?" I exhaled slowly, shaking my head. "I used to think war made heroes. Now I just think it makes survivors." I exhaled.

Torin was quiet for a long time. Then he said, "Survivors build things too."

I looked at him.

He shrugged. "It's not much of a legacy, I know. But maybe it's enough. Build something that lasts longer than the fight."

I thought about Aliera and the way her voice had cracked when she said she'd had enough of war. About Zac, whose laughter sounded too tired to be real. About Ivy and Dani, young and still learning what it meant to carry scars that wouldn't heal right. About the Dragons, the Fae, the Titans, all of us were just broken pieces trying to fit into the same story.

"What do you think comes next?" I asked.

Torin looked up at the high windows, where dawn was trying to bleed through the glass. "Rest, maybe. Then rebuilding. Maybe even a little living."

"Living," I repeated, the word foreign on my tongue. "Yeah. We could try that." I nodded.

He smirked. "You'll have to stop throwing yourself into death traps first."

I laughed, soft and hollow. "No promises."

The sound of Aliera's voice drifted faintly from down the corridor — calm, tired, alive. For the first time since the war began, I didn't feel the need to run after it.

Maybe Torin was right. Maybe survivors could build something.

Even if all that was left was the air we were still breathing and that had to count for something.

"You know," I said after a while, staring at the shattered ceiling above us, "I've never loved her without conflict in our lives. I can't help but wonder if it would have been different if we did." I let out a breath.

Torin tilted his head, wiping a smear of blood from his chin. "Maybe you can try now?"

I gave a half-smile, but it hurt to hold. "I think I've hurt her too much. But I'll let her decide and take whatever time she needs." My voice softened. "I can't thank you enough for diving in with me when this all happened. You're a true friend, Torin."

He grinned crookedly. "I've got your back. Always." Then, quieter, "So what's next?" He asked.

I thought for a moment, watching the faint gold glow of the torches flicker over the stone walls. "I know it sounds stupid," I said, "But I'd like to see Varsili restored. I miss the smell of the sea — its imperfection, its noise. It won't ever be the same, but I miss the towers leaning over the bay where Aliera waded for mussels and oysters. I think… that's where I start redeeming myself."

Torin nodded slowly. "And speaking of Aliera, what do you think she will do next?"

I rubbed a hand across my face, weary. "I can't decide for her," I said finally. "All I can do is give her a world that doesn't burn anymore. Maybe then, she'll choose to stay in it."

Torin smirked faintly. "That's the most poetic thing I've ever heard you say."

I huffed out a laugh. "Don't get used to it."

Outside, the distant hum of rebuilding filled the night. Dragons groaning, Fae voices echoing through the halls, the heartbeat of Antoli trying to live again. For the first time, I didn't feel like running toward the next fight.

"What about you and Ele?" I asked, glancing sideways at Torin.

He snorted softly. "Ugh, Farkli," He muttered, running a hand through his messy hair. "Ele hasn't been back since Astrid died. She misses home. I don't really have one… so I'll follow her wherever she wants to go." He smiled faintly — a little broken, a little unsure.

"I guess all the Foogals and Sporlings and Fauns will go home?" I said, more to the air than anyone in particular.

"Not necessarily," Came Thane's voice. He strode over, his boots echoing softly against the stone, and lowered himself beside us.

Torin's brow furrowed. "Why not?"

"The earthquake could have swallowed half of Tierra Hundida by now," Thane said grimly. "They might need to stay here. Orman is empty, and the Sonsuz is vast. If they can, I think they should stay, build something new."

Before any of us could respond, Vara and Titus approached with Zac in tow. They lowered themselves to the cold floor beside us, looking almost peaceful for the first time.

"We'll be going back to Vacia Isla," Vara said.

"You have family there?" I asked.

Her expression softened with a gentle nod. "Vacia Isla is unlike any of this… or *that*," She said, gesturing vaguely toward the window where the horizon glowed faintly. "It's abundant and beautiful. A free realm. We have cities beneath the water that no surface realm could ever mimic." There was pride in her tone but also longing.

"Time to go?" Titus asked, smiling at her.

"Our work is done here." Vara rose, bowing her head before turning to us.

Thane stood to embrace them both. "Don't be strangers."

Titus clasped my hand firmly. "Beau, I'm honored to have fought beside you."

"And you," I nodded, meeting his steady gaze.

"How will you return? Do you need the door?" Aliera's voice carried across the chamber as she approached, Jake, Ivy, Dani, and Roan trailing behind her.

"Yes, but we have our own," Vara said with a smile. "We'll find it. Stay with your friends."

She wrapped Aliera in a quick embrace.

"Come visit anytime," Aliera said, holding her tight.

"Of course," Vara said warmly. "I can't wait to see this place restored to its former glory."

She bowed one last time before she and Titus turned toward the light that shimmered faintly at the edge of the hall — their path home already calling.

"Roan," I said, catching his eye. "I could use a man like you in Varsili."

He met my gaze, and for the first time in days, I saw relief flicker across his face. Cress and Thira sat a little apart, close enough to hear. None of them wanted to go back to the ruin they'd left behind.

"Are our kind welcome here?" Roan asked cautiously.

Before I could answer, Cleo appeared from the shadows of the hall. "All who come in peace are welcome in Lexia." She said softly.

I raised a hand, laughing. "Hey! I'm taking this one. Get your own friends, Cleo."

She grinned. "I had to try. You're a fine warrior, Roan, but I do hope your fighting career is over and peace finds you."

"Varsili?" Aliera's voice lifted with curiosity.

"It deserves to breathe again," I said gently, meeting her eyes. I hoped she'd see the invitation there — a chance to start over, together.

Her eyes shimmered before she turned away, quickly brushing at them. "I hope it's all you dream it to be," She murmured.

"What will you do, Aliera?" Ivy asked quietly, her voice edged with the fear of parting.

"Antoli is the foundation of my people," Aliera said. "We've seen what happens when it's left to freeze. It needs to be guarded and rebuilt. Zac and I are the only Titans left to do it." She smiled faintly. "Azra and Irmak will stay, and Kieran too, with the young Dragons and those that came through the door. They're getting bigger — he'll have his work cut out for him." She forced a smile.

"I'll stay with you, if you'll have me," Marcus said, stepping forward.

"It's your home too." Zac shook his hand firmly. "Wouldn't mind giving one of those Dragons a try either," He added with a grin toward the girls. "You made it look like fun. And you too, Jakey."

Jake laughed. "I'm just along for the ride at this point."

Dani sniffled and wiped her cheeks. "How can I possibly go home and leave all of you here?" She cried.

"You could stay," Ivy said, hugging her tightly.

"I'll go with you, if that's what you want," Jake said, taking her hands in his.

"We'll never see them again," Dani whispered, her voice breaking as tears rolled down her face.

"You sure?" Ivy asked gently.

Dani let out a choked laugh. "I really miss plumbing," She admitted, half laughing, half crying.

The entire group burst into laughter, the sound a balm over the tension that had clung to us for too long.

"I miss cell phones, and Ubers, and tacos," She giggled. "But Jake — if you want to stay, I'll stay with you." She smiled.

Jake wrapped his arms around her waist and kissed her softly. "If you miss tacos that much, I'll go too."

Dani shook her head through her laughter. "No... that's selfish. Ivy and Aliera are here. Beau and Torin are here. This is our family now." Her voice wavered. "I think... I think we're meant to stay."

The hall fell quiet for a heartbeat — not with sorrow, but with peace. For the first time since the war began, everyone was exactly where they were meant to be.

Dani looked between Aliera and me, the tension heavy enough to choke on. "Maybe we should all give you two some privacy," she said, flapping her hands toward everyone else. One by one, they scattered, leaving the hall in an uneasy silence.

Aliera dropped her hands, wrapping her arms around herself as if trying to hold everything she was feeling in. I pushed myself to my feet — still sore, still barely standing, but mostly healed thanks to Ele and the Farklian hearths. I crossed the space between us. I cupped her chin gently in my hand.

"Aliera..." I whispered.

Her eyes were already puddles, and when they spilled over, she fell into my arms. I held her, and for a long time neither of us said a word. When she finally trembled against me, I lifted her easily, carrying her down the long corridor until I found a room that wasn't locked. The door clicked shut behind us, sealing us away, alone in the quiet.

I sat her on the bed and stayed kneeling in front of her. "If you want me here, I'll stay," I said softly. "But you have to tell me that's what you want. I won't decide this for you." I said as I held her hands.

She held my gaze — and then she moved. She climbed into my lap on the floor of the room and kissed me like it was our first time. Her fingers tangled in my hair, and I let my hands find her, tracing every curve, memorizing the warmth of her skin, the shape of her grief, the way her breath caught between us.

When we finally broke apart, our foreheads rested together.

"She said something to me," Aliera whispered.

My chest tightened. "What did she say?" I asked, though part of me didn't want to know.

"Sadness with him…sadness without him." The words sat between us like a shadow.

I swallowed hard. "I'm never going to kill anyone again. I promise you."

She sighed, shaking her head. "You can't promise me that. That's not who you are, Beau. We've both killed. And I'm forever changed because of it." Her voice wavered. "Sometimes I think… none of this would have happened to any of them if I hadn't tried to leave Varsili." She confessed.

"Don't think like that," I said sharply.

"Isn't it true?" Her voice cracking.

"I'm not the same person I was when I left Varsili," She continued. "I was human. Weak. Alone. And now I'm—this. A Titan! And I don't even know how to be one." Tears spilled again as her words became muddled and she took in a deep breath. "All I know is how to shell oysters and catch fish in the shallows." She cried.

I reached for her hand. "It's been over a year since that woman existed. You're a beacon now, Aliera. Ivy worships you. Dani thinks the world of you. They know you're not perfect — they love you for it. You're the one expecting too much of yourself. You think you shouldn't love me the way you do. And maybe you're right — you shouldn't. I've hurt you. I've hurt the people you love." My throat burned with the truth. "But there will never be another man who loves you more than me. Or one who spends every day proving that love isn't a place to die, it's a place to grow."

Tears spilled down my face before I even realized they'd fallen.

"I love you," I whispered.

She shook her head, voice barely a breath. "I can't, Beau. Not now. I need to be here, and you need to be there. Maybe one day, when the pain isn't so raw, when peace finally finds us, when the wounds turn to scars and are faded enough that we can forget how we got them. But right now…" Her voice broke. "I can't be who you want me to be."

I pulled her tighter to me, and we kissed. It was soft and infinite and unbearably sad.

And in that moment, I knew love didn't always get to choose.

Chapter Thirty One

ALIERA

I knew the decision I was making, I was letting him go, but if all the time we had left was tonight and I had to pay the price for it. It felt like the perfect place to die.

He kissed me and I kissed him back. It was desperate, it was slow and reverent as if we were learning each other all over again. Our hands trailed and explored one another in soft gentle touches that we knew couldn't last forever, but still we craved it. Demanded it.

I let my armor fall away piece by piece as Beau disrobed me. Pulling off my boots and unbuttoning the skintight suit that hugged my body like a second skin. I pulled at his torn clothes until they fell to the floor, and I was left tugging at his pants as he kicked off his boots.

"Shower…" I tilted my head to the small room in the corner of the bedroom. He picked me up and nodded and walked us into the space and warm water cascaded like magic over our bodies.

"That is cool." Beau smiled as water trickled down his face and between my breasts.

I tightened my thighs around his hips and kissed him gently, slower this time. The aching kind of kiss that says everything goodbye can't.

Our bodies slid together in a tangle of need and grief and devotion. I slid gently, knowingly up and down him as the water raced down my back and he leaned into the wall to steady himself.

"Beau…" My voice was ragged and desperate as I clung tighter to his neck and he held my thighs as we climaxed together.

I kissed him over and over again as he washed the blood and ash from my hair. The water didn't just mask the sound of our breathing, it masked the tears too as I shook in his arms.

His chest rose and fell with each pass of my hands cleaning the soot, and blood from his scales and skin. He would flinch when I unearthed a raw wound that had been scabbed by dirt and debris. He breathed through the pain, jaw clenched, hands gentle on my waist to steady himself, as though he was terrified of hurting me even now.

"Aliera," He whispered, barely a voice at all. But it was deep and warm, it was him.

I traced the line of his collarbone, where bruises bloomed like night flowers. "You're hurt."

"So are you…" His thumb swept beneath my eye, catching a tear the water couldn't hide.

"Why does this hurt more than any war." My lips trembled as the truth finally broke through me.

His forehead pressed to mine as if he could keep me together by proximity alone. "Because war never asked for your heart," He whispered. "I did. And I never should have."

Another tear slipped free. "Don't say that."

But he closed his eyes, pained. "If I had been anyone else… if I hadn't been the one who—"

"Don't." My voice cracked. "Please, Beau. Not now." My voice barely a whisper.

His hands framed my face with such gentleness it nearly undid me. "Aliera, I would give anything to rewrite the world for you."

I swallowed hard, chest tight, breath stuttering. "But you can't."

"I know." His voice broke on the words. "And that's why this hurts."

The water ran warm down our shoulders, our scars, our trembling bodies. It felt like the world had shrunk to a single heartbeat. His against mine, both frantic, both breaking, shattering into pieces we couldn't possibly fix.

"I'm going to miss this," I confessed, the words dragging out of me like splinters. He drew me in tighter, as if the strength of his arms alone could change destiny. "I'll miss you long after the worlds stop turning."

"I don't know how to walk away from you," I whispered. "You don't," he said softly. "You let me do the hard stuff." He stroked my cheek.

My breath hitched as grief clawed its way up my throat. "Beau…"

He kissed the corner of my mouth, then my cheek, then the place just below my jaw where my pulse trembled. Each one felt like goodbye.

"Sadness with you," I murmured.

He finished it for me, voice torn open. "Sadness without you."

My lips trembled in the kiss as I unravelled against those torturous words.

We slept together that night, one last time. And gods, it felt wrong to slip out of his arms at dawn. Every part of me wanted to stay there forever, to freeze time in the stillness between his heartbeat and mine.

Outside, the world was moving forward, away from the memory of war. The Fae had taken their wounded back to Lexia. Sina had ordered the Foogals and Fauns to finish burning the corpses before they followed the Sporlings north to Sonsuz. The air still carried the scent of ash, but beneath it was something gentler — the first whispers of peace.

I leaned against the balustrade and watched the sun rise. It was the first sunrise I'd felt in months that didn't feel like a battle.

Dani found me there, carrying two cups of tea. She passed one to me and leaned against the railing, shoulder to shoulder.

"Can I ask what happened?" She said softly, her voice full of compassion.

I exhaled a shaky laugh. "We remembered who we were before the wars," I animated my brows, so I didn't have to say the words aloud. "Then we talked." I sighed.

"And?" She pressed.

"We both know now is too soon." The words hurt to say aloud.

"Aliera…" Her tea fell from her hand as she wrapped her arms around me. "I'm so sorry."

"It doesn't mean never," I whispered into her shoulder. "Just… not right now."

She pulled back, brushing my hair behind my ear like a sister would. "Still, when you love someone, you want them with you always. I can't imagine saying no to what your heart wants." She said gently.

"It's shitty," I laughed through the tears. "Ugh, I'm sick of crying."

"You know, before I ended up here, I was running away from parts of my life. I was chasing excitement, new feelings." She confessed.

"What feelings?" I asked.

"I wanted to feel a love so powerful that it left me in ruins. I meant me, not you." She pressed her hand to my hair over my cheek.

"I don't wish it on you if it leaves you feeling how I feel now." I sighed.

"Then no more crying," She smiled.

"What will you do now?" I asked.

"Jake wants to follow the others to Varsili. If Roan's going, Ivy will too — and Jake isn't quite ready to stop babysitting her." She laughed. "But if you want, I'll stay with you for a while." She offered kindly.

"And upset Jake? He'd never forgive me." I hugged her tightly. "I'll be okay." I promised her.

From the shadowed halls, Beau emerged with Roan and Jake behind him, Torin and Ele were saying their goodbyes and suddenly my heart clenched.

"I guess this is it," I breathed. Dani stood aside.

He came to me without hesitation, his eyes soft, and steps slow. His hand found mine, and he pressed a kiss to my forehead. It was a silent farewell, heavier than words could bear.

He didn't speak. There was nothing left to say. But he pressed a folded note into my palm before stepping away.

I watched as he stood where the balustrade opened over the stairs, sunlight flashing against the curve of his jaw, the way the sun hit the blue of his wings, the wind lifting his dark hair as the Dragons rose into the east to escort him home. I didn't call after him. I just watched until the sky swallowed him whole.

When everyone had gone their separate ways, I returned to the room we'd shared — *my* room now. The sheets still held the warmth of us.

I sat on the edge of the bed and unfolded the note, tracing the ink with trembling fingers.

You are the ache that reminds me I once belonged somewhere. That once, before the ruin and the reckoning, my heart knew the shape of home. You are my home, not a place, not a realm… just me, with you.

The end.

✦ Author's Note ✦

This story has lived in me for years, six to be exact. It has haunted me in the quiet hours after midnight, in the moments when my life was more chaos then calm. In the car park at school pick up where I couldn't possibly note everything I dreamt of. It has taken different paths and grown with me, evolving through every season of my life, the same way those seasons have shaped me.

Home of the Harpies was never meant to be perfect, nor was it meant to be the second book. It was, however, meant to *feel alive*. It's a story about people who carry their pain like armor, who love too deeply, forgive too slowly, and somehow still keep fighting. It's a fantastical version of my life, minus the war and carnage.

Aliera and Beau are a version of myself trying to remember what peace feels like. Their ending isn't simple, because love nor life never is. Sometimes it isn't about happily ever after. Sometimes it's about surviving the ache long enough to see another sunrise.

If you've made it to this page, thank you for reading, for feeling, for believing in these characters as fiercely as I do. You've walked with them through blood and fire, and I hope, somewhere between the realms, you found a piece of yourself too.

To those of us who find love despite the wreckage. Here's to finding home, even when it's just in someone's arms.

With all my heart,

Vanessa Joyce

VANESSA JOYCE